What the critics are saying...

Believe In The Magic

4 stars "...Cait Miller has penned a paranormal romance that will keep you intrigued from the opening scene. With a dashing hero and a plot thick with action, sizzling love scenes, and bit of intrigue... I look forward to discovering more of Ms. Miller's talent..." – *BJ Deese, eCataRomance Reviews*

4 Hearts, "...I really enjoyed Megan and Jack's adventures and how they interacted. They both had a lot of personality, and it really made the story. I can't wait for the rest of the series, and I will definitely be on the lookout for more books from this gifted author..." – *Julia, The Romance Studio*

4/5 stars, "...The sex is hot and the couple seems to light up the pages. I look forward to reading more about the secondary characters and seeing how more of the pieces of this shapeshifter puzzle falls into place...." – *Ann Lee, Just Erotic Romance Reviews*

4/5 stars, "...Romance was, beyond anything else, the key element in this story. I'll definitely be reading books by this author again, and I'm really hoping to see Jack's friend Cameron's story. Give Believe in the Magic a chance if you want a sweet offering from Cait Miller.." – *Dani Jacquel, Just Erotic Romance Reviews*

STRAY MAGIC

Elizabeth Stewart

&

Cait Miller

Stray Magic
An Ellora's Cave Publication, January 2005

Ellora's Cave Publishing, Inc.
1337 Commerce Drive Suite #13
Stow, Ohio 44224

ISBN #1419951424

Edited by: *Martha Punches and Raelene Gorlinsky*
Cover art by: *Syneca*

Warning:

The following material contains graphic sexual content meant for mature readers. *Stray Magic* has been rated *S-ensuous* by a minimum of three independent reviewers.

Ellora's Cave Publishing offers three levels of Romantica™ reading entertainment: S (S-ensuous), E (E-rotic), and X (X-treme).

S-ensuous love scenes are explicit and leave nothing to the imagination.

E-rotic love scenes are explicit, leave nothing to the imagination, and are high in volume per the overall word count. In addition, some E-rated titles might contain fantasy material that some readers find objectionable, such as bondage, submission, same sex encounters, forced seductions, etc. E-rated titles are the most graphic titles we carry; it is common, for instance, for an author to use words such as "fucking", "cock", "pussy", etc., within their work of literature.

X-treme titles differ from E-rated titles only in plot premise and storyline execution. Unlike E-rated titles, stories designated with the letter X tend to contain controversial subject matter not for the faint of heart.

CONTENTS

Stray Thoughts

Elizabeth Stewart

Chapter One
October

For Sheridan Phillips, it had been one of those days.

A night of freezing rain and sleet had screwed up the morning commute, even before it had begun. She'd snagged her brand new pantyhose on the corner of her desk as she'd bent over to put her purse in the bottom drawer. Just then, her boss, The Prince of Darkness, had materialized, hands overflowing with files. "Urgent" files that had resulted in lunch being a cold turkey sandwich at her desk instead of a bowl of steaming, homemade soup at the café on the corner. At five o'clock, just as she was reaching for her computer's "off" switch, The Prince had reappeared at her desk.

"You know I wouldn't ask you to stay late," he began coldly, "if it weren't important..."

"Certainly, Mr. Duncan," she'd replied, trying with limited success to stifle a resigned sigh.

Now, having worked an hour and a half of overtime, stood all the way home on an overcrowded bus and carried a pair of wet, slippery plastic bags from the grocery store on the corner, she was finally dragging herself home. Inside the large foyer of her old-fashioned apartment building, she set the bags down and opened her mailbox. With one last effort, she managed to get up the wide flight of stairs to her apartment on the second floor.

Flipping on lights as she walked, she turned up the thermostat in the front hall, threw the mail on the coffee table, put the bags on the kitchen counter and moved on to her bedroom, peeled off her purse and jacket and slipped off her wet pumps. In the bathroom, she looked in the mirror and frowned.

Her short, curly black hair had been reduced to a mass of wet frizz and her "waterproof" mascara had run, forming a little bandit mask around her dark brown eyes. *I think it is time to look into different makeup*, she thought, as she wiped the black rings from her face.

"You're a mess," she chuckled, and shedding the rest of her wet clothes, tossed them into the hamper. She slipped into a comfortable pair of old gray sweats. Shutting off the light, she returned to the kitchen. By the time she'd finished putting away the few groceries she'd bought, the teakettle was singing its warm, cheery whistle and she'd put her frozen chicken dinner in the microwave.

Curling up on the sofa, she reached over and picked up her stack of mail. Gas bill. Electric bill. Phone bill. Notice that her car insurance was due. And a long white business envelop from Joanne Layton and Associates, Literary Agents. Immediately, her heart picked up its tempo as she slid her finger under the flap.

She'd sent her latest novel to them in the hopes of at last snagging representation.

"Dear Mr. Phillips," it began.

Her heart sank a little. Granted, with a first name like Sheridan (it was her mother's maiden name), she was used to being mistaken for a man. But it was obvious that whoever had written the letter hadn't paid much attention to her cover letter, synopsis or biography. It didn't bode well for their attention to the manuscript.

"We appreciate you taking the time to send your manuscript, Star Crossed. It's an interesting premise and certainly shows promise. However…"

She didn't need to read anymore. It was the standard rejection letter. She had enough of them to carpet her Ivory Tower. She'd been writing long enough not to get her hopes up when she submitted a new manuscript. Funny though, no matter how many rejection letters she got or how nicely they were worded, the pain never seemed to diminish. Miserable, she threw the letter back on the coffee table.

The bell on the microwave sounded the end of the cooking cycle. Somehow, though, the thought of food had suddenly lost its appeal. Mechanically, she got it out, put it on the small dining table and gathered the rest of her dinner, namely, a large glass of white wine.

She'd just sat down when she heard it. A soft sort of scratching noise was coming from the living room.

Curious, she got up and moved across the room. Her one-bedroom apartment was small, but it had a large living room window leading out to the fire escape. It faced another apartment building across the alley. Moving the drapes aside, she looked out.

At first, she didn't see anything in the cold, rainy darkness. She was about to chalk it up to her imagination when she saw the movement at the bottom of the window. A small black paw had reached up from the fire escape and was furiously scraping four little claws against the glass.

Intrigued, she unlatched the window and raised it a few inches. Immediately, the paw disappeared and the animal attached to it slithered through the small opening and plopped onto her carpet, shaking itself vigorously as it landed. A few of the cold, wet drops landed on her feet as she closed the window.

"Well, well," she smiled down. "Please come in and make yourself at home."

It was a huge black cat, almost like a miniature panther. Twenty pounds at least, twelve inches high and two feet long perhaps, lean and sleek. He looked up at her, not with the yellow, almond eyes she'd expected but with huge, round, sapphire blue ones. They studied her thoughtfully, something intelligent and wild in their depths. Even then she remembered thinking to herself that there was something almost unnerving about those eyes. Finally, with regal aplomb, he sat back on his haunches and curled his tail around his long front paws. He looked for all the world as if he'd been expected.

"All right," she told him lightly. "Since you asked so nicely, you can stay until it stops raining. Now if you'll excuse me, I was just having my dinner."

Sitting back down at the table, she picked up the breast piece of fried chicken and ripped into it. Crispy batter and tender meat filled her mouth, a trickle of juice dribbling down her chin. Wiping her mouth with a napkin, Sheridan reflected that it was the best thing that had happened to her all day and she closed her eyes to revel in the deliciousness of it.

She felt something soft and velvety rub gently on her calf. Looking down, she saw the cat at her feet, slowly moving his right front paw in a little circle, barely touching her skin. Inexplicably, a pleasant tingle flitted down her spine. And those eyes continued to watch her intently.

"Well, I'll say one thing," she said softly. "You certainly know how to ask for what you want. Most hungry strays would be up on the table, yowling at the top of their lungs and trying to stick their heads in the plate."

She ripped the crispy, heavily battered skin off the drumstick, laid it on several napkins from the holder and placed it on the floor, away from her leg. "Bon appetite"

A quick, cursory sniff and the cat attacked his dinner.

Well before she was finished, she felt that light touch on her calf again, eliciting the same pleasant tingle. Glancing down, she saw that the drumstick had been denuded of meat, the bone still sitting on the napkin.

"If this is a request for seconds," she told him casually, "I'm afraid you're out of luck. Since I wasn't expecting company tonight, I didn't get the extra portion dinner. Sorry."

Those enormous blue eyes gazed up at her, the paw never stopping. It was almost as if he were mulling over her words. And then she had a sudden urge, for that was the only way she could describe it, to get up, pour out a bowl of water for her guest and have some ice cream (chocolate chip cookie dough). Two scoops.

As she cleared the table and cleaned the kitchen, the cat sat quietly by her chair, nonchalantly cleaning his face and paws. He behaved as if it were perfectly normal to wander into a strange woman's apartment and invite himself to dinner.

"All right," she explained, setting a small bowl down on the floor by the refrigerator, "here's some water to wash down your dinner. You would, no doubt, prefer a snifter of brandy and a good cigar but I'm afraid you'll just have to settle for what you get."

Seeming to ignore her, he sauntered casually to the bowl and began lapping quickly. She reached into the freezer, pulled out the carton and got two scoops of ice cream.

Back in the living room, Sheridan resumed her position on the sofa, feet curled up under her, and began on her ice cream. In a few more moments, the cat strolled out of the kitchen and began a lazy, thoughtful inspection of her apartment, stopping to examine the small oak and glass entertainment center, bookcase, end tables and ladder back rocker.

To finish his circuit, he hopped gracefully up onto the coffee table, checking out the hand-tatted lace runner and simple crystal candlesticks. Running his nose along the base of both of the tall, cinnamon-scented red candles, he seemed satisfied. Finally, he came to her rejection letter, sniffing it once or twice. His nose twitched, whiskers bristling as if he'd smelled something objectionable. Abruptly, he raised his hind leg and peed on the offending letter, a small puddle forming before she could make any move to stop him.

Surprise, she knew, should have given way to shock or outrage. After all, she wasn't accustomed to strange animals relieving themselves on her correspondence. But instead, all she could do was laugh.

"Oh, that's beautiful," she giggled, "just beautiful. I mean, talk about poetic justice. When I think of all the times I've been pissed on by various and assorted editors and agents..."

Without looking back, he crossed the distance between the coffee table and sofa in one leap and sat down on the sofa cushion beside her. Gazing up at her, she was reminded of that old saying, "the cat that ate the canary". His whole being radiated satisfaction.

The small yellow puddle remained on the thick, heavy bond paper, not soaking through as she set the bowl down on the end table and gingerly picked up the letter, folding the corners up slightly and retreating to the bathroom.

After disposing of the paper and its puddle in the toilet and washing her hands, she came back to the couch. In the bowl, one of the scoops of ice cream was gone, bits of dough and chocolate chips pushed to the side, the scoop she'd been eating apparently untouched. The cat had moved to the hearth in front of her small fireplace, just licking the last of something off his paws.

"How the hell did you manage to eat all that ice cream in the three minutes I was in the john?" she asked incredulously.

He ignored the question. Instead, he turned his head to the empty fireplace then back to her.

"It would be a perfect night for a fire," she commented, the picture of a cheery blaze suddenly crackling in my mind, "but I don't have any wood. I was going to get some but...well, my life has been a little hectic lately." She paused and looked into those eyes. "If I'd known you were coming...."

Good God, she thought abruptly to herself, I'm talking to a cat! A stray cat no less.

"Oh boy," she sighed, dropping onto the couch. "I must really be losing my grip. First, you move in uninvited, and now you've got me talking to you like you could possibly understand me."

Shaking her head in mild disbelief, Sheridan smiled at her visitor. "Tell you what? It's been a really shitty day, even by the standards of my shitty life. I'm gonna go take a bubble bath. Maybe a little hot water and green apple bubbles'll help clear my head."

A few minutes later, she slid into a tub of hot bubbles, leaned back against her bath pillow, closed her eyes and sighed contentedly. Feeling her body relax, the cares and stress of the day seemed to leach away in the warm, sweet-scented water. Perhaps, she thought idly, if I lie here long enough, I can simply will everything away.

Lost in her own world, Sheridan didn't know exactly how long she'd been soaking when she became aware that she was being watched. It was that vague but unmistakable feeling that raises the hair on the back of your neck.

With a start, she opened her eyes and looked around.

He was sitting on the wide ledge of the tub, inches from her face. Slowly, he was moving his head from side to side, examining her with the same intense interest that he'd shown in the apartment and its furnishings. A tremor shivered through her. If she'd been standing on the bus or a street corner and seen some stranger staring at her as this cat was now, she knew she'd have gone looking for a cop.

"I'd invite you in," she joked weakly, "but I'm told cats don't like water."

Reaching out, he placed a paw softly on her cheek, leaning his head so close she could feel the brush of his whiskers. His eyes had narrowed slightly and were locked on hers. Combined with the feel of him on her skin, it was almost...sensual.

"This is ridiculous," she muttered, trying to shake off the feeling. He pulled his paw away but continued to gaze at her steadily, calmly.

Closing her eyes again, Sheridan tried to recapture the serenity she'd been enjoying but the unsettling presence of the little panther made that impossible. Eventually, she gave up but could feel those eyes on her every moment toweling dry, slipping on her nightie and padding out to close up the apartment for the night.

In the bedroom, she found him curled up on the bed, waiting patiently it seemed, for lights out and for her to join him. Carefully turning down the bedding, she slid between the sheets.

"It's still raining," she said, turning slightly to the cat, "so you can stay the night. But tomorrow morning, you're on the road again. Understand?"

He blinked those huge eyes once and then stretched out to his full length.

"Good night," she called, reaching up and snapping off the bedside light. Snuggling down under the warm comforter, she realized how sleepy she really was. Turning on her side, Sheridan closed her eyes.

Drifting off, the last thing she remembered was the feel of a furry paw laid gently on her arm and a narrow, rough tongue moving quickly across her cheek.

Chapter Two

"Okay, Cat," Sheridan grumbled, "rise and shine."

Impulsively laying her fingers on his soft side, she ran them over his silky fur. Instantly, those enormous eyes blinked open, wide awake and alert. Feeling his skin ripple under her hand, she watched as he stretched a little, trying to encourage her, she thought, to stroke more of his body.

He didn't purr. He was, she thought, not an animal given to purring. But there was a fleeting look of pleasure in his eyes. And the expression on that narrow, aristocratic face. She could almost imagine it was contentment.

"You know, I can't just keep calling you Cat or You. Especially since I have the feeling you've already made up your mind to stay. Still, I don't really feel as if I know you well enough to give you a name."

Sheridan grinned as he turned slightly, bringing her hand to his stomach. "And I certainly don't see myself calling you Max or Harry. I'm sure you do have a name though. I just wish you could tell me what it is."

She continued rubbing his stomach; his eyes partially closed in blissful enjoyment. Unexpectedly, he reached out and put a paw lightly on her arm, moving it again in that gentle, tender movement he'd used last night.

"Nick," Sheridan squealed suddenly, the name popping into her head like a bursting balloon. She had no idea where the name had come from, but looking down at him, she realized it was perfect.

That slender head moved up and down once, as if he were agreeing with her. At the time she remembered thinking the movement was just an odd coincidence.

"Anyway, Nick," she told him gently, "I've got miles to go and beasts to face. So what say we get this show on the road?" One last vigorous rub of his tummy and she was out of bed and padding for the shower.

As she stepped into the shower and stood under the hot water, she caught sight of Nick. He'd followed her and was now perched beside the sink, his long black tail hanging over the edge of the vanity, watching her through the clear glass shower doors. His dark blue eyes seemed to be taking in every inch of her naked body, every move she made. The look was so intense—and so sensual—she had to turn her head and close her eyes. It was almost as if she could feel firm but gentle hands gliding over her body as she rinsed off the soap.

Back in her bedroom, Nick leapt up on the dresser as Sheridan opened her underwear drawer. Immediately, an interested paw reached out and began feeling the satin panties.

Pushing the paw back, she glared at the cat with what she hoped was appropriate severity.

"Okay, Nick, I've shared my food and my bed with you. I've let you pat me and even watch me shower. But I absolutely draw the line at having you in my panties. Now if you want to watch me dress, I suggest you keep your paws to yourself."

The paw reluctantly returned to the bureau top.

When she was dressed, she went into the kitchen, Nick trailing behind.

"I always eat breakfast," she told him, pulling a bowl from the cupboard over the sink. "Since I was little. Unfortunately, I don't have time during the week for eggs and bacon, so unless you're into raisin bran, about the only thing I can offer you is a bowl of milk. Sorry."

Reaching into the cabinet for her cereal, Sheridan grabbed the box and was just about to close the door when she spied a small can in the back, almost hidden behind an unopened jar of applesauce. Perplexed, she took it out and examined it.

"Well, I'll be damned," she commented, holding the can out for Nick to see. "Salmon." She looked down at him questioningly. "Now where the hell did that come from? I mean, I don't remember buying salmon."

But if Nick was surprised, he didn't show it. He'd already settled himself on the floor by the refrigerator where his water bowl had been left. Apparently since dinner'd been provided, he expected breakfast was included too. Obviously he was used to traveling on the American Plan.

"You may not realize it, but this is definitely your lucky morning."

They ate their respective breakfasts in silence. When she'd finished putting the bowls and coffee cup in the dishwasher, put on her makeup and gathered her things for work, Sheridan came out into the living room. Somewhat surprised, she found Nick sitting by the window.

"Are you leaving?" she asked him, suddenly disappointed and yes, sad, that this stranger was apparently getting ready to drift out of her life as simply as he'd drifted in.

In answer, the cat raised himself on his hind legs and stretched up.

"Well, I guess that's clear enough." Unlatching and raising the window enough for him to reach the windowsill, he immediately hopped up, balancing himself lightly on the narrow ledge. For a moment he hesitated, turned his head and focused those beautiful eyes on her again. There was a pang in the pit of her stomach, and she had the thought that perhaps she should grab him and shut the window.

There was the sound of a door opening in the hall and Sheridan turned her head for a moment. Turning back, she saw that he was gone. Absolutely gone.

Sheridan opened the window enough to put her head out, craning to scan the fire escape up and down and the alley as far as she could see. But there was no trace of him anywhere. It was as if he'd simply vanished.

A blast of winter air blew through the window and she shivered. Snapping it shut with a thump, she gazed out the window again, confusion, uncertainty and a keen sense of loss all running together. With a final shake of her head, she picked up her briefcase and left.

* * * * *

"Well," Pat laughed, "at least it's a start.

"What's that supposed to mean?" Sheridan asked as she popped another bite of warm coffeecake into her mouth.

"That it's high time you picked up a stray male and got him into your bed. Now that you've taken the plunge with a cat, maybe you'll consider moving up to a real guy."

"Pat," she answered, trying to sound annoyed, "you're terrible."

"What?"

"You know damn well, 'what'."

"Look, Sher," she said seriously. "I know how bad it was. But he was a louse and a rat and it's been five years already. It's time to bury it and get on."

"That's a lot easier said than done," she tried to deflect. "Especially for a short, dumpy, middle-aged secretary with a dead end job and wannabe aspirations to a career in writing."

The other woman waved her hand and shook her shoulder length brown hair. "Don't be so hard on yourself. You're barely thirty-six, petite and at a hundred and twenty pounds and a size eight, hardly dumpy. And you know that without you, this place would fall apart. As for your writing, I personally look forward to the day when I'll be invited to cocktail parties because I knew you when."

"Will you please keep it down?" Sheridan hushed, glancing quickly at the open door of the office break room. "If I wanted the whole office to know, I'd post it on the bulletin board."

"I'm just trying to tell you, for about the umpteenth time, that just because one relationship went south, doesn't mean you have to hang it up for good. After all, Bruce and I are both on our second go around and we've been together fifteen years."

"You lucked out."

"You might too, if you'd give it half a chance." She leaned in and grinned mischievously, her hazel eyes shining behind her pale blue glasses. "There's this guy Bruce works with. Lou Magris. I met him at the office anniversary party in October. Great guy. Dark eyes. Brown hair. Built like a brick outhouse. Looks kinda like Harrison Ford."

"Part of Bruce's survey party?"

"Uh-uh. He's an engineer."

"I thought so," Sheridan sighed disgustedly. "Like I don't get enough aggravation from the engineers I have to work with. Now you're suggesting I get one to give me misery at home as well? No thanks."

Her friend made a face. "No, no. He's not a civil guy like here. He's a mechanical engineer. Works in a whole 'nother division. He and Bruce were standing in the cafeteria line and got to shootin' the bull about basketball. I could invite him for dinner on Saturday and you and he could get better acquainted. Whattaya say?"

"I say thanks, but no thanks."

"Why, for Christ's sake, not?"

"Because I couldn't hang on to the last man I was with. Hell, I couldn't even hang on to a stray cat. I've had just about all the males I can stand."

A young man's anxious face appeared in the doorway. "Sher," he hissed loudly, looking back over his shoulder. "Dracula's roaming the halls looking for you. And he's sharpening his fangs. I hope you got your cast-iron pantyhose on." Another furtive glance back. "Shit. I'm outta here," and he disappeared.

Sheridan stood up hurriedly, hoping to make her getaway. Unfortunately, she wasn't fast enough and the doorway was filled with a huge, dark presence.

"Mr. Duncan."

He glared down at her. At six foot four, two hundred and fifty pounds, he looked more like a defensive end than a professional engineer. Thinning iron-gray hair, worn in a "buzz" cut, mean, dark gray eyes and hard mouth. Cold disdain and an arrogant manner he always used with those he considered "lesser beings," combined with an unfailing ability to blame his subordinates for his screw-ups had earned him the undying hatred of virtually everyone he worked with. Only the Director, John Curtin, remained in his corner and that was mostly due to Duncan's first-rate ability to brown nose.

"I need the budget estimates for the Crane Project."

"Yes sir," she answered deferentially.

With an annoyed snort, he glanced at his watch. "I need them now." He paused ever so slightly. "If, of course, you're finished with your break."

Yeah. Right. Like you give a shit whether I'm finished or not, she thought bitterly. "I was just going back to my desk, sir. I'll have the estimates on your desk in a minute."

"And don't forget that draft for the Director is due by four. He wants a chance to look it over before I submit the final."

"Yes sir," Sheridan repeated. "You'll have it by noon."

"Be sure I do. You'll no doubt have to make changes after I'm finished proofreading it."

Stupid sonofabitch! "Yes sir." The words scraped in her throat like razor blades. *Just get the fuck out of my face* were the words that came to her mind.

Being finished with his underling, he departed, and the two women breathed a sigh of relief.

"I absolutely don't know how you do it," Pat remarked as she stood up so they could walk back to their desks. "I can't

24

stand being around that asshole. If I had to work for him…" She shook her head.

"You'd work for him the same as I do," Sheridan replied wearily. "And be glad for the job. Besides, I consider working for him to be research for a future book. 'All the Ghouls I've Known'."

"Jesus, Sher," Pat guffawed as they stepped into the hall and went their separate ways.

* * * * *

Sheridan heard the scratching as soon as she closed the apartment door. Part of her was annoyed, part relieved and glad.

"You have more brass than a cheap spittoon," she told him, slamming the window shut and re-latching it. "I should just let you sit out there and freeze your little balls off. Serve you right."

In response, Nick came over and began rubbing himself against her legs, his cold, wet fur momentarily chilling her. Looking up as if he hadn't seen her in years, those dark blue eyes were filled with what she could only describe as delight.

Needless to say, her heart melted. Bending down, she began stroking him under the chin with one hand and petting his back with the other. In a moment, he'd rolled on his back and she was rubbing his stomach. The same contentment appeared on his face that she'd seen that morning.

"Come on," she laughed after a few moments. "I don't know about you, but I haven't had my dinner and I'm starving."

Nick followed her into the kitchen, stopping to get himself a long drink of water from his bowl.

"I have lamb chops," she announced, opening the fridge. "I don't suppose there's any possibility that you actually eat cat food, is there?"

In response, Nick yawned disdainfully and walked back to the living room, planting himself in front of the fireplace again.

"Sorry," Sheridan apologized playfully, "but I still haven't gotten any wood. But you're right. A fire would be very nice and I'd like one too. Maybe this weekend."

For a moment, Nick gazed at her, the same thoughtful look he'd had when told there weren't seconds on the chicken. Like he was pondering something.

A moment later, the doorbell rang. Looking out the peephole, she recognized one of her neighbors from down the hall.

"Good evening, Mr. Fielding," Sheridan smiled at the elderly gentleman.

"Good evening, Miss Phillips," he replied with a smile of his own. He was a kindly looking old man with warm brown eyes and lots of snowy hair.

"What can I do for you?"

"Well, it's actually rather something that I might be able to do for you. With this damnable cold weather we've had, I purchased several bundles of firewood. However, this morning I was informed by my doctor that wood burning fires could be extremely detrimental, what with my respiratory problems."

"I'm so sorry to hear that."

"No need. One of the consequences of being old. However, since I can't use the wood, I'd like you to have it."

"Oh, Mr. Fielding," she breathed, "I couldn't possibly do that!"

"Why in heavens not? You're just about the only person I know in this building and you've always been very kind to me."

"Well then, at least let me pay you for it."

"Nonsense. It's a gift."

"But…"

"No buts," he responded adamantly. "I've brought two bundles for tonight and I'll have the superintendent bring the other four tomorrow." With that, he reached down by the side of the door and produced two large bundles of wood, which he placed on the floor just inside. "Enjoy."

After closing the door, she lugged the bundles back into the living room and over to the fireplace. She set them down and glanced at Nick. He'd moved to the side and seemed to be waiting calmly for her to build a fire. As he stared back at her, she saw that there was something knowing, a deeply satisfied look in his dark eyes. Something, as she'd thought before...unnerving.

The timer rang to announce the lamb chops needed to be turned under the broiler. The unexpected noise shattered the moment.

She and Nick ate a quiet dinner. Since he had two of the four lamb chops, he passed on dessert, opting instead to stretch himself out to his fullest length in front of the fire. Sheridan finished the dinner clean up, poured herself another glass of white wine and settled on the rug, propped on her left elbow just behind Nick. Absently, she ran her fingertips slowly along his soft side and watched the flames.

A quiet peace settled over them, as if lying here, basking in warm firelight with this wild animal was the most natural thing in the world. Yawning, she turned on her stomach, pillowing her head on crossed arms and closed her eyes.

"God, my back hurts," she complained softly. "I hate sitting at a computer for someone else."

Almost instantly, she felt weight settling in the dip at the base of her spine. A soft, furry weight. Moments later, a pair of velvet paws began gently massaging her back. Not that annoying kneading that cats do sometimes on your lap, claws extended. This was a delicate, deliberate movement. Gentle pressure in little circles. It was as heavenly as it was unexpected.

Occasionally, she felt Nick shift his weight and change his massage position. The sensation was both relaxing and sensual. Something about the feel of him against her skin made her think of strong, tender hands massaging away not only her sore, tired muscles, but the cares of the day as well.

Drowsing toward sleep, Sheridan remembered thinking that this was ridiculous. This was not a massage. It was the reflexive action of an animal. He hadn't understood her complaint of back pain. He couldn't have. It was a coincidence.

She yawned.

Just another coincidence, she repeated as sleep finally overtook her, Nick's paws still on her skin.

Chapter Three

Sheridan shivered, glanced groggily at the clock, pulled the comforter up around her ears, and burrowed deeper into the pillow. It was only six-seventeen a.m. Still another thirteen minutes until the alarm would ring. Even though she was no longer really asleep, she had no desire to stir from her warm bed.

Warm bed?

Her eyes flew open, head emerging from under the covers and looking around, confused and surprised. Beside her, Nick was sleeping soundly, curled into a tight ball, his back almost touching hers.

"How the hell did I get here?" she wondered aloud.

She tried to think. They'd been lying on the floor in front of the fire, Nick on her back, massaging her with his soft paws. She'd gotten drowsy. Obviously she'd fallen asleep but couldn't remember coming to bed.

Being careful not to squish Nick, Sheridan rolled slowly onto her back, still wondering what had happened. But try as she might, there just wasn't anything beyond the fire and the back rub.

Nick's face appeared in her field of view, his tongue lapping twice on her cheek.

"Good morning to you, too," she giggled, reaching her left hand out from under the covers and stroking him under the chin.

His sleek head snuggled under her chin, tenderly licking her throat and neck. Goose bumps rose on her bare flesh that she couldn't totally blame on the cold.

After a few admittedly delightful moments, she pushed him gently away. "Okay, Nick, enough. I need a shower, not a bath."

He pulled back a little and they looked at each other.

"You know," she whispered, lightly petting the top of his head with her fingertips, "you really are quite attractive."

Blinking once, Nick cocked his head slightly, and she again had the distinct feeling that not only was he paying attention to her but on some level he actually understood what she was saying.

"Those exotic eyes, jet-black fur, lean, muscular body. I bet you cut quite a swath with the ladies. I know if I was a lady cat..."

The sentence remained unfinished as the alarm blared and she reached over to turn it off. As she did so, something on the floor caught her eye. Or more precisely, somethings.

Scattered on the floor beside the bed were her clothes from the night before. Blouse, skirt, slip, bra, pantyhose, panties, shoes.

"What the hell?" Sheridan turned her head and glanced back at Nick. But before she could think further, another thought came to her. Quickly raising the covers, she was shocked to see that she was naked.

"I don't believe this," she shrieked. "What happened?"

Nick put out a paw and patted her bare arm, almost as if he were trying to comfort her.

"What the hell is going on? How did I get from the living room into bed? And what are my clothes doing on the floor? And why am I not wearing my nightgown?"

A look she could only call distress showed in Nick's dark eyes. Putting both his paws on her arm, he stretched up and licked her face again, one swift, tender pass of his tongue on her cheekbone.

"It's all right," she assured him, relaxing a little and touching her lips to the tip of his nose. "And thanks for your concern."

In a twinkling, the distress disappeared and she felt Nick's body relax too.

"Come on, guy," she told him firmly, throwing off the covers and putting her feet on the floor. "Time's a-wastin'."

* * * * *

"And the next thing I knew, it was morning and I was waking up in bed." Sheridan took a sip of coffee. "It was weird."

"How so?" Pat asked, reaching for another donut.

"Because I fell asleep in front of the fire. Fully clothed." Glancing at the doorway, she lowered her voice and leaned toward her friend. "When I woke up in bed, I was naked."

"Still don't see what your point is."

"It's winter, Pat. To save on the gas bill, I always turn the thermostat off at night and use my electric blanket. I wear my long flannel nightgown. Always," emphasizing the last word.

The other woman shrugged her shoulders as she nibbled on her chocolate donut.

"And when I get ready for bed, I always take my clothes off and put them in the hamper in the bathroom. But this morning, they...shoes, underwear, everything...were on the floor by my bed. Don't you think that's just a little strange?"

"I think you had a long, tiring day. You laid down in front of a warm fire with a full stomach and an extra glass of wine." She grinned maliciously. "Add that to a relaxing 'massage' by a good lookin' guy and the answer's simple. You fell asleep. Sometime later you woke up just enough to drag yourself into your bedroom, get undressed and fall into bed."

"I don't remember waking up," Sheridan insisted, becoming slightly irritated that her best friend wasn't taking her seriously. "And it wasn't a 'massage' as you call it."

"Coulda fooled me," Pat continued to tease. "The way you describe it, I was gonna ask if he makes house calls. I could use a good back rub myself."

"Ha, ha."

"Oh come on, Sher," her friend cajoled, "lighten up. You're acting like you were abducted by aliens, for Christ's sake. So you don't remember getting up and going to bed. It happens."

"Not to me," she retorted. "At least not after only a glass and a half of white wine."

"Okay, what the hell do you think happened? The cat carried you into your bedroom, undressed you and put you to bed?" Pat's teasing voice had taken on a slightly mocking tone.

Something icy blew lightly across Sheridan's neck and made her shiver a little. Suddenly, she no longer wanted to discuss the incident or Nick.

"Forget it," she snapped, picked up her cup and stood.

Pat looked up like she'd been slapped. "I'm sorry, Sher," she told her sincerely. "I was just kidding."

"Fine. Skip it. I have to get back to my desk."

Sheridan felt silly and a little ashamed of her behavior as she walked back to her desk. After all, realistically, Pat's explanation was not only plausible, but probably exactly what had happened. Still, it had been unsettling and she was mildly miffed that Pat had made light of it. And that crack about Nick picking her up, undressing her...

Stop it, she told herself firmly. Nick is a stray tomcat, albeit large enough to be a mini panther. Period.

As she sat down to resume typing the letter she'd been working on before the break, she tried to put the whole thing out of her mind. But before she could continue, Sheridan had to put on her sweater. It seemed her work area had suddenly developed a chill.

* * * * *

"So what is it exactly you do all day while I'm at work?" Sheridan asked, looking down at Nick as she latched the window.

Nick ignored her and made straight for the kitchen. As she followed him, she stopped only long enough to turn on the early news. Usually she didn't watch the news. Especially at dinnertime. Ruined her digestion. But she was anxious to find out what the weather forecast for the next day would be.

"We're having steak tonight," she remarked, coming into the kitchen. "I'm afraid it's top round and not T-bone but if you're going to live with a working girl, you'll have to adjust. However, as soon as I'm a rich, best-selling writer, I promise you filet mignon and lobster three times a day."

With a dismissive flick of his tail, Nick adjourned to the hearthrug to await a warm fire.

"Brat," Sheridan called after him.

As she was preparing the steaks, the doorbell rang. It was Brian, her superintendent's oldest son.

"Good evening, Brian."

He was tall, thin, gawky. Twenty-something, dirty blonde hair worn below his ears, pale blue eyes. Tonight he was wearing a pair of old, paint-spattered jeans and a much-faded University of Kentucky Wildcats sweatshirt.

"Evening, Miss Phillips," he replied, flashing a shy grin and studying his black high top sneakers. "My dad sent me up to bring you some wood from Mr. Fielding."

"Thank you, Brian," she smiled. "If you'll just set it in here by the door, I'll move it to the fireplace later."

"That's okay," he answered quickly, looking down at her. "I'd be happy to bring it in. These bundles are heavy."

"That's very nice of you, but I can manage. Really."

"Uh-uh," he shook his head. "Dad'd skin me alive if I did that. Besides, I can manage better than you. Been lifting weights."

"All right," she relented, and opened the door wide for him. "And thanks."

"No problem." With a grunt, he picked up a carrying strap in each hand and raised the two large bundles of wood.

"Please just put them down there," she pointed to the side of the fireplace.

With another grunt, he lowered them slowly to the rug, pushing them up against the wall, side by side. "Bring the others right away."

In a moment, he was back, stacking two more bundles on top of the first two.

"Uhm…Miss Phillips. Could I trouble you for a glass of water, please?"

"Sure, Brian. Why don't you sit down and rest for a second?"

"Thanks."

As she closed the fridge door, Nick ran up, tail held erect, waving frantically. Stretching as tall as he could, he pressed himself against her, his eyes wide and darker than she'd ever seen them.

"Meow!" he yelled loudly. "Meow!"

Sheridan had never seen him so agitated and was at a total loss.

She reached down with her free hand and tried to pet him but he jerked his head away and yowled more urgently.

"Anything wrong, Miss Phillips?" Brian appeared in the open archway between her little kitchen/dining area and the living room.

"I don't know," she admitted uncertainly.

Spying Nick, Brian grinned, squatted down and reached out an open hand. "What's his name?"

"Nick."

"Well hi there, Nick," Brian called brightly to the cat. "How ya doing, boy?"

Nick's head swiveled between Brian and her and she knew he was trying desperately to tell her something...something he obviously thought was important, but which she just couldn't understand. Finally, as if he sensed his mistress wasn't picking up his message, Nick lowered himself back to the floor and turned to face Brian.

Crouching almost flat on his stomach, ears flat against his head, teeth bared, Nick launched himself past the young man, clawing his hand as Brian made a grab for him. Sheridan caught a glimpse of him dash toward the bedroom before her attention was drawn back to Brian.

"Ouch!" he yelped, shook his left hand vigorously and stood up.

"Oh, Brian," Sheridan gasped. She set the pitcher of cold water on the counter and went to the young man. "Let me see that."

"It's okay, Miss Phillips," he responded, sticking the top of his hand in his mouth. "It's nothing."

She took his hand and examined it. Two thin, deep scratches about two inches long oozed blood, and a pair of twin red welts were already beginning to form.

"I don't think it's serious." She finished examining the injury and looked up at him. "But let me put some antiseptic and a Band-Aid on it."

"Oh no. It's all right." He grinned again. "Cats usually like me. Guess I must've scared him."

"Yes, well, Nick's not your average cat. I mean, he's really a stray. Just kind of drops in for food and a place to sleep out of the cold. I'm sorry."

"Like I said, no big deal."

"Well I feel awful just the same. At least let me give you that glass of water and a Band-Aid. Please."

"Well, okay. If it'll make you feel better."

"It will."

She handed Brian the glass of water, and watched as he folded his long frame onto the sofa. She went to bathroom to get the first aid items. As she crossed through the bedroom, she made a cursory search for Nick. Not seeing him, she got the antiseptic bottle, cotton balls and a Band-Aid from the bathroom. When she paused again in the bedroom to get something out of her nightstand, she felt her errant pet's presence even though she couldn't see him.

"Don't you think this is over, you contemptible little monster," she hissed. "Not by a damn sight. You're going to be yowling soprano when I get finished with you."

In the living room, Brian was sipping at his water and watching television. Calmer now, she sat down beside him and put the Band-Aid and all but one of the cotton balls on the coffee table. She flipped open the plastic antiseptic bottle, and drenched the soft material.

"Okay, this might sting a little."

It only took about three minutes to clean the scratches and apply the Band-Aid.

"There you go," Sheridan smiled when she was finished. "I can't tell you how sorry I am. But maybe this will help." From her pocket, she took a five-dollar bill and proffered it to him.

"Oh no, Miss Phillips," he protested, "I couldn't take that."

"Of course you can," she insisted, and pressed it into his palm. "Not just because Nick behaved abominably but because I really do appreciate you bringing the wood in and stacking it so nicely. Please take it."

"Okay. Thanks." He stared down at his shoes again.

"And on the local front, another woman in the Fairview Heights area was discovered this morning in her apartment, having been raped and beaten."

The announcement by the newscaster drew their attention to the television.

"Mary Dennis, thirty, of 52 West Elm, was found by police at about eleven o'clock this morning when, having failed to arrive at work or answer her phone, her worried co-workers phoned the authorities. When officers arrived, they found Ms. Dennis tied up in her bedroom, bruised, bleeding and unconscious. She was taken to St. Luke's Hospital where she's listed in stable condition.

"Ms. Dennis is the third woman attacked in her home in the Fairview Heights area in the last two months. The attacker is described as having blue eyes, approximately six feet tall, one hundred eighty pounds, muscular, dressed in a black turtleneck sweater, black pants and shoes and wearing a black ski mask and black gloves.

"All three attacks have taken place in broad daylight, two in the morning and one in the early afternoon."

"West Elm?" Sheridan repeated nervously. "That's less than four blocks from here. Two blocks closer than the last one."

"You don't have to worry, Miss Phillips. Especially not with that killer guard cat you got."

They both laughed and said their good byes. Then Sheridan went looking for Nick. She didn't have to go far.

"Olli, Olli oxen free, you miserable little bastard." She stood in the middle of her bedroom, arms folded across her chest, all the cold fury she was feeling reflected in her voice. She waited a few moments.

"Don't make this any harder on yourself. Trust me, this apartment…hell, this universe isn't big enough for you to hide in so you better just shag your sorry little ass out here and take what's coming to you. If you make me come looking for you, it's just gonna give me that much more time to think of how many different ways there are to skin a cat."

Slowly, a black pointed nose, whiskers and wary blue eyes emerged from the foot of her bed.

"What was that supposed to be?"

She'd expected him to slink out of hiding, cringe at her feet and begin begging for forgiveness. Instead, he still seemed to be nervous, agitated. And he made no move toward her.

"I don't know about you, but where I come from, attacking total strangers who haven't done anything but say 'hi' to you is considered very bad form."

Nick watched her, his whole body tense as a coiled spring.

"Well? Do you have anything to say for yourself at all?"

Suddenly, something uneasy rippled through her, breaking up and dissolving her anger. And Nick's anxiety seemed to be contagious. Concerned now, she took a step toward him. The face immediately disappeared back under the bed.

"Nick?" Sheridan called softly. She got down on her hands and knees and peered beneath the bed.

He'd retreated farther back, just out of her reach. There seemed to be nothing except two huge sapphires shining in the shadows.

Slowly, she slid her hand toward him.

"What's wrong, Nick?" she whispered. Suddenly, she was gripped by a strong need to touch him. He needed her and somehow, she needed him.

"It's all right," she soothed. "I'm sure you had your reason. I'm sorry I yelled at you. Just come out from there. Please." Sheridan's fingers stopped within inches of him and she laid her hand out flat, palm up.

Seconds dribbled by as she held her breath, waiting for this mysterious, independent, wild creature to decide if he was going or staying. As she looked into those eyes, she felt his need. And her own.

"I want you to stay," she told him sincerely.

More seconds. At last, he put out a tentative paw and laid it on her palm.

Fighting down an incredible urge to grab him, instead she brushed her thumb gently across his paw, trying to reassure him with her touch what she apparently couldn't with her words.

Gradually, Sheridan felt his paw creeping up her hand to her arm. He moved toward her. There was nothing for her to do but wait. Inch by inch, they moved out from the bed until she could sit up and hold him in her arms.

For several more minutes they sat there on her bedroom floor, Sheridan rocked him gently and felt his body slowly release its tension.

"How 'bout I finish getting our dinner and make a fire?" She grinned down at him. "But no wine tonight. Agreed?"

Nick stretched up and put his cold, wet nose on hers. Then he scrambled out of her grasp and scampered toward the living room.

Chapter Four

Nick and Sheridan fell into a comfortable routine.

No matter the weather or how late she worked, at the end of her day she'd find him on the fire escape, waiting for her to open the window.

Sheridan bought a litter box and tried to convince him to stay in the apartment during the day. "It's winter," she explained. "There's snow on the ground and that wind's like ice. And with my unpredictable schedule, you could freeze your cute little ass off waiting for me to come home."

But it was no use. Every morning, just before she was ready to leave for work, he'd go to the window and wait to be let out. A couple of mornings the weather was so bad she'd seriously considered just not opening it. For his own good, of course. But always he'd look at her with those eyes...part trust, part wild need...and she'd relent. And no matter what she tried, she never seemed to be able to see where he went. It just seemed that one moment he was there, the next he wasn't.

Occasionally, on the weekends when she was home, Nick would choose to stay in during the day, only asking to go out to answer the call of Nature. Other times, he would leave at his accustomed hour in the morning, not to return until night.

"If I didn't know better," she once scolded playfully, "I'd say you had another woman somewhere. Good thing for you I'm not any more insecure than I am."

Early on in their relationship, Sheridan discovered that for a stray, Nick's eating habits were, to put it mildly, eclectic. For one thing, he didn't do commercial cat food. Period. No matter how expensive the brand or enticing the label, all she got from him was a disdainful sniff and a dirty look. Raw meat was another no-no, everything had to be cooked—hamburger, roast, steak, chops. Apparently, he felt if it was good enough for her, it was good enough for him.

Beyond the expected taste for meat, Nick had other culinary peculiarities. Milk was for kittens and other sissies. Yet vanilla ice cream, banana pudding and cheese in any form sent him into rapture. Canned salmon? Certainly. Canned tuna? Not on your life. Meatballs with marinara sauce? Fine. Swedish meatballs? Don't be ridiculous. Mandarin chicken? Terrific. Sweet and sour pork? Forget it.

Sometimes after dinner they'd sit on the sofa and watch a little television. Nick liked for her to sit in the corner so that he could put his head and front paws in her lap and stretch his whole length, lying on his side. As they sat, she'd pet his head or stroke his body. Other times, they'd lie in front of the fire. Even on the nights when she'd adjourn to her computer in the bedroom to write, Nick would curl up contentedly on the left side of the desk and doze. Sheridan was amazed at how quickly and completely this little stranger had become such an important part of her life. And how lonely she'd been before his appearance.

No matter how long or rotten the day, she could close her apartment door now and not be alone. Nick gave her a companionship she hadn't admitted even to herself that she missed. He gave her someone to talk to and share a comfortable intimacy with.

In fact, since Nick had come into her life, Sheridan increasingly found herself at odd moments thinking that perhaps Pat was right. Perhaps it was time for her to try and make a new relationship.

"I'm glad you decided to stay," she told him one evening during a commercial break. "I enjoy having you around."

Instead of his accustomed lounging position, tonight, he'd curled himself in Sheridan's lap, his head on her stomach. At the sound of her words, he raised his head and gazed at her. A moment later, he stretched a bit and put his head between her breasts. The warmth of his body seem to warm her, too. She felt content and happy. Leaning down, she lightly kissed that adorable little nose.

"Thank you," she told him softly.

As if in response, he snuggled against her, stomach to stomach. His right front paw eased up and gently brushed her nipple. Immediately, she felt a very unexpected and very pleasant tingle.

The thought both surprised and disturbed her. It was ridiculous to have such a…a sexual response to something so innocent.

After all, Nick was just like any other cat, he enjoyed being stroked. That was one of the ways she expressed her approval, her caring for him. Wasn't it natural that he'd show his approval, his caring in the same way? And being a cat, he couldn't know what part of her he was touching. Licking. To him, skin was skin. It was the physical expression of their relationship, communicating their companionship and pleasure with each other's company.

The television program ended, the closing credits, squashed to unreadability in one corner of the screen, rolled quietly as the local news anchor appeared.

"Ahead on the news," she intoned seriously, "we have more highlights from today's press conference held by Police Chief Robbins concerning the Fairview Heights rapist. With the number of victims now five in less than three months, there are still no clues and no solid suspects."

"I don't know about you," Sheridan laughed as she clicked off the remote, "but I'm not interested in hearing about the Fairview Heights rapist right before bed. You ready to go?"

* * * * *

The stack of papers landed on Sheridan's desk with a heavy thud, the large black clip at the top making a sharp *ping* as it hit the laminate.

Startled, she jumped and turned her head from the computer. The Prince was standing just on the other side of the desk, his face a cold, mean mask.

"I've made the changes to this report," he announced pompously, nodding once toward the papers. Obviously he didn't think she was bright enough to figure out which report he meant. "There are major revisions. I have to have it before close of business."

Shit, she thought angrily. Out loud, she managed to keep a respectful tone. "I'll try, sir. But…"

"Don't try," he replied flatly. "Do."

Asshole.

"What I meant, sir, was that I'll do everything I can. But I can't stay late tonight. I have an important appointment."

Those beady little eyes glared down at her like a coiled rattler. "And I have to have this report. It's *very* important." His imperious tone and irritated grimace told her the rest. There was no doubt in his mind that his needs superseded anything in her trivial little life.

Glancing down at her desk, she stole a peek at her watch. It was ten of three. Her practiced secretary's eye told her the report was at least a hundred typed pages. Even putting aside the four "rush" jobs already on her desk and suffering the wrath of the other engineers was not going to save her from overtime.

"I realize that, sir," she answered carefully, raising her eyes to stare up at him. "and I'll stay until five-fifteen. But I really do have to be somewhere at six."

A touch of red appeared in that round, flat face and those full lips pulled tightly down. Sheridan felt like Oliver Twist standing with his empty bowl.

"That report," he hissed, leaning down into her face, "has to be finished…*tonight*. I'm sure you can cancel or at least postpone whatever it is you have to do." There was just the slightest pause. "No matter what it is, I'm sure it can't be more important than your job."

There it was. Her raises and even continued employment hinged on yearly reviews. And those yearly reviews depended solely on Jarvis Duncan. There was no recourse, no appeal. The Director, ensconced securely behind his closed door and faithful Administrative Assistant, was totally removed from the day-to-day operations of the office, relying absolutely on his supervisors' judgments, no matter how biased, vindictive or just plain wrong. And her yearly review was due in less than six weeks.

"Yes, sir," she sighed.

As he straightened up, she saw the merest hint of a satisfied smirk at the corners of his mouth.

For a second, Sheridan had a vision of running up and kicking him right in his wide ass, telling him to type his own fucking report and screaming "I quit!" at the top of her lungs. Wonderful as the mental picture was, it disappeared with Duncan's body as it rounded the corner back toward his office.

Someday, she thought bitterly, you're gonna get yours, you callous, tyrannical, blood-sucking, bastard! I'm going to write a book about this asylum and all the inmates. You and the rest of this crew of imbeciles and assholes'll be the laughing stock of the world and I'll be laughing the loudest. All the way to the bank!

Again her eyes fell on the pages, the print disfigured with scratch outs and scribbles. With a resigned sigh, she turned back to her computer.

* * * * *

"It's after six," Sheridan retorted, more than a small note of anger and frustration in her voice.

"I know what time it is," he said almost cheerfully, "and you know how much we appreciate you staying late to finish this."

He patted the sheaf of papers in front of him like a baby's butt. And she knew exactly how much her work was appreciated.

"But this is desperately important. So much so that George has agreed to wait in his office for it. And since you practically go by his building on your way home, I didn't think you'd mind dropping it off."

Of course, Sheridan thought, *you don't give a shit whether I mind or not*. Director John Curtin stood on the other side of the front counter, fake paternalistic concern on his face. Carefully casual, precisely cut and styled salt and pepper hair, name brand golf shirt covering his stocky chest, strong arms, his slight paunch bulging his designer slacks and belt. Only those impassive, disinterested dark brown eyes revealed his true nature. To him, she was no more than office equipment...the part of the computer that made the keys go up and down.

Nudging the papers toward her slightly, his voice took on the tone of an indulgent father trying to cajole a reluctant three-year-old to take her medicine. "I know that this is above and beyond, but you can add it to your overtime." The pretend smile got fractionally larger. "In fact, since it's dark and late and we know you want to get home, I'm giving you permission to take a taxi to the Cornwell Building and home and charge it to the firm." He looked like he had just delivered a royal pardon.

Yippee!

Knowing the only way she was ever going to get home was to capitulate, Sheridan nodded.

Curtin beamed and she had a picture of Nick's expression after he'd peed on her rejection letter. "Good. Good. Just make copies for Jarvis and me and you. Don't worry about the rest of the copies until tomorrow. Well, I've got to get home to Jean. I promised her we'd go for Chinese tonight."

"Sounds like a good idea," Duncan agreed. Of course, she thought acidly, he'd agree if John said the President was a Martian. "I better be getting home too."

"Well, good night, Sher."

"Good night, sir," she mumbled.

Turning back to his office, he took a step and then turned back to her, still wearing that ridiculous look of false concern. "And don't forget to call and have one of the security guards walk you out when the taxi comes. We wouldn't want anything to happen to you."

Sheridan didn't know whether to laugh or puke.

* * * * *

"If you'll wait a second," Sheridan hurriedly told the cabbie, "I'm just going to run in, drop this package off and come right out."

"Sure thing."

"Great. I'll be right back."

Opening her umbrella with one hand, she clutched her briefcase and made a dash from the curb to the entrance of the high rise, about twenty feet away. Her boots made a crunching noise as they moved quickly through the ice crust that had formed on the few inches of snow on the ground. A brisk wind was blowing the lightly falling snow.

After she signed in at the security desk, she took a quick ride to the thirtieth floor where George Wilkerson of Wilkerson, Dunby, Carlyle and Fisk, Civil Engineers, waited to take the report she'd brought. He gave her another, equally bulky package to return to the Director "on the morrow". In less than five minutes, she was back at her cab.

"Where to?"

"Six French Court," Sheridan replied, anxious now to get home to Nick. By now, he must be getting frantic, wondering where she was.

"Fairview Heights?"

"Uh-huh. Why?"

"Just heard on the radio. Big accident, intersection of Rosewood and Fairview. At least six cars. Cops, fire trucks, ambulances. The whole nine yards. Streets are blocked off in both directions. Closest I can do is Rosewood and Maple. Sorry."

Tears welled up and began silently spilling down her face. Sheridan was tired, angry, upset and just plain miserable. All she wanted was to go home to her warm apartment and curl up with the only being on the planet who cared whether she lived or died.

"Oh hey, lady," the cabbie yelped, concerned that he was responsible for the sudden fountain of tears. "I'm real sorry. Maybe if I drive up and tell the cops it's an emergency or something they'll let us through." He reached into the glove compartment and produced a tiny package of tissues, which he shoved in her direction. "You got kids or something?"

Shaking her head, she pulled out a tissue and wiped her eyes. The tissue immediately separated into soggy fuzz. "No, nothing like that. It's just that I've had a long day and walking seven blocks through the wind and snow and dark is not what I had in mind to top it off." She felt more tears.

"Maybe I could take you someplace else 'til the accident clears. A friend, maybe."

"No," she sighed, resigned to the inevitable. "Just take me as far as you can."

As it turned out, they didn't even get as far as the intersection. Because of the need for emergency vehicles to come and go, the police were turning traffic around two blocks from the accident. Getting out, she gave the cabbie the corporate account number (and a fat tip) and began trudging the nine blocks home.

By the time she finally locked the door behind her, Sheridan could feel the beginnings of a tickle in her throat and building pressure in her ears. Tomorrow, she would no doubt be in the clutches of a full-blown cold.

Good, she thought acidly. *First thing I'm going to do is go in and cough on Duncan and Curtin both.*

Nick came through the window as soon as it was open enough for him to slither in. He peered up at her questioningly, wet, cold and clearly glad to finally be inside.

"I'm sorry, Nick," she smiled, squatting down and taking him in her arms. "It wasn't my fault, really." She carried him into the bathroom, nuzzling him and stroking his wet fur. "Come on. Let's get you dried out and then we'll have some dinner."

* * * * *

"So then I ended up having to walk the rest of the way home. And I don't need to tell you how shitty it is outside. And on top of everything else, I think I'm coming down with a fucking cold." She threw another log on the fire and pulled the screen closed.

After towel drying Nick, Sheridan had stripped out of her wet clothes, indulged in a hot shower and fixed them both cheeseburgers. Now they were relaxing on the sofa, a roaring fire crackling in the fireplace as she explained why she'd been so late. Strangely, even though he'd been wet and shaking, Nick hadn't seemed the least bit upset. In fact, he'd seemed more concerned with whether or not she was all right.

Sheridan sat back down, Nick nudging his head against her hand, his signal that he wanted her to rub his head. Raising her hand, he laid his head on her thigh. Gently, she began to pet the top of his head with her fingertips.

"You know what?" she said, watching the flames.

Without moving his head, Nick looked up at her.

"I hate my fucking job. Typing those dry, boring, interminable reports. Babysitting those arrogant, conceited, moron engineers. Being at the mercy of stupid, lazy, vindictive bastards. Now, taking that crap on a daily basis, eight hours a day, five days a week, fifty weeks a year is bad enough. But, as an added bonus, I get to be under the thumb of King John and the Prince of Darkness.

"Sometimes I think they rub my nose in their perceived 'superiority' over me just because they can. Because it makes them feel 'big' and 'important'. And more and more it seems like the kind of day I had today is becoming the norm, rather than the exception.

"There are days when the only thing that gets me out of bed and into that hell hole is the need to support my writing 'til my writing can support me."

An evil grin appeared on Sheridan's face as she scratched his ear. "You know what I'd really like? I mean, besides becoming a best-selling author? I'd like to lose good ole Duncan. Not anything as permanent as being squashed by a falling piano, mind you. No, just something to get him out of my life for say, six months. I see him maybe being in a car accident and breaking a leg. Let him be laid up at home. Hire someone to replace him for a while. Maybe a decent human being. With a double digit IQ and a soul. What do you think, Nick? Is that wicked or what?"

He gazed at her thoughtfully, again seeming almost to be turning her words over in his mind. As if he understood her. For several moments he lay motionless, those dark eyes fixed on hers. Abruptly, he moved his head from under her fingers, stretched up, and that slender pink tongue found her cheek.

And even after all that had happened during the day, she felt calmer, more at peace. Like everything really was going to be all right.

Chapter Five

By morning, Sheridan was sick. But calling what she had a cold was like saying the North Pole gets chilly in December; it didn't begin to cover the situation. Hers was, to put it plainly, the mother of all colds.

"Fine friend you are," she grumbled hoarsely. "Leaving me on death's doorstep, no doubt for your other mistress."

Anxiously, Nick stretched up and patted the frosty window glass with his paw. Usually patient until they'd finished breakfast and she was ready to leave, this morning he'd seemed restless, eager to be out and away. Sheridan chalked it up to her cold. After all, what male would want to stay around a hacking, cranky female dragging around in her bathrobe and slippers, a comb having been run through her hair only sufficiently to make the bigger lumps lay down?

"You're all alike," she grumped as she fumbled for the latch. Her fingers felt like sausages, her brain seemed coated with peach fuzz. "Stick around for the steaks and strokes and then bail at the first sign of trouble." The window slid up a little and Nick hopped up on the sill, scattering some of the freshly fallen snow on the carpet as he landed.

"Traitor," she muttered as he jumped into the white blanket coating the fire escape, and landed up to his chest in the snow. He stood there a moment, an ebony blotch on a perfect white canvas. A huge sneeze rustled deep in her nose, giving her only enough time to grab a tissue from her robe pocket before it exploded, threatening to take the upper half of her face with it.

When she opened her eyes again, wiping her nose as quickly as possible, she glanced out to the fire escape. Nick had vanished.

* * * * *

Sheridan spent most of the day on the sofa, downing cold capsules, swilling orange juice, dozing and generally feeling shitty. The television was on, more for company than for entertainment. What with her stuffed head and not watching too much daytime television anyway, she had a lot of trouble following most of the shows, although she enjoyed the *Starsky and Hutch* rerun and the talk show where women were demanding their men take paternity and/or lie detector tests (most of them flunked). She also felt lonely and not a little pissed that Nick would leave her like this.

About six o' clock, Sheridan heard him scratching on the glass. "Glad you could make it," she commented as he scampered through the window. When he looked up at her, there was something…pleased, in the depths of those beautiful eyes. Immediately, he began to rub himself against her legs. It was not a grovel for attention; more like a celebration. Not knowing what was going on, but happy to see him, she bent down and picked him up.

After he licked her face, Nick settled into her arms and they went into the kitchen. For dinner, she heated him some leftover roast and had a cup of tea and some toast. The few dishes done, they curled up together on the sofa, Sheridan under the blanket, Nick on top, tucked snugly against her stomach, his head resting lightly on her arm.

As they lay together, it occurred to Sheridan that this was what she'd wanted in her marriage. The closeness of soul as well as body. Quiet calm. The certainty that at least one other being in the universe cared about you, wanted you to be happy. Someone, as the old saying went, who knew you for what you were and liked you anyway.

But there was more to this than mere companionship, she knew. Something that both excited and disturbed her. Her rational mind might try to dismiss it as the normal interactions of a pet with its owner, but her soul (and increasingly, her body) had begun to recognize the faint stirrings of longing. Something physical that seemed to respond to him almost in spite of herself. There was a faint stirring on the far horizon of her mind of something locked away and virtually forgotten.

It was as if Nick had suddenly reminded her how much she missed having someone special to share her life. And her bed. He'd made her remember the tingle a warm caress or a fleeting kiss could bring. The wonder of two bodies joined in the physical expression of love.

Much as she was trying to deny it, it was as if Nick's very presence had awakened her need, her desire, for a man in her life.

The stray thought suddenly transformed itself into a video in her mind. Soft, cool sheets. Moonlight through an open window. A man and a woman, naked, wrapped in each other, lips and hands on heated flesh, moving together toward the goal of their growing passion.

Sheridan's eyes popped open and she realized that she was sweating, her heart racing, a strange feeling making her dizzy and lightheaded for a moment. Instantly, she felt a soft paw on her arm and two blue beacons of concern looked anxiously up at her.

"It's all right," she assured him with a grin and rub on the top of his head. "I was daydreaming. Probably had a fever spike."

Nick continued to gaze at her, his velvet fur brushed gently on her skin.

"Well," she yawned, "I don't know about you, but I can't keep my eyes open. I'm going to take some more cold medicine and call it a night."

As if on cue, Nick yawned too, stood and stretched from his front claws to the tip of his tail. Without another sound, he jumped off the sofa and began to stroll for the bedroom. When Sheridan came out of the bathroom, he was on his side of the bed, chin resting on his outstretched front legs, eyes half closed.

"Good night, Nick. I'll try not keep you awake with my hacking all night."

* * * * *

Sheridan took another two days off. Truth be told, she could have gone back to work after one more day, but what the hell? As she viewed things, it wasn't like the office was going to come to a screeching halt without her. They could always find another warm body to keep the computer keys moving.

Once she started to feel human again, she didn't even mind daytime television. Especially since the sun had come out and the temperature began to soar toward the middle teens. And most especially because Nick decided to stay home with her. She worked on a short story she'd been trying to finish, made a crock-pot of beef stew and watched a romantic video. Like most men she'd ever known, Nick had seconds of the beef and slept through the video.

Facing work the next morning, Sheridan and Nick decided to make it an early night. In the bathroom, she took two cold capsules so she could sleep and, shutting off the bathroom light, went into the bedroom. Nick was in his accustomed place, curled up, his eyes half closed.

Slipping between the sheets, she gave him a few last strokes on the top of his head.

He rubbed this head against her palm, licking the tips of her fingers.

"Good night to you, too."

* * * * *

At the time, Sheridan remembered thinking that the dream was a combination of the cold medicine and the sexy video. After all, just because she was divorced and alone didn't mean that she'd forgotten completely about romance and sex. Later...well, later the dream was only one of many things she'd wonder about.

For one thing, she didn't normally dream. At least not things she remembered afterwards. Sometimes bits and pieces, but never whole stories. And certainly not with the reality and depth of detail this one had.

Something moved slowly, gently, tantalizingly over her face, ears and neck. Sheer silk. Butterfly wings. Softness that made her skin tingle.

As she opened her eyes, Sheridan was surprised to see that her bedroom wasn't dark. Candles, all shapes, sizes and colors flickered around the room, a heady mixture of aromas wafted through the air. And the softness gliding effortlessly over her was fingertips.

Interested but strangely not alarmed—it was, after all, only a dream—Sheridan turned her head on the pillow. Her lips and nose brushed an unfamiliar face .She could see black hair, enormous dark blue eyes, slender nose, high cheekbones, and full lips, smiling mysteriously at her from a sleek oval face.

"Hello, Sheridan," he murmured. It was a deep, husky voice.

"Hello," she replied casually. "Do I know you?" Now, of course, it sounded incredibly stupid, but at the time, it seemed an appropriate question.

"Very well," he chuckled, "but not nearly as well as you soon will."

As she looked into those eyes, she felt she did know him somehow. She just couldn't remember. "How do I know you? What's your name?"

"Shhhh. You think too much. You need to feel. This is a dream. Let yourself go, Sheridan." To make his point, he put his mouth on hers, and ran his tongue along her lips until they parted, almost by themselves. Swiftly, hungrily, he explored every part of her mouath as his fingers continued to play over her warm flesh. The combination of sensations sent shock waves of half-forgotten pleasure rolling through her.

Carefully he pulled back the covers and pushed them to the foot of the bed. The expected blast of cold air didn't come. Those unbelievably soft fingers moved down her chin and throat and stopped on the top button of her sunflower flannel nightgown. In a moment, it was sliding over her head and off the edge of the bed. Still, she wasn't cold. In fact, her body was very warm.

The stranger had suddenly shed his clothes, black pants and shirt she thought, and was lying against her, his skin smooth and glistening in the candlelight.

"You are so beautiful," he said tenderly. "I wanted you the first moment I saw you." Leaning over, he kissed her again, still gently, still searching with his tongue. As his bare chest connected with her breast, he took her other nipple in his fingers and began to roll it between his fingers, feeling it harden in response.

"Where…? What…?" The words formed but were lost in the burst of pleasure of his touch on her breast.

"Don't talk," he repeated, more breathlessly than before. "Just let me touch you. Taste you. I knew the moment I first looked into your eyes. I could have snapped my fingers and had you then, but I needed for you to want me as I want you. I knew how frightened, how bitter you'd become. Cut yourself off. I had to steal into your life so you could come to trust me. Care about me. Love me."

Small, wet kisses trailed down from Sheridan's lips as he changed his position slightly to expose her breast. Quickly, his tongue brought that nipple to the same hardness that his fingers had accomplished on the other side. The feel of his tongue playing over the sensitive area made her gasp with delight.

"That night you fell asleep," he breathed. "You were so beautiful in the firelight. Your skin pink and flushed. Little lights in your dark hair. I picked you up and you were light as a feather as I laid you on this bed. It was like unwrapping a beautiful Christmas present. Every layer of clothing revealed another part of your exquisite body. Your feet. Legs. Arms. Breasts. Ass."

She felt his hand slide down from her breast, across her stomach and into the black curls below her belly button.

"I ran my hands over your body and it was like satin, and I wanted you so badly my body ached. But I knew it wasn't right. That you weren't ready. Now you are." His fingers moved farther south, finally reaching their goal.

Sheridan's body quivered as he massaged her clit. It had been so long since a man had touched her, loved her… All she could do was make little mewling sounds. He seemed to know her body exactly. She could feel the heat and excitement building rapidly inside her.

His mouth moved from her breast, followed his fingers south, and marked his journey with kisses and flicks of his tongue down her stomach. The feel of his hot breath as he wound his way through her pubic hair made her squirm, but he never faltered. He gently nudged her thighs apart and settled between them, her private, intimate secrets now exposed to his gentle exploration.

Finally, his mouth arrived to replace his fingers. As his tongue began fondling her, Sheridan couldn't believe the sensation. This hadn't been something her ex had been comfortable with and her knowledge of this particular expression of physical passion was extremely limited. She was afraid that the combination of his attention and the length of time since she'd been with a man would bring her to climax in another breath.

Perhaps he sensed her urgency as he slowed his tongue, and moved slightly from the pleasure point and began to suck gently on her wet flesh.

"You taste so good," he mumbled, his voice now only a harsh whisper. "Like sweet, warm honey. I've dreamed of how you'd feel. Smell. Taste. My wildest dreams, though, pale with the reality." That tongue began to massage her again, alternating long, slow, delicate strokes with quick, furious pressure.

Sheridan's head was spinning, her body trembling with the intensity of feeling. Never had she experienced such passion, such physical pleasure, even in her marriage. She felt as if she were going to explode, literally.

"That's right," he encouraged, taking his mouth from her only long enough to take a breath. "Let me give you this gift. Release yourself to me and let me feel your passion, your joy."

She felt her body tense, grabbed the sheet with one hand and his hair with the other. For a moment, she was struck by how soft and silky his black hair was and then everything was blotted out in a moment of shattering bliss. She made some kind of noise, her back arched, rainbows and stars fountained through her like victory skyrockets. It felt like she was suspended in some kind of perfect web of pleasure.

When it was over, Sheridan lay on her back, panting like an exhausted animal, unable to move. Completely, thoroughly, utterly drained. When she could finally think again, she opened her eyes. All she could see were those incredible eyes watching her over her own pubic hair. She didn't need to see his mouth, she could see the smile of satisfaction in his eyes.

After a few moments, he touched her hips and rolled her gently onto her stomach. She couldn't have resisted even if she'd wanted to. Tenderly, he pulled her to him, raised her hips so that she was on her hands and knees, face turned to one side, resting on the pillow. She felt his hot, erect cock rub against her ass.

"You have the most beautiful ass I've ever seen," he breathed. "Round and white and perfect." To make his point, he bent down and kissed each cheek.

Sheridan was so wet he slid in effortlessly. Again, this was not a position she had a great familiarity with. Having married young, a virgin, her ex had insisted on being in charge of this area of their lives just as he ruled all the other aspects. He had very definite ideas about sex and this hadn't been included in them.

"You feel so good," he mumbled. "Just like I knew you would. Relax. Feel me. Feel yourself."

There were so many sensations. Not just the heat of him filling her to bursting but the friction of his body rubbing against her ass, his hands kneading her cheeks. And even though she had just come, she could feel herself beginning to build again. It was something that had never happened to her before, but the feeling was unmistakable.

Again, he seemed to almost read her mind. "It's the position. Most humans don't understand that we're animals. This is how we made love for millennia. The really sensual, sensitive nerve endings are in the front not the back. When a man mounts from the back, he contacts with those places. You feel it, don't you?"

Some kind of noise came out of her, that same sort of animal in heat sound she'd made before. But she didn't care now about anything except the feel of this man inside her and the waves of pleasure that were cresting and shuddering through her body.

Sheridan became aware that his strokes were getting harder, faster. She felt his body slapping against hers, the sound of wet flesh grinding together, his fingers digging into her cheeks. And instinctively, she began to rock back and forth, in sync with this stranger in their timeless dance of passion.

"Oh…oh…" he moaned, gripping her tightly. As the first tremors of his climax arrived, they touched off her own. The fireworks erupted again, as brilliant and shattering as the one just passed, joined with this dream creature in an experience more passionate, more wonderful than any that had ever taken place in her real world.

Spent, he slipped out and fell to the bed beside her. He pulled her to him; they lay together, eyes closed, and listened to their hearts return to normal rhythms, bodies slick with a sheen of passion. As their breathing became more regular, she felt herself slip back to sleep. Of course, the rational part of her brain told her she'd been asleep all along. This whole thing was just a dream.

She put out her hand, and felt his warm soft hair under her fingers.

"Thank you," she mumbled dreamily as she stepped off into blackness.

Sheridan thought he answered her but couldn't clearly make out the words. It sounded, for all the world, like a deep growl. Or maybe even a purr.

Chapter Six

Not surprisingly, the candles, exotic scents and romantic stranger were gone when she opened her eyes the next morning. Even her flannel nightie was in place, buttoned all the way to her neck. Beside her, Nick was coiled tightly against the morning chill, blue eyes closed. She lay for several blissful minutes, reliving the dream in her head. It had been so real...so... Well, not like any dream she'd ever had before.

Sighing heavily, she flipped off the covers and stood up. Nick opened his eyes but made no effort to move from where he was. Normally, the slightest movement would rouse him. This morning, however, he seemed perfectly content to stay where he was. Only his eyes moved, watching her as she yawned and stretched.

"Good morning, Sleepyhead," she teased. "Are you getting out of bed this morning or have you decided to sleep in?"

His whiskers fidgeted a little and the pink tip of tongue showed but nothing else.

"Suit yourself. You know where I'll be if you want me."

Just as she was stepping into the shower, he roused himself enough to saunter into the bathroom and take his spot on the vanity so that he could watch her. This morning, though, he didn't seem to be studying her with the same intensity that he usually did. Perhaps the novelty of seeing her naked was wearing off.

"Don't forget," she told him after breakfast as she moved over to the window to let him out. "I have to stop at the grocery store tonight so I'll probably run a little late. I've decided though, that if King John and the Prince of Darkness pull another dirty trick like sticking me with the errand girl routine,

I'll call the super and have him let you in, no later than six. It's too damn cold for you to have to suffer because I work for a group of assholes. See ya tonight."

* * * * *

Diana Kessler always reminded Sheridan of a little girl. It wasn't just her short size. At five foot one, barely one hundred pounds, she was smaller even than Sheridan, although they shared the same age. Mousy brown hair which never changed shade or length, cut short and curly, matching mousy brown eyes, pert nose, rosebud mouth, round face. She looked like one of those illustrations of ten-year-olds from 1940's elementary readers.

She was one of those girls who's voted most popular in the seventh grade and then disappears without a trace in high school. Not stupid exactly, just not quite the sharpest knife in the drawer. Prone to giggles. Incurable flirt. The kind of classmate that set your teeth on edge at twelve. At thirty-something, divorced, saddled with elderly, demanding parents and no life of her own, she was virtually unbearable.

To most of her fellow workers, that is. Fortunately for her, though, not to the Director, Mr. Curtin.

Six and a half years earlier, Sheridan had been hired a week ahead of Diana, who'd come aboard as Executive Administrative Assistant to the then-head of the Large Projects Department, Miriam Cutler. Ms. Cutler had been the primary reason Sheridan had put aside her reservations about working with engineers and signed on as Administrative Assistant for the Design and Construction Division. Smart, funny, competent, she was that rare combination of professional engineer, good administrator and people person. Like most of the peons below Professional Engineer rank, Sheridan adored her.

"MC", as she was affectionately called, could really churn out the work. Nothing was more important than getting the job done. As she'd told Sheridan the day she was hired, "We're busy here. All of us. The learning curve's very steep. Don't ever hesitate to ask questions, but I'm afraid I need someone who can hit the ground running." She imagined Diana had gotten the same speech, only in spades.

For months, Diana would arrive at work to find her desk covered with correspondence, reports, files and written instructions. In the few spare moments Sheridan had, she often took things to help, not her, but the Director. Twice, Diana confided to her, on the brink of tears, that she wasn't sure she could cut it. Being the new kids on a definitely cold block, they'd gravitated together. At one point, Sheridan had even been naive enough to believe they were friends.

Unfortunately, Miriam Cutler had two major flaws — she was a woman in a profession and a firm dominated by men and she was better than any three of them put together. Firing her outright would have left the company open to a lawsuit and might have made the partners look bad. But Sheridan had been around the block enough, and so had MC, to recognize the pattern — unreasonable work demands and schedules, getting the shit jobs and clients, increasing pressure, personally and professionally. Remarkably, she stood it for almost a year. Then, abruptly, she made the announcement at the weekly partners meeting that she was leaving for another firm.

She'd accepted a vice-presidency with a firm far larger and more prestigious than theirs, taking several clients with her. In less than two years, she'd made partner. Much later, they'd learned that the firm's partners had approached her.

With King John's ascension to the throne, Diana's fortunes had risen too.

It began innocently enough. Weekly lunches away from the office, "to discuss our work." Lunches that rapidly stretched to two hours. A remodel of the Director's office and his Assistant's office. Complete rain outfit and steel-toed construction boots — all custom-made because of her small size — so that she could accompany the Director "out in the field". Conferences, official functions, even "management training" for her. All at the company's expense. Rumors about the lengthy closed door meetings in his office were widespread and colorfully speculative.

Inevitably, their relationship inside and outside the office began to make itself known on the grapevine. King John and Princess Di became Sugar Daddy and the Cupcake. Mostly the office staff wondered among themselves how the Dynamic Duo escaped the watchful eyes of the partners. And Mrs. Curtin.

More and more, Diana found herself cut off from the rest of the women in the office. Take, for instance, girls' lunches. They excluded her, making plans in whispers and leaving the office solo or in pairs, meeting up at the selected restaurant and then slinking back again separately. The general consensus was that they had to kiss her ass eight hours a day, they weren't going to do it on their own time. And it was well known that whatever you said to her, you might just as well go into the Director's office and say to him.

Now, Sheridan and Diana's paths crossed only when she had work to delegate or in the office break room. Even at that, Sheridan was usually in before she was and they had their breaks and lunches at different times and different locations. Which was why Sheridan was surprised when Diana came through the break room door that morning as she was making the first pot of coffee.

"Oh, Sher," she gasped, her eyes wide, "I'm so glad you're back."

Translation: I actually had to work while you were out sick.

"It was awful!" she exclaimed. "Just awful."

Sheridan couldn't imagine why. Diana had a whole clerical staff to dump work on while she was gone. Unless, of course, there'd been a real emergency with the Prince and she'd screwed up.

"What?" Sheridan asked, suddenly curious to know what minefield she might be walking into.

"Jarvis," she squeaked excitedly. "Mr. Duncan. He was in a terrible accident."

Something cold prickled down her spine and Sheridan felt her stomach tighten with a nameless dread.

"Accident?" she repeated timidly.

Diana nodded emphatically. "That first day you called in sick. He was driving to work and lost control of his car and slammed right into a light pole. The fire department had to come and cut him out of his car and the ambulance took him to the hospital. He broke his left hip, both leg bones and his ankle. Got a concussion and some sore ribs. Doctor said he was lucky to be alive."

Instantly, her words came back to her. "I'd like to lose Duncan." The tightness in her stomach became a hard knot.

"Is…is he going to be all right?"

"Oh yes, but he'll be away for at least four to six months. The doctor said he'll be in a wheelchair and then on crutches and he wants Jarvis…Mr. Duncan…to rest and stay off his leg until it's completely healed."

She breathed a sigh of relief. "Well, that's good. I guess it could have been worse. Driving on these icy roads can be treacherous. How did it happen, do you know?"

"John and I went to see him as soon as he was able to have visitors." There was a slight but unmistakable note of superiority in her tone. "He said he was driving along, when all of a sudden a cat darted into the street, right in front of the car. He slammed on the brakes and swerved to avoid it. Said it was odd because he has anti-lock brakes on his car and they should have kicked in and they just didn't and he went smack into the light pole on the driver's side. Probably because of the ice."

"A…cat?" Sheridan could barely get the word out.

"That's what he said. A big, black cat. Ran right out in front of him."

The room suddenly listed to port and her head got light. She put out a hand to catch herself, and for a moment she had the distinct feeling she was going to faint.

"Sher, are you all right?" There was sincere concern in Diana's voice and face.

Nodding, she got hold of herself and took a deep breath. "Yes. Thanks. I just felt a little dizzy, that's all. Probably the cold medicine."

"Are you sure? You look awful. Maybe you ought to sit down. Even go home."

"No," Sheridan assured her, smiling thinly. "I'm fine. I just need a cup of coffee, that's all."

Patting her hand, Diana smiled that idiot smile of hers. "Well, take it easy. Rich is taking over Jarvis' projects until we can get a temporary replacement in. He's going to contact everyone and see about extensions. Things should actually quiet down for a few days."

Back at her desk, Sheridan stared at the blank screen, her mind racing. A cat. A big, black cat.

It wasn't possible. It had to be a coincidence.

Another coincidence.

Since Nick had come into her life, it seemed that coincidences had become the norm. It also seemed that whatever she asked for, including a near-fatal accident for the Prince, she got. The thought sent another cold shiver through her.

Her mother's voice echoed from her childhood. "Be careful what you wish for. You just might get it."

* * * * *

Sheridan had never paid any attention to the little place, tucked between a small shoe repair shop and a second-hand record store, between a delicatessen and the office, about three blocks away. Now, standing in front of the ornately painted front window, she was torn between going in and simply walking on.

BELL, BOOK AND CANDLE
Everything Occult

Perhaps this was another coincidence. She'd walked down this street, past these stores dozens of times and never noticed this one. Why had she stumbled onto it now, seemingly by accident?

Timidly, she moved to the door and went in.

If someone had asked her a few days earlier, Sheridan would have said that a store dealing in the occult would have been tiny and cave-like, tended by a decrepit, shriveled hunchback. Bell, Book and Candle, on the other hand, was large and brightly lit, crammed with bookshelves and posters and candles and crystals in all shapes and colors. And the only person she saw working was a twenty-something, nerdy looking young man in thick black glasses who was apparently trying, with limited success, to grow a mustache. At the sound of the door opening, he looked up and smiled.

"Hi," he greeted her warmly, "what can I do for you?"

Suddenly, her mind went blank. The young man, identified by his pocket name badge as "Ed", continued to look at her expectantly.

"I...I'm a writer," she stammered finally. "I'm doing a story. Kind of...fantasy, I guess. I've never done anything like this before and I...I need some information. For research."

"Sure," he chirped. "Whatcha need?"

"Are there...creatures that can change from...animals...to...people?"

If the question surprised him, he didn't show it. "What category?"

"Excuse me?"

"What category of creature are you interested in?" The look on his face told her that she obviously didn't know even the simplest thing about the subject.

"I'm...I'm sorry. I didn't know there were categories. As I said, I've never done this before." She tried to smile. "I'm afraid I'm a rank amateur in this area."

The kid relaxed a little and that annoying smile widened. "Oh that's all right. We get all kinds in here." He frowned. "I assume you're talking about "earth" beings and not aliens. Aliens are a whole 'nother subject."

Right.

"Yes, I guess so."

"Well then, in that case, there are three major kinds of beings that change from humans to animals and back. The first is shape shifters. They're really neat. They can change into any kind of shape they want, whenever they want. You know, like Ricky the Slasher in the Mall Crawler movies. Especially *Mall Crawler Three – Red Christmas*. He looked at her like she should know what he was talking about.

Not getting anything but a blank look, he forged on. "As far as animals are concerned, wolves are the usual choice, but, like I said, they can do whatever they want. Then there are familiars, companions to witches. That's where you get your traditional Halloween black cat. Sometimes they change into people, but usually they stick strictly to the animal shape. Finally, there are witches themselves. They usually change into animals when they're hiding or when they want something."

"Want something?"

"Oh yeah," he grinned. "Witches are very powerful but sometimes they like to do things on the sly. I mean, who's gonna pay any attention to a dog or a cat or a bird? Also makes a hell of an escape route."

That lightheaded feeling engulfed her again, and it was all she could do to remain upright. But there were things she had to find out.

"What about warlocks?"

"You mean male witches?" he replied.

"Isn't that what a warlock is?" Sheridan was becoming more and more confused.

"That's what most people think," he continued seriously, "but it's not true. Actually, the word warlock means 'oath breaker'. It comes from the witch hunts...the Burning Times as they're known. It meant anyone who was a traitor to the Craft. A male witch is just that...a male witch."

"Oh. Well then...can...can witches...grant wishes?"

"Piece a cake."

"Even read minds?"

"Oh sure."

"Can," she could feel her throat closing up, "can...witches make...make love with...humans?"

The kid lit up like a pinball machine gone "tilt".

"Are you kidding? Ever read about Zeus and Lido?" He laughed and turned slightly. "If you're interested, we have this book called *A Super Natural High: The Witch's Kama Sutra*. Got pictures and everything. It's right over..."

Chapter Seven

The hunt.

There was nothing like it, he thought as he moved silently, deliberately, through the shadows, every muscle taut, every sense keen and alert. It pumped adrenaline into an otherwise dreary life, tapping into something primeval and urgent. Something very much like life and death.

Prey.

He knew the best places to seek it out, even in this broad, sprawling city. Even in the light of day when the grazers were out, heedlessly going about their placid, herd lives, believing that their very numbers gave them safety.

But a cunning hunter knew all the tricks. Could follow a promising trail, sometimes for days, watching, waiting to find the weak, the straggler, the unwary. Pick his own moment to strike, leaping out and going for the jugular. Watching the prey struggle, hearing it bleat pathetically, the terror in its dull little eyes as the reality sinks in, sharp and inevitable as fangs.

A tremor of excitement rippled through his lean body, the familiar excitement beginning to bubble up like magma waiting to erupt, driving him on like something ravenous inside. Something that couldn't, wouldn't be denied even if he'd wanted to. And he most certainly didn't want to.

Sometimes it seemed to him that stalking and the game of strategy was more thrilling, more satisfying than the taking itself. In a little while, the urge would be filled, the need sated.

All around him, the little apartment buildings and houses converted to flats, rose up. A working class place, neat and tidy but past its prime. Narrow, residential streets, deserted by jobs and cold in the midmorning quiet. Alleys and fire escapes giving secret, hidden access to carelessly unlatched windows and unlocked doors. Prime hunting ground that had already yielded prey and that was still fat with ripe bounty.

As he prowled his hunting grounds, the need in his belly grew, heightening the urgency with every step, spreading the fire to his blood. He knew what to look for. The seemingly harmless, insignificant signs that others, less crafty, might overlook. The telltale signs of laziness, carelessness or stupidity that would bring him what he sought.

Patience. He must have a little more patience. Be careful. Watchful. In his jungle, it was only a momentary lapse, a heartbeat and the predator became the prey.

A little while longer…

* * * * *

Sheridan had a vague recollection of darting…running…out of the shop, desperate to be away from the grinning young man and his shape shifters and witches and Halloween cats. She didn't even remember how she got back to the office or what happened that afternoon.

It seemed that in a wink of time, she was trudging slowly up her front stairs, three plastic grocery bags hanging heavily from her arms. Because of the Prince's accident, all projects had been suspended until a replacement engineer could be brought in. Rick Yung, the Senior Engineer under Duncan, had enough difficulty managing his own projects; being in charge of the division was out of the question. So things had ground almost to a halt and she'd left the office on time for a change.

In the apartment, she set the bags down and went to the window. Dusk was just settling, the first lights in the surrounding buildings coming on. Nick wasn't waiting for her. Scanning the fire escape and the alley and not seeing him, she stepped away and went into the bedroom.

Part of her was actually relieved. With everything that had happened, she wasn't at all sure she wanted to spend any more time with this mysterious stranger she'd opened both her home and heart to. But part of her, perhaps only because he'd become such a part of her life, was definitely saddened that he wasn't in his usual place to greet her.

Six o'clock came and went. Then seven and still no Nick. Sheridan could feel the bitter cold through the closed glass of the windowpane as she peered into the darkness. He should have been home by now, she thought, growing more anxious with every passing minute.

Going into that occult shop had been a mistake. This whole business about humans changing into animals and back was just so much hooey. Having abandoned fairy tales, religion and science fiction long ago, it was ridiculous for her to have even listened to such idiotic notions. Ed had simply been parroting back a lot of superstitious nonsense.

Why was she worried? She was an intelligent, educated, reasonably sophisticated woman. Nick was a stray cat. Hell, in the strictest sense of the word, he didn't even really belong to her. When spring came and the weather was warmer, he might decide to resume his street life fulltime. Right now, as she stood there fretting, he might be enjoying some other good-hearted soul's generosity. A lonely, childless couple with a huge, warm fire and goose liver pate.

Just before eight o'clock, she heard a familiar scratching at the window. Jumping off the sofa like a jack-in-the-box, Sheridan almost broke an ankle in her haste.

"Well it's about damn time," she growled at him. "Where the hell have you been?"

Instead of jumping in as soon as the window was open, he seemed to hesitate a moment on the sill, glancing first at her and then uncertainly down to the floor, about two feet away. Gingerly, he finally made the leap, landing crookedly on his front paws and immediately picking up his right rear leg.

Sheridan's heart clutched as she bent down and scooped him into her arms. On the sofa, she eased him into her lap and quickly began to check him out. Carefully, as gently as she could, she ran her fingers along his body, feeling it tremble under her hand. As soon as she touched his right rear leg, he pulled it away and made a move to get away.

"Okay, Nick," she soothed, holding onto him a bit tighter. "I'm sorry. I didn't mean to hurt you. But you have to let me see what's wrong." He looked up at her, pain, fear and his natural wildness in the dark depths of his eyes.

"You have to trust me, Nick," she whispered softly into his face. At the same time, she released her grip on him, only stroking his head with her fingers.

For another moment she felt the tension, the anxiety in his body. As she watched, she suddenly saw his eyes clear, his body relax. He'd decided to trust her.

"I'll try not to hurt you, Sweetheart."

Blinking, she stopped, her hand poised over his leg, amazed that the term of endearment had slipped out so effortlessly. Or how comfortably. Instinctively, she knew in that moment that they'd passed an important milestone and was inexplicably glad. Looking into his eyes, she had the feeling Nick was too.

At first, she didn't see anything wrong. No blood, skin scraped bare of fur, no obvious wounds. But as soon as she touched his leg again, he flinched. She didn't feel or see any swelling but he was definitely in pain.

"Well," she pronounced when she'd finished her cursory exam, "my diagnosis is that you've done something to your leg. Tomorrow, you go to the vet. In the meantime, you make yourself comfortable on the sofa and I'll get you some dinner. Considering your delicate condition, I think we can bend the rule about not eating in the living room this once."

"I'm glad you're home," she told him sincerely, smiling and scratching his ears. "I missed you. And don't get a swelled head, but I was worried about you."

In a few minutes, she presented Nick with his portion of the sea bass she'd bought for dinner and some water. As he was finishing up, she brought a small bowl of vanilla ice cream and set it down for him. In apparent thanks, he stretched and rubbed his head against her palm.

"You're welcome."

* * * * *

"Ms. Phillips. I'm Dr. Montgomery." He glanced down at the manila folder in his hand. "And this, I would guess, is Nick." With a broad smile, he held out the long, slender fingers of his right hand to the cat's nose, moving with confidence but not so as to scare him.

Nick, unhappy about being there at all, sniffed the unfamiliar hand suspiciously.

"You're a big boy," he commented to Nick.

Looking at Sheridan with clear, kindly brown eyes, he asked, "What seems to be the matter today?"

"I'm not really sure," she admitted. "When he went out yesterday morning, he seemed fine but when he came home last night, he was favoring his right leg. Couldn't put any weight on it and when I touched it, he practically hit the ceiling in pain. I didn't see anything and it didn't seem to affect his appetite last night or this morning. And he was in good enough shape to give me quite an argument when I went to put him in the carrier this morning to bring him here. I borrowed it from a neighbor and I think he smelled Mrs. McCauley's cat, Emma, on it."

The doctor laughed heartily. "Well, let's see what we can see." Gently, he reached out and began stroking Nick head, seemingly in the most casual manner, but actually feeling along his skull and jaws, down his chest and front legs, moving carefully back toward his right leg. When he reached it, he'd moved one hand to Nick's body, pinning it to the exam table and gingerly putting the other hand on his hip. Immediately, Nick tried to struggle free and get off the table.

"Okay, boy," the doctor told him quietly, "I know this isn't the fun part. I'll try to get this over with as quickly and painlessly as possible." His fingers ran expertly over Nick's leg from claws to body.

"You did fine," he chuckled, releasing Nick and glancing at her. "You, too." She felt a little silly as she reached out to comfort her cat.

"I'll want an x-ray just to rule out a hairline fracture," he said professionally, "but it looks to me like a fairly severe soft tissue injury just above the knee. A sprain or a deep muscle bruise, maybe. Nothing serious but I'm sure it's painful and he'll have to stay off it until it heals."

"A sprain?" she repeated, dumbfounded. "But how?"

"I take it Nick here isn't a housecat?"

"Not really," she agreed. "He's a stray who sort of adopted me a few weeks ago. Pretty much comes and goes as he pleases."

"Well, it's pretty hard to keep a tomcat at home. This could be anything. Misjudged a leap, had a fall and landed wrong. Happens sometimes, even to cats. Might have gotten his leg caught somewhere and hurt it getting loose. Heck, he could even have been sideswiped by a bike or a car."

The doctor scribbled something in the chart. "If you'll wait a minute, my nurse will be in to get that x-ray. Soon as it's developed, I'll look at it and be back with the results."

* * * * *

"Bummer. He gonna be all right?"

"Oh yeah. Vet gave me some painkillers for him. Not enough to put him out completely, but he's definitely floating. Doesn't even bitch about staying inside. But after practically ripping your hand open that night, I wouldn't think you'd care," Sheridan chuckled.

Brian grinned. "Ah, it wasn't that bad. Male cats are real territorial. Probably didn't like another man being around his woman."

Inexplicably, she felt a blush rising. To hide it, she turned back to laundry basket and resumed sorting her dirty clothes into the machines. "So, what are you up to these days?" She was suddenly anxious to change the subject.

The young man shrugged the shoulders of his tattered white tee shirt. "Not much. My dad says I should go to college. I got a cousin who's a computer tech. Me? I hate that kinda crap."

"Well, you're young yet. You have lots of time to decide what you want to do with your life."

Bending down, Brian picked a pair of her panties off the laundry room floor. "You dropped these." He held them out to her, the small piece of satin between his index and middle fingers.

"Thanks," she answered quickly, grabbing them and dropping them in the washing machine. "And thanks for helping me haul this stuff down here."

"No sweat. I told my dad they oughta put an elevator in this place but he says it's too tough for a guy his age to get another job so he's not gonna tell 'em."

"It's all right, Brian. It's not like this is a fifty story high rise. Besides, as the Yuppies say, 'it would wreck the building's ambiance'."

"Yeah," he agreed with a shy laugh, "that sounds about right."

"Well, I better get going. I've still got a lot of stuff I need to get done." Sheridan began gathering up her laundry things.

"I thought you were off on the weekends."

"Only in that I don't have to go into the office. On the weekends I have to clean house, do laundry, shop, do errands. All that stuff I don't have time for during the week. Not to mention my writing."

"You write?"

"A little."

"Cool." It was the ultimate adolescent accolade. "Like what?"

"Nothing you'd know." For some strange reason, the subject embarrassed her. Like the young man had accidentally stumbled into a private part of her life. "I mean, I've had a couple of short stories published in emagazines, but I'm still shopping my novel around. Someday, though."

His eyes got round and he leaned forward. "What's it about? The book, I mean."

"A mystery." The embarrassment was growing. "Hey. Thanks again for the help. See you."

Upstairs, Nick was stretched out on the sofa, his eyes only half open. Hearing the front door open and close, he twitched his ears, his eyes opening another millimeter.

"Boy, if you could see yourself," she kidded, squatting down to stroke his side. "You're higher than a Macy's Thanksgiving balloon." Gently, she pecked his nose. "Talk about 'feeling no pain'."

As she stood up, the phone rang. It was Pat.

"Hi, Sher," she said brightly. "Just calling to see how you and the cat are."

"I'm fine," she smiled. "Nick's floating about four feet off the sofa."

She laughed. "Then I guess his leg isn't bothering him?"

"What leg?"

Another round of laughter.

"Look, I need to ask you a favor."

"Sorry, Pat, I'm not interested in meeting this guy from Bruce's office."

"Wrong, Smarty. That would be me doing you a favor. No, Mommy Dearest is coming for dinner tomorrow and I was wondering if I could borrow your rug cleaner. I understand it's not going to do any good because she hates my guts and thinks I'm a pig, but it'll give me something to do beside stick pins in a doll."

"Come on, Pat," Sheridan teased her friend, "Bruce's mother's not that bad. I met her at your Christmas party, what…two years ago? She seemed perfectly nice."

"That's because you're not married to Bruce," she answered tartly. "Honestly, I keep hoping she'll croak but if it's true the good die young, that makes her practically immortal."

"Okay, Pat, I get the idea. Sure, you can borrow the cleaner."

"You're an angel, Sher. I promise to do a kindness for you sometime."

"It's nothing, Pat. You've done a lot for me over the years, far more important than the loan of a mere appliance. Glad to do it."

"Okay if I come by in about an hour and pick it up?"

"I'll be here."

"Thanks. You're a lifesaver. See you then. Bye."

"Bye."

* * * * *

"So you're Nick," Pat commented, leaning down and inspecting the dozing cat. He opened his eyes a little, blinked at her, and closed them again.

"You're right," she giggled, standing back up and turning to her friend. "He's in another time dimension from the rest of us. You're also right about him being gorgeous. Looks almost like one of those black panthers you see in the movies, only smaller. And those eyes! I don't think I've ever seen a cat with such blue eyes. I'll bet they're beautiful when he's actually awake."

"They are," Sheridan agreed, setting down the bulky rug cleaner she'd lugged from the hall closet. "I think he must be part Siamese. That sleek body and those big blue eyes."

"Well, he's a definite keeper. Bitch about the leg, though."

"Could have been worse, I guess. Doctor says he'll be fine as frog's hair in a week. Gotta stay off that leg though. That's why Dr. Montgomery gave him the heavy-duty stuff. Not just to kill the pain but keep him home for a few days as well."

"Whatever it is, it seems to be working. That cat isn't going anywhere. Anyway, thanks for the loan of the cleaner. Probably won't get it back to you until next weekend. Unless you need it sooner. If you do, I can bring it to the office."

"Weekend's fine."

"Speaking of the office as we were, what's the latest medical update on the Prince?"

Sheridan shrugged a little. "According to Cupcake, he'll be in the hospital until at least next week sometime. Been hinting strongly that the department, or at least me, should go and see him. Cheer him up."

Pat's nose wrinkled up like she'd just smelled burning cabbage. "You actually gonna do it?"

"Bite your tongue. I have to put up with him in my jugular vein on the company's time. No way on my nickel."

"What's a little brown-nosing among friends," she insisted sarcastically. "After all, if memory serves, you should be coming up on your yearly evaluation soon. A dozen roses and a pint of good whiskey might go a long way towards erasing some of your more egregious sins. Couldn't hurt."

"In the immortal words of Methuselah, he should live so long."

"No shit." Pat and Sheridan roared with laughter. Wiping her eyes, she patted the other woman's arm. "Look, I really gotta be going. Thanks a bunch for the cleaner."

She swiveled her head to the sofa. "Take care of yourself, Nick. We must do this again when you get back."

Later that evening, Nick and Sheridan shared some roast chicken for dinner. Still on the sofa, he chewed the meat like he was doing it from memory, those eyes vague and faraway. Perhaps selfishly though, it was easier for her to see him a little drifty than in pain.

"Don't worry, Nick," she soothed as she laid him carefully on their bed and prepared to turn in herself, "it won't be for very long. You'll be out tomcatting again before you know it. Good night."

Chapter Eight

"And this is Sheridan Phillips," Diana giggled. "She's the Administrative Assistant for Design and Construction Division. She works for you, of course, but she does all the administrative work for the entire division. Sher, this is Jim Eldridge. He's going to be taking over as Assistant Director of Design and Construction while Jarvis is laid up."

"Ms. Phillips," he smiled warmly, extending his hand to her.

"Mr. Eldridge," Sheridan replied shaking his hand. It was a firm, friendly shake. "Please call me Sher."

"And I'm Jim. Seeing as how we're all part of the same team, I don't see any need for a lot of formalities."

Diana did a double take, surprised that a member of management, even a temp, would utter such an unthinkable sentiment. Sheridan figured she'd make a point of telling John so that he could set Jim straight. Here, there was no teamwork. Only those in charge and the peons. Still, in spite of her natural cynicism, she had a feeling she was going to like her new boss, even temporarily.

As they made the tour of the office, she watched him out of the corner of her eye. Forty-something probably, full, wavy brown hair—what was known as "Dishwater Blonde" in Sheridan's youth—deep gray eyes, perhaps five-ten, well built, husky but not fat or paunchy. Not devastatingly attractive, but with a nice face and a kind smile.

About two hours later, she was surprised when her intercom flashed.

"Sher. This is Jim. Could I see you in my office, please?"

"Certainly, sir." Picking up a yellow pad and pen, she shook her head slightly. Please? From someone in this office above the rank of janitor? Unbelievable.

"You wanted to see me, sir?" She stood respectfully in the doorway.

"Yes, Sher. Please, come in." He smiled and motioned to a chair in front of his desk. Uncertainly, she moved to the chair and perched uneasily on the edge.

"Is there something I can do for you?" she asked timidly.

"Yes," he replied warmly, "several things."

Sheridan poised her pen over the paper and looked at him expectantly.

"The first thing you can do is stop calling me 'sir'. As I said, I'm not one much for formalities. Jim's fine."

"Yes, sir…" She felt red rushing to her cheeks. "I'm sorry. Jim. It's just that, well, I've never really been on a first name basis with any of the management staff here."

"Well you are now. At least for the next six months or so. I'm going to be relying on you quite a bit, especially in the beginning while I'm feeling my way. I'll need help to understand how everything is done around here from the format of reports to where the coffee is. I'd also like to have your input on how you think things might be improved. From an administrative standpoint."

Her mouth must have dropped open because he smiled and leaned back in his chair. "You look surprised."

"I am," she managed to stutter. "No one ever asks the opinion of the administrative staff about how to run the administrative end of things. I thought there was some kind of managerial rule against it."

Jim laughed. A deep, hearty, friendly laugh. "Not that I know of," he answered, "but it probably seems that way sometimes. No, I believe that the only way to run any enterprise is to hire the best people you can and then let them use their expertise and knowledge to do it. I assume you were hired because someone thought you were the best person for the job. You've been here a lot longer than I have and I assume you've been doing your job. I also assume that in the what...six years you've been here, you've probably also had one or two thoughts about how the job might be improved. Am I right?"

Still stunned, she could only nod.

"Well, I'm interested in knowing those things. Streamline the workflow. Reduce or eliminate as much paper as possible. Stop duplication of effort and get the job done quickly, efficiently, and, hopefully in budget. So, if you've got a few minutes, I'd like to talk."

Sure, she thought amiably. After all, any minute now the alarm's gonna go off and I'll wake up.

They spent almost an hour in his office, discussing office procedures, personnel, projects. They also talked about football, good seafood restaurants and vintage cars. And they laughed, something Sheridan thought was against company policy. It was like being paroled after solitary confinement.

Walking back to her office, she felt positively giddy. As she turned the corner back down the hall to her desk, she had the stray thought that not only was she free of Jarvis Duncan for six months, but Jim Eldridge was a really decent human being. With a double-digit IQ and a soul.

* * * * *

"How's Nick?"

"Getting there," Sheridan answered, washing down a bite of barbecue chicken sandwich with a sip of tea. "Limps around a little. Once in awhile he goes over to the window and looks up at it. Mostly though, he's so high, he doesn't do much besides just float around near the ceiling."

"How long he gonna be outta action?" Pat picked up the other half of her turkey sandwich and glanced at the break room clock. They still had more than half an hour before lunch was over.

"Dr. Montgomery said he should stay on the medicine and off his leg for about a week. I'm gonna start weaning him from the dope in a couple of days. He should be out and about by the weekend."

"You ever figure out what happened?"

She shrugged and wiped a dollop of rich, red sauce from her chin with a paper napkin. "With a stray, who knows? I'm just glad he managed to get home. The thought of him being hurt, out in the snow and the cold, alone…" A sharp pain stabbed in her chest and she couldn't finish the sentence.

"Hey, it's all right," her friend soothed, patting her gently on the arm. "It's easy to love an animal. Even a stray cat."

Love. It was not a word Sheridan had used to Nick, or even to herself. But it was exactly how she'd come to feel about him. And how she knew he felt about her. The touch of his paw, his tongue, the look in his eyes when he looked at her.

"Yes," she told Pat softly, "it is. And I do love him."

"Good. It's high time you tried loving someone. And that gorgeous cat of yours is a start. Now why don't you let me invite Lou Magris to dinner?"

"You can invite anyone you want to dinner," she laughed.

Pat's face brightened. "Now you're talking."

"Just don't expect me to show up so you can play matchmaker."

Immediately the other woman's face fell. "But…"

"Don't 'but' me," Sheridan insisted. "You're so bad, every time I see you I can practically hear 'The Wedding March' coming out of your ears. But I'll tell you what. When and if I ever decide to take the plunge again, I'll definitely bring my business to you."

"Very funny," Pat retorted sourly.

"Look, Pat," she teased, "I have to wade back into this whole thing gradually. It's been five years, for Christ's sake. Let me see how it goes with Nick. If it turns out I don't screw up this relationship, maybe I'll let you set me up with a man. Okay?"

"Do I have a choice?"

"No."

"Okay."

* * * * *

At five minutes to five, Sheridan saw Jim heading toward her desk with a fist full of papers.

Oh well, she thought wearily, she'd known it was too good to be true.

"Getting ready to go home?"

"Yes sir…Jim. Unless you need something."

"Oh no." He placed the papers in her inbox. "These can certainly wait until tomorrow. I'm not much on overtime. Don't like it myself." He grinned. "Besides, if you abuse your staff by crying 'crisis' too often, it gets very hard to convince them to help you when you really do have a problem. Anyway, you have a good night and I'll see you in the morning."

"You too si…Jim."

* * * * *

"Hello, Nick," she whispered softly, rubbing his head lightly.

He was lying on the sofa, asleep. At her voice and touch, he roused himself enough to open his eyes. It seemed to take him a moment to focus. Moving his head under her hand, he laid a paw softly on her leg.

"I don't need to ask what you've been doing all day," she laughed. "Well, enjoy it while it lasts 'cause tomorrow I'm gonna start cutting you off. By the weekend, you'll be back to earth. You think you can hover long enough to eat some dinner?"

They had leftover pot roast for dinner and banana pudding for dessert. As they ate, she told him about her day, including her meeting with Jim Eldridge. He seemed more interested in his pudding than in her talking but he listened politely, nonetheless.

"He really is something," she finished, gathering her plate and wineglass from the table. "Intelligent, kind, professional. Generally a good guy. I have a feeling that after working for him for six months, the Prince of Darkness will be a hundred times worse."

She smiled at Nick, happily lapping up pudding from his perch on the sofa. "I don't suppose there's any chance the Prince would decide to retire and sail to Tahiti, is there?"

Nick looked up for a moment, continuing to enjoy his dessert, that same vague look in his eyes.

"I didn't think so. Still, a girl can always hope, can't she?"

When dinner was over they settled on the sofa in front of a cheery fire. Sheridan watched a romantic comedy as Nick relaxed, alternately snoozing and enjoying having his stomach rubbed gently.

During one of the commercials toward the end of the movie, the early news talked about a special report on the Fairview Heights rapist. Something "exclusive" to their newscast. She wasn't actually interested but at the end of the movie, she wasn't quite ready to go to bed so decided to stay up and watch the weather report.

"Channel Six News," the anchor began solemnly, "has learned today that the police have what may be a significant new clue in the Fairview Heights rapist case. Linda Sanchez has been following this story since the first rape almost four months ago and joins us now with the update."

The picture changed to an earnest looking young Hispanic woman standing outside the local police headquarters.

"Four days ago, the Fairview Heights rapist struck for the seventh time in less than four months, attacking Sylvia Jones of Carolton Avenue. As in the past rapes, the rapist escaped, leaving no clues. However, within hours of the rape, rumors began to circulate around police headquarters that the rapist may have injured himself while leaping from the fire escape of Ms. Jones' building.

"Unconfirmed reports indicate that a man dressed in black sweater, pants, gloves, shoes and watch cap, was seen limping badly by at least two people at about one p.m., less than ten minutes after police believe the attack occurred. The man was seen going rapidly west on Tenor Street, which backs to Ms. Jones' apartment building, less than a block from where the man was seen.

"Police refuse to comment, saying only that this is an ongoing investigation. However, I talked with Mr. Hu Lin, owner of Lin's Market, one of the people who saw the man."

Video film of the interview began rolling.

"Mr. Lin," the reporter asked seriously, "can you tell us what you saw?"

"Yeah. About one o'clock Tuesday afternoon, I'm bringing in some stock round back at the delivery entrance. In the alley. As I'm picking up a box of tomatoes, I look up and at the end of the alley, I see this man. He's coming from Tenor and while he's trying to walk fast, I can see he's limping real bad. I think maybe he's hurt so I put down the box and yell to him. 'Hey. You need help mister?' He doesn't answer, just limps away. I run out to the end of the alley, but I don't see nothin' but a stray cat sittin' in a doorway across the alley."

"Did you get a good look at the man?"

"No," Mr. Lin admitted sadly. "Tall. Skinny. All dressed in black. Even gloves."

"Thank you, Mr. Lin."

The reporter came back live. "We also have an interview with Elsie Brewer, the other witness."

More video, this time of a small, stout, gray-haired black woman standing on the tiny porch of an old house.

"Mrs. Brewer, can you tell our viewers what you saw that afternoon?"

"I was just comin' back from the senior center. I go every day fer the free lunch. Anyway, I was on my porch here gettin' my keys outta my purse so I could open the door when I see this here fella across the street there," she pointed a gnarled finger to her right.

"From the direction of Tenor Street?" the reporter prodded.

"Yeah. Looked ta me like he just turned the corner from the alley. Anyway, he seemed ta be tryin' ta walk fast but he was limpin' somethin' fierce."

"Did you get a look at the man?"

"Naw. I don't see real good anymore. Need new glasses but I can't afford 'em an' I can't git a new pair from Medicare 'til next March. I could tell he was a big man, though skinny-like. White fella. An' all his clothes was black. Even his gloves."

Once again, the reporter reappeared.

"Police will say that the attack on Ms. Jones appears to fit the pattern of the Fairview Heights rapists but refuse to speculate on whether the man seen by Mr. Lin and Mrs. Brewer may have been the assailant. However, rumors within the department persist that officers investigating the rapes believe the man to be a solid suspect."

"Linda," the anchor's voice came through, "Do police have any clues as to the identity of this man in black?"

"The police aren't saying anything," Sanchez answered. "They aren't even admitting the man has anything to do with the case. But in light of descriptions given by the rape victims of the attacker as tall, slender and dressed all in black, the method of entry and exit for all the rapes being fire escapes and that the man was seen in the vicinity of the latest rape shortly after it's believed to have happened, it does present an interesting picture."

"Too bad the stray cat in the alley can't tell us what happened," the anchor laughed.

"Too bad, indeed," the reporter cackled in agreement. "I guess he was the only one who actually saw what happened."

Inexplicably, as if a cold wind had blown over her, Sheridan shuddered. Feeling the tremor, Nick opened his eyes and looked up at her. Instead of the vacant, spaced out look she'd come to expect, there was a flicker of that mysterious, wild, unnerving something she hadn't seen since his injury. She shivered again.

Gently, Nick put his paw on her arm and patted it.

If it was meant as reassurance, it failed and she shuddered a third time.

Chapter Nine

For the next few days, Sheridan kept a wary eye on both the evening news and Nick.

Despite Channel Six's insistence that "unsubstantiated rumors" continued to circulate about the mysterious man in black and his possible connection to the rapes, there was nothing concrete. The Chief of Police even went so far as to deny the whole idea of a possible suspect.

Nick's normal, independent self re-emerged almost as soon as his mistress began weaning him from the pain medication. After his enforced confinement, an impatient restlessness seemed to settle over him, causing him to pace aimlessly through the apartment and stare glumly at her as she closed the door behind her each morning.

As the day approached when he would be well enough to return to his street ways, the vague feeling of dread she'd had the night of the newscast grew steadily into a full-blown but still nameless terror.

"Of course you're afraid," Pat said firmly. "You love Nick and he was hurt and you're afraid it might happen again. You told me yourself how the thought of him being hurt and not being able to get home made you sick at your stomach." She smiled and patted her hand. "Welcome to parenthood, Sher."

"You don't understand," she replied.

"Sure I do," the other woman continued, reaching for a second chocolate chip cookie from the basket on the break room table, "I've owned dogs, cats, parakeets, a hamster and even a white rat when I was eleven. Named him Hank after my oldest brother. At eleven, I thought he was a rat too. One thing I've learned is that animals are easy to love. Easier than most people I know."

Sheridan tried again. "Sometimes...sometimes when I'm talking to him, it's like...like he can understand me. Knows what I'm saying."

"Sure he does. Our little Boston Terrier, Jack, knows exactly what we're talking about. He's crazy about riding in the car. If Bruce or I even say 'ride', he goes completely bonkers. We even tried spelling it. No dice. Soon as we do, Jack runs right over to the front door and starts jumping up and down and barking. No doubt Nick understands you too. It's part of the bond. Don't try to understand it."

"But...but it's like he knows what I'm thinking. I can see it in his eyes."

"They all do. That's how they wrap you around their paws and get you to do anything they want."

"And whenever I want something...wish for something...he knows. And it happens."

"Look, you're alone. He's become family for you. Cats especially seem to understand people. It's part of their mystery. And part of their attraction for us. Trust me on this. You're having a very natural reaction."

"There's nothing natural about this," she insisted, frustration seeping into her voice.

"What's that supposed to mean?"

"I...I don't know. There's just something...weird going on here."

Pat leaned forward, interest and concern on her face. "I don't understand. Weird how?"

Throwing a cautious glance at the break room doorway, Sheridan leaned forward also. Pat was her dearest friend. She'd shared things with her that she would never have confided to anyone, even her family. They had a strong friendship but at that moment, she wondered if it was strong enough for this.

Taking a deep breath, she jumped in. "From that first night when he just…materialized on my fire escape…my life hasn't been the same. I mean, how did he get up to my second floor living room window anyhow? And the salmon. I know that can wasn't in my cupboard. I know it for a fact. Yet, as soon as I told Nick I didn't have anything for him to eat…presto! Instant salmon.

"He wanted a fire that first night. Don't ask me how I knew. I just did. The next night I told him I still didn't have any wood. The words weren't out of my mouth when my neighbor arrived with two bundles of wood and my super's son brought four more bundles the next day.

"So I made a fire and laid down in front of it with Nick and a glass of white wine. I complained that my back hurt and the next thing I know, he'd curled up on top of me and was giving me a back rub. Then apparently, I fell asleep because the next thing I know, it's morning and I was in my bed, naked, and all my clothes were strewn on the floor by my bed."

Her voice lowered almost to a whisper as she continued. "You remember when I told you about that shitty night when I had to work overtime and then I had to deliver that stupid report for King John? I ended up walking nine blocks in the cold and dark because of the six-car smash up and the cab couldn't get through?"

Nibbling on her cookie, Pat nodded. "The night you caught cold."

"Right. Well what I didn't tell you was that night, after I got home, I was telling Nick about all the shit and I told him I wished the Prince would have an accident. Specifically, a car accident that would break his leg and keep him out of the office for six months and that he'd be replaced with a nice, smart boss. Next morning…zap! Not only did the Prince have a car accident that broke his leg in three places and will keep him out of the office for six months, but the accident happened because he swerved to avoid hitting a cat and his anti-lock brakes suddenly didn't work. A big, black cat.

"Then there was the dream. The one I told you about with the candles and the dark-haired stranger. It was so...so sensual. And real. If I didn't know it was a dream, I'd swear it...it actually happened. Only I know it didn't. But there was something about him...the feel of soft black hair and the way he touched me and those blue eyes...It was like I knew him. Or maybe like I should know him. Something familiar but not..."

She shook her head, trying to clear it enough to find the right words to make Pat understand. To explain how she felt. Pat looked at her intently but kept silent, sensing the story wasn't over.

"Anyway, a few days later, for lunch, I walked over to that deli on Twelfth. Now I've been there dozens of times but as I was walking back to the office, I discovered this little store called Bell, Book and Candle. It deals in the occult. I swear I've never seen that shop before. It was like it just suddenly appeared there. Anyway, on some kind of freak impulse, I went in and asked if it was possible...for people...beings of any kind, to change into animals...and back again."

Again she watched Pat's face. If her friend was shocked or amazed, she didn't show it.

"So this overage Harry Potter told me about shape shifters and familiars and witches. Apparently people changing into animals and back again is a fairly common phenomenon in the science fiction and fantasy realm. Unless, of course, you're talking about aliens but as I understand it, they're an entirely different story and you don't want to go there. At any rate, witches are not only adept at changing back and forth between animals and humans, but can also read minds and grant wishes.

"Then Nick came home late, limping from having hurt his leg. The vet said it could have been from being sideswiped by a car or getting his leg caught in something or by leaping off something and landing wrong. The vet gave him some heavy-duty painkiller to keep him at home while he healed.

"Finally, I heard on the news that another woman was raped about six blocks from where I live. Two witnesses say they saw a man dressed all in black limping away from the scene. That was the same day Nick came home limping. And there haven't been any rapes since Nick's been home, under the influence."

Several moments went by while she watched Pat digest what she'd just said.

"Are you telling me," she ventured uncertainly, "that you think your cat, Nick, is some kind of shape shifter or witch who lives with you as a black cat and reads your mind and grants your wishes at night and who changes into a part-time serial rapist in the daytime? Except, of course, when he changes into a man who carries you into your bedroom, undresses you and makes mad, passionate love to you?"

Condensed into a few words, it sounded even more ridiculous than even Sheridan had imagined. Still, it was a fairly accurate assessment of the situation.

Feeling the blush rising, she nodded once and took a hasty sip of tea.

"Jesus, Sher," she groaned, "you really are losing your marbles! You know that, don't you?"

"I know how this sounds, Pat…"

"Yeah," she agreed. "It sounds like you're a shrieking nut case!"

"All right," Sheridan shot back, beginning to feel angry, "how do you explain all this?"

"I explain it the same way any other normal, sane human being would."

"And how's that?"

"A combination of coincidence and a really active imagination."

"What?"

"Look, Sher. It's very simple. Take the salmon, for instance. Haven't you ever bought something, stuck it in the fridge or a cupboard and then forgotten about it? Or how 'bout the other way around?

"Last Thanksgiving, I got stuck with Bruce's mother for dinner. I was just about to put dinner on the table when I went to the cabinet to get the two cans of whole cranberries I bought especially for the old battleaxe. They weren't there. I mean, I turned the entire kitchen upside down and couldn't find them.

"To this day, I am absolutely convinced that I bought those cranberries and I have no idea what happened to them. For all I know, the Good Cranberry Fairy came during the night and took them for some underprivileged cranberry freak. It's the same thing. You bought the salmon and forgot about it. End of story."

"Okay, that might explain the salmon," she persisted. "But it doesn't explain everything else."

"You're serious, aren't you?"

"Yes. If I'm being so ridiculous, you explain it."

"Okay, I will.

"The wood. Nick was out in the cold all day. Of course he thought a fire would be nice. He curled up on the rug in front of the fireplace. Your neighbor stopping by just when you'd finished talking about the wood was a fluke. He knows you work during the day, so he came by when he thought you'd be home. And it doesn't take a medical degree to know that wood fires can be very hard on people with respiratory problems. Especially elderly people. Simple.

"After you built the fire, you lay on the floor and drank a second glass of wine, which you usually don't do. The cat massaged your back and you were tired after a crappy day. You fell asleep. You woke up later and were still groggy. Stumbled into your bedroom, stripped and fell into bed.

"As for wishing The Prince of Darkness would break his leg, to know that bastard is to hate him. Hell, if wishes came true, he'd long ago have fallen onto an upturned wooden stake or slid headfirst into a vat of boiling oil. I mean, that night can't possibly have been the first time you wished Duncan would die or quit or at least break a leg."

"No, but it's the first time I ever said it in front of Nick."

"It was a coincidence, Sher," Pat replied, exasperated. "Nothing more."

"What about the accident being caused by a cat?"

"Do you have any idea how many cats there must be in this city?"

"A big, black cat."

"Okay. Do you have any idea how many big, black cats there are?"

"What about the anti-lock brakes?"

"What about them? You think this is the first time in automotive history that anti-lock brakes have failed? It was icy. Who knows? But whatever happened, you can be sure that you didn't 'wish it' on him, Nick or no Nick."

"The Bell, Book and Candle?" Sheridan pushed.

"Bullshit," Pat snapped. "Pure and simple. I can't believe that you'd even entertain the notion of something so ridiculous. This is the twenty-first century, for Christ's sake! You might just as well read tea leaves.

"And I'm not surprised you never noticed it before. Those little stores down there come and go like stray dogs. I remember there was a little boutique down there about a year ago. Pricey crap. Six months later, it was a dog-grooming parlor. Same thing with your occult store. It probably wasn't there six months ago and it probably won't be there six months from now.

"You let that writer's imagination of yours get the better of you."

Sheridan was beginning to feel sillier with every passing moment, but didn't seem able to stop herself. There was no point in discussing the rapes or Nick's limp or the newscasts about the mysterious man in black. But there was one more thing.

"The dream," she whispered. "What about the dream?"

"Yeah," Pat grinned, "The dream." She was silent for a few seconds. "Listen, sometime when we're both half in the bag, I'll tell you about this dream I used to have after I was divorced but before I met Bruce. About Han Solo and his Wookie."

"From *Star Wars*?" Sheridan was more than a little surprised.

The grin got broader. "I won't go into it now, but trust me, it gives a whole new meaning to the phrase, 'May the force be with you.'" She winked and they both laughed.

And as they got up and went back to their desks, Sheridan felt better although she couldn't have said exactly why.

* * * * *

It was like Nick's injury had never happened. No trace of the limp remained and he jumped off the windowsill and onto the carpet like a panther bouncing down from a jungle tree limb. Immediately he came over and began rubbing back and forth against her shins, looking up with those bright blue eyes.

"Good evening to you too," she laughed, reaching down and stroking him gently. That sleek black head slid beneath her hand, moving quickly as she rubbed. She could tell that he was as delighted to see her as she was to see him.

"Let's have some dinner. I've got chicken."

Nick scampered ahead of her into the kitchen, pausing only long enough for a long drink of water.

When dinner was over, Sheridan went in to her computer to work on her latest book, Nick trailing after. Instead of taking his usual place on the desk, he curled up on the bed. It was as if he knew she needed to concentrate and didn't want to disturb her.

Funny how he always seemed to know what was on her mind. What was important to her. He seemed to understand how much her writing meant to her and never interfered or complained when she wrote, even for hours at a time. Even her ex-husband hadn't understood or been so patient.

Sometimes, when the words wouldn't come, writing was absolute hell. Sitting at the computer screen trying to make the words come by sheer force of will. Write six words, change five and then erase the whole shitty mess. But other times, when the words flowed sweet and clear as cherry wine and she could hardly type fast enough to keep up with them, writing was heavenly. But no matter whether it's piss or bliss, writing was something she needed to do, the same as she needed to breathe or eat. And the worst day writing was always better than the best day working.

This particular night was one of those "cherry wine" occasions. The words seemed to spill out of the computer by themselves, immersing her in her work. By the time she came up for air and looked at her watch, it was past ten o'clock.

"Sorry, Nick," she yawned, moving to the bed and sitting down beside him. "Must have got carried away. You're a good sport to let me work. Better than my ex. He hated for me to work when he was home."

Those brilliant sapphire eyes watched her, seemingly intent on her words.

"You know, considering what happens when I wish for things in your presence, I probably shouldn't say this, but do you know what I'd really, really like? More than anything else in the world? I'd like to be a writer. A real, honest-to-God, published-and-somebody's-actually-read-it writer. Being rich wouldn't be bad either." She scratched his ears and planted a quick peck on his nose. "You think you can handle that?" she giggled.

Nick reached up and lightly patted her cheek.

"Thank you, Nick. I'm gonna hold you to that. Now, how 'bout we hit the sack? I don't know about you, but I'm bushed."

* * * * *

"Sheridan."

The voice was a whisper; so soft in her ear it might have been in her mind.

"Sheridan."

"Who's there?" she mumbled groggily, turning automatically to the sound.

"It's just me," the voice replied, a tender kiss fluttering on her cheek. "I know it's late, but I need you."

"Need me?" she repeated, trying to clear the last of the sleep out of her brain. "For what?" She saw now that it was the man from her erotic dream and that curiously, she was neither surprised nor alarmed to see him poised at the edge of her bed.

"Let me show you."

In a twinkling, both the bedclothes and her nightgown were gone. There was the feel of air moving against her bare skin, but no coldness. In fact, she had a distinct feeling of warmth.

Leaning over, the dream lover slid his arms under her and in one fluid motion, swept her into his arms as lightly as if she were a child. Immediately, she felt his naked skin against her own. As she wrapped her arms around his neck, he leaned down and kissed her, long and passionately.

When she opened her eyes again, they were in her living room, a fire blazing cheerfully in the fireplace, candles in ornate silver holders dotting the rug and the furniture, a fat, down-filled quilt before the fire. Gently, he laid her on her back, sinking into the warm comforter as he slid a thick pillow under her head.

"I…" she started but he put a finger to her lips.

"Shhh," he told her with a beautiful smile. "You don't need to know anything. Just enjoy."

Reaching behind him, he took two tall, thin, crystal flutes and balanced them between the fingers of his left hand. With his right, he took a champagne bottle from an exquisite silver bucket on the floor and poured the pale, bubbling liquor into the glasses. Finishing, he replaced the bottle and held out a glass for her.

"To my eternal Sheridan," he toasted lovingly. "Then. Now. Always."

They clinked glasses lightly and drank. She remembered thinking that this dream was so real she could even feel the bubbles tickling her nose as she sipped.

When the glasses were drained, he took them, set them back by the bucket and then stretched out on his side next to her, propping himself with one elbow and running a fingertip of his other hand along her cheek.

"You are so beautiful," he told her quietly. "In the morning, rumpled and yawning in that dreadful, baggy nightgown of yours. Eating cereal in one of your ugly, ridiculous suits with your silly briefcase. Sipping coffee and reading the newspaper. Nibbling popcorn and sniffling at some old movie. Talking back to the stupid people on television. Making those funny little faces you make when you're pounding away at your keyboard. But mostly, when you lie here beside me and let me feast on your nakedness like ambrosia."

As he found her mouth again, he took her nipple between his fingers and began lightly playing with it, feeling it grow hard and responsive under his touch.

"I try to be patient," he explained breathlessly between kisses, "but I've waited so long and I want you so much that just being with you isn't enough. I have to have all of you, even if it's only stolen moments in your dreams."

"Who are you?" she whispered hoarsely. "Why...why do you bring me these dreams?"

"Not now. In time, you'll know and understand everything. All you need right now is to just let yourself go. Believe in the dream and let me give you love."

Sheridan felt the hardness of his erection rubbing against her thigh and the feeling seemed to intensify her own building passion. Whoever...whatever this dream lover was, he was right about one thing. All she cared about at this moment was joining with him.

Slowly, gently, he turned her away from him, dropping kisses across her neck, shoulders and back like garlands of tiny flowers. Curling up against him like spoons in a drawer, she felt both safe and wild. He made her feel as she'd never felt before, even in her marriage bed.

"I love the feel of you," he mumbled into her hair.

With one hand busying itself on her breasts, she felt the other slide her stomach, over her ridge and down between her legs. Without coaching, she moved her leg upwards and balanced on his thigh. His fingers immediately found their goal, skimming over her wet clitoris and down inside her. As he worked, she felt him hard and tight, moving ever so slowly against her back.

Waves of heated passion rolled over her with every move. It was so foreign and yet so thrilling. So unknown and yet so right.

His fingers moved gently out of her as he readjusted his position so that his shaft came up from behind and slid inside. The feel of him as he glided in and out inflamed her already swollen, sensitive area. It was a sensation like nothing she'd ever known and she was caught between never wanting the exquisite suspense to end and reaching the climax she knew would be like an explosion of body and soul.

The rhythm of their movements was becoming swifter, more urgent.

"Come for me, Sheridan," he growled behind her. "Come for me."

"Oh!" she cried, now almost unable to catch her breath. "Oh...ohhhhh..."

"Dear God," he moaned as she felt the quivering inside, unsure if it was her or this wonderful creature.

They rocked together for a few more moments and then she erupted, no longer conscious of or caring about anything, even her partner, as she shattered into a million slivers of pleasure, each one glistening for its own brief moment, creating a cascade of fire through every molecule of her being.

The embers of their passion died away, but they made no move to untangle, choosing instead to float back to earth in their comfortable position. Through her sated exhaustion, Sheridan felt sleep slowly closing around her, wrapping her in blissful contentment, just as the arms of her dream lover were wrapped around her now.

"Thank you," she mumbled.

"My pleasure," he replied with a peck to her cheek. "My pleasure."

Chapter Ten

Sheridan gladly turned loose of her silly suspicions and fears about Nick and gave herself over to the pleasure of his company. He, in turn, seemed to enjoy the lessening of stress and overtime of her job, joyfully greeting her at the end of her days, and quietly spending their evenings together.

Jim Eldridge was like a breeze of cool, fresh air through the stale, fetid prison of her job. Quickly, calmly, efficiently, he began making some long overdue changes.

His first priority was doing away with what he called "needless" meetings, memos and written daily updates.

"If you need to tell me something, call, come by my office or e-mail me. Enough already with the paper!"

Next was forcing Rick Yung into seminars on time management, organization and business writing.

"Look," he'd told him, "you can't find your desk for the paper, your office looks like someone launched a Polaris missile from a flea market and you are not being paid by the word."

In fact, he made them part of the next year's goals in Rick's written evaluation. And set up what he called, "measurable standards".

Time management. Rick was to attend, in no more than ninety days from the date of the evaluation, a seminar, approved by his supervisor (Jim). In no more than ninety days from the end of the seminar, Rick was to demonstrate to his supervisor's satisfaction a reduction in amount of time to return phone calls (no more than twenty-four hours), reduction in time to answer correspondence (no more than five working days) and an adherence to deadlines (work would be turned in on time).

"It's very simple," he'd explained to his dumbfounded subordinate. "You've been getting away with this so long, you probably think it's an acceptable way to conduct business. You're about to discover that's not the case, at least with me. You will either meet what I consider to be reasonable standards of professional business conduct and receive your yearly raises in a timely fashion or you'll continue your current practices somewhere else. The decision is totally up to you."

He was, in short, understanding, professional and a thorough pleasure to work for. Well, at least for Sheridan he was.

That's not to say that they didn't have their disagreements or that one or the other of them didn't make mistakes. But there was no sarcasm, no superiority and no snobbery. He treated Sheridan with respect, both as a human being and a professional capable of doing her job. They were not exactly friends but not enemies, either.

And he formed a kind of buffer between King John and Princess Di and Sheridan. From the beginning, he made it clear that while he had no problem with her "helping out," requests would go through him. And he always seemed to have enough work for her to do that his standard reply became, "I really can't spare her right now."

Winter's grip remained firm although the snow had stopped and the daytime temperatures had begun to crawl back into the middle thirties.

Sheridan got a postcard from Brian, who had taken a temporary job at a ski resort, telling her that he liked the snowboarding and the snow bunnies and not having to listen to his father bitch about college.

There was quiet scuttlebutt along the office grapevine that the Prince of Darkness' recovery wasn't going as well as expected and that six months might very well be an optimistic estimate of his return.

With her latest story finished and polished, Sheridan sent it off to an editor, promising herself she wouldn't worry about it.

Even the Fairview Heights Rapist seemed to have taken a holiday.

It was the best her life had been in a long time. She should have known it was too good to last.

* * * * *

It was a Saturday. Nick and Sheridan had had their breakfast and he'd gone out. Since she was planning a quiet day at the computer, after her shower she'd slipped into an old, comfortable pair of faded red sweats and started her weekend housekeeping ritual.

Having cleaned the kitchen and the bathroom, she was vacuuming. Being inherently lazy, she had one of those big uprights with the super long cord. That way, she could plug in the cord in the living room and vacuum from the bedroom out to the living room and end up in the foyer closet where she stored the beast.

With the noise of the vacuum and her concentration on the rug, she didn't even know he was there.

The blow landed at the base of her skull, one sharp, well-aimed "whack" that sent blinding pain shooting through her whole body. She didn't remember making any noise except a sort of "whoosh" as the air escaped her lungs. Strong arms grabbed her under the armpits and locked around her chest as her body sagged toward the floor. Black arms and hands wobbled in her blurry vision and she had a sensation of moving backwards.

Stunned, she tried to swim back to alert consciousness up through the gray fog swirling around her brain. But there were only those black limbs and the feeling of being dragged. Finally, she felt herself being thrown onto the sofa, landing with a dull thud that reactivated the pain and sent the world spinning again.

She felt pressure on her chest and stomach as a large black figure loomed over her, jiggling and dancing as she tried to focus. Sheridan struggled to move the weight, opening her mouth to get much needed air into her lungs. A black ball raised up and hurtled toward her face, her dizzy brain registering it as a fist only as it struck her mouth. Something thick and warm trickled down her cheek toward her neck. This new pain raised the level to agony and she felt herself slipping sideways toward the welcome darkness hovering at the edge of her vision.

The dark hand appeared again, slapping her mouth again but this time with something sticky and wide. Suddenly, her air was reduced to the little that seemed to be dribbling down her nose, not nearly enough to keep her alive. Inside, she could feel her frightened heart racing, lungs screaming.

A force, rough and strong, grabbed her arms and pulled them up above her head and she felt something being wrapped tightly around her wrists, pulling her arms down toward the floor. She was too weak and dizzy to try and move them back.

Two black fists appeared in her runny vision. One reached up and buried itself in her short hair, yanking it so hard her half-open eyes flew wide, almost by themselves so that she could see the small silver blade in the other hand.

All the other sensations…pain, surprise, dizziness…disappeared at that moment, washed away by the tidal wave of terror that engulfed her as the full horror of her situation crystallized. In that split second, she understood that it was, indeed, possible for one's blood to run cold.

A black face, featureless except for the eyes, leaned down, so close she could feel his breath on her skin. Looking into those cold, clear blue eyes, she could almost see the smile she knew was there. The anticipation. The excitement at her helplessness. She wanted to scream…tried to…but her mouth refused to work, as if soldered shut by her own fear.

Sheridan felt the flat side of the blade, cold against her cheek as he placed it delicately, softly and began to move it slowly down, easing it along her jaw line to her chin and down to her throat. When the blade reached the hollow, she felt it stop, the tip tracing little circles, pressing a little harder with each one. A small, strangled, pleading noise escaped her unbidden, as if her body was reacting to this horror on its own.

There was something that sounded almost like a chuckle from the black body on top of her, the hand released her hair and another fist appeared, blotted out immediately by the searing pain of her left eye and the darkness that covered that part of her sight.

The blade continued its journey, reaching the neck of her sweatshirt. She felt, rather than heard the material tearing in a sort of jagged line down her front, revealing more and more of her skin. Her bra front opened, a black hand peeling away the cups to expose her breasts. He examined them closely, taking each one in turn, grabbing and twisting, obviously relishing her pain and squirming. And in those eyes, she saw a growing excitement.

Next, the blade cut into her sweatpants, the elastic waist parting, the blade making its casual way over her stomach, catching the edge of her panties and splitting them as it did so. At her crotch, the blade disappeared, replaced by the black hands that tore the legs quickly down the seams, leaving her naked and helpless.

Smooth, cold, black leather fingers ran over her body from neck to thighs, pinching, poking, and once even punching her in the stomach. Not hard enough, she could tell, to make her pass out. Just to hurt her. This was his foreplay, as important, if not more so, than the act itself. Strangely, though, all that she could really feel was the absolute and overwhelming terror inside. It was as if everything else had been gobbled up by this huge monster.

In a reflex of self-protection, Sheridan shut her one remaining good eye. The other was swollen shut from the blow. Instantly, she felt a sharp slap and the point of the blade at her throat. Opening her eye, she could see anger in those blue eyes. He wanted her to watch.

If she could have been sick, she would have. Even the thought that she might choke on her own vomit and die was preferable to this. But she guessed her will to live was stronger than she imagined, even under these horrific circumstances.

He lifted himself up onto his knees, and she saw him reach for the brass fastener at the top of his dark pants. A moment later, she heard the sound of a zipper slowly being lowered.

Sheridan must have momentarily passed out, because when she realized what was happening, it seemed that many minutes had passed. With her half-opened right eye, she saw a different scene before her.

Like a marionette suddenly jerked by its strings, the black figure above her seemed to rise up over the back of the sofa. She heard a growl and a grunt. She tried to turn her head see what was happening, but a stab of pain stopped her. There was nothing but blurred shapes moving at the far edge of her tunnel vision.

Two black shadows intertwined and melded, heaved to and fro behind the sofa, moving back and forth, cursing and groaning. The shadows seemed to be locked together, unable to separate.

How long they danced, she didn't know. It seemed an eternity. Suddenly, she heard the sound of glass shattering, and cold winter air washed over her bare skin. And then the blood-curdling scream of something wounded, dying, cut short in mid cry.

She teetered on the brink of blackness, terrified, alone, in physical and emotional pain that threatened to swamp her very being.

"Sheridan."

Like a rope to a drowning man, the voice came out of the dazed, frightened night and found her.

"Sheridan."

A face, indistinct and blurry, swam close to her face. Huge sapphire eyes shone out and she felt suddenly that she was all right. She wanted to speak, to reach out but couldn't. All she could do was look into those eyes and draw their strength.

"I'm sorry," he breathed heavily. "Dear God, but I'm sorry. I never meant for this to happen. That first night when he came here, I felt the evil in him like a tangible thing. He kept it in that innocent shell, but I knew. I tried to tell you but I couldn't make you understand. I wove a spell of protection around you but I knew that the evil would feed on the terror and the pain and grow stronger and stronger so I went out to look for him. Stop him." As he spoke, Sheridan felt gentle hands carefully cutting the bindings on her hands until she was free. She concentrated on the tender sound of his voice, reaching out like a buoy that kept her from being swept under the dark sea of pain and terror surrounding her.

"I followed his trail, the stench of him marking every step. I wanted to catch him, keep him from hurting anyone else. Stomp out the evil. Kill him.

"He was clever, though. I almost had him once but I missed the jump from the fire escape and hurt my leg. I was trying to get home but the police came and were looking for me, not him, so I had to hide under a car for hours and hours until they left and I could get back to you. I never thought he'd actually..."

She felt a warm, soft touch as he pulled at her tattered clothing, trying to cover her as best he could. "But he won't hurt you. No one will ever hurt you again.

"I...I can't stay," he whispered hoarsely. "I...I've used up everything. All my strength...my time. But I don't regret it, Sheridan. Not for an instant. I've waited a thousand years for you. I can wait a little longer. I found you once. I'll find you again. I promise. And don't worry about your writing. You don't need me to grant your dream. You have the power inside you to make it come true. You always have."

The face was growing blurrier, the voice weaker. Somewhere, far away, it seemed she could hear muffled voices and the distant whine of sirens.

"Good bye, Sheridan." Soft lips brushed lightly along her cheek. "You won't remember this talk when you wake up, but know in your heart that everything will be all right now. Everything. I love you."

The image and the voice faded away as she fell into the blackness.

Chapter Eleven

The police found Brian's body in the alley under Sheridan's fire escape. Cause of death was officially listed as a broken neck. In their haste and relief to have the Fairview Heights Rapist case closed, publicly they skimmed over the autopsy report which revealed that his clothes had been "ripped to shreds" and that there were deep scratches and bite marks on his face and body, in many places, right through his clothing.

"We believe," Chief Robbins later read from his statement at the televised news conference, "that the rapist entered the apartment through the fire escape window. To facilitate his escape, he left the window unlatched and open a few inches. As he was attempting to rape Miss Phillips, her cat, a large black male, weighing some twenty pounds, returned home, squeezed through the open window and attacked him. Surprised and frightened, the young man tried to free himself and flee. In the ensuing struggle, he accidentally crashed through the window and off the fire escape, breaking his neck. Investigators later searched the young man's room and found several pairs of black leather gloves like those used in the attacks and a detailed diary of his rapes."

The police chief refused all questions from the media.

Except for a black eye, some bruises and scratches and raw places on her mouth and wrists from the duct tape, Sheridan was physically okay. The doctors insisted that she stay overnight in the hospital "for observation," whatever the hell that meant.

As she waited in the Emergency Room to be admitted, Sheridan met Detectives Arnold Thoreau ("no relation") and Gwen Swift.

"We know this is a difficult time," Detective Swift told her gently, "and we know that you're tired and that you need your rest. We just need to ask you a few questions and then we'll get out of your hair."

"All right."

Detective Thoreau took out a small spiral bound notebook and a stub of pencil. Flipping through some pages, he paused and looked at his partner, nodding to let her know that he was ready to start.

"Ms. Phillips," she began calmly, "Can you tell us, in your own words, what happened? Take all the time you need to. If you need to take or break or want to continue some other time, we'll understand. But we would like to get as much of the story, as many details as we can now, while things are still fresh in your mind. You'd be surprised how fast a lot of this will fade."

Tears blurred her remaining vision as the horror show began another replay of the attack. It hadn't stopped since the moment the police had broken down the door and actually saved her. The thought that this nightmare might "fade" hadn't occurred to her.

Something soft was pressed into her hand. It was a large, white, man's handkerchief. Using it to wipe away the tears, she saw the detectives waiting patiently, looking sympathetic and understanding.

Handing it back to him, Sheridan smiled limply and took a deep breath.

"I'd let my cat out and I guess I didn't lock the window," she whispered. "I was in my bedroom running the vacuum..."

* * * * *

When the doctors and the police had finally finished with her, a pair of young orderlies took Sheridan's gurney upstairs to the sixth floor and helped her into bed. It was a nice room, private, painted a bright sunny yellow and with a view of the grounds. A tray appeared but the sight of food made her sick at her stomach and it disappeared as quickly as it had arrived.

There was a telephone in the room but the nurse said the police had asked that it not be connected and that Sheridan not have visitors for twenty-four hours, to spare her the pressures of the media.

"Good thing, too," the old nurse sniffed derisively. "They're camped out down in the lobby like a flock of vultures. They'd be up here circling if they could. You wouldn't believe what I've seen those idiots do to try and get to a patient. Bribe staff. Impersonate doctors and nurses. One lunkhead even tried pretending to be a window washer and came down the side of the building. You'd think grown people would have more sense."

"I would like to call someone," she pleaded, "a friend. Please. Isn't there something I can do? A pay phone even."

"Sorry. Doctor's orders are that you stay in bed, no visitors, no phone calls."

Seeing her distress and the tears beginning again, the nurse relented.

"There, there," she soothed, cradling Sheridan's hand in hers as if she were comforting a small child. "The doctor doesn't want you getting all upset and neither do I. But I'll tell you what I'll do. Give me the name of the person you want to hear from. I'll leave word at the desk that if they call, we can route it to you through the intercom feature of the phone. Supposed to be for in-house calls only, but we've been known to bend the rules in a pinch. Bright and early tomorrow, we'll get the phone turned on and then you can talk to them yourself. Okay?"

"Oh yes. Thank you. My friend's name is Pat. Pat Kellogg." Sheridan quickly rattled off Pat's phone number.

"Got it. Now you have to rest." She smoothed the linen and plumped the pillow and left Sheridan alone.

As soon as she was gone, the hideous event came screaming back, floods of tears doing nothing to diminish the awful scene or the excruciating details. They did, however, finally exhaust her and she fell into a restless, fitful sleep.

* * * * *

"Ms. Phillips?"

Sheridan nodded uncertainly.

"I'm Karen Webley," she smiled warmly, handing over a small white business card.

Karen Webley, M.S.W. Rape Counselor. The last two words seemed to leap off the card and slap her face. There it was. In cold, impersonal black lettering.

Rape.

The nightmare was real.

"I brought you a cup of really bad hospital coffee," she was saying, placing a white Styrofoam cup on the bedside table. "Mind if I sit down?"

"Miss Webley," Sheridan began wearily, "I appreciate you coming. I'm sure it's part of your job. But please, I'm just not up to talking about it now. It's too…" She felt the pictures starting up even as she spoke and had to shut her eyes and fight against them.

"Please," she answered gently, "call me Karen. And I understand absolutely how you feel."

"How could you possibly know how I feel?" Sheridan snarled, suddenly overwhelmed by anger and frustration and misery. "You think just because you have a degree in hand holding that you can come in here and tell me you understand! You can't possibly know how I feel!"

"Yes I can," she countered quietly. "I can understand because I was raped too."

The revelation was like throwing cold water on Sheridan, stopping her abruptly. She stared at the other woman, not comprehending or even believing what she'd just heard.

"It's part of the reason I do this. Because someone was there for me when I needed them, I try to be here for someone who needs me. I know you don't want to talk about it now and that's all right. You probably need to cry more than anything else. But you will want to talk sometime. And when you're ready, you have my number. I'm available day or night."

"I'm...I'm sorry," Sheridan croaked.

"Don't be," Webley reassured her. "It was a long time ago. And difficult as it may be for you to believe now, it's possible to survive even this. I know. I did it. So can you."

"I...I..." The words disappeared in a fresh tide of tears.

Gently, Webley put her arms around Sheridan and held her as she wept.

"Go ahead, Sheridan," she whispered. "Let it out. Let it all out. You can't start to heal 'til you do."

* * * * *

"Sher," Pat yelped into the phone. "Oh God, I'm so glad to hear your voice."

Sheridan could hear the tears in her friend's voice. It was almost worse than hearing her own.

"I'm all right," she whispered back without conviction.

"There was a special news bulletin on television," Pat continued, racing her words through the story at break-neck speed. "As soon as I heard, I tried calling your apartment but there wasn't any answer. Then I made Bruce drive me over there because I was shaking and screaming and the police and the media and a crowd of people were all outside your place and I told the policeman I was your dearest friend and you'd want to see me and they said you'd already been taken to the hospital. They told me it was Saint Luke's but when we got over there, the nurse told us that you were really at Carver General so we went over there and they told us you couldn't have any visitors or any phone calls and I started to cry and the volunteer called up there and I told the nurse who I was and she said she'd put me through but only for a minute. Oh God, Sher!"

The tears flowed in earnest. Sheridan couldn't do anything but listen in silence to her friend weep. After a few moments, Pat honked, sniffed loudly and took a deep breath.

"Okay," she announced firmly. "I am all right now."

"Good. I need you to do something for me."

"Anything, Sher. Anything."

"Go to my apartment," she explained quickly. "By now the police should be finished with it. Nick will be frantic. Please, go and let him in. I've got some leftover meatloaf in the fridge. Warm it in the microwave, no more than thirty seconds, make sure he has fresh water and tell him I'll be home as soon as I can."

"But, Sher," she answered patiently. "The police will have boarded up the window by now and…"

"I don't care," she shouted. "If it's boarded up, tear it down! Just get Nick into the apartment. I can't…won't…leave him out all night. He won't understand."

"Listen to me, Sher. The police think that Nick…that Nick jumped this guy and that while he was trying to get Nick off him, they crashed through the window and into the alley." She paused, waiting to see if the significance of what she was saying was sinking in.

"They didn't find Nick. Just a small pool of blood that wasn't human. If Nick was hanging onto this guy when he fell and he didn't have time to get free…"

"No!" Sheridan screamed into the phone. "Don't say that! Don't even think it! Nick isn't…he couldn't be."

"All right, Sher," she agreed, resignation and compassion in her voice, "whatever you say. Just promise me you'll try to get some rest. Okay?"

"Okay. Thanks, Pat. And I'm sorry."

"It's all right. I understand."

* * * * *

Pat arrived the next day as soon as she was allowed in. Seeing her best friend, it was everything she could do not to burst into tears again. Sheridan's left eye was swollen shut, a huge black and purple starburst mushrooming out toward her forehead, cheek and the bridge of her nose. She was pale as the sheets she was lying in.

"Oh God, Sher," she squealed, throwing her arms around her friend. But Sheridan had other things on her mind. Breaking away from her friend, she looked up.

"You look awful," Pat murmured.

"I know," Sheridan agreed weakly. "I went in the bathroom last night to use the john. I almost passed out from fright when I saw this face staring back at me in the mirror. Doctor says it could have been worse. I didn't even get a concussion from Brian hitting me. Thank God for this thick Irish skull."

"Well at least it's over and you're going to be all right. As soon as you've got yourself together, we can get out of here. Bruce is waiting downstairs in the car. Since the news ghouls are roosting out front, the hospital let us come in the back way and we can go out the staff entrance."

"That's nice," Sheridan sighed. "I'm not up to answering any more questions."

"Well, Bruce is going back to work but I'm taking a couple of days off to look after you so anything you want, you just ask. So let's get you back to the house and settled in the guestroom so you can rest. Later, you can make a list of things...clothes, toilet articles...and Bruce will go by your place and pick up whatever you need."

But Sheridan shook her head emphatically.

"I have to see about Nick," she told Pat firmly.

"Be reasonable, Sher," Pat sighed. "I told you. Nick wasn't there. The window's boarded up and I checked the fire escape myself. I left the meatloaf though."

"He might have been scared by all the police and people and noise and stayed away," Sheridan insisted. "Then he couldn't get back in because the window was boarded up."

A picture came to her of Nick...hungry, cold, confused...scratching desperately at the plywood, unable to understand where she was. Why she didn't come home to him.

"If you don't want to take me," she snapped, "I'll get a cab. But I have to get back to the apartment."

"All right, Sher, all right. Don't get upset. We'll take you by the apartment so you can check on Nick. But you can't stay there. Not after...after what happened. You shouldn't be alone now. You need someone to take care of you."

"Pat..."

"Just for a few days, Sher. To humor me. Please?"

"All right. Anything to get out of here."

* * * * *

Surreal.

It was the only word Sheridan could come up with as she stood amidst the debris of the battlefield that had so recently been her safe, cozy living room.

Reddish brown splotches spattered her beige carpet, ranging from dot sized to one almost the size of her hand near the window. Glass from one of the shattered doors of her entertainment center was sprinkled like ice shards on the rug.

The small brass reading lamp that had stood on her round oak end table now lay on the rug, its cream-colored pleated shade crushed and bearing the dirty print of a large shoe. Discarded bandage wrappers, a short length of thin plastic tubing and even a latex glove littered the area in front of the sofa. Someone had pushed her coffee table almost to the fireplace, knocking over one of the crystal candlesticks, breaking the candle in half and leaving it dangling forlornly over the edge.

Instead of the expected plywood, a shiny new window admitted the winter sunshine, bathing the room in bright light, only adding to the unreal quality of the scene.

"I'm sorry about the mess," Pat apologized as she stood beside Sheridan and surveyed the damage. "I probably should have straightened up when I was here last night but I only just popped in to take care of Nick and...well, I guess I just wasn't paying any attention."

"It's all right," Sheridan mumbled mechanically. She had a stray thought that she'd spent a lot of time in the last two days uttering those words to a lot of different people. Idly, she wondered how often she would have to say it before it became true again.

"Last night," Pat was saying, "the glazier was tearing out the plywood and getting ready to put in a new window. Said the building owner was afraid of vandals or burglars or just curiosity seekers. Paid him extra to replace it on an emergency basis."

Slowly, Sheridan drifted to the window and stared out. The fire escape was empty except for a small plate of drying meatloaf and a bowl of water. With a little difficulty, she managed to get the window open enough to put her head out and look down into the alley. Immediately, she regretted it.

Directly beneath her, the remnants of a white outline could still be seen on the dirty ground. The only thing she could make out clearly was a foot and a leg, both jutting out at an unnatural angle.

A wave of nausea rolled over her. Pulling back, she sagged, feeling too weak even to stand up anymore. Pat was at her side in a second, guiding her gently into the bedroom and helping her to lie down.

"Look, Sher," she said anxiously. "I told you, you shouldn't come here. That you should let me take you home and put you to bed. So now you lie here and rest. Just tell me where your bags are and what you want me to pack and we'll get the hell out of here."

For a moment, Sheridan tried to focus but could do nothing but stare back at her friend.

"Okay," Pat replied finally, "don't worry. I'll take care of it." And she turned quickly for the closet.

Looking around her bedroom, it was like nothing had ever happened. Everything was exactly as it had been in that last moment before her world had been shattered forever.

Only the carnage in the living room marked the horror, the terror of what had happened. Only it showed the physical disruption, the pain and shambles that her life had suddenly become.

But here, in this room, time had simply stopped. Like those clocks that mark the exact moment of horrendous disasters like earthquakes and stand silent forevermore, this room remained exactly as before.

Slowly, she stretched out her fingers and tentatively touched the handle of the vacuum cleaner, standing beside the bed precisely where it had been when the blow had landed and the nightmare had begun. It felt solid and real. Maybe this was the reality and the other, the living room, the fantasy. Perhaps all that was necessary to end this, make everything as it had been again, was simply to close the door and stay here.

Somewhere in the background, she could hear Pat muttering to herself as she rummaged in the closet and bureau.

Shutting her eyes, Sheridan turned her back on the vacuum and tried to turn off the attack video playing in her mind. Being in this place that had once been her haven, her refuge, seemed to exacerbate the horror. As if the entire apartment had somehow absorbed a terror, an evil that permeated the very air.

Where are you, Nick, she thought desperately. I need you!

The irrational thought popped into her head that if he were there, curled up beside her, he could somehow make everything all right again. He'd snuggle tightly against her, put a velvet paw on her arm to reassure her, run his rough little tongue over her cheek and gaze up at her with those beautiful eyes.

Nick's face formed in her mind, blurred and indistinct. As if she were seeing it through rippled water or cracked glass. Only his eyes were clear...bright and reassuring as the blue beacons of a lighthouse at the entrance to safe harbor. The sight of them seemed to calm her, ease her white-knuckled need to flee this place.

And for the first time since the nightmare had begun, Sheridan had the tiniest glimmer of hope that things would, eventually, be all right.

Chapter Twelve

Brian was buried as quietly as the ghoul press would allow. Barred from the church services and the private cemetery, they had to content themselves with pictures of his parents and younger sister scurrying to and from the waiting black limousine, trying to shield themselves from the prying lenses and shouted questions. And if Brian had any friends, they were conspicuous by their absence.

Seeing the two-minute snippet on the evening news, Sheridan was reminded of something her mother had told her as a child: "If there's no one there to mourn you, you'll never rest in peace." She wondered if any of them, herself included, would ever find peace again.

With a simple, two line, handwritten note, his father quit his job as super and the family moved away, where, no one was ever quite sure.

After all the suffering, destruction and finally death that he'd brought into so many lives, it seemed almost anti-climactic. The proverbial whimper.

Now, all that remained for those left behind was to try and put the fragments of their brutally disrupted lives back together.

* * * * *

"And why not, may I ask?"

"Because, Pat," Sheridan answered wearily, "nice as your guest room is and as wonderful as you and Bruce have been, I can't stay here forever."

"No one has said forever," Pat corrected gently, shifting her weight on the edge of the bed. "Just for a little while. Until you're well. The doctor gave you a practically open-ended excuse from work and you've got all kinds of sick leave. What you need is to rest and relax for a while."

"I'm not going to get better lying around here watching television and dwelling on...on things I'd just as soon not dwell on." She sighed and looked down at her hands, picking at the quilt on top of her. "Sometimes I don't know which is worse, the flashbacks in the daytime or the nightmares."

"Oh Sher." Pat leaned over and took the other woman in her arms. "I'm so sorry. I feel so...so helpless. I'd do anything..."

"I know you would." She smiled a little. "And you have. More than you can know. But it's time I try to move on. And that means being on my own again."

"But..."

"But nothing, Pat. My mind's made up."

"Where will you go?" she asked anxiously. "You can't go back to your apartment. I mean..."

"I know what you mean. And I don't have any intention of going back there."

"Then where will you go? What will you do?"

"I've been thinking about that. A lot. And I have three things I want...need...to do. One, I need to find Nick. Next, I need to find a new apartment. And lastly, I need to work on a new story that seems to have arrived full blown in my head and which is screaming frantically to get out."

The corners of Pat's mouth curled down and Sheridan cut her off before she could speak again.

"I know what you think about Nick. I know what everyone thinks. But I know it's not true."

"How can you know?"

"Because," she whispered, "if Nick were...were dead, part of me would be too."

Pat felt her throat close up, and her heart clutched for her friend. Sheridan was in the worst kind of denial. She'd refused to talk about the attempted rape to anyone. Not to the counselor or even to her. It was as if she'd decided that ignoring it could somehow make it go away. And her refusal to accept the truth about Nick was obviously part of the whole denial process. There was no use in trying to make her see reason.

"What do you plan to do?"

Sheridan immediately brightened.

"I'm going to make posters, have them printed up and plaster the city with them. I'm going to offer a reward. Nothing gets people's attention like money."

"All right," Pat relented. "If that's what you want, you can use the computer in the den."

So for days, Sheridan paid one of the neighborhood teens to check her fire escape morning and night for Nick. She papered the city with flyers offering a substantial reward. Vets offices, the humane society, every pet shop in the area got a notice. In the days following his disappearance, she saw every large and not so large, male and female and neutered, black, dark gray, light gray, spotted and tiger tabby for miles around. But no Nick.

At the end of many long, frustrating days of posting notices, talking to strangers, looking at cats and searching alleys, Sheridan would drag back to Pat's house, lock the guest room door and collapse onto the bed, wracked with tears until she finally dropped into a restless sleep.

Some nights, she'd dream of Nick, having fought to save her life...crippled, bleeding...crawling off somewhere to die alone in some filthy, garbage-strewn alley. Once in awhile, though, he'd come home to her, leaping onto the carpet and rubbing himself joyously against her legs at the reunion.

Most nights though, at least once, she'd relive the attack in all its horrible, minute detail, bringing her wide awake, heart racing, body trembling and sweating, shame and disgust and terror hanging on her like a dirty cobweb.

And the tears would flow again.

* * * * *

Sheridan happened upon the apartment quite by accident.

One afternoon, while she was posting a flyer about Nick on a community bulletin board in a small neighborhood grocery, she noticed a handwritten ad for an apartment. Since the building address was just around the corner and she was finished for the day, Sheridan decided to take a chance and go see it.

The address turned out to be a wonderful old Victorian home, painted a cheerful sunshine yellow with crisp white gingerbread trim. A turret at the right corner of the house rose to a point above the gray-shingled roof. Huge, stately maple trees on either side framed the house and the empty flowerbeds in front, waiting for spring. Snow carpeted the front lawn, split perfectly down the middle by a wide cement walkway leading to the front door. On the wide veranda porch, an old-fashioned swing completed the picture.

Pushing the doorbell produced a wonderful, resonant, bell sound from deep inside the house, audible even from the outside. A moment later, the door swung open.

"Yes?" asked a tall, nice-looking elderly woman with snow-white curls and bright, dark brown eyes.

"Hello," Sheridan answered awkwardly. "My name's Sheridan Phillips. I saw the ad about the apartment in the grocery store around the corner. I'd like to look at it, if it's still available." She glanced down at the scratch paper in her hand. "Mrs. Farnsworth, I think?"

A warm, friendly smile appeared on the other woman's face. "I'm Maude Farnsworth and yes, the apartment's still available. How many of you are there?"

"Just me."

"That's good. The ad says one bedroom and that would be one person or a married couple. I don't want a family of seven or college kids playing Musical Roommates. Too old for that."

"I can certainly understand."

"Come in." She stood aside and Sheridan stepped into the large, comfortable entry hall, dominated by a huge grandfather clock and a dark, antique hall tree.

"Thank you."

"It's the second floor, front," Mrs. Farnsworth was saying as she closed the door. "This way." She led the way up the front stairs, carpeted in a rich burgundy, complementing the turned white spindles and thick dark banister.

Upstairs, they turned immediately to the right, Mrs. Farnsworth taking a ring of keys from her apron pocket.

"Carrie, the former tenant, up and eloped last weekend."

Putting the key in the lock, the old woman turned the doorknob, opened the door and stepped aside for Sheridan to enter.

"Nice young man," she commented as they moved into the large living room. "Been going together for a long time. He's in the service and got a transfer to Hawaii. Can't blame her. She said she was sorry to be leaving without proper notice but when you're young and in love…"

Sheridan gasped in delight as her eyes fell on the turret alcove, the curtains open to the long circular windows, sunlight spilling into the room.

"It's beautiful," she breathed, moving to the large alcove and glancing out toward the front yard and quiet street beyond.

"It is nice," Mrs. Farnsworth agreed, coming to stand beside her. "This turret is the reason Ralph and I bought the house originally," she commented wistfully. "That was almost forty years ago. Place was a big, old, rundown eyesore but we loved it the second we saw it. Real estate agent and all our friends thought we were crazy. We spent our first night having dinner in the downstairs turret alcove."

Sheridan could see that the old woman was seeing another time, gazing out the window and looking at the past. She waited silently for the other woman to return from her nostalgic journey.

"At any rate," she resumed quietly, turning to face Sheridan again, "when Ralph died five years ago, it was convert the house to flats or lose it. This one was the first one rented. Not very big as you can see. Kitchen's through there, small dining area. The living room's large and even though the fireplace is small, it's nice on a cold winter's night. Except for my flat, which is directly downstairs, it's the only one with a fireplace. There's a little veranda outside the French doors there." She nodded to the far side of the living room. "Not much to it but there's room for a lawn chair and a couple of potted plants and it's nice in the summer heat. Bedroom and bath are over there."

"It's exactly what I'm looking for," Sheridan told her when they'd taken a short, quick tour of the apartment. "Could I fill out an application?"

The older woman waved her hand as if to dismiss the whole notion. "Oh, good heavens, that's too much trouble. I've got a little personal information form and a rental agreement downstairs. Got both of them at the stationery store."

"Well, I'm sure you'll want references and to do a credit check."

"You employed, Miss Phillips?"

"Yes, ma'am. I'm an Administrative Assistant for a civil engineering firm." She hesitated a moment. "I'm...I'm on temporary disability leave right now but I'm still getting a full paycheck."

"You have a place to live now?"

"Yes. An apartment on French Court in the Fairview Heights area."

"How soon would you like to move in?

"I was hoping to move out of my apartment as soon as possible."

"How 'bout next weekend? I have the painters coming in on Monday and I expect the place will be ready by Saturday."

"That would be wonderful," Sheridan breathed, hardly able to believe her good luck.

"Good," the other woman announced with a firm nod of her head. "That's taken care of." She put out her hand. "As long as we're going to be neighbors, you can call me Maude."

"And I'm Sheridan," she smiled reaching out and taking the other woman's hand. It was a surprisingly firm handshake.

"Now, let's go downstairs, have a cup of tea and get the paperwork out of the way."

At the top of the stairs, Maude turned to her and frowned slightly. "There is just one more thing," she said firmly.

For a moment, Sheridan was afraid she was going to go back on her promise of the apartment. "Yes?" she replied warily.

"Do you like cats?"

The question took Sheridan completely by surprise. "Yes," she managed to stammer out. "I'm…I'm very fond of cats. I had one I loved very much until…until very recently."

"I'm so sorry to hear that," Mrs. Farnsworth told her, patting her gently. "I only asked because of Asia, my calico. She's like me. Old, crotchety and set in her ways. Had her since she was a kitten. Before we had to convert to flats. Still thinks she has the run of the place and pretty much comes and goes as she pleases. Your veranda is one of her favorite haunts when the weather's nice. Just wanted you to know. In case you don't like cats or are allergic or something."

Breathing a sigh of relief, Sheridan smiled. "Asia sounds wonderful. I can't wait to meet her."

So the next Saturday, with the help of a rental truck, Pat, Bruce and several of the people she worked with, Sheridan left one part of her life and began another.

Avoiding the living room in her old apartment, she scurried quickly into the kitchen, immersing herself in wrapping and packing her dishes, glasses and cookware. Having already discussed the subject with her friends, she listened as they began packing and hauling her things down the stairs.

There wasn't really very much. Most of her clothes and personal items had already gone over to Pat's. Rocker, coffee and end tables, bureau and mirror, bed, computer equipment and desk, television, VCR and stereo, and dining table and chairs were the main things. Because she couldn't bear to look at them, the sofa and entertainment center had been consigned to a local thrift store. They'd been picked up the day before.

She'd received a formal letter from the owner of the building—well, actually his lawyer—stating that in view of the "unfortunate incident", she would not be held responsible for the stain damage to the living room carpet or the emergency repair of the living room window.

Also, in return for her written assurance that she "would not seek to find the building, its ownership or management in any way responsible for the problem", they would, barring any damage beyond normal wear and tear, be happy to refund her security deposit and provide a positive reference to any future landlord.

Opening the cupboard, Sheridan was momentarily startled to see two large cans of salmon. She'd bought them the last time she went to the store before...

Tears blurred the shelves, making a multi-colored smudge.

Oh God, Nick!

Sheridan slumped against the counter, her shoulders sagging as sorrow overwhelmed her again.

She couldn't stay here. Even her love, her belief, her need for Nick couldn't overcome the horror that Brian had brought into this place. Just being here now, in the daylight, the apartment filled with sun and other people, the evil seemed to be pressing in on her, threatening to suffocate her. It was taking every ounce of strength she had to fight down her panic-stricken urge to run.

But she couldn't leave, either. This had been where she and Nick had made their home, shared their lives. This was where he'd return. Where he'd expect her to be waiting. If she left, she'd be abandoning him. It would be admitting that he wasn't coming back. That she'd lost faith in him. In them.

Could he…would he, ever be able to understand? Forgive her?

Nick, she screamed in her mind. *I need you so much.*

* * * * *

Sheridan stared out into the unfamiliar blackness of her new bedroom.

After clearing out her old apartment, they'd all piled in their respective vehicles and begun the reverse process at the Victorian. Everyone had *ooohed* and *aaahed* over her flat, especially the turret window. She'd insisted that her computer desk be put in the alcove, where it fit perfectly. Gino, one of the interns from the office, had immediately set about hooking it up for her.

When all the furniture had been placed and the boxes stacked in various rooms, Sheridan had paid for buckets of fried chicken, all the trimmings, cola and beer. They'd sat on the living room floor, talking and laughing, trying just a little too hard to make the transition seem festive. Carefully, they sidestepped any hint that the move had been caused by anything more than the normal transience of everyday life. In fact, Pat had commented again how much more she liked the Victorian than the old place. Someone else told her that it would be a shorter, more convenient commute to the office.

Finally, they'd all drifted away, saying their goodbyes, wishing her well in her new place and hoping to see her back at work soon. Exhausted, she'd deadbolted the door, checked to make sure the windows were locked and gone to bed.

But even the physical exhaustion could not coax her body to shut down and sleep. Like the monster in the closet of her childhood, Sheridan's mind knew the nightmare of the attempted rape was waiting just over the threshold of dreams to leap out and attack her as it did every night. As it did in her unguarded daytime moments. And the fear of that monster had become almost as terrible as the event itself.

There was no way to keep the beast at bay except to stand guard against the enemy, sleep. Dwell on the new story. Fill up her brain with scenes and people and words. Tomorrow she would begin putting them all down in the computer. But tonight they must stand, like a palisade battlement, against the monster lurking beyond wakefulness.

"Sheridan."

The whisper was so faint, she wasn't even sure it hadn't been the wind. Or perhaps even her imagination.

Lying on her back, she glanced up to the headboard where the large red numerals of her alarm clock glowed upside down...four minutes after three. She must have dozed off because she was still feeling fuzzy and tired. And the moon, which hadn't been visible when she climbed into bed, was shimmering through the window, bathing everything in a soft, silvery glow.

"Sheridan."

"Who's there?" It was her voice but it seemed to be coming, not from her mouth, but her mind.

"I didn't mean to wake you," the voice told her softly. "I know you haven't been sleeping very well and I know you need your rest. I just wanted you to know that you weren't alone. You'll never be alone again."

She felt tender lips brush hers even though she couldn't see anyone, anything in the darkness.

"I...I don't understand," she mumbled.

"Don't try," the voice shushed. "Just know it. Don't be afraid. Nothing will ever hurt you again."

Fingertips ran gently down her cheek as the lips found hers again. Unexpectedly, Sheridan felt herself shiver...not with fear but with a sudden burst of warm anticipation. It was a sensation she'd thought dead. Murdered by Brian in her apartment that Saturday afternoon.

Slowly, the lips traveled down under her chin and into the hollow of her throat.

"You have the most beautiful body. Your skin's ivory velvet. You don't need to cover it, hide it from me. Especially not in our bed."

Her nightgown disappeared and she could see her naked flesh against her floral sheets, pale and almost luminescent in the moonlight.

He lay on his side next to her, lean and handsome as he'd been in the other erotic dreams. Smiling down at her, caressing her spirit with his love as sweetly as he did her body with his hands and mouth.

"How did you find me?"

"I never left you," he breathed, leaning over to cup her breast in his hand and bringing her nipple to his mouth and suckling gently.

"Oh!" she yipped as the sensation shuddered through her.

"It's all right now," he assured her as he fondled her, running his hand across her stomach and down her inner thigh. "There's no fear in our bed. Only pleasure. Don't be afraid, Sheridan. Let me love you."

"Please...no...don't!" she protested, the all too familiar fear of a man's touch rushing up to engulf her.

"It's all right, my love," he soothed, continuing to touch her skin and brush light kisses along her lips and cheeks. "I would never hurt you. Much as I love you, want you, it's not my time yet. You're still too frightened. The pain's too fresh. But you need to start again. Need to start back down the road to trust. And you need to rest."

"I can't," she whimpered into his bare chest.

"Let me love you, Sheridan," he coaxed tenderly. "Let me give you pleasure to wipe away the pain. Bring you contentment and peace, in your body as well as your spirit."

As his mouth found hers again, his fingertips found her soft, pink clitoris. Delicately as butterfly wings, he ran them over it, feeling her tremble under him.

"I love you," he mumbled hoarsely between kisses.

Almost in spite of herself, Sheridan felt her terror and revulsion being melted by the heat being generated inside her by this mysterious, caring apparition.

"Who...who are you?" she murmured, her eyes closed, her body rocking slightly.

"In time," he growled as his mouth moved in a zigzag down her body, dropping kisses to mark his passing. "When we find each other again, you'll know me. For these few moments we have together now, it doesn't matter. All that matters is you."

The face disappeared into the thick black curls of her pubic hair and she felt his mouth on her, like gasoline suddenly causing a small flame to erupt into blazing fire.

"Oh God," she squealed again, barely able to breathe as he worked his magic on her. It was like nothing she'd ever known, even in their dreams before. Then, he'd seemed to know her needs, her desires exactly. And these repeat performances seemed to have honed, have sharpened all his skills.

His tongue made long, slow sweeps, laying flat and covering her full, tender bud completely. These he combined with short, rapid ice cream cone licks, placing his mouth over her, inhaling like a vacuum. The combination raced through her, uncontrolled lava, spinning her head and vaporizing thought. There was nothing but the exquisite pleasure blotting out everything else.

Sweeping toward climax, her body shivering and trembling, the phantom kept pace with her, never losing contact with her skin. Sensing she was almost there, he made one last frantic attack that sent her crashing down into a vast ecstasy that rolled and crested and totally engulfed her.

Lying back on her pillow, her eyes closed as she tried to regain her senses, she felt him against her again, cradling her in his arms like a child, slowly kissing her forehead and hair.

Reaching up to touch his face, Sheridan half opened her eyes and smiled. "I want you," she whispered. "I need you."

"Not now, darling. We have all the time there is. Besides, I should leave you and let you rest."

She grabbed his hand and held it firmly. "Don't leave me," she pleaded anxiously. "Stay with me. Be with me."

"I don't want you to be afraid, to hurt you, even accidentally."

Silently, she reached down and touched his shaft, straining at attention. "You want me," she breathed, "as much as I want you. Please."

"I...I don't know," he hesitated.

"I need you," she repeated, sliding her legs apart and pulling him to her.

Gently, with agonizing slowness, he did as she asked, feeling her wet body slip over him like a perfectly fitted velvet sleeve, bathed in pleasure.

"Are you all right?" he asked fearfully. "I'm not hurting you, am I?"

"You feel wonderful," she responded, closing her eyes and losing herself in the sensation of him inside her. Squeezing as tightly as she could, Sheridan pulled him to her, feeling his strong, muscled body cover hers, shutting out the pain and the terror of the rape and replacing it with warmth and caring.

Playfully, she stroked his butt, pushing on the firm flesh as she ground him to her as hard as possible. She wanted him to come now, to return to him some measure of the joy he'd given her.

"Sheridan," he breathed harshly. "Dear God, darling! Oh...oh!"

She felt his body shudder and shiver above her as she wrapped her legs around him, trying to take as much of him as she could, wring out every last drop of pleasure from him. She felt the warm gush of his semen as it spurted deep within her body. Feeling him inside of her, knowing at last that Brian hadn't robbed her of the gift of giving and receiving physical pleasure, she felt an enormous weight being lifted from her body and soul. A new sense of freedom.

"Sleep now," he whispered. "All the nightmares have been banished. Tomorrow, you'll feel better and can start again. Remember how much I love you and that we'll always be together."

Drifting away, Sheridan felt warm and safe.

* * * * *

It was a little past eight when Sheridan finally opened her eyes, yawned deeply and stretched a long, feline stretch from fingertips to toes. She couldn't remember when she'd slept so well or so soundly. Certainly not since the attack.

And she'd had a dream. She couldn't remember what it had been but the warmth of it hung around her like a fuzzy blanket. For the first time in what seemed like ages, she actually felt rested and refreshed.

After a shower and a bowl of cereal, she considered her options. Except for a few personal items, kitchen and bath necessities, and her clothes, practically everything she owned remained scattered on her living room floor. Her furniture, including her new sofa and entertainment center, had all been placed on moving day. So, realistically, she should spend this first day unpacking and straightening up.

Instead, she went to her desk in the sunlit turret alcove and sat down. Rummaging through a nearby cardboard box produced her desk set, including mouse pad and wrist rest. A few more moments and she was ready. Switching on the machine, she went to her word processing program and typed a title at the center top of the blank page.

As she worked, Sheridan began to feel as if someone was dictating the story in her mind; all she was required to do was write it down. Even with her hard-won typing speed, the words gushed out so fast she had trouble keeping up with them. The cherry wine seemed to be spewing out of a fire hose.

When she looked up from the computer again, Sheridan was shocked to see it was already past noon. Lacing her fingers together, she stretched her arms out in front of her as far as she could, trying to relieve the cramping in her hands and shoulders. Turning her head from side to side, she stretched her tired neck muscles.

It wasn't often, she thought as she scrolled over the finished pages, that she got so caught up in something. Even as her body begged to be released from the computer, her mind was anxiously spinning out the details of upcoming scenes, demanding that she remain in her chair and type.

And it was good.

She didn't ordinarily say that about her work. Usually she was her own harshest critic, inspecting every word, every phrase with an eye toward possible improvement. Nothing ever seemed to satisfy her unless it had been tuned and tweaked, as Pat said, "past all reason".

But as she read her words, they seemed perfect, saying exactly what she wanted, exactly the way she wanted it to say. It was better than anything she'd ever done before and it brightened her spirits enormously.

Standing, she glanced around the messy apartment again and a flicker of uncertainty flashed in her brain. Maybe she really should clean up a little. But as she moved to the kitchen for a cup of tea, the thought was gone, pushed out by the ongoing novel unraveling in her brain.

Chapter Thirteen
January

Per usual, it turned out the office grapevine was right. Duncan's leg failed to heal properly making it impossible for him to sit or stand for long periods of time or to clamber over excavation and building sites. Instead of a leave of six months, he retired and Jim Eldridge became permanent.

After sending Sheridan to school, at the company's expense, Eldridge promoted her to Senior Administrative Assistant for Design and Construction. Granted, her office wasn't as big or as nice as Diana's, but then, she wasn't required to sleep with the boss, either. With the raise she got after her evaluation, she was able to afford a dependable used car and no longer had to ride the bus.

Her free time was taken up almost completely as the book spilled out. Sometimes she wrote until after midnight, dragging into the office yawning and bleary-eyed. Weekends were spent holed up at the computer, the answering machine picking up her phone messages. When she wasn't actually at the computer...driving to work, pushing her grocery cart, sorting her laundry...the book whirled relentlessly along, demanding virtually every minute of her time and energy. Only the recurring nightmare of Brian's vicious attack could push the flowing story from her dreams.

In fact, the story went so well, that in record time it was finished. She spent several days going back over it, making mostly technical revisions but not changing the story. Finally, polished to her satisfaction, she put it in a large manila envelope, took it to the post office and sent it on its way. Now there was nothing left to do but wait.

* * * * *

Winter slowly passed away and spring began creeping in. The first crocus appeared in the garden downstairs. Trees began to sport the beginnings of green buds. Flyers that Sheridan had put up about Nick yellowed and faded. All around her, the world seemed bursting with new life. And she knew it was time.

"Hello, Karen," she said timidly into the receiver. "This is Sheridan Phillips. I don't know if you remember me or not. We met in the hospital a few months ago. You said if I ever needed someone to talk to…"

"Certainly I remember you," she replied cheerfully, and Sheridan could almost see her smiling at the other end of the phone. "I'm glad you decided to call."

"I…I was wondering if…if…" Sheridan suddenly found that she couldn't get the words out, a feeling of panic suddenly washing over her.

"Would you like to make an appointment and come in?"

"Yes," Sheridan breathed gratefully. "I'd like that very much."

"Good. Let me check my schedule."

"Karen?" she blurted out anxiously.

"Yes?"

"I…I'm so frightened. I don't even know what to say."

"That's perfectly all right, Sheridan. And perfectly normal. Don't worry about it. Just come in and we'll see where it goes from there. You don't have to say or do anything that doesn't feel comfortable. I'm here for you."

* * * * *

The warmth of spring gave way to the heat of summer.

Sheridan saw Karen once a week for an hour. Sometimes she talked. Sometimes she was silent. And sometimes she cried. Karen encouraged her to join a group of women who'd been raped so that she could find support and understanding from women who'd been through it too. Women who were in all stages of recovery, from Monica, more than a year since her assault, to Cheryl, less than two weeks after.

They spoke of fear and anger and helplessness and rage. Karen shared her story of being assaulted by a college acquaintance in her dorm room after coming over on the pretext of studying. When she'd gone to the police, the young man had cheerfully admitted having sex with her but claimed it was consensual and that she'd invited him up to her room. Amidst a lot of smirking and innuendo, the case had been dropped.

Unable to cope with the situation, she'd gone home to be confronted by suspicion, snide comments and doubt, even from her family. Six months later, a suicide attempt had brought her to the hospital and the attention of a lady named Grace. She'd been raped and had formed a support group. It had taken almost another year for her to coax Karen to join them.

She also met Jennifer, a middle-aged housewife with frizzy brown hair, and Carly, a twenty-seven year old cocktail waitress with sad green eyes. They hadn't known him personally, but both of them had been Brian's victims too. Listening to them, Sheridan found herself appalled and revolted and furious. This vicious animal, masquerading as a harmless young man, hadn't just violated their bodies; he'd violated their lives, their homes. Along with their dignity and self-worth, he'd stolen their security, their sense of safety. And she began to understand that she truly wasn't alone.

They'd learned to take back their lives from the monsters that invaded them. And if they could survive, she told herself, then so can I.

Slowly, the nightmare began to subside.

* * * * *

One Saturday afternoon, Sheridan and Maude were sitting under the shade of a huge old maple tree in the backyard, sipping homemade lemonade when the postman arrived.

"Afternoon, Maude," he chirped merrily. "Miz Sheridan."

"Good afternoon, Mr. Kim."

He was a short, stocky man with neatly trimmed black hair, bright, shoe-button eyes and a ready grin.

"I got a registered letter for you, Miz Sheridan," he told them, taking the white business envelope and a green postcard out of his pouch. "Just sign here." He handed the postcard to her and pulled a pen from his shirt pocket.

She scribbled her name and they exchanged mail.

Maude leaned over and looked at the return address. "Sanderson Publishing," she read aloud.

Normally, the envelopes were thick manila mailing ones, her manuscript returned with a short note. This one, however, was thin.

Carefully, not daring to breathe, Sheridan put her thumb under the flap and ripped it open.

"Dear Miss Phillips," it began.

"I'm pleased to inform you that your manuscript has been accepted for publication…"

Sheridan didn't remember much after that sentence. When she'd read the letter four times herself and had Maud read it twice to be sure, she went into shock. And when she got to the part about being paid "an advance," well, let's just say there had probably been days she'd been happier but she couldn't think of one off the top of her head.

"Oh Sher," Pat squealed delightedly into the phone, "that's absolutely wonderful! I'm so happy for you! When will it be published? I can hardly wait."

"Well," Sheridan laughed, "not right away. I mean, there are all kinds of rewrites I'll have to do. They will send the manuscript back to me by overnight express. I figure it will take me a month to get the revisions finished and back to the publisher and then there's the cover art and the printing. But they'd like to hurry so they can get it out for the Christmas season."

"Christmas season? But that's months away."

"Not when you're trying to get a book out."

"Boy. Now I can tell people that I know an honest-to-God, published writer. I'm going to put my autographed copy on the coffee table."

"There's something else, too. I'm dedicating the book to 'Pat, for always being my friend'."

The line fell silent for several moments.

"Pat?" Sheridan asked. "Are you still there?"

"Oh Sher," she replied, emotion tearing up in her voice. "I don't know what to say. I'm so honored."

"Not as honored as I've been to have you for my friend. There've been lots of times when I'm sure I wouldn't have made it without you. I'd just like to tell you thanks."

Chapter Fourteen

Fall came again, leaves tumbling gently from multi-colored trees, the sun a sort of hazy gold, the air warm but with a hint of the coming winter. With an advance and a two-book deal, Sheridan finally had the money and the confidence to quit her job.

Going into the office early one crisp autumn morning, before she put her purse away, she took out a white envelope, walked resolutely into Jim Eldridge's office and set it on the top of his desk. She knew he had an appointment and wouldn't be in until at least after ten.

Coming out of the break room about ten-thirty, she literally ran into her boss.

"May I see you in my office for a moment?" he asked quietly.

"Certainly."

Settled comfortably in his chair, he held up the single piece of white paper.

"You're resigning." It was a statement not a question.

"Yes, Jim," she replied simply.

"You say it's for 'personal reasons'."

Sheridan nodded once.

Is it something you can discuss?" Although serious, he seemed genuinely interested. "I don't mean to pry, but if there's a problem, I'd like to know what it is. If there's something I can do, I'd like to try."

"I've sold a book," she told him. "It's going to be published soon and with the advance I got, I think I can make ends meet until the royalties start coming in. Also, my publisher says he thinks it should do pretty well but he wants to get as much publicity as he can for it. He's talking about me making a book signing tour."

Eldridge leaned back in his chair and sighed with relief. "I didn't know you were a writer."

"It's not something I bring to the office," she replied with a little shrug. "I try to keep my personal life away from business hours. Besides, I've been writing for a very long time and this is the first real success I've had. I guess I just didn't want to jinx it."

"Well, of course I'm very pleased for you, but selfishly, I hate to lose you. You're an excellent Administrative Assistant and a darned nice person to work with. I'm going to miss you."

There was a sincerity of feeling in his voice, a depth of emotion that surprised her. Something more than a boss losing an employee. Something personal. For a moment, she was touched with a pang of regret she didn't understand.

"Thank you," she answered softly. "I've enjoyed working with you, too. That's not something I say to everyone in this office."

He chuckled and leaned forward again. "No, I don't suppose it is. And I'm flattered. Have you told anyone else?"

"Not formally. I mean, you being my boss, I felt I owed it to you to tell you first. Let you break it to John and the others. Of course, Pat knew because she's my best friend and I told her when I first got the acceptance for publication in the summer. She thought I should give notice back then, but I didn't want to leave until everything was settled for sure." Sheridan paused and looked down at her lap for a moment. "I would appreciate it, though, if you could perhaps suggest that all things being equal, I'd just as soon the office not do anything. A going away party or something like that."

"Oh?" He raised a quizzical eyebrow. "Why's that? I'm sure the people you work with would like the opportunity to say good bye."

"I don't like parties and people making a fuss. With few exceptions, the people I work with are just that; the people I work with. I'm sure in the two weeks that I'm going to be here, I'll have a chance to say good bye privately to everyone who matters."

"All right then. But I hope that you'll let me take you to lunch."

"That isn't necessary."

"Perhaps not. But I'd really like to. And not as boss to secretary but as Jim to Sheridan." He smiled broadly. "Please."

"I'd like that," she returned his smile. "Thank you."

"Good. Sometime next week. Thursday, maybe."

"Thursday would be terrific."

"Okay. I'm seeing John this afternoon, right after lunch. I'll give him the news then."

Reaching across the desk, he extended his hand. "I'm serious, Sheridan. I wish you nothing but success with your writing career and I'll expect an autographed first edition."

"The book's not going to come out for a few months yet," she replied taking his outstretched hand, "but when it does, I'll be happy to give you a copy."

"What's the title?"

"That's sort of a secret," she responded shyly. "Publisher wants to keep it under wraps until the big announcement."

"Well, what's it about?"

Sheridan's smile dimmed somewhat and her eyes took on a faraway, wistful look. "I guess you could call it a love story."

* * * * *

News of the book and Sheridan's departure ripped through the office like Montezuma's Revenge. It seemed as if the words weren't out of Jim Eldridge's mouth before Diana was out at her desk.

"Oh, Sheridan," she mewled, "I think that's just the most wonderful thing!" She practically quivered with excitement. "Why didn't you tell us before?"

Because, she thought caustically, *I get enough abuse in this place about my work; if you'd known I was writing, you and the rest of the inmates in this asylum would have been on me unmercifully.*

Aloud, she waved her hand and smiled demurely. "It's no big thing," she lied smoothly. "Just something I've been fiddling with in my spare time."

"Well, you just have to tell me all about it," Diana giggled, fairly squirming in anticipation.

I'd rather eat ground glass.

"Not much to tell, really. My publisher has asked me to keep the title and the details to myself until the official announcement, hopefully, sometime before Christmas."

"That's so exciting!" she squealed. "You'll have to give me an autographed copy when it comes out."

Sure, Sheridan mused wickedly, *in another lifetime.*

"And John too."

Of course. You can sit in his lap and he can read the big words like "cat" to you. Sorry. No pictures.

"Certainly."

A shadow crossed the other woman's face and she frowned, sticking out her lower lip like a spoiled child.

"Jim also said you didn't want to have a going away party," she pouted.

I'll celebrate when I'm finally released.

"No," Sheridan admitted. "I'm just not much on parties."

"Well we can't just let you go with nothing," Diana insisted. "You have to let us take you to lunch. Or a cake at the very least."

Not in this lifetime, you stupid bimbo.

"We'll see."

By the time Diana had retreated back to her office, other staff members had begun dribbling by Sheridan's desk to check on the news and ask about the book. She did little besides confirm the accuracy of the report and say something vague about the book's tentative Christmas publication.

Late in the afternoon, the dreaded summons came from King John.

"You wanted to see me, sir?" Sheridan stood uneasily in the Director's doorway, yellow tablet and pen in hand.

"Yes, Sher," he smiled. "Come on in and sit down." He waved to a chair on the other side of his huge, oak veneer desk.

Sheridan perched on the edge of the chair and looked at him, bracing for whatever he might have on his devious mind. With her resignation, he'd now lost the terrifying power of employment over her and seemed to have shrunk in stature. Still, she would be in the office for another two weeks and he was still capable of making her life miserable every minute of the remaining time.

"So, Jim Eldridge says you're leaving us," he began in that damned paternalistic, faintly superior tone he often took with her. "Going to pursue a writing career." He made it sound like she was a dim bulb six-year-old running away to join the circus.

"Yes, sir," she replied simply. She'd learned from hard experience not to get drawn into these no-win conversations with this pompous jackass. Just let him talk and get it over with so she could get out of there.

His grin got wider. "Guess all those press releases I had you write finally paid off."

You mean all the press releases I wrote that got printed under some hack reporter's by-line and that I never got credit for, she thought bitterly.

"I suppose so."

"What's the book about?" Before she could open her mouth, he made a face. "Hope it's not one of those romance things. Don't like to read all that sex stuff."

Don't like to read it, just like to do it with your bimbo secretary.

"I can't really say what it's about," she countered. "Publisher wants to keep it under wraps for awhile."

"Oh. Well, we can't have you breaking orders, as it were," he chuckled dryly. "But I expect an autographed copy. Might be worth something someday."

To John Curtin: tyrant, bonehead, adulterer and general-purpose pain in the ass. May you rot in hell!

"Of course, sir," she smiled limply.

"Well, you better get back to your desk. I'm working with Diana to pull together a list of all the projects that will need to be completed in the next two weeks and I'd like you to give her a list of your duties so that we can get started on finding your replacement."

Out in the hall, Sheridan released a breath she hadn't realized she was holding. He hadn't congratulated her or even acknowledged how marvelous the accomplishment had been. There'd been nothing but thinly veiled contempt and his usual demeaning, disrespectful attitude. His concern was that she finish up her work and make sure her slot was clean so that a new body could be inserted quickly and cleanly. Not much for almost seven years of her life.

And at that moment, Sheridan realized that she was free. Truly free. Whether or not she did her job was no longer of any consequence. Even if she failed to come in at all. The worst John Curtin could do to her was to fire her. It was the worst thing he'd ever had the power to do to her.

She was a writer now. A real, honest-to-God, published writer. With any luck at all, she would never have to return to being a secretary. And, worst case, even if she did, there would always be need for someone to make the word processor keys go up and down. After all the years of fear, she'd finally been liberated by the simple knowledge that there would always be another job.

Several people working in their offices and cubicles looked up in questioning surprise as the sound of rollicking, giddy laughter passed through the hall from the Director's office back to the front desk.

Sheridan's going was as simple and quiet as her coming. No crocodile tears, no feigned regret, no cake. She was gratefully, gleefully, leaving one life for another. And with the exception of Jim, who she believed was truly glad for her, she had no doubt that everyone else, including John and Diana, were almost as happy to have her gone as she was to have left.

* * * * *

Snow was on the ground when the book came out.

Sheridan held her first book signing at a large bookstore downtown, the first Saturday in December. She remembered stopping and staring in delighted shock when she first saw the display in the front window, complete with a recently done glamour shot photo. "Come meet Sheridan Phillips," it trumpeted, "local writer and author of the best selling novel, *The Cat Who Came to Dinner.*"

That first signing was a big thrill. Sitting at a three-by-six table draped with a beautiful, white linen cloth reaching almost to the floor, she watched, awestruck, as people began lining up, all of them clutching copies of her book. As she signed her name, total strangers smiled and spoke to her in glowing terms. It was like a dream come true.

The signing had been scheduled for only two hours, but because of the demand, she'd stayed an extra forty-five minutes, basking in the warmth every moment.

When the signing was finally over, they adjourned to a nearby hotel where her publisher held a small reception for members of the news media to get acquainted with the city's newest celebrity. There was white wine and bottled water and canapés as people milled around. She did short interviews with people from three of the early news shows and a longer one with the book critic for the local paper. Near the end, the publisher announced that Sheridan would be doing several other local book signings and that after the first of the New Year she'd be embarking on a national book signing tour to cover fifty cities in sixty days.

Not having traveled very much, she was ecstatic. First class flights. Suites in five star hotels. Meals in the best restaurants. And all at her publisher's expense. It was absolutely too good to be true.

As it turned out, it was.

* * * * *

"This is Mary Baxter," her publisher's rep was saying as they shook hands. "She'll be your tour administrator. Make sure you get to your flights on time, take care of baggage. Hotels. Signings. All the details so you can sit back and take care of the book buyers."

"Happy to know you, Miss Phillips," she said crisply, putting out her hand. "I've read your book and found it quite enjoyable." There was no trace of enjoyment that Sheridan could detect in the other woman's voice. "I'm looking forward to working with you."

Sheridan was struck by the grayness of her new companion. Tall, thin to the verge of gaunt, iron-gray hair pulled up into a tight topknot at the crown of her head, dull little gunmetal eyes peering suspiciously out of a gray, sunken face. A line of dark red lipstick marked her mouth and two spots of light pink blush highlighted her cheeks. She felt that Mary was older than she was, but it was difficult to say whether she was an old forty or a young sixty. Even her severely tailored, mannish jacket and skirt were a charcoal hound's-tooth.

"I'm happy to know you, too, Miss Baxter. I've very excited about the tour."

"Well," she responded in an authoritative alto voice, "that's because you've never been on tour. You'll get over that soon enough."

The rep laughed nervously. "Now, now, Mary," he chided lightly. "Let's not scare Sheridan before she's even had a chance to get her feet wet."

He turned to face his slightly perplexed author. "Don't worry about a thing. It's just that these tours can get to be a real grind. I mean, what with the travel and sleeping in strange hotels and eating on the run. But you'll enjoy it. Really."

It seemed to Sheridan he was trying just a bit too hard to convince her.

"At any rate," Miss Baxter continued, "here is your overall itinerary for the tour." She handed Sheridan a thick sheaf of paper, stapled neatly. "This is the general list of cities and the dates you're scheduled for appearances." Another sheaf of papers. "And these are the schedules for specific cities. Purely FYI. I'll actually be handling the day-to-day details. Of course, with the winter weather, the length of the tour and your basic unforeseen circumstances, there'll be changes, but don't worry about them."

"Don't worry about a thing, Sheridan," the rep assured her with a pat on the arm. "Mary's been doing this forever. You couldn't be in better hands if your mother was running the show."

"I suggest, Miss Phillips," the older woman told her, "that you look over the schedule for the coming week. You'll find, I think, all the details in order. I pride myself on my organizational skills. If you have any questions or have any special requests, don't hesitate to let me know. I'll do whatever I can to accommodate you."

The tone of her voice made Sheridan feel that anything that deviated from the carefully arranged schedule would not be met with enthusiasm.

"I'm sure everything will be fine," she answered lamely.

"Now, about your luggage, Miss Phillips."

"I have a set, thank you."

Miss Baxter eyed her like a schoolteacher when a small child gives the wrong answer.

"I was going to suggest that one or two pieces of soft-sided luggage would be sufficient. I've also included a list of clothes and toilet articles you might want to pack. A few well-chosen pieces that can be mixed and matched and accessorized properly reduce the baggage considerably. And since you'll be traveling with your laptop as carryon, you might want to consider carrying your wallet, identification, money and other small items in a large fanny pack. This allows you to have everything handy without having to worry about a purse. You can pack your handbag in the your luggage."

The rep was right. It was going to be like traveling with her mother.

"I'll be sure to look over the list."

"Very well, then. The tour begins next Monday. You can check the schedule for the exact time the car will arrive to take you to the airport. I'll meet you at check-in." She extended her hand once more. "Until Monday, Miss Phillips."

"Until Monday."

Chapter Fifteen

"Good morning, Miss Phillips," the voice at the other end of the line chirped. "This is your six o'clock wake up call."

"Mmmm" Sheridan mumbled as she set the phone back in its cradle, rolled back into her pillow and shut her eyes.

How could it possibly be six o'clock in the morning already? It seemed she hadn't been in bed more than fifteen minutes.

What day is this, she wondered groggily? Wednesday? Thursday? And where was she? Chicago? Minneapolis?

Her exhausted brain, balking at the strain, went as blank as a crashed computer screen.

Wearily she pulled herself to a sitting position on the edge of the bed and glanced at the small message pad lying next to the phone. "Welcome to the Wilton House" it read in bright emerald ink across the top. "Cincinnati's finest address."

Okay. She now knew where she was. Reaching over to the nightstand, she picked up the wrinkled, creased paper lying there. Flipping about halfway through it, she stopped at the page marked, "Cincinnati."

8:00 a.m. – Breakfast with the Ohio Ladies Literary Guild

9:30 a.m. – Book signing at a local bookstore

11:30 a.m. – Interview with local television talk show

Noon – Lunch and rest at hotel

1:30 p.m. – Book signing

4:00 p.m. – Book signing

6:00 p.m. – Publisher's cocktail reception

7:30 p.m. – Dinner with representatives of the local media

9:00 p.m. – Airport

10:30 p.m. – Flight to Miami

That meant that even if there weren't any last minute changes, she wouldn't see bed again until midnight. Of course, she hadn't been to bed before midnight since she'd started this merry-go-round from hell so why should this be any different. And they were only a little past halfway through the tour. Sheridan had given up hope that she would ever see her little apartment again.

The phone rang again and Sheridan sighed heavily. It was Warden Mary making sure she was actually awake.

"Good morning, Mary."

"Just checking," she announced. "Have you showered yet?"

"No," Sheridan replied, trying to stifle a yawn. "I thought I'd have a cup of coffee first."

Silence.

Sheridan could see the matronly face pinched into a disapproving frown. "Yes, well don't dawdle. The car will be here for us at seven-fifteen. We need to go all the way across town and the driver told me last night that commuter traffic is always bad at this time of the morning."

"I should think forty-five minutes is overkill," she replied, a tad more tartly than she'd intended. As usual, Miss Baxter went right on, apparently oblivious to everything but the task of getting her charge from one place to another.

"Perhaps," she agreed shortly, "but we don't want to be late. I'm sure there will be introductions before breakfast."

"No doubt."

"Well, I'll let you go. I'll come by your room at seven sharp. We need to run over the day's schedule. And if I might suggest, Sheridan, you wear the white, long-sleeved dress shirt with the small ruffles, navy gabardine pantsuit and matching pumps."

"Fine."

Dragging into the bathroom, Sheridan flipped on the coffee maker as she passed the vanity, being careful not to glance at herself in the mirror. Standing in the hot shower, she tried to rouse herself. Even her special "energizing" mandarin shower gel failed.

True to her word, Mary appeared at Sheridan's door at seven straight up. Meticulously dressed, bright-eyed and bushy-tailed, she sat down at the small table, opened her ever-present briefcase and produced a piece of white paper.

"I assume," she began briskly, "that you've looked over today's schedule of events."

Sheridan took another sip of coffee. Even though it was her second cup, the caffeine just didn't seem to be kicking in.

"Uh-huh," she muttered. "Not that it makes any difference. The only thing that changes is the name of the city and the bookstores."

As usual, Mary ignored her. "Here's the list of names of the officers of the Literary Guild. I've gone over them so I'll introduce you. There'll be a few minutes of mingling before the actual meal. Just smile and nod."

"I know the drill."

"I've made sure they understand that we have to be at Crosley's Books by nine-fifteen for introductions and publicity photos. They've promised to start breakfast promptly. Fruit cup, bacon and eggs, cottage fries, toast and coffee. Then you'll be asked to say a few words to the group. I think the speech about encouraging reading and an early appreciation of literature in the schools is your best option. Short and on point."

Looking up, she quickly scanned Sheridan from head to toe. It was clear from her expression of mild disapproval that the author had again failed to pass muster, but there was nothing she could do but bear up courageously.

"If you're ready, Sheridan, I think we should go."

Goody, she thought as she set her cup down on the table and reached for her tote bag, another shitty day in Paradise.

* * * * *

"But you promised!" Sheridan wailed. "It's on the schedule."

"Don't whine," Miss Baxter replied calmly, "it's not ladylike. And besides, you know that the schedule is not carved in stone."

"I need to rest," she insisted. "This is the first lunch hour...the first lunch minute I've had since we started this torture marathon. I'm exhausted."

"What you need is publicity." There was a hard edge forming on her words. "In case you've forgotten, selling books is the whole point of this little exercise. This radio show reaches people all over the state and being invited for an interview, even at this late moment, is important."

Knowing she was beaten, Sheridan sagged back into the car seat and glanced out the window at the passing city skyline.

"How long is this going to take?"

"Approximately a half hour, on air. He'll ask you about the book and a little about yourself and then take some calls. Nothing you haven't done before."

"With travel time, that pretty much eats up my entire lunch."

"Unfortunately, yes." Baxter sounded annoyed, not regretful.

"Then what am I supposed to eat?" Sheridan pouted. "Or do I have to give that up for the duration too? I mean, just think how many more book signings and interviews I could do if I stopped eating. And sleeping. You could just wind me up in the morning, stick a pen in my hand and off we'd go."

"Granted," she agreed icily, "that would make things considerably easier, especially my job. However, since that's not possible, I suppose we'll just have to muddle through as best we can. I shall personally make sure that you have a turkey sandwich on whole wheat, no onions, no mayo and a side of cranberry sauce, a bag of sea salt potato chips and a large ice tea waiting for you in the car so that you can eat on the way to the interview. I trust that will satisfy you and conclude this tantrum."

"I'll bet no one treats Danielle Steele like this," Sheridan muttered under her breath.

"I would imagine not," Baxter said, gazing out the window, "but you are most certainly not Danielle Steele."

* * * * *

They'd spent three days in San Francisco, using it as a sort of home base to travel all over the Bay Area, towns and stores and people having long since blended into a sort of continuous blur. After three grueling days in Los Angeles, though, Sheridan could finally see the finish line. Two more days and it would be over. Sunday night would find her sleeping in her own bed.

"My fingers are killing me," Sheridan moaned softly, waving her fingers a little in front of her. "I think I have terminal writer's cramp." Lying back on her pillow, she closed her eyes and felt the thump in her hands keeping time to the beating of her heart.

"You need a hot bath and a good night's sleep."

Miss Baxter was seated at the table across the room, poring over the next day's schedule.

"Probably. Only problem is I haven't had a good night's sleep in almost two months."

Unexpectedly, she heard the other woman chuckle.

"What?" Sheridan asked, opening her eyes and propping herself up on her elbows.

"I was just thinking how excited...how positively giddy you were that first morning when you found out about the tour."

"Oh. That." She lay back down.

"Yes, that. You seemed to think it was some kind of pleasure jaunt instead of a business trip. A very long, trying business trip."

"I suppose I was pretty naïve," Sheridan admitted. "But boy have I learned."

"Well that's the important thing, isn't it?"

The other woman's voice was suddenly soft...kind almost. Immediately, Sheridan turned her head and looked at her. She was actually smiling.

"I don't understand."

Getting up, Miss Baxter came and sat down on the bed next to her. "I've watched you these last fifty-eight days, Sheridan Phillips. When I first met you, I thought you were a silly little girl. Especially in light of your age and...well, the circumstances of your life. More than once, particularly in the beginning, I was sure you were going to fold. That you just didn't have what it takes to hang in there when the going gets tough. In fact, I fully expected you to call the publisher and have me removed after that radio interview incident in Cincinnati. You just didn't seem to have a clue."

"I didn't," Sheridan told her, feeling a shameful blush coloring her face. "I thought the publisher would put the book in the stores and people would trample each other to buy it and success would just sort of shower itself on me. Writing's a solitary pursuit and writers tend to live in their own little world. I had no idea how competitive, how downright cutthroat, the real world of publishing is. Or how fortunate I was that my publisher was willing to gamble so much on me."

The smile got wider, warmer. "That's what I meant about learning, Sheridan. It's been a real pleasure to watch you grow these last few weeks. Like seeing a beautiful plant bloom into a magnificent flower. I look forward to seeing what you'll produce in the future."

"I know now that I couldn't have done it without you. When I think of the hotel and plane reservations, coordinating the book signings and the personal appearances. All the endless details that I didn't have to worry about because you were doing it for me. I feel more like a spoiled brat than a beautiful plant."

"Well, it's almost over now. And as long as we're on the subject of changes in the schedule, I guess now is as good a time as any to let you in on another one."

"Go ahead," Sheridan laughed. "I'm steeled for anything."

"Good. Because our last stop has been canceled and we're leaving a day early."

"You're kidding!"

"You don't think I'd kid about something this important, do you?" Miss Baxter laughed too.

"Oh God," Sheridan shouted, "How? What happened?"

"Well, I'm not exactly sure, but from what I could gather, a disgruntled former employee of the chain which owns the bookstore where you were scheduled to be, burned down the main warehouse, including all several hundred copies of your book which hadn't yet been delivered. And because the warehouse was gone, the other stores in the chain were understandably reluctant to let the store have any of their remaining stock. So, no book signing."

"That's wonderful. Oh, I mean that's awful. I mean..."

Both women dissolved into gales of laughter. Holding each other, they laughed for several minutes, the pressure of the tour now past and a new friendship forged.

Finally, Sheridan reached over and pulled a handful of tissue out of the box and handed some to Miss Baxter.

"At any rate," she told Sheridan, "I've already changed the reservations. You'll be home by Saturday evening."

* * * * *

"Sheridan."

"Mmm?" she mumbled into her pillow.

"Sheridan."

The voice was nothing more than a whisper, as if a soft summer breeze had murmured her name.

Turning toward the sound, she opened her eyes.

Seated on the edge of her bed was the phantom of her dreams, leaning over her so closely she could practically feel his lips on her cheek. In his hand he held a single, long stemmed rose, the color of fresh blood.

Instead of the surprise she'd felt before at her mysterious night visitor's appearance, Sheridan felt immediately warm and safe.

"Hello," she told him gently, reaching up to run her fingertips lightly along his face.

"Hello, my love," he whispered in response, slowly drawing the flower down the curve of her cheek and across her lips, laying it finally in the hollow of her throat. "You are so beautiful."

The delicate scent seemed to envelop her, the feel of the petals on her skin like warm silk. Around the bed was an aura of soft, muted light, like candles or the moon, but she couldn't see any source for it. As before, she became aware that her nightgown was gone and that they were both naked.

He put his lips on hers, tasting the warm flesh like a hungry man savoring a fine meal. Quickly, her lips parted, her tongue dancing with his as he searched every corner of her mouth.

"I knew you'd come," Sheridan said breathlessly between kisses.

"I've missed you so much." His voice was already hoarse with building passion. "The feel of your skin. The musk of your body. The taste of you. You can't know the torture of being so close to you but not being able to hold you. Kiss you."

"I don't understand."

"There's no need," he assured her, playing the rose across her breasts, breathing in the scent as he bent to her. "The waiting's almost over. It's almost time. Soon we'll be together. Forever."

Whatever thought she may have been trying to form disappeared in a burst of pleasure as his mouth found her nipples, each in turn, his tongue darting over their sensitive tips, suckling like a contented baby. Her back arched and she felt his hand slide beneath her, tenderly cradling her ass.

"Feel the pleasure," he coaxed. "Know what it is to be loved…in all the ways that two people can love."

She felt the hardness of him as he rubbed against the hard bone at her crotch. It made her temperature climb, her pulse quicken.

"Tonight is a celebration. Not just of our love and our bodies, but of you, my darling. You've been like a sad, ugly little caterpillar, crawling on the ground with the rest of the insignificant creatures, never knowing or even suspecting the secret inside you. In your dark chrysalis, you thought you'd died. That your life was over. You didn't realize that your life was only just about to begin. And now, see what a magnificent, beautiful butterfly you've become. You can have anything you desire. The whole world is laid out for us, my love. All you have to do is spread those remarkable wings and fly."

Gripping him tightly, Sheridan raised herself up slightly and they rolled over, her lover now on his back.

"All right," she grinned down at him, "if this is a party and I can have anything I want, I'm going to start with you."

"What would you like?" he chuckled.

Leaning down on him, she rubbed her breasts over his bare chest as her tongue sought out his mouth.

"I don't know," she panted, pulling away just enough to speak, "but I'm sure we can think of something."

Beginning at his mouth, Sheridan planted small, delicate kisses over his chin and down the front of his throat. At the hollow, she paused, sticking the tip of her tongue into it and tickling him. Moving to the side, where his neck joined his shoulders, she nipped him lightly, using her mouth to form a vacuum and suck furiously.

"Oh...oh..." he sighed, squirming a little under her.

"You can show that nice hickey to all your dream friends," she told him, giggling and nibbling at his ear.

Resuming her trip, she traced a line to his chest, stopping to fondle and kiss his nipples, feeling delight and her own growing passion as they responded to her touch. More kisses brought her to his erection, straining at attention in the nest of his black pubic hair.

Slowly, lovingly, she took his shaft in her mouth, using her tongue to make tight, quick circles around the head, tasting the slight salt of him.

"God, Sheridan," he whimpered as her attentions turned up his own heat. "You make me feel so..." She heard him moan again, felt his body quivering under her.

"Not just yet," she laughed as she released him and traveled back to his mouth.

Carefully, gently, she straddled him, taking him inside, feeling his hardness fill her completely, the heat of him radiating out.

"You feel so good," she sighed, gazing down at him. Almost by itself, her body began moving slowly up and down, rubbing the most sensitive parts of her over him, every movement rippling exquisite pleasure through her.

Through half-closed eyes, he watched her, his face a mirror of her own dreamy bliss. For long, sensual moments they moved together, like two pieces of an intricately entwined puzzle.

It was, she thought, the most intimate, most intense encounter with this dream creation yet. As if she could simply wish anything and have it instantly granted.

"You're thinking again," he teased, taking her breasts in his hands. "Just be here, right now. Surrender yourself to the moment."

Moans and small sounds of animal lust were all that she could manage in answer.

Their movements quickened as she felt the first shivers of climax. Inside, she felt him nearing the end too. Lying down on him again, she took his head in her hands, kissing him hard and furiously, their rhythm escalating.

"God...oh God, Sheridan..." he called, his body writhing under her.

He met her passion with equal intensity, throwing his arms around her, kneading her ass as they fought to bring their bodies closer. Passion exploded into heat, sending tidal waves of ecstasy racing through them. Like a bolt of lightning suddenly erupting and cooking earth into glass, it fused them for a moment into one being, their bodies and spirits joined in a perfect moment of shattering bliss.

For a long time they lay together, not moving, bathed in the exhilaration and exhaustion. She felt him all around her, inside her. His fingers lightly brushing her back, his lips occasionally touching hers.

"I love you," he whispered.

"I love you," she replied, snuggling against him like a small child.

"Good night, my love."

As she drifted into satisfied, peaceful sleep, Sheridan thought she felt something small and wet lap quickly across her cheek.

Chapter Sixteen

Sheridan arrived home just as dusk was settling in. Pushing her large tapestry bag with the toe of one foot and shifting her heavy computer shoulder bag, she managed to pull her key out of the door. As soon as it clicked shut and locked, she slid the computer case and handbag carefully to the floor, heaved a sigh of relief and headed for the kitchen to put the teakettle on.

Dear Mrs. Farnsworth, true to her word, had collected her mail and piled it in neat little stacks on the coffee table. She'd even gone through and thrown out the flyers that had expired. Fortunately, her newly acquired business manager had attended to the mundane details of the rent and her monthly bills. A sealed manila envelope bearing the manager's return address sat by itself, her name and "paid bills" printed in a thin, precise hand on the front.

The red light on the answering machine was blinking an angry, insistent red. With a sigh, she dropped onto the sofa. Screw it, she thought wearily, they've waited this long, they can wait a few minutes longer.

When the teakettle began singing, she was almost too tired to answer. Rousing herself, she'd just opened the cupboard and pulled out her favorite mug, when she heard the noise.

At first, she wasn't sure she hadn't imagined it. Flicking off the burner and moving the kettle, she stood perfectly still, straining into the darkness outside.

It came again. A distinct scratching at the window.

Her mind whirled. She'd waited, hoped, for so long. No, it wasn't possible. After long, lonely months, she'd forced herself to face the fact that Nick was... And even if he wasn't, it'd been so long... How could he possibly know where she was? But then, how had he known where she was the first time he'd found her?

Bolting to the living room window, she threw back the curtains and flung it open to the small veranda beyond.

Surprised, she found herself looking into a dark blue chambray shirt.

"I...I'm sorry," said a tenor voice above her head, "I didn't know anyone was home."

Looking up, Sheridan saw a slightly abashed stranger grinning shyly down at her. At least six feet tall, long, oval face, dark sapphire eyes, a lean, strong look about him.

"I...I heard the scratching..."

He held up a small wire brush. "Painters were here today to finish this side of the house. Left about an hour ago. I've been nosing around to make sure they did the job right."

His nose wrinkled up slightly, like he'd smelled something bad. "Think because Maude's an elderly woman alone, they can get by with anything. I noticed there were paint splatters on your window. I'll have the painters come back and take care of them tomorrow."

"Thank you," she mumbled, trying not to stare into those beautiful eyes.

"No problem. That's what you pay your rent for."

He grinned a lopsided, boyish, impossibly sexy grin.

"If I'd known you were going to be home, I'd have used the front door," he laughed. "I thought Maude said you'd be gone until Sunday."

"I was supposed to, but the last stop on my tour was canceled, thankfully."

"Tour?"

"Uh-huh. Book signing tour. Fifty cities in sixty days."

"Sounds interesting."

"Brutal, yes," she replied sourly and rolling her eyes, "interesting, no. Mostly it's plane, hotel, store, store, store, hotel, plane. Talk shows and rubber chicken dinners just in case you should actually have six minutes to yourself when you're awake. You get where you have to check the name on the towels in the hotels to remember where you are." Feeling somehow at ease and relaxed with this stranger, she leaned against the window frame.

"I thought you looked familiar," he told her, those amazing eyes twinkling down at her like two evening stars in a twilight sky.

And now that she looked at him more closely, she had an eerie feeling of familiarity too. Not so much the face or the body, but his manner, his being. For a moment, she had a feeling of déjà vu. As if they were repeating something.

"You're the woman who wrote that book, about the cat. Sharon Something."

Immediately, she felt a flush of embarrassment. "Yes, that's me, Sheridan Phillips," she admitted shyly.

"Yes, Sheridan. Sorry for the mistake. I saw you on one of those morning talk shows about three weeks ago, I think. I'm sorry, I haven't read the book yet. The station house was supposed to get a copy when it first came out but you know how it is, getting anything from the bureaucracy."

"The station house?"

"Yeah, I'm a firefighter and paramedic. Station Four, two blocks down on Webster."

"And a house inspector in your spare time?"

"This?" He glanced at the wire brush and dropped his hand. "Oh no, I'm just doing Maude a favor. She and Mom were best friends when I was growing up. I spent many a night in your turret."

"Really?"

"Oh, hey," he continued hurriedly, "I mean when I was a kid. Before Ralph died and Maude had to convert the house to apartments or lose it."

He looked wistfully across the room to the alcove where Sheridan's computer desk sat. "Many's the night I dreamed I was a knight in shining armor, riding up to this castle on my white steed to rescue the fair princess trapped in the tower by the evil dragon. I used to look up sometimes and even imagine I could see her face in the window."

"That sounds very nice."

"Yeah. Later I thought I wanted to live here. Get married and raise six kids."

"Six?"

He laughed again.

"I come from a big family. Seven of us. Four boys and three girls. Maude used to say we were so close we were like a litter of kittens. Guess that's why I wanted so many myself."

A few more moments went by and then he seemed to snap out of it. "Yeah. I really loved this house when I was a kid. In fact, next week I'm finally taking the plunge and moving into the flat right across the hall from you. If I hadn't been away in Alaska on a fishing trip when this one came up, I'd have grabbed it. You're lucky. Personally, I think this is the best flat in the place. Maybe the whole city."

"I know. But I'm sorry, I mean about you not getting it."

"Don't suppose you'd consider a swap?" he teased.

"Not on your life," she shot back, now feeling very comfortable.

"Well, I'm glad to have met you," he told her, "since we're going to be neighbors and everything. Sorry I scared you though. Next time I'll ring the bell and come through the door like civilized people."

"I'm very glad to meet you," she assured him. "And don't worry. You didn't scare me. Just sort of startled me is all."

The conversation lagged for a few moments.

"Well," he sighed, "I guess I better let you get back to what you were doing. Hope I didn't catch you in the middle of dinner."

"Oh no, I was just making myself a pot of tea. Too tired to cook. Probably call out for a pizza later."

He grinned again. "You know, I was just thinking about a pizza myself. Supreme. Everything on it."

Sheridan smiled too. "Except green peppers and anchovies. I loathe green peppers and anchovies. Extra cheese though. And Parmesan to sprinkle on top."

"Pineapple?"

"Mmmm."

"Look, I know this really great little place down on Third...."

"Willie's," she added.

"Yeah, Willie's." He seemed genuinely delighted that she knew the place. "Since we're both in the mood for pizza and we're practically neighbors, what say we split a Jumbo Supreme with everything..."

"Except green peppers and anchovies."

"Right. Except green peppers and anchovies."

After everything that had happened, this should have been the place where all Sheridan's fears and embarrassments reared their ugly heads and she suddenly came to her senses.

She'd let Brian into her life because he was a friend, and he'd betrayed her. Who knew what kind of person this stranger was. The prudent thing was to say a polite, "no thank you" and get rid of him as quickly as possible. And Sheridan had always prided herself on doing the prudent thing.

But looking into those kind, beautiful eyes, she knew in her heart that not only was she safe, but she was doing the right thing.

"Sure," she answered cheerfully.

"Terrific. Can I come in and use your phone to call Willie's?"

"Help yourself. Phone's on the end table by the sofa."

Nimbly, he folded his tall, slender frame through the window, landing on the carpet like a feather.

"What would you like to drink?" he called after her as she went into the kitchen.

"Iced tea, please. The biggest they have."

Sheridan heard him on the phone as she put away her tea things.

Coming back into the living room, she tripped on a small throw rug, lurching forward and catching her leg on the sharp corner of the end table.

"Damn!" she screeched, forgetting her company.

In an instant, he was beside her.

"Here," he ordered firmly, "sit down on the sofa and let me look at that."

"It's all right, really," she countered. "I'm such a klutz."

"You can never be too careful," he insisted, taking her arm and guiding her to a sitting position on the sofa. "It's the little things that always turn out the worst."

Squatting down, he put out his hand and began gently stroking her calf with his fingertips. A delicate, soft, circular motion that both surprised and soothed her. Again, that feeling of déjà vu rolled over her. And she felt a small but distinct flutter down her spine.

"Looks like just a good, solid whack," he told her, gazing up. "Red mark. Probably be a bruise and sore tomorrow." Those fingers on her skin were making her positively giddy.

"If you'll excuse me," she finally managed to get out, "I think I'll go and change. I feel like I was born in these clothes."

"Sure," he said, standing up and stepping back so she could rise too. "Pizza won't be here for another half-hour. Take your time."

Quickly Sheridan changed out of her traveling suit and into a pair of comfortable old blue jeans and her favorite red tee shirt. She was also careful to brush her hair and put on fresh lipstick.

When she came back into the living room, he was standing by her desk looking through a copy of her book.

"Sorry," he apologized again, "incurably nosy. My mom used to tell me, 'Curiosity killed the cat.' I don't know, though, I'm still here."

He held the book up and pointed to the picture on the back of the dust jacket. "Sheridan? I don't think I ever knew a Sheridan before. Especially not a good looking woman."

That blush came creeping back and she hoped he couldn't see it from across the room. "It was my mother's maiden name. Family tradition."

"It's nice. I like it."

"Well maybe if you tell me your name, I'll like it too."

Putting down the book, he crossed the room to where she was standing in a few long strides.

"Sorry. I forgot we haven't been formally introduced. My parents were from Russia and being the oldest son, I got a traditional family name, too. I'm Serge Feodor Nescovatnovich."

Surprise must have registered on her face because he laughed.

"Don't worry. Even I still have trouble pronouncing it."

"That's quite a mouthful," she agreed, shaking her head slightly. "How do you say it again? Slowly."

He laughed once more, those dark eyes glistening and beautiful.

"Skip it. Just call me Nick."

Epilogue

"So Mrs. Nescovatnovich," Nick teased, "isn't this the place in the novel where the hero turns to the heroine and says, 'alone at last'?" He watched her with love-filled eyes as she put down the phone.

Sheridan shook her head as they embraced. "Only in those gooey, bodice-ripper romances," she laughed.

"Ripping some bodices sounds like a great idea. After all, I didn't bring you to this romantic suite in this fabulous tropical paradise hotel so that you could spend our honeymoon on the phone to your publisher and lawyer. Let them get their own women."

"Yes, well," she countered between passionate kisses, "when you see all those zeros on the check from the movie company, you might not begrudge me a few minutes out of the rest of our lives."

"I thought you took care of all that before we left."

"I thought so, too. Even my publisher was surprised when the bidding war for Cat started. He thought the movie rights would go relatively cheap. And for me to be asked to adapt it for the screen, especially being a first-time author, is practically unheard of. I mean, just think. This time next year, I could be standing up on national television saying, 'I'd like to thank the Academy…' "

"Wrong," he nuzzled her neck. "This time next year, you're going to be holed up somewhere with me saying, 'I'd like to thank my husband for the best sex I've ever had'."

"Mmmm…" was all she could muster as a reply.

"So, let's get this honeymoon on the road."

Without another word, he picked her up and threw her over his shoulder like a sack of potatoes.

"Hey!" she shrieked, caught somewhere between laughter and surprise. She was even more surprised when she felt his hand caress her raised ass.

"This is how we firefighters do it," he told her, turning from the living room of their suite, carrying her quickly through the bedroom and into the bath.

Sheridan gasped as he set her back on her feet and watched with pleasure as she surveyed the scene.

"Oh, Nick. It's...it's unbelievable! Gorgeous. Absolutely gorgeous!"

The two-person whirlpool tub sat sunken as in a Roman bath, whirred jets and streams of bubbles churned like a boiling cauldron. Around the rim, candles of all colors, shapes and sizes threw a warm, romantic glow over the room and a bouquet of exotic scents filled the room. Through the rectangular window, a huge yellow moon seemed painted against the black night, illuminating the tops of palm trees below.

Gently, he reached for the sash of her light satin robe, sliding it down her arms and into a raspberry-colored heap on the floor. As he kissed her deeply, his fingers found the spaghetti straps of her pale burgundy baby doll negligee, dropping it on top of the robe. She hadn't bothered putting on the wisp of lace that served as underpants.

Without parting from him, she opened his thick, white hotel robe to reveal his naked body underneath.

"After that long plane ride and talking so much on the phone," he whispered as his robe was shed too, "you must be exhausted. What you need is a good relaxing massage and a soak in the tub."

He took her hand and they stepped carefully into the roiling water, finding seats so that they could look out the window.

"That moon is beautiful," she sighed, laying her head on his chest and running her fingers along his smooth, lightly tanned skin.

"It should be," he replied softly, brushing the top of her hair with his fingers. "I ordered it especially for you. I told God that everything had to be perfect for my Sheridan. I'm glad you approve."

"You're spoiling me," she laughed.

"Nothing could ever spoil you, my love," he responded seriously, looking down into her face. "I just want the chance to spend my life seeing that you get the perfection you deserve."

They shared another long, passionate kiss.

When they parted, he slid away from her a few inches and she saw a bottle of champagne chilling in an ornately decorated silver bucket sitting on a silver tray along with two tall, slender, delicate flutes. As she watched, he held the flutes between the fingers of his left hand and poured the champagne with his right.

A fragment of dream flitted through Sheridan's mind and again she was struck by an odd feeling of déjà vu. As if she and Nick were repeating something she knew they hadn't shared before. After all, it had only been six whirlwind months since Nick had appeared at her window until this morning when they'd stood together in Maude Farnsworth's front parlor, Pat sniffling at her side, and taken their vows.

"You're thinking again," he chided gently as he handed her a glass. "You think too much. You should just relax and let it be." He kissed her tenderly. "What shall we drink to?"

"I don't know..." she mumbled self-consciously. "I...I've never been very good at that sort of thing."

"Then let's just drink to us."

They clinked glasses lightly and drank deeply.

"I have a little present for you," he announced, setting his glass down and reaching behind him.

"Oh, Nick," she began. "You've already given me..."

"Not nearly enough." He produced a small velvet box and held it out to her. "For you, love."

"Oh, Nick," she gasped as the box opened to reveal a square-cut emerald of several carats set in a wide, gold band. It was simple, elegant and perfect. "It's magnificent! Emeralds are my favorite, even more so than diamonds. How did you know?"

Taking the ring from the box, he held it up for her and smiled. "I know everything there is to know about you, my love," he told her tenderly. "The diamond was for our engagement. But this is special. This is a token for you to wear against your skin and know that I'll never be any farther from you than this ring. And look inside."

Squinting in the candlelight, she turned the ring until she could make out the tiny printing inside. "Sheridan. Always, Nick." Overcome with emotion, tears welled up in her eyes.

"Don't cry, Sheridan," he said anxiously, wiping a tear with his thumb. "I can't stand it when you cry."

"I'm only crying because I'm so happy," she assured him, kissing his cheek and smiling limply. "I always do. Obviously there's at least one thing you didn't know about me."

"I guess you're right." He slid the ring onto the third finger of her right hand. "That makes it official. Now, why don't you turn around and let me rub those beautiful shoulders of yours?"

Turning, she settled back against him as his strong, gentle hands began to manipulate the muscles in her neck and shoulders. It was heavenly and she closed her eyes, sinking into the massage like a fluffy cloud.

"You are so beautiful," he murmured, his lips brushing the nape of her neck ever so gently. "Your velvet skin. Perfect breasts. Your scent. The feel of your round, firm butt." She felt his growing erection against her lower back and instinctively responded by pushing herself harder against him.

His hands moved down from her shoulders and around to the front of her chest, each hand forming a cup over her breasts.

As he manipulated her nipples and continued to nibble on the sensitive flesh of her neck, she felt her own arousal stirring.

Unable to stand very much of his attention, she curled her body around to face him, gently pushed him into a sitting position and moved into his lap, straddling him on her knees.

Silently they embraced, opening their mouths and letting their tongues run wild with the other. She had the fleeting thought that he tasted like champagne and that this too was familiar — but not quite.

Raising herself, she felt him slip smoothly into her, taking him up completely and feeling the full, hard heat of him. As she moved up and down, his shaft found her clitoris, making her almost giddy with the sensation. This was not something that she'd ever done and yet it seemed perfectly natural, perfectly right with Nick.

Taking a breast in each hand, he pulled her gently forward, suckling her, alternating his tongue and the vacuum of his mouth to stimulate her.

Bracing herself on the rim of the tub with both hands, she looked down into his eyes, half closed and dreamy with the pure physical joy of the moment. She saw herself in those dark eyes, a reflection of the man she loved and the pleasure at their joining. It was as if they'd been together always, and knew each other's secret places of passion.

For long moments, there was only the sound of the water swirling and bubbling around them. They moved together perfectly, their skins slick as wet seals, nothing but their kisses and their building passion.

"Sheridan," he moaned softly, grabbing her ass and squeezing. "You feel so good…"

She knew he was close because the first shivers of her own climax were rippling through her.

"Nick," she gasped, their movements urgent and furious, creating their own splashing whirlpool around them. "Oh…oh…"

Her back arched as waves of sensual fire washed over her, each one carrying her to another, higher plain. Inside she felt Nick, his body locked in a spasm of fulfillment, his face buried between her breasts.

Sagging together, it was several minutes before their heart rhythms and breathing returned to normal enough for them to speak.

"You are," he whispered hoarsely, "the most wonderful lover a man could ask for. Every time I'm with you, I think that it can't be any better, that there can't be any higher heights. But you always surprise me. Bring me something more."

"I don't claim to be very experienced," she replied quietly. "Believe it or not, I was a virgin when I married. I didn't know anything. Not that he really knew anything either. But you...you just seem to bring out something in me that I didn't even know was there. I can only say, 'thank you'."

"Anytime, my love, anytime."

Nick kissed her and reached for their glasses. As they lay in the soothing water, sipping their champagne and enjoying the afterglow of their lovemaking, the niggling feeling that had been just over the horizon of her mind finally arrived in Sheridan's consciousness.

"You know," she mused, "now that Cat's a success, I have to start thinking about the second book in my two-book deal."

"When we get back. For these two weeks, you belong, body, mind and soul, exclusively to me." Nick kissed the back of her neck and the sensation made her shiver.

"Yes, but sooner or later I have to write something. I mean, I took the money already."

"There's lots of time," he assured her, his hands moving down her back. "You're going to write lots of books."

Taking a deep breath and opening her eyes, she turned to face him. "I...I was thinking about following it up with a kind of adult fairy tale," she said uncertainly, searching his face. "About a male witch and a human woman who meet and fall in love."

So there it was. From the beginning, there in her apartment when he'd first asked her if she'd like to share a pizza, he'd seen the shadows flicker in her eyes, the unspoken questions on her lips. He'd always made sure there'd been something to distract her, turn the subject. But he could see in her face now, it was time for the truth.

"A fairy tale," he repeated.

Sheridan nodded.

Nick took her hand and kissed it. "I suppose then, like all good fairy tales, it should probably begin, 'Once upon a time'."

"I guess that would be as good an opening as any," she agreed.

"Maybe I can help you with it." He paused, as if thinking of his words. "Well, then, once upon a time, there were a race of beings who, for ease of explanation, I guess you could call witches. These powerful beings shared the physical world with their human neighbors and yet were apart from it. They weren't really immortal, but their life spans were so long in comparison to mortals it seemed as if they were.

"And so, a long, long time ago, there lived a young witch who grew up in a family of these powerful beings, happy and content with his parents and siblings, learning the ways of the world and how to use his power.

"As adolescence overtook him, though, a strange thing began to happen. He began to dream of a woman. Always the same dream. He'd be walking through a beautiful garden, down a path to a dark pool. Bending down, he'd see the reflection of a beautiful woman, smiling and beckoning him. Not understanding the dream, he asked his mother about it. She smiled and told him that he was seeing his one true mate, the woman who would share his life forever. He asked her where he'd find her but his mother just smiled and told him that when he did, he'd know."

Nick's face had taken on a sad expression that Sheridan could never remember seeing and she suddenly regretted opening this door. But it was open now, and there was no way to close it until the end of the story.

"So the young witch grew to manhood and began searching for his mate. He searched this world and lots of others. He was restless, never able to settle down and feel at home because he had to find her. He looked into the faces of countless women…witches and mortals and demons alike, always hoping, always seeking. Clinging to the belief that one day, he'd turn a corner and there she'd be."

Kissing her fingers again, he smiled a little and she saw her reflection again in the depths of his incredible blue eyes.

"And in the best fairy tale tradition, one day that's exactly what happened. The witch was walking down a street when he happened to glance into the front window of a restaurant, and there she was. Sitting at a table by herself, she was scribbling madly on a yellow legal tablet. He stood transfixed, utterly spellbound by her, filled with a love he'd carried and nurtured for a thousand years. And when she looked up, with a faraway, thoughtful look in her beautiful eyes, his heart almost burst with longing.

"His first thought was to race into the restaurant, sweep her off her feet and live happily ever after. But he realized that there'd been someone before him. Someone who'd hurt her so badly she'd shut the door to her heart, barred it and would have spurned his attentions out of fear and misunderstanding."

She saw herself sitting at Max's many a noon, eating a solitary lunch and working on her writing, oblivious to anything or anyone around her.

"Of course, he could have snapped his fingers, enchanted her and had her fall head over heels in love with him. But that wasn't what he wanted. He wanted her to love him for himself, as he loved her. So he began trying to find a way into her life that would keep him near her, show her how much he cared and give her a chance to fall in love with him.

"As he watched her, he began to understand how unhappy, how lonely she was, that her need for love and companionship and her ability to give and receive it was as great as his. So he shadowed her, waiting, hoping, for his chance. One day, he saw her sitting in the park eating her lunch. A stray cat came by, a scrawny, pathetic little thing that came over because he smelled her sandwich. Instead of shooing him away, she took the roast beef out of the uneaten part of her sandwich and gave it to him. With that simple act of decency and kindness, the witch knew then how he'd come into her life."

Almost in spite of herself, Sheridan smiled. "So one raw, rainy winter's night," she finished, "the witch changed into a black cat and invited himself into her apartment."

Nick grinned. "Makes a nice tale, don't you think?"

She eyed him with amused suspicion. "I have a couple of questions…purely from a writer's point of view."

"Such as?"

"What happened to the witch when the black cat went out the window, saving his love from the Brian?"

"For a witch, taking another shape, especially an animal, takes a lot of strength and energy. That's why he needed to spend a lot of time away from the apartment. He had to return to his plane, his real shape. Like recharging a battery. But fighting Brian and then falling through a second story window essentially destroyed the cat shape, smashed the battery. Since the cat shape was gone and the man shape didn't really exist—at least not in her human plane of existence—he could still be with her, but not in any real, tangible way she could understand."

"Except in her dreams."

"Because in her dreams, nothing was 'real' anyway. He could come to her, be with her, in his true form."

"Then how does the witch keep his human shape without recharging his batteries back on his own plane?"

"Simple. The human shape is how the witch really looks. It's his own shape made visible in her reality." Nick grinned and ran a fingertip lovingly down Sheridan's cheek. "He doesn't need to recharge his batteries except after he's been making mad, passionate love to his wife."

"And everything else? The human woman's landlady? The other firefighters? They all have stories, memories of the witch in his human shape."

Snapping his fingers, Nick laughed. "What is life really, except recollections? Don't you think any witch worthy of the title could conjure up a whole lifetime of memories and stick them in people's heads, even if they weren't real? But if an old woman remembers a young boy and his family or a group of firefighters remember a buddy, who's to say that the little boy or the buddy didn't really exist? After all, they say the worst thing about Alzheimer's is that it takes your memories and hence your life, before it kills your body."

"So the man never really existed? It was just another shape, like the cat. And people only know him because the witch put the memories in their minds."

"It's a little more complicated than that, but yes, simply put in fairy tale terms, that's about right. The witch knew his love had moved into a new apartment and that she'd recovered from the attempted rape because they made wonderful love. He knew then it was time to start laying the groundwork so he could manufacture a 'chance' meeting with her. So he moved to this plane of reality, gave the landlady some comforting memories and a good friend. He gave the firefighters memories too, so he could get a job. And not to sound too immodest, especially for a fairy tale, but he's damned good at being a firefighter and paramedic in the bargain. It was important to the witch that his beloved see him as a functioning, contributing, caring man. He wanted to be worthy of her."

"So, the witch and the human woman live happily ever after?"

"If the witch has anything to say about it." Sheridan smiled at the loving arrogance in his voice.

"And what about children?" she persisted. "I mean, can a witch and a human mate? And if they do, what will their children be? Human? Witch? What?"

Nick kissed her passionately, feeling her melt in his arms.

"I have no idea what the offspring of a witch and a human will be. How do any two people know what their children will be? But whatever they are, I know they'll be terrific because what better gift can parents give their children than a strong, happy, loving home?"

He grinned wickedly. "And trust me. Witches have absolutely no trouble mating with human women. Especially a beautiful, warm, giving woman like the one in my arms. In fact..."

They shared another long, passionate kiss.

"Anything you say, Nick," she breathed between kisses. "Anything you say."

About the author:

Liz began her career at age three when she started telling her own stories to her dolls and favorite stuffed bear. Her older sister taught her to write at six so she immediately began writing down her stories and reading them to her family. At seven, she decided to become a writer. She won several creative-writing contests in grammar school and by the time she'd moved on to high school, she was working on the school newspaper and had a "lending library" of her popular stories that circulated amongst her peers. Her first paying writing job was in her teens working for the local newspaper, interviewing celebrities who appeared at the local theater-in-the-round.

Liz married, had children, and took a "real" job while she went to college at night, finally earning her degree in Business but never giving up her writing. During this time, she continued to learn her craft and hone her skills. Five years ago, she decided to devote herself to writing seriously. In that time, she's had several short stories published and finished four novels. Her work ranges over several genres from romance to the paranormal.

Elizabeth welcomes mail from readers. You can write to her c/o Ellora's Cave Publishing at 1337 Commerce Drive, Suite 13, Stow OH 44224.

Also by Elizabeth Stewart:

The Academy
Harm's Way
Hearts of Steel anthology

Believe in the Magic

Cait Miller

Prologue
Two years ago

Like the cover of a romance novel, the young couple lay intertwined with each other on a heart-shaped bed, modesty safeguarded only by the closeness of their bodies and the tangle of the red satin sheet. The gold of their hair and of the rings on their fingers glinted in the light from the candles that flickered over them. Clothes lay scattered around the room, and a table by the window held the remains of two meals. On the nightstand, an open bottle of champagne rested in a bucket of swiftly melting ice next to two empty champagne flutes.

They did not stir when the door opened, slept on soundly even when he entered the room. He regarded the scene with grief, anger and satisfaction. The drug had worked.

For a moment he felt regret for what he was about to do but he smothered it mercilessly as he raised the gun in his gloved hand. The woman—no, creature—before him was no longer the little girl for whom he had had such hopes and dreams. His daughter was dead, the male she was wrapped around had seen to that. She was like *him* now and they would both have to be put down. He knew there were others. They could only be the work of evil. No human could do what they did. And so it was up to him to free their souls from torment.

In the end the decision was easy.

Chapter One
Today

The insistent buzzing of the dreaded alarm sliced through Megan's brain, signaling her that it was time to start another day. Groaning softly she stuck an arm out from beneath the covers and slapped at the button on top of the clock until there was blessed silence. "Oh God...it can *not* possibly be time to get up yet." It was warm and cozy under the quilt and she had had an unsettling night full of dreams she couldn't recall. They had left her feeling unrested and groggy. Sticking her nose out from beneath the covers, Megan checked the digital alarm clock and saw that it was indeed six a.m. She flung back the quilt, swung her bare legs over the edge of the mattress and stood up, pulling the faded oversized T-shirt down over her backside as she rose and stumbled blindly to the bathroom and into the shower.

Forty-five minutes later, Megan pulled her ancient car into the parking lot at the side of the beachfront Seaview Hotel, a two-story monument to Scottish tourism complete with the distinctive blue and white flag of Scotland on the roof. Painted the color of sand, the narrow building had thirty rooms stretching to the back. The restaurant with its large glass conservatory was at the front, and the main door leading to the reception area at the side.

It was early September and the sun was already on its way up, though a wispy mist still hung over the sand and only a few ambitious — or stupid — people were visible jogging or following jubilant dogs.

Megan swallowed the last mouthful of coffee from a travel mug before clumping it onto the dashboard. She could have made the drive to work in her sleep, which was probably just as well considering she almost did. "I am definitely not a morning person…which of course explains why I choose to work the breakfast shift," she grumbled sarcastically to the tired blue eyes that looked back at her from the rearview mirror.

She climbed out of the car and headed for the staff locker room to stow her bag, pulling her damp curly dark hair into a ponytail, and checking her white blouse and short black skirt and tights as she went. Actually the seven-until-four shift wasn't so bad despite the uncivilized time she had to get out of bed. It meant the rest of the day was hers to do what she pleased. Anyway, she had been tired for so long now she was almost used to it, it was her own fault for going to bed late nearly every night. Briefly she thanked the god of all waitresses that she was on holiday for two weeks after today.

Danny, the brusque Irish chef, had already started cooking when she passed through the hot kitchen with all its gleaming stainless steel appliances—someone must already be down for breakfast. Short and nearly bald under his crumpled hat, Danny had been there as long as she could remember. Faded blue amateur tattoos climbed up his arms beneath his rolled-up sleeves. Megan turned a blind eye to his teapot filled with dark beer sitting on the counter behind him, as most of the staff did. Danny was an alcoholic, but he did his job and was loved by customers and staff alike. They had stopped trying to change him long ago.

"How is it going, Dan? Are we busy?"

"What time d'ya call this?" he growled without turning away from the bacon sizzling under the grill. He was notorious for being at least an hour early for work and it was his standard reply. Megan grinned and walked on. If she was half an hour early he would still say the same thing. He loved her really.

As she approached the dark wooden doors to the dining room she became aware of a building sense of trepidation. Frowning, she pushed open the door and froze. Sitting alone directly in front, watching as if he had expected her, was the most gorgeous man she'd ever seen. He looked to be in his early thirties, just about the right age for a twenty-six-year-old waitress, she thought whimsically. Although he was seated she knew he must be tall, but then, at five-foot-three everyone seemed tall to her.

In seconds her gaze ran over his short black hair and the sharp planes of his clean-shaven face to his broad shoulders and a fantastic chest covered by an indecently tight T-shirt. Through the shirt, a shadow of dark hair was just visible. She suffered a small pang of disappointment that the table blocked her view of what promised to be a lower half as heart-stopping as the rest of him. When she brought her eyes back up to meet his silver gaze, her head felt as if it were buzzing and the rest of the room faded away from them.

The spell was broken when his mouth curved in an insolent smile as if he knew exactly what she was thinking. She felt the heat rising in her face and turned away to pick up an order pad.

Ah, but I do, Megan.

Megan's eyes snapped back to his face as the deep American voice floated through her head, but his eyes were on the newspaper on his table and his face impassive. *You have got to get more sleep, Meg*, she thought, shaking her head.

You had trouble sleeping last night? Me, too. Maybe we should try together.

She narrowed her eyes and looked at him again but he seemed to be paying her no attention. *Get a grip, Megan. Telepathy is impossible, it's just lack of sleep…or too much television and far too many vampire romance novels… You will go over there and take his order and he will not have an American accent.*

There was only one other table occupied in the dining room. She decided to play it safe and headed over to the elderly couple to take their order, ignoring the word *coward* following in her wake.

Jack Douglass raised his eyes from his newspaper and watched her talk cheerfully to the people at the other side of the brightly decorated restaurant. Her Scottish accent was surprisingly easy to follow when he had been struggling to understand people since he arrived. They were discussing local tourist attractions, but her thoughts were chaotic as she tried to rationalize what had just taken place. The only other Scot he had ever been able to understand with ease was a good friend whose mother was American. She had influenced her son's speech enough to slow him down and it appeared that someone had done the same for this woman.

He closed his eyes, inhaling deeply. His sharpened senses were tuned to Megan now and he easily picked out her unique scent from the multitude of others in the dining room. No perfume, just soap and her own skin. Now that he was in her presence magical energy zipped between them, an almost tangible force. It made his skin tingle and the hair on his arms stand up, like a storm was coming and the air was filled with electricity.

Jack allowed himself a small satisfied smile. He knew he shouldn't toy with her but she was broadcasting her thoughts so loudly that he had been able to pick up more than he had anticipated. More than he had with the other women he had found, and he hadn't been able to resist teasing her. Nearly two years spent searching worldwide medical databases for records of women with the mark that declared their compatibility as a mate. More than a dozen wasted journeys where he had been tempted again and again to just give up and accept the inevitable.

It had all been worth it. He had finally found Megan Cartwright—in Scotland of all places! Although given that this was where his kind originated, he should probably have expected it. It hadn't taken long for him to make a few inquiries and find out everything he could about her.

When he'd first seen her picture she had taken his breath away—she was beautiful. He still couldn't believe his luck. He had known that she was the one the moment he was in her presence, linked with her mind, smelled her scent. The constant shiver of energy over his body as his magic reached out for her only confirmed it. It was a feeling he had begun to doubt would ever come.

The urge to mate had become more difficult to ignore. He had searched for so long now that sleeping and eating, never mind working, were becoming impossible. Perhaps the cruelest part of the mating cycle was that any time he had tried to gain relief by seducing a woman, he would find himself utterly repulsed and unable to even force himself to touch her. No matter how attractive he found her, it was apparent that only one of the marked would do. Several times now, he had been faced with women who could have given him that relief. Resisting the temptation had been harder than he had expected, but to give in to it would have meant giving up his hopes and dreams for the future.

It felt like his own body was betraying him. Now he was hungry and horny and temptation was once again standing ten feet in front of him pretending she couldn't feel him. This time though, he could take what he wanted. An erection pressed painfully against his jeans as he thought about claiming Megan at last. He couldn't wait to see the birthmark on the inside of her thigh—see it…touch it…taste it…

He waited patiently for her to approach his table. He had to physically touch her to begin the process that would bind them together. A physical conduit to allow his magic to spark the dormant magic in her body to life, sort of a metaphysical jumpstart. Once that process had started there would be no going back, he would begin to transform unpredictably. It was almost as though the bond drained some of the energy he needed to control his change. He had only experienced the transformation once before—at puberty, as all the males of his kind did—it had *not* been an enjoyable experience. Not only was it painful, but he had also hated the loss of control over his own body when he changed and when the primitive instincts overtook his senses.

There would be only a short time—days, maybe as much as a week if he was lucky—in which to fully claim Megan. Unless he completed their bond he'd begin to transform more and more often, and eventually he would become trapped in the other body for good. His heart pounded with fear at the thought. He had to be successful. His father had assured him that once he claimed his mate, his body and mind would no longer fight the transformation. He'd have complete control of it, allowing him to choose when to change and stopping the pain. Of course, his father also claimed that what he was able to do was a gift, one he and his mate would learn to revel in.

Jack sincerely doubted it.

He thought fleetingly of the effect the bonding would have on Megan before dismissing it—she would adjust, the same way he would have to. She was attracted to him—he hadn't missed the appreciation on her face when she'd first entered the dining room. The sexual attraction between a shifter and one of the marked was always strong and for some that was enough. Even though it might mean spending the rest of your life bound to a woman who wanted to screw you every time she looked at you, but hated you while she did it. If he had to lose control over his body and his mind then at least he would be able to have some control over the reason why. He had grown up hearing his mother tell the story of how she and his father had met and fallen instantly in love. They had been married for thirty-five years now and seemed to be as happy together as ever. Jack wanted what his parents had. A Dearbh Ceangal. The Gaelic phrase literally meant "true bond". Where the mated pair were compatible in every way, soul mates. He now knew that he and Megan Cartwright could have that, if only he could persuade her of the same.

Finally she turned her attention his way again. "Can I take your order?"

She stood by his table, and though her voice and expression were friendly she was broadcasting her confusion and tension loudly. He made her uncomfortable even though she was convinced her imagination was running away with her.

Skeptical as she was, Jack realized convincing her otherwise was going to be difficult. "I'm fine, thank you. I just had coffee and something from the buffet." He gestured to the table brimming with fruit and cereal and smiled wryly as he thought of the struggle it had been to eat that much. He had already begun to lose weight, it would be nice to get his appetite back.

Shock and suspicion chased quickly over her face as his accent registered. Jack paused a moment, excitement and fear coursing through his veins—he was glad for the table as it hid the condition of his body. "Jack Douglass." He offered his hand, refusing to be deterred when she did not immediately take it.

After a moment's hesitation she decided she had no alternative and pressed her palm to his. "Megan Cartwright. Pleased to meet you, Mr. Douglass."

"Jack, please." He tightened his grip on her hand as she tried to withdraw it. Taking a deep breath he looked into her blue eyes and focused his mind on hers. He became aware of an aura of color surrounding her body. When he flicked a glance at their clasped hands he saw the silver of his own aura mingling with the white of hers. It was a spectacular sight and part of him mourned the fact that he would be the only one to see it. His vision blurred and he felt a sharp pain as a jolt of power surged through their joined hands.

When his vision cleared he saw the colors burn intensely for a second before fading. Megan gasped and pulled her hand away, quickly turning her back and walking into the kitchen.

Jack made no move to stop her. She had obviously felt the energy generated when they merged. She wouldn't be aware of any other effects. He, on the other hand, would. The prickling shimmer of magic that had filled the air between them was gone now but his skin still tingled and he felt lightheaded. It was done.

He stood on shaky legs to leave the dining room. He needed the privacy of his own room to recover properly. It would take a blood exchange between him and Megan to complete the bond and to do that he needed to get closer to her.

Their newly formed link and his other senses should allow him to track her when he was ready. Her scent was now imprinted into his brain, marking her even more strongly as his. Besides, he thought wryly, he had her address.

All he had to do was seduce her.

Piece of cake.

Megan stood with her back against the kitchen door, heart pounding, and absently soothed her tingling hand. What had just happened there? There was no way Jack Douglass was telepathic. *Ridiculous*! But she could not deny he had indeed had an American accent that sounded frighteningly like the one she had imagined as she entered the dining room. *It was a lucky guess, coincidence…that is all*, Megan told herself. She wasn't entirely convinced but there was no other explanation she was prepared to accept. Her mind was made up as her heart slowed to its usual rhythm. There was no need to see him again after today, and it was a small town but not too small to avoid Jack Douglass. She'd be on holiday and he would no doubt be gone by the time she returned.

Settled at last, she took a deep breath and went back to work, telling herself she was glad his seat was now empty, and ignoring the pang of disappointment from deep inside.

* * * * *

Jack awoke to find the pink and gold light from the setting sun shining through his hotel room window, painting the cream walls with color and giving glowing life to the dark wood furniture. He felt his mate's presence in his mind, an awareness that was difficult to describe, both comforting and arousing. A slight breeze stirred the curtains at the open window, bringing with it the scent of the sea and the distant sound of music from a car radio. He had slept the whole day away! By the time he had returned to his first-floor room after breakfast, his head had been reeling with dizziness and exhaustion had him dragging his steps. After hanging the *Do Not Disturb* sign and locking his door, he had kicked off his shoes, flopped down fully clothed on the green plaid duvet of the king-size bed, and been asleep in minutes.

While the room was no longer spinning around him, he still felt slightly lightheaded. Mind you, that could be due to the fact that he had gone all day with only some cereal and coffee when his body had already been lacking in fuel. Room service would definitely have to be his first priority… *Okay, second,* he thought as his bladder reminded him of this morning's coffee. Cautiously, he raised himself to his elbows before swinging his legs to the side of the bed and slowly standing. The corner of his mouth curved in satisfaction when everything stayed where it should be. He stretched, groaning as the muscles in his back protested, before walking into the bathroom, scratching his chest absently.

Minutes later Jack emerged and headed for the phone on the nightstand to order lunch.

I'm hungry.

The feeling took him by surprise. It had been so long since he had enjoyed a meal that he was tempted to order the whole menu. Restraining the impulse with difficulty, he asked for soup and a sandwich instead. He had not had any appetite for a couple of weeks. Had in fact had to force himself to eat and knew that gorging now would only make him ill. This was yet another unsettling part of his heritage. While he could perhaps have ignored the desire to mate for longer, he could not go as long without food or sleep. Part of him had realized that he was basically starving and exhausting himself but the other part was pining for a mate. As the mating cycle progressed, those instincts had grown stronger and the appeal of food had declined. He knew that had he not found and linked with one of the marked, the rational—human—part of him would have eventually been overcome and he would have very slowly died.

It was the itching that stirred him from his reverie. The itch on his chest had gradually spread to the rest of his body. Instantly Jack's mind flashed back to that long-ago night when he was a teenager, and he knew that he was changing. Panicked, he threw off his clothes and watched as thick black hair forced its way from beneath his skin. He held his trembling hands up as his nails darkened and grew into sharp claws and his fingers seemed to shrink back into the now rough black skin of his palms. His eyes closed while his scalp tightened and his ears burned, but he knew the worst was still to come. Sweat sluiced down his face and back, he groaned low and hoarse, words beyond him, as he felt the burning sensation again just above his buttocks and knew he now had a tail. The pain began in his face and mouth then spread downwards as teeth, bone, muscle and joints reshaped themselves. His whole body was in agony…

Gradually the pain subsided. He fell forward as his back and hips became unable to support his upright position and he realized he was standing on four paws. Jack padded over to the full-length mirror on the wardrobe door and regarded with resignation the large animal staring back at him. All at once he was surrounded by sights, sounds and smells that even his normal sharp senses had been unaware of. It was difficult to associate the sleek black cat with himself, even having been surrounded with shifters all his life. For his kind the transformation was a very private thing and he had never actually seen it happen. The only memories he had of his own transformation as a boy was the pain of the shift and a confusion of alien urges and images of hunting. The animal's strength of will had swept him away until he didn't know who he was anymore.

His eyes closed as he again fought a battle against the instincts more familiar to this body.

With the knock at the door and the call of "room service" the battle was lost and the only thought in Jack's mind as he turned for the open window was *mate*.

* * * * *

Megan trailed into her flat just after sunset, kicking off her shoes and hitching up her skirt to peel off her tights, not even pausing as she tossed them with her bag through the open door of her bedroom. Wincing at the resulting crash, she carried on to the living room and dropped onto the threadbare blue couch with a groan, resting her feet on the small table in front of her. "It's time you learned to say 'no', Meg. N. O. Say it with me, it is not a difficult word. The next time that little weed of a manager asks you to work an extra shift... You. Say. No." She let her head drop onto the back of the couch. "And here you are, talking to yourself again!" *Maybe*, she thought with a smile, *I should get a cat or two. Then all the kids could call me "Crazy Meg, the cat lady who talks to herself", while they hide in the bushes sniggering at me. At least there would be a little bit of excitement in my life.*

In truth, she reflected grimly, she could not afford to say no to any extra shifts no matter how sore her feet got. The rent on the flat took up most of her paycheck and the rest just seemed to disappear into thin air. She liked the freedom her job gave her, but it might be time to look for something else that paid a little better. She studied the room around her, eyes touching on the pale blue walls with the framed posters adding splashes of color. The floor was just plain wood that she had sanded and varnished. A wooden coffee table she had also refinished sat on a woven rug in the same blue as the walls.

The rest of the furniture in the room was also secondhand, fixed to the best of her ability. Except for her CD player—which had been a Christmas gift to herself this year—and the small television and VCR she had won in a supermarket raffle last year. She smiled to herself as she remembered how she had choked on a grape she had just liberated from the fruit and vegetable display when her name had been announced over the supermarket loudspeaker. For a moment she had been convinced that security cameras were focused on her, the grape thief. She had not pinched another grape since, that's for sure.

However, despite the state of her finances she had every intention of ordering takeaway for dinner. She had earned it and she had not eaten since lunchtime. Thus justified, she mentally— because she could definitely not be bothered moving—flipped through the menus for her favorite Chinese and Indian

takeaway and the nearby pizza place. *Decisions…decisions…
Okay, Chinese it is…* Fighting off another attack of the guilts, she
reached for the phone and ordered Mandarin chicken and fried
rice.

As she replaced the receiver a silver picture frame on the
table caught her attention, bringing to mind the eyes of Jack
Douglass. Unconsciously her fingers caressed the place on her
hand where she had felt that very strange jolt of pain when he
introduced himself. Her lips quirked as she thought of that lean
muscular body. The man was definitely hot. She could feel that
heat even now. It was just a shame he had such a detrimental
effect on her mental health. Overactive imagination or not, no
one else had made her hear voices in her head. Still, he was
worth a fantasy or two, since she had no intention of ever seeing
him again. She pried herself out of the hole she had sunk into,
cursing the broken springs of the couch, and headed for the
shower.

Chapter Two

The transformation made the trip to Megan's apartment a little more difficult than Jack had anticipated. Her scent outside the hotel had been faint, diluted by the oil and fuel scent of her car and the passage of strangers' feet. It made her harder to track and the animal in him wasn't exactly interested in following street signs. It was a miracle he hadn't been spotted. Lost in shadows, the journey through the small town had been both terrifying and fascinating.

As an adult he found that his sense of self was not so completely lost to the stronger personality of the cat. Once he became more accustomed to the new sensations, he regained some of his human perspective—it was sort of like sitting in the backseat while someone else was driving. He was aware that his actions and the things he was feeling were not normal, but there was nothing much he could do about it. Jack suspected that in time, if he felt strongly enough, he might be able to overrule the animal, but tonight he had not had much success. He was still more than a little disgusted that he had crept in the open kitchen door of a restaurant and stolen a big chunk of raw meat. He tried to tell himself it was just like eating a rare steak, only bigger... He snorted softly to himself...might've even worked if he didn't usually prefer his meat well done.

He crouched now, unseen, on the fire escape outside his mate's bedroom window. The room was nothing like he expected. Where he had thought she would surround herself with vibrant colors, he discovered that her room was pale lilac with white accents and a polished wood floor. As he watched through her lacy white curtains, she came out of the adjoining bathroom. His heart almost stopped. She was completely naked, her creamy, damp skin slightly flushed. As she reached up to loosen her corkscrew curls from the clip on top of her head, her lush breasts were thrust forward, displaying tempting pink nipples. His fascinated gaze caressed her gently rounded stomach, lingered on the soft dark hair at the apex of her thighs, before continuing down the length of her legs. His searching eyes returned to the spot high up on her left thigh where he knew her birthmark lay, despite the fact that it was out of sight.

She began smoothing lotion onto her hands, arms and shoulders with long strokes. Her nipples puckered to points as she spread it onto her breasts, and his tail twitched from side to side as it dangled over the edge of the platform. She sat on the bed and lifted first one foot, then the other to rub the lotion there, then worked it up her calves and thighs. Her head was tilted back, eyes closed. Finally she relaxed back onto the pillows, dipped her fingers into her moist center and began to slowly tease herself.

Jack felt his claws extending, curling round the metal of the fire escape, as if to physically restrain himself. He focused on Megan's thoughts and saw it was him she fantasized about, and his control slipped another notch. He felt the sighs of pleasure she released and tension grew in his body along with frustration. When she took herself over the peak with his name on her lips, it took all his willpower to prevent himself from crashing through the window to get to her side as instinct demanded.

The doorbell rang, shattering the atmosphere. He growled low in his throat at the interruption. Megan turned to the window, head tilted to one side, a frown creasing her forehead, and he silenced himself abruptly. The bell chimed again and she quickly rose, pulled on a robe, bent to retrieve her purse from the floor and went down the hallway to the door.

Jack snarled when a few moments later she passed the open bedroom door carrying a delivery bag of food. Disappointment and anger swirled through his veins. It made the thick hair bristle on the back of his neck and he battled the cat's desire to roar out its frustration. It didn't want to leave—hell, neither did he—but he couldn't approach Megan in this form anyway. He rose, tension in every line of the cat's lithe body, and started down the fire escape determined to return for her in the morning.

* * * * *

"Good morning, Megandear!"

Megan paused with one bare foot on the stairway to freedom and groaned silently, rolling her eyes.

It's seven-thirty in the damn morning! What the heck is she doing up at this hour and how did she hear me? Slowly she turned back to the flat next door to her own and faced Mrs. Timms.

Lucille Timms was a small bird-like woman who could have been anything from eighty to a hundred and eighty. She was the most conscientious neighbor Megan could ever wish for. She was also nuttier than a fruitcake. Her wispy, shoulder-length hair was blue-rinsed today and held in place on top of her head by two blue ballpoint pens crossed like chopsticks. This morning she was wearing an off-the-shoulder blue and silver ball gown with a flared skirt, and on her feet were huge Tweety-bird slippers. Her face was heavily made up with dark red lipstick and silver eye shadow. At least the colors all pretty much matched today.

"Good morning, Mrs. Timms," Megan replied, resigned.

"Is it not a glorious morning!" Mrs. Timms exclaimed in her upper-class English accent. Her eyes took in Megan's strappy sundress, stuffed-to-the-brim straw bag, and the sandals she carried in her hand in the vain attempt to sneak past the door. "Are you off to the beach? How lovely. What a pretty dress you have on! Why don't you have your shoes on, Megandarling, you'll catch a chill."

Megan remained silent since she wouldn't have been able to squeeze a word in edgewise anyway, and waited for a break in the flow.

"George and I are off to the palace for a ball, it's the most exciting thing!" George was Mrs. Timms' husband. He had been dead for twenty years according to her son, whom Megan had met on one of his infrequent visits.

"Mrs. Timms…" She stopped, closing her eyes briefly. What was the point of distressing her, she would have forgotten again in about twenty minutes. "Yes," she smiled. "I am going to the beach. That's me on holiday now and I intend to relax."

Mrs. Timms beamed innocently at her. "Wonderful, Megandear. The weather is so lovely all the young men will have their swimsuits on and you will be able to pick out a good one. My George is hung like a horse, you know." Megan gaped at her, astonished, while she blithely continued. "I have a devil of a job fending the ladies off him when we go to the beach."

"Mrs. Timms, I really have to go or all the best spots on the beach will be taken," Megan hastily interrupted.

"Oh yes, you had better get on then. Have a lovely day, Megandear."

They exchanged goodbyes and Megan headed for the stairs again before she could hear anything else about George's attributes.

The sky was clear and blue, the air just beginning to warm up and the beach still empty of tourists when Megan arrived a couple of hours later. She had stopped off at the Sunday market first to pick up some fresh fruit and vegetables. It had been fun to search through the car boot sale as well, before the crowds made off with the best bargains.

After parking her car, Megan grabbed her bag and made her way between the sand dunes to her favorite little cove, knowing it was unlikely anyone would bother her there. Despite what she had said to Mrs. Timms, she hadn't expected the shore to be crowded, especially here at the very end, far away from the shops and cafés where people tended to gather.

She spread her blanket and sat down with a sigh of satisfaction, slipping off her sandals and digging out a book and the fruit she had bought for breakfast. It had been another long night filled with very little sleep, but this time she was perfectly aware of who and what she had dreamed of. Jack Douglass and hot, sweaty, mind-numbing sex—it was her own fault for indulging herself last night. She had never been so affected by a man before, particularly not one she had hardly even spoken to. Damn, even the thought of him made her squirm. Finishing her fruit, she lay back on the blanket and closed her eyes, prepared to soak up some vitamin D.

A few minutes later a shadow fell over her face, disturbing her contemplation of the back of her eyelids, and her eyes blinked open. There, as if her earlier musings had conjured him, was Jack Douglass.

"Hello again," he grinned at her while his eyes did a slow sweep of her body. "Megan, isn't it? From the hotel?"

Megan sat up quickly but resisted the urge to cover herself—she was fully dressed, after all—and raised a hand to shade her eyes while she looked up at him. "Mr. Douglass, good morning. A little out of the way of things aren't you?" *In other words, what the hell are you doing here?* She gave him a once-over of her own. He was dressed in a pair of khaki trousers and a white polo shirt. Barefoot, he carried a pair of battered trainers in one hand and a rolled-up towel in the other. Silver-framed sunglasses hooked in the open collar of his shirt where she could just see a hint of crisp dark hair. She had been right in the restaurant—he was tall, around six feet, give or take a couple of inches. He towered over her.

"Jack," he corrected, drawing her eyes back to his face. "I prefer to be away from the crowds and it looked kind of secluded up here." He looked at her assessingly. "You don't mind if I join you, do you? I promise I'll stay out of your way."

Yes, I mind! She shrugged. "Suit yourself."

Megan watched dry-mouthed as he spread his towel out a few feet away and whipped off his shirt, revealing a muscular golden body only slightly marred by the fact that his ribs were clearly visible. As if he'd recently lost weight. *Why is he so thin when the rest of him is obviously fit?* There was a sprinkling of dark hair over his chest, tapering into a thin line past his navel and disappearing into the waistband of his trousers. Heat rushed to her face as she imagined tracing that trail with her tongue. Jack cleared his throat and her gaze flew back to meet the molten silver heat of his. Heat flushed her face. Hastily she tore her attention away from him and picked up her book. Stretching out on her side, she opened it to her bookmark and settled in to ignore temptation.

Jack drew a deep breath as he tried to bring his body back under control. When Megan finally acted on those erotic fantasies, she was going to kill him. Was it possible for a man to expire from an excess of pleasure? He didn't know but he was very willing to experiment. He studied her in silence. Her hair was once again caught up in a clip, though a few renegade strands had escaped to frame her face. The white dress she wore emphasized the paleness of her skin and he noted the dark shadows under her eyes. She had slept poorly again last night; he had, too.

It had been an eventful night, he thought wryly. He had just managed to get back to his room when he had begun to change back. It had hurt just as much as the first time. He shuddered as he remembered the pain and disorientation. As if all that had already happened hadn't been enough to disturb his sleep, he then realized something his father hadn't told him about the bond with Megan. They shared dreams. He had come closer to a wet dream last night than he had since he was a teenager. He had tried in vain to block her as he did with her thoughts, but it seemed that dreams worked differently. If this was how close he and Megan were now when the binding was not complete, what would it be like when they were one? The thought caused a wave of arousal and anticipation to wash through him.

His thoughts were interrupted by Megan's sigh as she gave in to her curiosity. "So, Jack, are you here on business or holiday?" She closed her eyes and laughed. "I cannot believe I actually just asked that."

"At least you didn't say business or pleasure," he answered with a smile. "Actually, I'm here on…family business, but I'm sure I'll find the pleasure too." He let his eyes caress her body suggestively, grinning at the color that flooded her face. "What about you? Not working today?"

"Nope. I'm on holiday now too, for a couple of weeks."

"Then you could show me all there is to see in the area, huh?" He read the hesitation in her expression. "Please, spend the day with me." *What harm could it do?* he whispered into her mind. "We can do anything you'd like."

"I'll think about it," she conceded, and gave her attention back to her book. Resigned, Jack lay back on the towel to enjoy the sunshine. He would have to take some kind of action soon, but he was reluctant to force things too quickly. He had a feeling this was going to be difficult enough. Megan did not seem the type to just give in to anyone's demands.

After a while spent in companionable silence Jack began to shift uneasily. The hair on the back of his neck prickled and he glanced at Megan to find her eyes were still on her book. Someone was watching them. He sat up and looked around— there was no one visible, but he could feel eyes on him. It was probably nothing, someone hoping for a cheap thrill, but it made him uncomfortable. While he scanned the little bit of the beach he could see, the feeling passed and he guessed that whoever it was had found something more interesting to watch. He looked at Megan and saw she too was examining the shoreline uncertainly.

Abruptly she looked at him and announced, "All right," even as he heard her mind protesting. *This is a really bad idea, Megan. He could be a serial killer.*

He stifled the laughter that tried to escape and smiled at her instead. "Thank you. I promise I will take good care of you."

Megan looked uncertainly at his amused face. "Yeah, that's what I'm afraid of," she grumbled under her breath. *Either that or I will lose what's left of my mind and take care of you instead.* The man was a stranger, going with him was no doubt dangerous. She certainly was not the most trusting of people but oddly enough she just wasn't afraid of Jack, and the more time she spent around him the more she wanted him.

At a loss as to what to do with him now that she had agreed, she suggested the first thing that came into her head. "Why don't we go to The Cliffs for lunch then decide what we want to do?" Almost at once she wished the words back. The Cliffs bar and restaurant was a place she ate at occasionally because it had a wonderful view and an excellent lunchtime special. It was also four miles outside of town, which meant she'd have to be alone in a car with this stranger. *Stupid, Megan.* Even as she tried to think of a way to get out of it, he was holding out a hand to help her up.

"Sounds good," he said, pulling her to her feet.

Yes it does. That's the problem.

* * * * *

They spent the rest of the afternoon wandering around various car boot sales after Jack discovered Megan's fondness of it. She had laughed at his dumbfounded expression at the term and patiently explained that they were like "an open-air market crossed with a rummage sale".

The day passed quickly and as he got to know her, Jack realized he could not have made a better choice to be his mate. She was open and friendly and shared his dry sense of humor. It had been a very long time since he had enjoyed a woman's company as much.

Their conversation didn't tell him much more about her life than he already knew, though he found himself wishing he had waited to hear the details from her own lips instead of reading them in a report. She was an only child whose parents died when she was eighteen, leaving just enough to clear up bills and leave a small nest-egg—for a drought she said, since this was Scotland and rainy days were common. The rest of her family was scattered all over the world and she really was not close to any of them.

They took their time over dinner and coffee. Jack was bemused by the fact that he couldn't even remember afterwards just what they had eaten.

Despite his preoccupation with Megan, he had gotten that same feeling that he was being watched on several occasions throughout the day. He never actually saw anyone, though, so he concluded that Megan's presence was making him paranoid. He knew that there could be other shapeshifters out looking for a mate. It would be the ultimate irony if, now that he had found a woman he believed he could spend the rest of his life with, someone else were to come and steal her away. Another blot on the landscape of his sunny day was that, in the back of his mind, he was constantly aware that he might change.

Megan glanced covertly at the man sitting in the passenger seat gazing at the sun setting over the sea as they approached the Bay. She was glad she had followed her instincts and agreed to go with him, and wasn't ready to see the day end.

Megan parked the car in front of her building and turned to face him. "Would you like to come back to my flat for a drink?"

Jack smiled slowly at her. "Sure, I'd love to."

Well, that's fairly promising. Her heart beat a little harder as she considered the possibilities. *Oh yeah, there is no way he is going back to the hotel tonight.* She was astonished at her own brazenness, this just wasn't like her. True, he was sex on legs but she had known the man less than a day and she wanted to throw him on the ground and ravish him. If the looks he had been sending her all day meant anything, he felt the same way.

They climbed out of the vehicle and she looked at Jack again in the fading light. "Are you allergic to something?"

"What?"

She nodded at his hands. "You've been scratching them for the last few minutes."

His gaze flew to his hands and she watched as what looked disconcertingly like panic traced over his features. "Uh, no. Megan... I have to go..." Even as he spoke he was backing away.

"But, I thought you were coming up for a drink?" She frowned at him, puzzled.

"I know, but I can't... I just remembered something I have to do."

"Jack..."

"Thanks for today. I'll call you in the morning."

Before she could get another word out he walked swiftly around the corner and Megan was left standing alone in front of her door, anger gradually overtaking bewilderment.

Well, that's just great! There is only one thing to do when you are this pissed off at a man. Ice cream, followed swiftly by chocolate and vast quantities of apricot brandy. After all that, she'd be too sick to think about how angry she was at Jack Douglass. Turning on one heel she marched purposefully in the direction of the twenty-four hour minimarket nearby.

By the time Megan had made her purchases her temper had simmered down a bit. Maybe she had misread his signals. *Yeah, right.* As her mind replayed the events of the day it occurred to her that she had talked a lot about herself while learning very little about him. She knew that he belonged to a close-knit family and that he had one younger brother. He mentioned that he was here on family business for himself and his parents, but he had hinted that he had his own fairly successful company. He was a strange one, all right, but that didn't seem to matter to her hormones. At least nothing weird had happened—well, until now that is... *Maybe he has performance issues...* The thought made her snort in disbelief.

She had just stepped off the kerb onto the deserted road when the sudden roaring of an engine and the screech of wheels made her heart slam into her throat. Her feet seemed to be glued to the concrete as she squinted against powerful headlights that were all too close and getting closer. Before she had time to draw breath to scream, something slammed into her, pushing her out of the path of the oncoming car. A glimpse of black was all she caught as she made solid contact with the pavement and the car sped past in a blur of white paint and red taillights.

Megan lay stunned on the concrete, her heart was racing and breath coming in whimpers which quickly turned into soft groans as various body parts began to ache in protest. Only two facts were able to penetrate her adrenaline-soaked brain while she pushed herself into a sitting position. Someone had nearly run her down. Someone had saved her life. "GOD DAMMIT! Where did you get your license!" she yelled belatedly at the empty street. Tremors racked her body as she checked her injuries—a skinned elbow, a bump on her head and a bruised backside. Her white dress would never be the same again. Lucky, compared to the alternative.

Slowly she picked herself up off the ground. Spotting the plastic bag containing her emergency rations, she limped over to investigate their condition. *It was a measure of her emotional state that the sight of the intact bottle of apricot brandy and tub of ice cream started her sobbing.*

By the time she reached her flat she had pulled herself together, more or less, although it had been a relief to see no light shining under Mrs. Timms' door. Her face felt hot and her head ached from the crying jag. She was dirty, her hair was probably standing on end and she'd discovered more sore muscles than she knew she had as she climbed the stairs.

To add to her problems she was horny. *Damn him for running off like that! I need a drink, a really, really big one*, she sniffed. She considered and dismissed the idea of calling the police. There would be absolutely nothing they could do since she hadn't seen much and there had been no one else around. It had probably been stupid young boys joyriding, and they would be long gone by now. Besides, she did not think she could face any more trauma tonight.

She made her way through the living room to the kitchen, stopping on the way to pull off her sandals and open the window to let some air in. After she poured her drink she took it and the tub of ice cream and a spoon back to the living room. Intent on fighting with the lid on the tub, she was in the middle of the room by the time she raised her head. Her triumphant expression froze as she came face to face with an enormous black panther.

Chapter Three

Megan noisily sucked in air for a scream that froze in her lungs. The cat stood in front of the open fire escape window, tail twitching, eyes focused intently on her face. Cursing inwardly at the stupidity of leaving the window open even a little bit, she made a mental note to never do it again...if she lived.

The sheer size of the body under that sleek black coat was breathtaking, not to mention the power evident in those muscles. Megan whimpered as she caught sight of the sharp claws just visible on its feet. "Holy crap, someone up there has a really sick sense of humor. When I said I should get a cat, this is not what I meant!" she whispered. The cat snorted and her heart lodged in her throat.

Slowly she raised her glass to her lips, ice rattling as her hand shook, and downed the drink before setting everything on the edge of the table between her and the animal. Cautiously she began to edge towards the hallway door, stopping abruptly when a low rumbling growl filled the room and the cat narrowed its eyes at her. "Okay Meg, stay calm, who do you call when you have a panther in your living room? RSPCA? Cats Protection League?" A hysterical giggle slipped past her lips before she could prevent it.

Without taking her eyes off of the cat, she reached out to the table again in search of the phone, but as her hand made contact with the receiver the cat growled again. Megan snatched her hand back, "Okay...nice kitty... No phone calls, huh?" Her voice quavered, rising with her panic. The cat's ears swiveled towards her and it fell silent again. She eyed the beast warily as it sat down, displaying some impressive equipment. *Okaaay, so you're definitely a boy cat.* "So, what do we do now?" The cat tilted his head at her as she talked. "We can't just stay here all night, besides, I really need to sit down. I had a little mishap a while ago and I'm a bit s-s-s..." Her mindless chatter stuttered to a halt as the panther got to his feet and prowled around the table towards her. Closing her eyes she stood motionless as he brushed past her, not daring to even move her head to see where he was going. Suddenly something bumped into her butt and she let out a startled shriek. She spun around, hands raised to ward off an attack, only to feel that same bump on her hip this time. Cracking one eye open, she peered down to see the cat nudging her with the top of his head. Incredibly, she realized she was being urged towards the couch.

Jack pushed Megan again. He couldn't believe he was actually doing this but after that car had nearly hit her he really needed to be with her, make sure she was all right. The cat's instincts also said he had to be with his mate, to protect her. The need had overrun his caution and before he knew it he had been standing in her living room. Now he had to do something to calm her down, because she was clearly terrified. Talking to her mentally might just shove her over the edge—she had been through too much already tonight. No, he thought, it was better to let her get used to the cat before he revealed he was also telepathic...and a shapeshifter.

He watched as she inched down onto the couch, then he sat on the carpet in front of her so that their eyes were level. Her hands were clenched together in her lap and the knuckles turned white as he slowly bent his head towards them. He ran his rough tongue over her fingers, tasting the salt of her earlier tears, then nudged her hands with his nose. Megan gasped, "You want me to touch you?" He glanced at her face and laid his head in her lap as she gingerly unclasped her hands and touched his head. Gradually she grew bolder and she began to explore his soft fur and the sensitive skin beneath it. When her fingers found the sweet spot behind his ear and scratched, he could not contain a groan of pleasure. The fingers froze but when he continued to rest his head passively on her thighs, enjoying the sweet scent of her body, she carried on with her investigation.

Megan smiled wonderingly. *He's so soft. God, I never imagined I'd ever get a chance to experience something like this.*

Jack unashamedly eavesdropped, catching her thought as she ran her hands over his shoulders. The purring startled them both, it was an unconscious reaction and he made no attempt to stop it. Megan laughed delightedly, earlier fear all but forgotten.

"You like that, huh? Where did you come from? You're so tame, someone must be looking for you." *There must be someone I can contact to see where you escaped from.* Deliberately Jack projected a picture of pacing in a dirty, too-small cage. *Tomorrow is soon enough*, Megan told herself.

She ran her hands along his spine, brushing the fur the wrong way and smoothing it back, causing his skin to twitch at the strange feeling. *Black as midnight... Black...* Her hands paused again and he lifted his head as he anticipated the conclusion of her thoughts. "Was that you?" she whispered. "No way, now I'm being crazy." He met her gaze and saw the knowledge in her eyes.

"Okay, I've had enough, I'm going to bed." She stood up with a groan, picked up her tub of ice cream, and gestured to the window, "I don't know where you came from but it would certainly be easier if you'd go back there."

It probably would be wiser if he left, but he found himself walking to the hall doorway instead. Megan followed him, stopping on her way to toss the half-melted dessert into the freezer. "You can't stay here, what would I tell the neighbors!?" He ignored her and continued into the bedroom. "I can't afford to feed you!" He sat at the foot of her bed and waited. "All right, dammit, but I *am* calling someone in the morning!" She marched into the bathroom, closing the door firmly. A few minutes later he heard the shower start up.

Megan moaned in pleasure as the hot water sluiced over her battered body. She could hardly believe the events of the last couple of hours. *Maybe I'm suffering from a head injury and this is all an hallucination.* She half-expected to come to at any minute and find herself still lying on the pavement outside. Had that blur of black been the cat? It certainly seemed intelligent enough and its speed would explain why she hadn't seen anything before she hit the ground. It made as much sense as finding the huge creature in her living room. Where had it come from, and why her flat? Someone had to have trained him so he was probably valuable. It was possible he had escaped from a cage like the one she had pictured earlier. She knew that she would have to return him but the thought made her stomach hurt. Quickly she finished her shower, dried off and pulled on the nightshirt hanging on the back of the door. *Maybe he'll be gone.*

She walked back into her bedroom to find the cat stretched full length on her bed. "Oh, no way! Get off of there." When he ignored her she pulled futilely on the corner of the quilt. He raised his head from her spare pillow and she swore she could read amusement in his eyes. Panting and exhausted, she gave up and crawled into the other side of the bed. "You better not have fleas," she mumbled. Her eyes drifted shut and as she tumbled into sleep, the word "*Goodnight*" whispered into her mind.

The street was dark and deserted. Jack noticed little else as he raced for the safety of the streetlights ahead. Behind him he could hear the scream of an overtaxed engine as the car sped after him. Glancing over his shoulder he saw the headlights gaining and desperately tried to convince his body to go faster. His throat burned with the rasp of his breath, his chest tightened from the want of oxygen, his paws felt raw from the friction of the concrete. Sanctuary seemed no closer. Movement caught his eye and he turned to see his mate running alongside him.

In the shadows to the side, Megan could see the cat keeping pace with her and tried to call out to it, but it merely looked at her with familiar eyes and vanished. Hearing the rasp of someone else breathing, she looked again to the shadows and saw Jack. His face hard with determination, he reached for her hand and ran with her towards the streetlights. Her legs ached and trembled with the strain and she imagined she could feel the heat from the engine close behind them. Heart pounding, she pushed on. Just as she thought all was lost they tumbled into the golden pool of light and all was silent.

Then the burning began, the light that before had represented safety turned on them and heat engulfed them, dissolving the clothes from their bodies so that its hungry flames could reach their skin –

The nightmare released Jack from its grip with a suddenness that left him disoriented. Still in his feline form, he lay on Megan's bed. Beside him, she too quieted as if now that he was awake the fire had been deprived of fuel. Another wave of heat washed over him, and he realized that he was on the verge of shifting again and the illusion of fire had been his addition to the dream. He had only intended on staying with Megan until she fell asleep but as he glanced towards the room window he saw the lightening of the dawn sky. Checking one last time that she now slept peacefully, he slid off of the bed, padded silently through the apartment and out of the window.

* * * * *

Having safely retrieved his clothes and other belongings from the hedgerow where he had hurriedly stuffed them last night, Jack returned to his hotel room. He was exhausted from the shift and his cock ached with lust for the woman he had left. He had to have her, she was his.

If he were a normal man, he thought bitterly, he would be waking up warm and satisfied beside Megan right now. He pulled on clean jeans and a soft black shirt. Then again, if he were a normal man he would probably never have met Megan. He didn't even want to consider that.

The thought brought to mind Megan's accident last night. Being the cat did have some advantages. Quick as he was as a man, he could never have reached her in time. His hands trembled as he remembered how close it had been, his tail had actually brushed the car as it passed. Megan believed it had been joyriders and she was probably right, but Jack recalled the times yesterday he had felt they were being watched. Still, who would want to hurt her, and why? The answer was, of course, no one.

He dismissed it from his mind for the moment, resolving to be more vigilant—just in case.

In the meantime, he had to go back to her apartment. He had some explaining to do after abandoning her last night and he had no idea what he was going to tell her. Whatever else happened, he was determined to make up for the unfulfilled promise of the night. He swore; it all might have been over if the change had not got in the way. It was only going to get worse as his transformations came more frequently. He was rapidly running out of time.

* * * * *

Megan sat at the dark wooden table in her kitchen drinking coffee and refusing to feel disappointed that the cat had been gone when she woke this morning. It was for the best really, this way she wouldn't have to feel guilty about turning him in. Of course that would not stop anyone else from doing it. She only hoped he would be okay.

The knock caused her to jump. Hissing in annoyance, she licked the cooling drink off of her fingers and placed the cup on the draining board before making her way to the door. It was still early and she could not think of anyone who would be knocking at her door at this time unless, her expression brightened, it was the postman with her latest book order. She opened the door and the look of anticipation slid off her face. *Jack.*

"Hi." He stuck his hands in his pockets and his gaze took in her fitted blue T-shirt and tight jeans.

She ignored the resulting spark of heat. "Morning," she replied, her tone more of a statement than a greeting.

"I need to apologize and explain about last night."

Megan waited, one hand on the door. *This had better be good.*

"I had to call my parents." As she stepped back inside and began to close the door he continued in a rush. "Really, they're on vacation. This was the last chance to speak to them for the next week because they'll be staying at their cabin and it doesn't have any phones." As he spoke, he edged past her into the flat. "I promised I would call and update them on the business." They stood facing each other in the narrow hallway, bodies nearly touching.

"That is just about the worst excuse I have ever heard, so it must be true. I felt like an idiot, Jack." Megan shut the door, resisting the urge to slam it, and headed for the kitchen, knowing he would follow.

"I'm sorry." He stood so close behind her that she felt his breath stir her hair, causing a shiver to chase down her spine. She stepped away from him, taking a clean mug from a cupboard and pouring him a cup of coffee. She turned abruptly to hand it to him only to discover those fabulous eyes of his had been fixed to her backside.

"I'm up here, Jack." She refused to be affected by the heat she saw in his gaze when he lifted his head.

"Those are really great jeans." His voice had deepened and she swore she could feel the vibration of it as their fingertips connected on the handle of the mug. *Okay, maybe I'll be a little affected.* His eyes held both heat and that trace of amusement. "I like your T-shirt, too. It really draws attention to your...eyes." Megan's face flushed and she could not help but smile at his outrageous comment as she looked down and saw that, without the constriction of a bra, the thin fabric outlined her nipples.

Jack placed the untouched coffee on the worktop and slowly advanced as Megan began to back away from him.

"I'm still angry at you."

"I know." She found herself backed against the table as Jack continued to stalk her. Excited butterflies fluttered in her stomach. He was so overwhelmingly masculine, he seemed to fill her little kitchen with his presence. He placed a hand on either side of her body, trapping her in a loose embrace. She could smell him, soap mixed with an indefinable scent that was all his own. Her heart began to beat a little faster and she moistened her lips in anticipation.

His hands moved to her waist and he bent his head and brushed her mouth with his own once, twice. His tongue traced her lips demanding entry and when she complied, he responded with a hunger that belied his initial gentleness. His hips pushed against hers, the hard length of his erection bulging behind his jeans. Her tongue thrust and dueled with his for control of the kiss as her hands came up to grasp his shoulders. Hands slid up beneath her T-shirt to cup her breasts and a bolt of heat shot straight to her core as his thumbs brushed over her nipples.

She gasped and Jack broke away from her lips long enough to pull her top over her head. Her hands went immediately to his shirt, quickly unbuttoning it and sliding it off of his shoulders to drop to the floor. He unfastened and stripped off her jeans and panties while she explored his powerful shoulders and hair-dusted chest, his breath caught when she ran her nails lightly over his nipples. She watched as they beaded, then caressed his firm buttocks as she pushed his underwear and jeans over his hips. He caught the waistband before it could slip to his ankles and groped in his pocket for a foil-covered condom. She took it from him, opened it and began smoothing the thin latex onto his cock with shaking hands. He groaned and moved her hands back to his shoulders and finished sheathing himself with a practiced stroke.

"I want you too much," he murmured, "and if you touch me like that it'll be over before we get started." Catching her waist he lifted her onto the table, drawing her knees apart to make a place for himself. The shock of the cold surface on her buttocks made her suck in her breath. She leaned back on her elbows. Jack dipped his head to her breasts, suckling one while his fingers teased the other, switching to give each equal attention. He lifted his head and met her eyes as he blew gently on her engorged nipples, causing her back to arch in a silent appeal for the damp heat of his mouth again. His hands gripped her hips and Megan's eyes flickered closed while he kissed his way down the center of her body, pausing to swirl his tongue in her navel. She whimpered in frustration when his mouth brushed teasingly over the curls at the apex of her legs and down to nuzzle and nip the inside of her thigh where her birthmark lay. A chocolate-brown blotch about the size of a ten-pence coin orbited by smaller spots, it vaguely resembled a paw print. Her mother had once told her it was inherited from her side of the family. *What the heck am I doing thinking about my mother!*

Jack's mouth left her but before she could catch her breath his hand released her hip and she felt one long finger slip into her, testing, before it was joined by another. Impossibly, she felt her cheeks heat further as he discovered how wet she was. Her eyes flew open and she cried out as she felt his tongue part her so that he could close his lips around her clitoris, sucking gently as he thrust his fingers in and out of her. When she felt her muscles begin to contract she brought her hands up, fisted them in his hair and dragged his head back up to her mouth for another desperate kiss, tasting herself.

"I want you inside me when I come," she whispered.

For an instant Jack's thick, hard cock slid against her own swollen flesh, his hips bucked against hers and his body quivered with restraint. "Not yet." He moved back and his fingers thrust into her once again.

She moaned into his mouth as he circled her clit with his thumb, his tongue mimicking the action of his fingers. Her breathing growing frantic, Megan raked her hands through his hair and over his shoulders and back. His mouth drew a damp path around to nibble on her lobe, his breathing harsh in her ear and his voice strained as he whispered "Now!" and pressed his thumb hard on her clit.

Megan groaned as she flew over the edge, her body convulsing as she felt his cock filling her with one slow thrust. Her legs wrapped around his hips, they began to move together, faster and faster until she felt Jack reach his own completion, his shout filling the room, followed by her own in another shattering climax.

The world faded back in slowly. Megan stroked her hands down the muscles of Jack's back, reveling in his weight and the heat of his breath on her neck. Jack groaned softly and she chuckled, hardly believing she had just taken part in a kitchen-table sex scene. "I don't think this table was designed for this, you know."

He lifted his head and met her eyes. "Do I look like I care?" Conveniently her hand was stroking his tight buttock and she slapped it once hard. "You will if it collapses underneath us." He yelped and she soothed the sting.

"Okay, that's true," he smiled at her as she felt his cock harden inside her again. Her body tingled with the knowledge. "Guess we better be quicker this time."

Chapter Four

"What's wrong?" Jack's own mind was spinning, but he was aware of Megan's turmoil as they lay together wrapped in a cotton throw. Temporarily sated, they had stumbled as far as the living room couch where they had both drifted into sleep.

"Nothing," she replied. "I'm just worried about the cat."

It was now early afternoon and when they had woken up Megan had told him about her strange feline visitor of the previous night. He noticed with mild amusement that she left out a lot of the details. He ran his fingertips lightly along the creamy skin of her arm. He could not believe he hadn't performed the blood exchange. He'd had plenty of opportunity—you couldn't get much closer than they had just been. Hell, he could even do it right now. It didn't take much blood from either of them, just a few sips, and it would only be once. The thought of drinking someone's blood—even Megan's—made him feel faintly sick. Since he was not looking forward to the process much himself, he knew there was little chance of Megan doing it voluntarily. The problem was he didn't want to force or trick her into it anymore.

He wanted her to choose to be with him.

He wanted her to trust him.

"You think he will be all right?" She lifted her head from his chest to look at him.

"I'm sure he's fine."

"But anything could have happened to him." She sat up, holding a corner of the throw over her breasts with one hand. "He could have been hit by a car, or someone could have captured him, maybe he's locked up in a cage. D'you think it would be on the news?"

His amusement faded and he watched helplessly knowing that her distress was his fault. He made his decision — it could be dangerous, but if he wanted her to trust him this would be the first step. "Megan," his voice wavered a bit. He grasped her shoulders as she reached for the television remote intent on turning on the news. Clearing his throat he looked into her eyes and tried again. "Megan, I need to tell you something." She looked at him, impatience turning to wariness as she studied his face. He took a deep breath. "I'm a shapeshifter…the cat in your apartment last night was me."

For an agonizing instant there was complete silence in the apartment. Jack watched Megan's face, seeing astonishment, disbelief and finally anger reflected there before she spoke.

"That is not funny, Jack. I don't know whether you are trying to make a fool of me but I'll give you the benefit of the doubt and believe that was meant to be a joke." She flung the edge of her cover towards him and stood frowning, hands on her hips, oblivious to the fact she was naked. Afternoon sunshine filtered through the half-closed vertical blinds at the window, bringing out red highlights in her hair and illuminating her pale skin.

Jack's mind went blank as he gaped at her. *God, she's beautiful.*

"I realize you probably think I'm being stupid, after all, he is just an animal. But Jack, there's something about him…" her voice trailed off. "Are you even listening to me?"

He brought his attention back to her blue eyes, appalled at his daydreaming, and his nerves once again overtook his hormones. She looked down at herself…*naked*…and abruptly whipped the throw from where it was bundled on his lap, eyes widening at the half-erect cock, which hadn't quite got the message from his brain. As she put the barrier of the coffee table between them, he grabbed one of the small cushions from the couch and covered himself, feeling ridiculous. She didn't believe him. It almost was funny…almost.

"Megan, I wasn't joking."

She narrowed her eyes at him, shifting her attention from the material she was tucking in above her breasts and studying him. "My God, you are serious, aren't you!?" He nodded. "Well, that is wonderful!" Hitching up the throw with one hand so she wouldn't trip, she began to pace up and down the length of the small table, gesturing wildly with her free hand. "The first guy I have sex with in three years and he turns out to be certifiable." She shot a glance at him as she passed. "This is what I get for sleeping with someone I met two days ago. Guess that makes me nuts, too." She stopped and pointed a finger at him. "This is your fault, you know. I never do this, then you come along with that body and that smile and those fuck-me eyes."

His brows lifted at the uncharacteristic curse. "Megan, I am not crazy. It really is true. I am a shapeshifter and I turned into the cat that was in your apartment last night."

"Fine, prove it," she challenged, folding her arms.

He thought for a moment. "You wear a nightshirt to bed."

She shook her head. "Too easy. Besides the fact that half the population probably does, you could have seen that lying on the end of my bed." Skepticism was clear in her expression.

"You told me I 'better not have fleas' before you climbed into bed with me." Jack watched the battle in her eyes as she absorbed the fact that there was no way he could know that unless he had been there, but as he was rapidly learning, she was a true skeptic.

Anger darkened her eyes again as her mind provided the logical answer, "You spied on me! You were on the fire escape!"

Jack's thoughts immediately went to the night he *had* watched her from the fire escape and knew guilt was evident in his face before he could suppress it.

She spun around and started towards the kitchen. Briefly he considered using telepathy but quickly discarded the idea. She would only consider it to be another way he could have known what happened last night. It was bad enough she thought he had been physically spying on her, she would probably go up in flames when she discovered he could read her thoughts. He followed her and discovered her stumbling over the end of her makeshift robe as she retrieved his clothes from where they lay scattered around the floor. "I was not spying on you."

She ignored him, muttering under her breath, Scottish accent broadening with every angry step so that he caught only the occasional words. "Idiot... Dammit... Crazy..."

Jack strode over to her and tossed the cushion onto the kitchen table—it wasn't as if she hadn't seen everything he had anyway. Then he pulled her gently up by her shoulders to face him. He felt his clothes brush against his abdomen as she clutched them in between their bodies. "I know because I was here. What do I have to do to prove it to you?"

Megan's gaze met his and he knew he was not going to like what came next. "Show me." He released her and took a step back as she continued. "Change into the cat right here, right now, and I'll believe you."

He closed his eyes, acutely aware of his failure to complete the bonding. "I can't."

She thrust his clothes at him. "I didnae think so!"

He took them without protest and dressed as he spoke. "I don't control when the cat comes. There is no pattern to it." She watched him silently and he continued. "That's why I left in such a hurry the other night. The scratching was a sign that the change was coming."

She tilted her head. "Or it could just have been allergies." she said.

"Okay, so how do you explain a wild animal saving your life then coming to your apartment and spending the night on your bed?" he asked, frustrated.

"Well, obviously he was tame and well-trained."

He shook his head. "Will you at least give me time to prove it to you? I want to see you again, Megan. I need to see you." Jack followed as she started towards the door. He thought she looked a little less skeptical but that could just have been wishful thinking. They stood face to face once more by the front door and Jack couldn't resist tracing one finger down her flushed cheek. He could see her anger, hurt and confusion. Her voice was clipped as anger again won the battle.

"I'll think about it, but for now I want you to leave." She reached behind her and opened the door.

"All right, I'll go, but I won't wait around for you to call, Megan. I want you and I am going to have you." He stepped out the door, wincing as she slammed it shut behind him.

Megan slumped against the wall by the door, closed her eyes and let her head drop back with a thud as the anger began to slip away. *I really hope Mrs. Timms was out walking with George,* she thought with a sigh. *I will never hear the end of it if she saw Jack leaving. I can't even think about her reaction if she heard us shouting or...other things.* At the thought, her eyes flew open and her temper flared again as she pushed away from the wall and headed for the living room.

"What was he thinking? Does he think I am stupid?" Angrily she swept around the room gathering her discarded clothes and straightening the cushions on the couch. "Actually, I take that back. He doesn't think it, he knows it. I believed that poor example of an excuse, after all." When she tripped over the end of the throw again, she tossed it on the floor in front of the washing machine and continued her tidying frenzy naked. Thankfully she came to her senses just as she was contemplating dragging the vacuum cleaner out of the cupboard. "See what he's done to me?! I almost vacuumed!" Dragging her hands through her tangled hair, she caught her reflection in the mirror on the living room wall. She looked like some kind of fanatical nudist, her cheeks flushed and her curly hair like a bird's nest. *How come Julia Roberts' hair never looked like this after she spent all night rolling around with Richard Gere?*

"Okay, maybe I overreacted a bit," she said to her reflection, "After all, the man can't help it if he's got a few screws loose." Megan would be the first to admit that she could have a short temper, but it was not like her to blow up like that. She could only assume that her insomnia was catching up with her.

A long, hot bath followed by dinner restored her humor but also gave her too much time to think. When she found herself alternately fantasizing about Jack and watching the fire escape window for the cat, she knew she had to do something. Hands on hips she surveyed her empty flat, picked up the phone and did what women have no doubt been doing for centuries when having man troubles. She called on her best friend.

* * * * *

"All right, care to tell me exactly why I am going to work tomorrow with a hangover?" Jayne Davis was tall and slim with fair skin, fiery red hair and light green eyes that Megan admitted she was a little jealous of. She had come straight from work and was still wearing black trousers and the bright green shirt with the company logo in red on the pocket.

They had been friends since they had been three years old and their mothers had met on the beach. After a short disagreement when Jayne dumped a bucket of sand on Megan's lap, the toddlers had become inseparable. The car crash that had killed Megan's parents had also killed Jayne's mother. The two couples had decided to go out for the evening but Jayne's father had to work late and was going to meet them later. It was Megan's dad who had been driving the car when it skidded on ice and hit a railway bridge, killing him and the two women. Jayne's father had never forgiven himself for not being with them and had begun drinking. Four years ago he got drunk one last time and crashed his car into the same bridge and died.

Jayne had retreated from everyone but Megan. A gifted artist, she gave up her teaching post at the nearby university and took a job at a supermarket. No matter what Megan said to her, she no longer joked about "drawing her way around the world" as she had once. In fact, she rarely went out at all. When she wasn't at work or with Megan, she spent all her time reading.

Megan retrieved two wineglasses from the cupboard before turning to answer her friend. "I told you I needed to bitch about a man."

Jayne leaned against the counter and studied her. "Yes you did, what you did not tell me was which man." She tilted her head. "Nor did you tell me he made you cry. What happened and who is the guy?"

She had always been able to tell Jayne anything but, strangely, Megan found she was reluctant to tell her what exactly had happened. It was ridiculous but in the back of her mind was a little voice saying *what if...* "Did I tell you I was almost run over last night?" She knew it was a pathetic attempt at stalling. Jayne had known her too long to fall for it.

"No, you never mentioned that either and I would like to hear it, but first I want to hear about the man. Stop trying to change the subject."

Megan opened her mouth to tell her it was part of the subject before deciding to start at the beginning. Finally she said, "I met him at work." Guiltily, she glanced at the kitchen table and heat crept up her cheeks. Jayne's eyebrows lifted, she picked up the bottle of wine she had brought in one hand and the two wineglasses in the other and shepherded Megan into the living room. Megan turned on a CD and sat on one end of the couch while Jayne shoved the coffee table out of the way and sprawled on the floor, leaning her elbow on the other end.

"Tell me," she said, simply.

"I do not think I will ever be able to sit at your kitchen table to eat again!" They both looked towards the item of furniture in question then at each other and dissolved into laughter.

"You are just jealous," Megan stated as she reached for the half-full bottle of wine and filled both glasses.

"You bet I am. I swear to god, Meg, if you have found a real live shapeshifter, you will have to fight me for him. You'd probably win, too. It's been so long since I dated that I've forgotten how." Jayne lifted her wineglass and saluted her with it.

Megan shook her head, ignoring the dating comment. Jayne knew her feelings on the subject and this was not the time to fight about it again. Jayne could have her pick of men. It used to be a challenge to find a night when she wasn't out. "Come on, Jayne, this is not one of the paranormal romances you like to surround yourself with."

"Hey!" Jayne interrupted, "You read them too!"

"All right, okay, but this is real life and people do not turn into animals. Jack really seems to believe what he's saying and I just don't know what to do about it."

Jayne looked at her. "Has he hurt you?" Her eyes promised retribution at the mere thought.

"No. Well, not physically."

"Face it, he hasn't really hurt your feelings either. You're mostly angry at yourself for sleeping with a near stranger."

Megan considered that for a moment in silence before stating softly, "That's it, though…he doesn't feel like a stranger. I feel as if I know him. It's really bizarre, Jayne." She watched the knowing smile appear on her friend's face. "Not in a warm, fluffy way," she preempted. *Definitely too many romances.* "I'm not talking star-crossed lovers here. More like… Oh! I don't know but it does not feel like we just met."

Reading the message loud and clear, Jayne laughed quietly and changed the subject. "Do you think he is dangerous?"

"No. I don't know why I believe that, but I do."

"Well then, you have three choices. Never see him again, see him and put up with this little quirk in his personality…"

"Quirk!" Megan exclaimed.

"Yes, quirk, like you talking to yourself all the time."

"Everyone talks to themselves," Megan said defensively.

"Yes but not everyone has whole conversations," Jayne stated calmly.

"Okay, what's number three?"

Jayne took a sip of wine before meeting Megan's gaze. "Believe him."

Megan stared at Jayne for a moment while her words seemed to echo in her head. "What do you mean, 'believe him'?" she exclaimed.

Jayne moved to the couch beside her. "He could be telling you the truth."

"Jayne, if there were real shapeshifters, don't you think someone would have told the rest of the world by now?" Megan smiled and voiced her earlier thought, "You are clearly reading far too many of those books."

Jayne dipped the tip of her finger into her wine and ran it around the rim of her wineglass, drawing forth a clear tone. "I just want to believe in the magic. Meg, you're being given the chance to do that. Aren't you the one who is always complaining that nothing exciting ever happens to you?"

"Yes, but..." Megan broke off, shaking her head.

"He's offered to prove it to you, Megan. What are you going to do if he does?"

That was a question Megan was not ready to answer. She looked at her friend's serious expression and said flippantly, "Then I suppose I'd better buy a cat flap."

Jayne studied her briefly then accepted the subject change, her lips quirked. "From what you told me about last night... I think you already have one!" Both women laughed uproariously.

"Jayne! Oh God, that's disgusting!"

* * * * *

Frustrated, Jack paced the floor of his suite and tried to think what could possibly have gone wrong. *Megan had thrown him out!* This was not the reaction he had expected the first time he told someone that he was a shapeshifter. It was a secret he had never shared with anyone before and a tremendous risk, and now she wanted proof. Although it had always been part of his life, he had never really had to deal with the mating and transforming part of his heritage before. Up until now he had just been able to enjoy the benefits like his enhanced senses, speed and stamina. So far nothing was going as he had planned.

Megan filled his thoughts in a way that was unfamiliar to him and although he wanted to put his trust in her, he was still afraid of her reaction when she saw him change. She might be his Dearbh Ceangal but at the moment she just thought he was a lunatic. What would she think of him then? It really made no difference whether he told her now or later anyway because once they were mated, she couldn't help but find out. Maybe this would give her some time to get used to it. Then again, perhaps she would run as far and fast as she could and he would spend the rest of a very short life as a cat.

Jack suddenly wanted nothing more than to talk to his family. Unfortunately, his parents really were on vacation. Every year they retreated to their mountain cabin and it didn't have a phone—they relied on a friend in a nearby town for contact in an emergency. The cabin was one of his father's favorite places for that very reason. Head of a major computer software company, he enjoyed getting away from the ringing phones. Another reason he loved the cabin so much was that he could shift whenever he felt like it—as Jack had recently discovered for himself, it was not easy for a huge cat to go undetected in a town or city. He knew there was little his parents enjoyed more than running together in the surrounding woods.

Then there was his gregarious brother, Nick, who embraced his animal side. Nick had been one of the few people who understood his determination to find his true mate and Jack missed his support. He would never have gotten himself into this situation. Nick was more the kind to take what he wanted and answer questions later. Jack had always warned his younger brother that his approach would get him into trouble. *A year is too long to be out of contact with your family.* Nick had come here to

Scotland a year ago to bring some new computer software to Cameron Murray, a family friend. It could just as easily have been couriered but Nick, being Nick, had decided he would deliver it personally. He had joked that it was time someone prodded the reclusive Cam into leaving the house again and tried to badger the man into picking him up from the airport. Their friend had dug his heels in and refused, telling Nick that if he was so desperate to see Scotland he could rent a car and drive.

Nick had never arrived.

Jack pushed away the worry that tried to surface when he thought of his absent sibling. Nick was alive, he would feel it if he wasn't. Jack was going to pound him into the ground when he finally appeared. He shook his head and returned his thoughts to the present. He would give Megan until tomorrow, and after that she had better get used to his presence because he wasn't leaving her side until he could prove his case.

Chapter Five

Jack was surprised to find the blinds on Megan's windows were closed when he looked up at her apartment. He had the impression that she usually woke early. He had waited as long as he could stand before leaving the hotel, hoping to give her some time to cool down. He couldn't remember whether they had shared their dreams last night, but given his state of arousal this morning, he could only assume that they had. As he stood on the sidewalk, he became aware once more of the prickling feeling that told him he was being watched. It had happened a few times over the last couple of days and he wondered if he really did have a rival. *Paranoia…* Cautiously he glanced back at the windows above, assuring himself that all was clear, and headed into the building.

A few minutes later Jack was still standing outside her apartment door. He had knocked twice and received no answer. She was definitely there, he could feel her presence. It was possible that Megan was just ignoring him but there was no way he was leaving without making sure she was okay. Kneeling on the rough doormat, he called in her letterbox. "Megan, I know you're in there. Are you okay? Answer the door." Along the hall a neighbor's door opened a crack. "I'm not leaving until you open the door." Getting to his feet, he raised his hand to knock again, but the door flew open and Megan stood before him.

"What the hell are you doing?" she hissed.

"Hello to you, too." Jack replied wryly. He wasn't sure whether to laugh or hug her as the teddy bear on the front of her nightshirt suggested. Her curly hair was standing on end all over her head. She was pale as a ghost, had dark circles under bloodshot eyes and she was fuming. If the look on her face hadn't told him so, then her accent would have. He wondered fleetingly if she was aware that the more angry she was, the more Scottish she sounded. It probably wasn't the best time to ask.

"Can't I die in peace?" She glared at him. "Never mind...just come in," she said wearily and shuffled away, her knee-length bed socks falling to her ankles. "And don't slam the door!"

Jack followed her down the hall and found her perched on the couch in the dim living room with her head in her hands and her elbows resting on her knees. A rush of emotions filled him. They pushed out the brief flare of amusement and made him catch his breath at the intensity. He wanted to protect her, comfort and soothe her, then throw her onto the couch and take her. Instead he merely sat beside her. Her hair had tumbled forward to cover her face, leaving the nape of her neck bare and tempting him to press a kiss to the vulnerable skin. Taking his life in his hands, he asked carefully, "Hangover?"

She raised her head enough to glare at him. "What do you want, Jack?"

"I told you I would be back." He couldn't resist stroking a finger down her pale cheek. "Why don't you go take a shower and I'll make some coffee. I'll even try to find you some aspirin."

Megan stood resignedly and ran a hand through her hair. "All right, I have some questions for you anyway." He watched her walk her away, confused by her easy acceptance. She paused at the door and looked back at him. "Cupboard above the coffee machine."

"Huh?"

"The aspirin." The door closed behind her with a click.

Megan wiped off the steam and looked at her reflection in the bathroom mirror. "I cannot believe I answered the door looking like this." Her head was still splitting but at least the nausea was fading. She and Jayne had finished the bottle of wine between them and then moved on to her bottle of apricot brandy. Their serious conversation had dissolved into innuendo and laughter and it had been very late when Jayne caught a cab home.

Megan had stumbled to bed with the room revolving around her and thought about Jayne's words while she waited for sleep to claim her. In the end she had decided that if Jack showed up again it wouldn't do any harm to listen to what he had to say. She had also realized that there were a lot of questions she wanted to ask him, she just hadn't expected to be hungover when he appeared. Smiling, she stripped off her nightgown and socks and wondered how he would have reacted if he had known she had nothing on underneath. *Why can't I control my hormones around the man?* She stuck her hand into the shower to test the temperature and stepped under the hot water with a groan of pleasure.

When Megan walked into the kitchen a while later, her hair was still damp but she was a little more presentable in jeans with an oversize white shirt. Jack sat at the table with a cup of coffee. At the opposite place, buttered toast, hot coffee and two headache pills waited. She sighed and sat down. Neither of them spoke while she finished the toast and took the pills. Jack looked as good as ever. *Doesn't the man ever get messed up?* His well-worn jeans hugged his body and he had on another polo shirt, this one pale gray. Before she could ask, he got up to refill their cups, then sat back down and gave her his attention again. Megan sipped the coffee, wondering where to start.

"So tell me, Jack, how did you become a shapeshifter?"

He looked at her warily. "I didn't actually 'become' a shapeshifter. I was born one. My whole family are shapeshifters."

She tilted her head. "Do you all turn into different animals?"

"No, just cats, but not all the same type." Jack met her eyes, his expression grave.

"How did that happen? Are you all under a curse... Did one of your ancestors get on the bad side of a witch?" she said, playing along. "Oh! Are you from..." she glanced towards the ceiling, "...up there?"

Jack sighed and shook his head. "Honey, if you're not going to take it seriously, there is no point in doing this now."

"I'm sorry, Jack, but you have to admit this is a little hard to believe."

"I know and I'm living it. No, we are not aliens, we are as human as you are... We just have the ability to change shape. We actually come from Britain originally, although we were more common in Scotland. There are shapeshifters all over the world now." He paused a moment, his expression thoughtful. "How do you feel about psychics?"

Megan regarded him with suspicion wondering where this was leading. "Okay, I know that there are some con artists out there but I think there are some who are genuine."

"Psychics are people who have mental abilities they can't explain and you don't think they are aliens."

She couldn't argue with that but in her mind there was still a big difference between shapeshifters and fortune tellers. "If there were shapeshifters all over the world, I should have heard something by now. Unless you are all living in the back of beyond—which you're clearly not."

"You have, you just didn't know it. Haven't you ever seen stories in magazines or newspapers about sightings of big cats? The most well-known is probably the Beast of Bodmin Moor."

Yes she had, come to think of it. She had to admit, his arguments were very convincing. *Okay, so it's a well-researched psychosis.* "That was you guys? And I thought we just had really incompetent zoos," she said flippantly. "So how often do you transform? Is there something that triggers it?"

"I told you before, the change comes when it comes. There is no pattern to it."

"Then it can happen any time? That must be inconvenient, particularly when you were a child. Growing up is hard enough without worrying if you are going to turn into a cat in the middle of classes."

Jack watched her. She was getting too close to the things he didn't want to discuss yet. He would have to tread carefully. "We only shift once in puberty, it's triggered by all the hormonal changes in the body at that time. Regular shifting doesn't start until later in life."

"Really? Wow, and I thought I had hormone troubles to look forward to." She flashed him a quick smile. "When did you change the first time, as an adult I mean?"

"Very recently." Jack felt his cheeks and the tips of his ears grow warm, and lowered his head to stare into his mug of coffee. Embarrassing as it might be, it was easier to let her believe her assumption. He didn't want to lie to her any more than he already had, but until he had convinced her he was a shapeshifter, she would never believe she was his mate. He ignored the devil on his shoulder that urged him to just get it over with and tell her everything now. One world-changing revelation at a time was definitely the best way to go.

"I have to admit that I am *maybe* a little less skeptical, Jack, but my mind just doesn't want to accept this. I'm afraid seeing is believing."

He lifted his head and studied her face. He was relieved that she had let the subject of his first change go so easily, but she still didn't believe him. Letting his gaze caress her face, he said, "I am going to prove it to you, Megan, I just hope you are ready for it when I do. In the meantime, I will be staying very close to you."

Megan swallowed, her throat suddenly dry, and whispered, "How close?"

Jack stood and moved around the table to crouch between her knees, his voice deepened. "As close as I can get. You could even say I'm going to be a part of you." His hand lifted to sift through the hair at her temple. "You smell like strawberries today," he said softly. "You always smell so good."

Megan's heart fluttered at the hunger in his voice and her nipples peaked under her shirt as desire washed through her. She ran her fingers over his smooth cheek, drawing his attention back to her face. Their bodies were just inches apart, she could feel his warm, coffee-scented breath brush her lips and felt a trickle of moisture between her legs. Jack's nostrils flared and his pupils dilated and she somehow knew he could smell her arousal. When his hands clenched where they rested on his thighs but he made no move to touch her, she realized that this time it was up to her. The knowledge went through Megan's body like lightning. She fisted her hands in his hair and crushed her mouth to his, her heart pounding in her ears. When he opened his lips for her, she slipped her tongue inside to duel with his. His palms were warm under her shirt where they rested at the base of her spine.

"Yoo-hoo, Megandear!" The voice registered gradually in Megan's foggy brain followed by the tapping at the door. Jack groaned in frustration as she pulled away to rest her forehead on his. They were both breathless. Glancing down she saw Jack's cock pressing impatiently against his fly and her fingers itched with the need to touch it. Jack must have read the intention in her face for a strong tremor ran through his body. "Do not answer it," he growled.

"I have to, it's my neighbor. She probably knows I'm here."

Jack recalled the open door when he had stood in the hallway. "Make that definitely," he said, she looked at him and he shrugged. "She saw me in the hall."

This time it was Megan who groaned. "You have no idea what you have just done." She pushed Jack's shoulders causing him to lose his balance and land on his butt with a startled "Hey!" then stood and headed towards the door. "But you are about to find out." Jack sat on the floor for a moment trying to bring his aching body back under control before getting slowly

Cait Miller

to his feet and following his mate. He paused halfway down the hall when she opened the door.

"There you are, Megandear, I was beginning to get worried about you!" The elderly woman who stood before Megan was certainly...eye-catching. She wore a yellow and orange striped top with purple polka dot cycling shorts. On her feet were a pair of yellow flip-flops with two-inch soles and large sunflowers stuck onto the straps. Her wispy silver hair was floating around her shoulders and there was a large pair of spangly purple sunglasses on her face. He was sure he heard his jaw hit the floor. He looked on fascinated as Megan blushed becomingly.

"I'm sorry to have worried you, Mrs. Timms. I'm fine, I just didn't hear the door."

"George and I are going to the beach, Megandarling, and I was just wondering if you had a picnic hamper we could borrow. I seem to have misplaced mine."

"No I don't, I'm s—" Mrs. Timms didn't wait for the reply as her gaze shifted down the hall and landed on Jack. "Oh! This must be your young man!" Jack smiled and approached the two women, struggling not to laugh at the whole situation. "Mrs. Timms, this is Jack Douglass...a friend." Her blue eyes dared him to contradict her as he reached to shake her neighbor's hand.

"Nice to meet you, ma'am."

Mrs. Timms' hand fluttered to her chest. "Oh! You're an American, Mr. Douglass!"

"Yes, ma'am, and please call me Jack."

"How lovely! George and I had an American staying with us for a while during the war." She glanced at the empty hallway to her left. "Didn't we, dear?"

Puzzled, Jack looked at Megan who shook her head imperceptibly.

"He was such a nice young man, very good company. George didn't really spend much time with him, did you dear? He was always at work, he works for the government, you

237

know." She looked Jack up and down. "You Americans are all so...big." Jack heard Megan gasp and struggled not to laugh as Mrs. Timms continued brightly. "What are you doing in Scotland, Jack?"

He gave her the same answer he had given Megan. "I'm here on family business."

"Really? What business is your family in?"

"Computers. My father's company makes software. Mine makes the computers." He saw the surprise on Megan's face before Mrs. Timms spoke again.

"Oh! Do you know the Internet? I just love it, you can get such interesting pictures on there!"

Megan interrupted desperately, "Mrs. Timms, you had better go before the beach gets too busy."

"My, my! Yes, you are right! Let's go, Georgedear." She turned and took a few steps down the hall before stopping abruptly. "Oh Megandear! I almost forgot, I told Miss Appleton downstairs that I would ask if you had seen a stray dog around. She says she saw a big black dog on her fire escape!" she laughed. "I promised I would ask but it was probably her imagination. You know I think she is a little touched, poor dear..."

There was so much in that statement that Megan was clearly not sure what to react to first. Jack resolved to take more care in the future. "Ah, no... I definitely have not seen any dogs."

"All right, Megandarling, I'll see you later. You too, Jackdear. Cheerio!"

Megan shut the door and turned to face him. "Mrs. Timms is a little... Okay, who am I kidding? The woman is more than a few sandwiches short of a picnic."

"So I gathered," he chuckled. "Who's George?"

"I'll explain later." She looped her arms around his waist so that every inch of her body was touching him, bringing his body to full alert.

"Now, where were we?" she murmured.

He laughed softly and returned her embrace. "I believe we were about to take part in another one of those kitchen table sex scenes."

Blue eyes met silver. Megan smiled. "Maybe I should invest in a stronger table."

"Maybe you should. Do you think we will ever make it to bed?" In answer, she slipped her hand into his and led him down the hall to the bedroom.

Jack stopped just inside the door, folded his arms to prevent himself from reaching for her and leaned one hip negligently against the doorframe.

She stood at the foot of the bed, her eyes scorching him. "What are you doing, Jack? Come here." She reached her hand out to him, her voice husky with desire.

Jack shook his head, keeping his face impassive as his body ached to be inside her. This time he wanted to take her slowly. Make her scream his name. He knew she was wet for him, the scent of her desire tormented him. "Take your clothes off for me, Megan, I need to see you."

Surprise lit her eyes briefly but her hands were already moving towards the buttons of her shirt. She fixed her gaze to his face and unfastened it slowly from top to bottom. She lifted one shoulder then the other and let the white top slide down her arms to pool on the floor at her feet. Her hands lifted to cover her breasts coyly before sliding slowly down to the waistband of her jeans. The rasp of her zipper was loud in the silence of the room and in a moment she stood before him in a white lace bra and high-cut panties. Her hair spilled over her shoulders in stark contrast to her creamy skin. Berry-red nipples were peaking against the sheer, lacy cups, and he glimpsed the silken curls between her thighs.

"Touch me," she whispered.

Jack felt a bead of sweat roll slowly down his back when her tongue moistened her lips. This was his mate. No longer able to tolerate the distance between them, he crossed the room and walked slowly around her, caressing her with his eyes before pausing in front of her. But he didn't touch her. Not yet. "Take them off."

She raised a brow but said nothing. His hard-on throbbed insistently against the fly of his jeans as she obeyed him. "Lie on the bed."

Obediently she crawled onto the white duvet, her curvy ass swaying seductively, pausing to give him a heat-filled glance that told him she knew exactly what she was doing to him. She reclined against the soft pillows, one hand resting low on her belly, legs parted just enough to tease him. Reminding him of the night he had watched her pleasure herself.

As if she had read his thoughts her hand slipped down and she caressed herself gently, just barely touching her mound. His body surged with excitement. It took all his restraint to strip slowly when every nerve ending screamed at him to rip off his clothes and plunge into her. With hands that trembled, he sheathed his rigid erection in a condom and knelt between her thighs. Placing his hands on either side of her, he bent and kissed her with a slow carnality, thrusting his tongue into her mouth with deep leisurely strokes, a portent of what was to come.

Megan reached out for him and he stilled abruptly. "Ah, ah…hands off." He waited until she gripped the duvet, he didn't know if he could last if she touched him. When he raised his head he saw that her cheeks were flushed and her breathing had quickened. He lowered his head again this time to her breasts, drawing first one, then the other into his mouth, rolling her sensitive nipples between his lips before suckling them until she moaned with pleasure and began to move restlessly. He paused and lifted his head. "I've been meaning to ask you something…"

"Now!?" she demanded, incredulously.

Jack nuzzled the soft curve of her belly, ignoring her. "Why is it that your accent is so easy for me to understand?" He dipped his tongue in her navel and she gasped.

"Ah! I've, uh, worked in the restaurant for ten years."

"And?"

"We get a lot of tourists." She moaned as he traced the tips of his fingers along her sides. "I've-learned-to-slow-down-and-speak-clearly." Jack chuckled at the rush of words and slid further down her body.

"Jack." She whimpered in protest when he kissed his way towards his ultimate goal. She had stopped him from making her come this way before. "Not this time, honey... This time I intend to finish what I started." He brushed a kiss across the crown of her sex before running the tip of his tongue lightly along the seam of her labia from top to bottom and back. She moaned and tilted her hips as he parted her and swirled his way around her swollen clitoris, sucking gently on it. Her body trembled under his hands. The taste of her inflamed him, causing his own hips to buck against the bed in search of relief.

He grasped the smooth cheeks of her ass and raised her hips, pushing his tongue inside her, thrusting in and out in a sensual mimicry of what his body cried out for. Her hands gripped his head this time, holding him to her instead of pushing him away as she lost herself in the sensations. He felt her inner walls begin to spasm and clench around his tongue, her breath coming in gasps.

"Oh God, Jack!" Megan cried out, her head tossing on the pillows, body arching off the bed. He gripped her hips and held her in place as a rush of hot fluid filled his mouth and bathed his chin.

She collapsed back onto the mattress panting softly, her lashes dark against pink flushed cheeks. Jack thought he had never seen a more beautiful sight. He licked his lips clean as he trailed the length of his body up along the length of hers until his marble-hard penis rested against her damp heat. "Let me come inside you," he murmured and kissed her deeply, sucking her tongue into his mouth, letting her taste the salty sweetness of her own release.

It felt like every muscle in his body was drawn tight in anticipation. He could feel Megan's heart pounding hard within her chest as it rose and fell beneath his, his cock pulsed with the rapid beat of his own heart. Slumberous blue eyes locked with hungry silver while he slowly penetrated her and sweat beaded on his brow as he resisted the urge to take his own pleasure quickly. Megan wrapped her legs around his hips and gripped his shoulders, pressing her face to his neck and breathing deeply of his scent.

She nipped his earlobe and whispered, "Please...please...."

Blood rushed in his ears, all of his senses focused on the hot clasp of her body around his cock as he moved. He felt the tension in her as he built her up towards the peak once more, muscles tightening, hips rising off the bed to meet his. Her nails dug into his back, panting breaths becoming desperate moans with every thrust.

He felt her come, her body clenching tightly around him as she threw back her head and screamed. Tremors shook him and sweat rolled down his back, his own release approaching with the speed and power of a freight train. His buttocks and thighs grew taut with need. With an animalistic growl, he gave in to his body's demands, pistoning his hips faster and harder until he followed her in a burst of heat and light.

Chapter Six

Megan lay in Jack's embrace, her head resting on his chest watching the afternoon light filter through her bedroom window and listening to the slow beat of his heart. Heat radiated from his body and his chest rose and fell silently. He was fast asleep, unfortunately, Megan couldn't say the same. She could not believe she had given in to the desire between them again—for someone who was usually very cautious about sex, she didn't seem to have any trouble throwing herself at Jack. Their discussion earlier had made one thing clear to her, that he believed absolutely in his story and he was not going to go away until he had her convinced, too.

That was another thing...why was he so desperate to make her believe? After all, they had only met a few days ago, they didn't have what you could call a relationship and yet he was determined to tell her this secret. She had a feeling there was something else he wasn't telling her, but what could be worse than being a part-time cat? It gave her a headache to think about it. In the meantime, her independent streak was emerging again, now that her thoughts weren't clouded by lust.

Megan didn't like to be forced into anything, she had been taking care of herself for a long time and if Jack thought he could force himself into her life he was very much mistaken. Time to pull herself together and try to beat this...irrational attraction, it was frightening the way it always seemed to push everything else out of her head.

She needed her own space and it didn't look like he was going to give it to her. With that in mind, she eased herself out of his arms, freezing when he stirred, only daring to breathe when he settled onto his stomach. Silently she crept from the room.

In the kitchen she dressed quickly in wrinkled clothes from the clean laundry basket, glad for once that she had shoved it in the cupboard until she could be bothered to sort everything. She glanced longingly at the fresh hot coffee in the pot then pulled a plastic grocery bag from the recycle drawer, wincing at the noise, and filled it with clothes as well. Amazed she had gotten this far without Jack hearing her, she retrieved her shoes and bag from the living room and wrote a quick note on the message pad on the coffee table.

When she glanced into the bedroom on her way down the hall, she saw that Jack was stirring restlessly and had thrown the covers off. He was gloriously naked, the soft white of the sheets emphasizing his rich gold skin and midnight black hair. His cock nestled between his thighs, almost as impressive flaccid as it was erect. There was a dull flush of red along his cheekbones and as she watched he grimaced as if in the grip of a nightmare. Second thoughts assailed her but she pushed them ruthlessly aside and turned away—it was only for a few days. At the end of the hall, she took the door key from the hook on the wall and let herself out of the flat closing the door gently behind her.

Jack woke abruptly, confused for a moment by his surroundings, knowing something had disturbed him but not sure exactly what. He glanced around the room and memory returned in a rush. *Megan.* He glanced at the bed beside him, finding it empty. There was no sound from the bathroom and he felt her presence nearby so he assumed she must be in the living room, probably drinking the coffee he could smell. Although why she would want to drink coffee when the apartment was so damn hot was beyond him. He swiped at the bead of sweat that trickled down his jawline. His thoughts trailed to a halt as he finally took stock of his body to find that it wasn't the apartment that was hot—the sheets he lay on were cool on his skin—it was him.

Jack sat up and a tremor of apprehension washed over him. This was it, Megan was about to find out that he was telling the truth. Still, he didn't move and he was disgusted at himself for his weakness until finally the onset of the itching in his skin spurred him on. As he headed for the front room he realized that it wasn't just the bathroom that was silent, it was the whole apartment—the living room and kitchen were both empty when he entered them. The paper on the table caught his attention and he stopped his search to scan it.

Jack,

Had to go away for a few days, need some space to think. The door will lock again when you close it behind you. I'll give you a call at the hotel when I get back.

Megan

Scratching furiously now, he reached for the link with his mate only to feel her presence in his mind rapidly become fainter. He knew then that it had been the sound of the front door that had awakened him. He raced to the window and saw her car pulling away from the front of the building. *She was leaving!* Anger bubbled through him. If Megan thought he was going to sit around and wait for her to get in touch, she was very much mistaken. Heedless of his nudity and the ache of his joints he started for the front door, thinking only of catching up with her. He made it as far as the hall before the change swept through him. The pain of it doubled him over and forced him to the floor, the snarl that escaped his throat more feline than human.

When it was over he lay on his side panting, his tail twitching with agitation. *Why now?* He rolled fluidly to his paws and stalked to the door. There would be no exit through there. He glared at the small round doorknob with a heat that should have melted the metal. In his present form there was no way he would be able to turn it to open the door—his paws were too big and he wouldn't be able to grip the smooth metal with his teeth either. Besides even if he did manage to turn it, as high as it was he'd have to lean his front paws against the door to reach it, meaning he would not be able to pull the door open.

Growling in frustration he prowled through the rooms checking the bedroom window and the living room windows to find they too were shut tight. He began to pace up and down in front of the window as he fought the cat's desire to break out of its confinement and go after his mate. There was absolutely no doubt in his mind that Megan would not appreciate him smashing her window. It would attract too much attention anyway, so he put it to the back of his mind as a last resort. Anger surfaced as he acknowledged he was trapped in the apartment until he changed back, and he had no idea how long that would be.

* * * * *

Two hours. Two damn hours he had prowled Megan's apartment while the frustration and anger of the cat had pummeled him until he had thought he'd go mad. They mingled with and heightened his own irritation making it difficult to fight against his animal instincts. So he found himself slipping into its behaviorisms again and again. He had to complete the bond with Megan soon, before he lost himself completely.

The rain that now soaked his clothes as he stood outside the apartment had started an hour ago and had almost been the final straw. It obliterated any scent trail he might have followed. All he could do was check places she might have gone, starting with the most likely—her closest friend. As the rain began to trickle down his neck he pulled out his compact cell phone and called a cab. Jayne Davis lived on the other side of town and he was in no mood for any further delays.

Within half an hour he was standing in front of another small apartment building. Satisfaction and relief filled him along with the knowledge that she was here, that she couldn't hide from him. *Not that she knows that*, he thought with a twinge of guilt. The rain was heavier now, storm clouds bringing darkness early and cooling the August day so that he shivered slightly. He ignored it though and stood in the deserted street as his mind and senses were filled with her, causing his cock to harden with anticipation.

He never even saw the attack coming.

There was a moment of hot burning pain in his left side before the two men wearing woolen masks pinned him against the wall. One held a switchblade in front of his face while the other tried to pull his wallet from his pocket. They said nothing, but when he looked into the cold eyes of the one with the knife he knew that they meant to kill him. They were both as tall as he was and thickly muscled, and had he not been what he was they could have held him easily. With a growl of rage, Jack twisted his wrists from their grip, causing both men to stumble back with gasps of surprise. Low snarls rumbled in his chest as he took a step towards them. The two exchanged a terror-filled glance at the inhuman noise and fled. As Jack started to follow, fiery pain spread through his abdomen and he sank onto the wet pavement.

For an instant he thought he was going to change again. Then he saw the spreading stain on his pale shirt and realized it wasn't just rainwater he could feel trickling down his side, soaking the waistband of his jeans. He touched his fingertips to the wet fabric, gleaming black in the orange streetlights.

Blood.

He needed to move, he couldn't just sit here in the street waiting for his attackers to come back. Worse, a passerby might come along and call an ambulance and there was no way he could be admitted to hospital. Besides the fact that his body healed abnormally quickly, there was just too much danger of him shapeshifting. Grimly he struggled to his feet, gritting his teeth against the pain as he clutched his side and made his way into the building.

By the time he had climbed the two flights of stairs that led to Miss Davis' apartment he was pale, sweating and exhausted. He knocked on the door then leaned against the wall beside it, fighting the desire to slide down it to rest on the floor. *It's just a flesh wound, Jack. If this was the movies you would have chased down the bad guys then run up those stairs.* His lips quirked in grim humor at the thought. He heard the lock turn and he pushed off the wall to face the door as it opened.

How did he find me? He heard the startled exclamation and saw the surprise on Megan's face, before she started to slam it closed again. Moving more quickly than was wise, he stepped forward to block it. Agony shot through him and his vision grayed around the edges. He moaned as he crumpled to the floor thinking ruefully that he seemed to be spending far too much time on the ground lately.

"Oh God, Jack, you're bleeding! What happened?"

His side throbbed with the beat of his heart and he could feel the warm trickle of blood on his chilled skin. He looked at Megan's shocked face as she knelt beside him and lifted his stained shirt. *Wonder what she would say if I asked her to do the blood exchange now? After all, why waste it?* Jack dismissed his idiotic musings and raised his head enough to look at his side. The wound was low on the left side of his abdomen just below his ribs, thin and about two inches long. Dark red blood seeped from it steadily, dripping down his side and onto the polished wood flooring. He picked up Megan's thoughts easily as she realized that it was a knife wound.

"I had a little argument with a couple of guys downstairs. They thought they should have my wallet and I disagreed," he said wryly. He had his suspicions about the incident but he wasn't ready to share them yet. If he had the energy he would have kicked himself for not paying attention to his surroundings. So much for his enhanced senses.

She pulled a drying white T-shirt from the radiator on the wall behind her with trembling hands and pressed it firmly to the cut. Jack gritted his teeth against the hiss of pain that wanted to escape. "I need you to hold this in place while I call the police and an ambulance."

He gripped her hand. "No. No police and definitely no hospital."

She met his gaze. "What? Jack, you were mugged. You are bleeding all over Jayne's floor!"

He tightened his grip. "Please, Megan. I told you what I am, I heal quickly. The guys will be long gone by now, so what good will calling the police do? I'll be fine, it's not as bad as it looks." Grimacing, he sat up and took the makeshift bandage from her. "Look, the bleeding's already slowed down." Megan studied him for a moment, concern and reluctance evident on her face, but she couldn't force him to go to the hospital.

Even in his present condition his body started to respond to her presence. It was ridiculous, wearing a pair of wrinkled gray sweatpants and an equally crumpled sweater, she wasn't exactly dressed to impress. The baggy clothes hid all of the enticing curves he knew she possessed. His mouth almost watered in anticipation of discovering them again. His fingers itched to pull the band from her hair and run his fingers through the riotous curls.

Oblivious to his wayward desires, Megan's business-like tone brought him back to earth with a bump. "Come on, let's at least get you out of this doorway before one of the neighbors see us. If you won't go to hospital, I want you here where I can make sure you are okay." She helped him to his feet.

In the living room Megan covered Jayne's couch with a few towels before handing him another. "Get out of those wet clothes and lie down," she ordered. Jack arched one black brow at her but wisely said nothing. Heat rushed to her face but she ignored it. After all the man was injured, she shouldn't be thinking about sex. Anyway, it wasn't as if she'd never seen him naked before. Hell, she had run her lips and tongue over most of that body just a few hours ago. When he eased out of his shirt she was relieved to see that the bleeding was definitely slowing. Her brow creased in puzzlement, in fact, the cut didn't look as bad as she had first thought. It still needed to be stitched, though. "Please, lie down. I'll get the first aid kit." Taking his wet clothes from him, she fled to the kitchen.

When she returned a few moments later, Jack's lean, sleekly muscled body was sprawled on the couch. He was still pressing the T-shirt to his side and had draped a towel across his hips hiding his burgeoning erection. *I am not disappointed,* Megan told herself firmly as she knelt on the floor beside him, but part of her hungered for that cock.

His short, coal-black hair had been soaked, but he had obviously dried it with one of the towels since the damp strands stuck up in spikes. It should have looked comical but instead it only added to the air of wildness that clung to him. This time when he peeled the T-shirt away she could see the bleeding had almost stopped and had begun to clot, sealing the cut. Jack said nothing when she started to gently clean the wound and his skin, but she could see the muscles in his jaw tighten and knew he was gritting his teeth against the sting of the antiseptic. "I can't believe this has happened, Jack. I mean, this isn't paradise, there are occasional bag snatches but I have never heard of anyone being assaulted with a weapon during a robbery. Especially not in this part of town… This is a good area."

"There's a first time for everything," he replied, his voice betraying none of what he might be feeling.

Finished cleaning the cut, she applied some butterfly strips to close the edges. Blood still oozed slightly from it but it wasn't actively bleeding anymore. Jack had been telling the truth when he said he healed quickly. The implications of that made her slightly uneasy. "I suppose so… I still think we should call the police and report this. I know they won't be able to do much for you but they should know in case these men go after someone else." He didn't answer and she sighed in frustration and looked at him. "Jack." His molten eyes pinned her for endless seconds before he finally spoke. "No."

A trickle of sweat rolled down his impassive face, catching her attention. She followed its path down to his hair-dusted chest and frowned as it was followed a wave of goose bumps.

"Are you all right, Jack?" When she looked at his face again, it was a little flushed and his gaze seemed to be focused inward. "Jack?" *I knew I should've just called an ambulance… God, what if he's got internal injuries…*

She started to get to her feet, gasping in surprise when Jack's hand shot out and grabbed her wrist. A shiver ran down her spine when she noticed he was scratching his neck and chest with his other hand. His words of the other day echoed in her head. *"The scratching was a sign that the change was coming…"*

"You are about to get your proof, Megan." His low voice startled her and she dragged her eyes back to his face. He released her wrist and Megan backed away a couple of steps while he climbed slowly to his feet, shedding the towel to stand naked before her.

"He's offered to prove it to you, Megan. What are you going to do if he does?" "Shut up, Jayne," she whispered under her breath. He was shivering now, and his chest rose and fell as his breathing sped up and he pressed his hands to his stomach and hunched over.

"Jack, talk to me, tell me what's happening. You're scaring me a little here."

His skin seemed to ripple and darken and as thick black fur pushed through his pores, he spoke to her through gritted teeth. "Please, don't be afraid, Megan. I won't hurt you." His voice was guttural, almost unrecognizable, his eyes glowed with an inner fire and intensity and he reached out to her with a clawed hand.

Megan let out a startled shriek and clapped a trembling hand to her mouth. Frozen to the spot, she couldn't have moved even had she wanted to, her chest rose and fell rapidly with shallow panicked breaths. Fascinated and horrified, she watched his fur-covered ears change shape and move towards the top of his head. Jack groaned as his face and jaw thrust forward to accommodate razor-sharp teeth and she saw a tail curl itself around him. The groan changed to a low rumbling growl as the transformation swept down the length of his body. His entire frame was reshaping itself so brutally she expected to hear the bones snapping but the only sounds were Jack's panting breaths and growls of pain.

Her heart tried to beat its way out of her chest as finally he fell forward onto all fours, feline head bowed low and his chest heaving. Megan dropped to her knees like a puppet with its strings cut. Standing before her was the huge cat that had spent the night in her apartment, just as Jack had tried to tell her. His hair was the same midnight black as Jack's and he looked at her with Jack's quicksilver eyes.

Holy crap! She rubbed her hands over her face.

"Oh my God! Jack?" She whispered tremulously, "Is that you?" The cat—*Jack*—raised his head and...nodded!

"Oh my God! I can't believe I just...you just..." Reassured by the very human response, she crawled over to him on hands and knees and lifted a trembling hand to stroke his jaw.

"That was amazing and, and...terrifying, but..." She looked into his eyes. "I'm sorry I didn't believe you, Jack."

He rubbed his face against her palm. The gesture was so feline Megan's lips twitched into a reluctant smile. "Are you okay? It looked so painful." Suddenly she remembered his knife wound and ran her fingers down his side until she found the butterfly strips caught in his fur. She found the cut nearby and discovered though her fingertips came away spotted with blood, the cut was about half the size it had been. She raised her eyebrows in surprise when Jack nudged her out of the way to lick the wound clean. He obviously still understood her but twice now he had behaved like a cat... The ringing of Jayne's phone shattered the uneasy silence and interrupted her thoughts. Jack's body tensed at the noise, ears twitching he stared at the phone. Rising slowly, she answered it. When she glanced back, he had returned to his task.

Chapter Seven

Megan's phone conversation was only background noise as Jack struggled with the fact that he had actually shifted in front of his mate and she hadn't run screaming from him. After all the time he had spent agonizing over it, the reality was hard to accept. She had been afraid, certainly, but had trusted him enough to believe he would not do her any harm. The knowledge made his heart clench and sent a rush of warmth through his veins.

The crash as Megan slammed down the phone interrupted his thoughts and brought his head up. He realized with a shiver that the cat had taken over and had been busily tending its wound while he had been preoccupied. "That was Jayne calling from her cell phone. She'll be home soon…we have to get this mess cleaned up. She will flip when she sees her favorite T-shirt. I have to hide it!"

Jack cocked his head and watched her silently as she raced around the living room lifting the shirt, towels and first aid supplies. *I knew it had been too easy*, he thought wryly. She headed for the kitchen and he padded after her quietly, just in time to see her closing the door of the washing machine. He gave brief consideration to the fact that his clothes must be in there too, so he would have nothing to wear when he shifted back. She turned from the washing machine, her hand flying to her heart when she saw that he was standing behind her.

"You have to leave!" She was right. However reluctant he was, he couldn't let her friend see him like this. He felt the cat's determination to stay with her but before he even thought to fight it back she changed her mind. "No! You can't, there's only one way out of this apartment. She'll see you! You have to hide!" He watched from the living room doorway as she took some cloths to the hall and cleaned up the blood from the floor before throwing those in the wash too. Her thoughts were muddled and confused but he knew that she felt guilty about something.

He doesn't need to know.

Okay, that was annoying. What good was the ability to read someone's thoughts if what you heard was so often only bits and pieces? Megan passed him again this time going from the hall into what he assumed was a bedroom.

"Come on, Jack!"

Tail twitching and eyes narrowed, he followed her, making a mental note to ask her later just what it was that he didn't need to know — unless he picked it up before then.

One step into the room and Jack froze. He hadn't taken much notice of Jayne's apartment so far other than to note that it was larger than Megan's and that the furniture was new rather than used as his mate's seemed to be. He couldn't help but notice this room, however. The cream-colored walls were lined with bookcases, most of which were filled with books. In the corner by the window was a plump two-seater sofa, a tall lamp was lit behind it and a small table stood beside it. Perfect for spending hours absorbed in a book.

Megan stood at the wall opposite the sofa, by the open door of a walk-in closet. It contained only a few boxes and some spare bedding and pillows high up on some shelves, nothing hung on the rails under them and the carpeted floor was clear. It took a moment for the implications of that open door to sink in — she expected him to hide in there! The cat snarled at her, with the natural resistance to captivity of any wild creature. Jack was aware that he had very little choice. He could not leave the apartment, not without letting Jayne — or worse, one of her neighbors — see him in his feline form. The decision was made for him when he heard the rattle of keys at the front door. He stalked reluctantly into the closet and Megan closed the door behind him. There was just enough room for him to turn around or stretch out on the floor.

Although it was dark, the small amount of light which seeped under the door and the exceptional night vision of the cat allowed him to see quite clearly. Not that there was anything to see. The cat was not happy and Jack knew it was going to take a lot of energy to keep it contained and quiet. The change last time had only lasted a couple of hours and he hoped that would be the case this time, too.

The slight ache in his side reminded him of his wound and he shifted to ease it. The attack bothered him. It didn't seem like a random mugging. In his distracted state, they could easily have stolen his wallet and run before he could react. Sure he would have caught them easily, but they couldn't know that. Megan's comments about the unlikelihood of it happening only confirmed his suspicions. Those men had meant to kill him, but what he didn't know was why.

He cast his mind back to the events of the last few days and his anger rose as he remembered his sense that someone was watching them and then recalled the hit and run. The near-miss still had the power to scare him. At the time he had dismissed it as an accident, but what if it hadn't been? Rage, dark and ugly, filled him when he considered the possibility that someone could be trying to hurt his mate. While it wasn't impossible that something had been missed, his investigation of Megan had not revealed any enemies. It was more likely to be his fault. He had made his share of enemies in the past and what better way to get to him than to hurt someone he cared about? The only problem with that theory was that his enemies were more likely to try to kill his business than a person. Besides, why target Megan? They couldn't know how important she was to him. As far as anyone else knew, she was only a waitress he had just met.

Once back in his human form he was going to have to do some poking around, try to find out who could be after them and why. In the meantime, he would stick close to Megan and be vigilant. She was his and no one was going to take her from him.

He felt the cat's restlessness rise again, it growled softly and he shifted his focus back to the present. He was aware of

Megan's chaotic thoughts and the muffled voices of the two women as they moved about the apartment. He listened intently to both to assure himself that all was well.

"Did you hear something?"

Megan jumped, nearly slicing her finger instead of the chicken breast. She looked at her friend and smiled. "Just my stomach."

Laughing, Jayne resumed chopping up the mixed vegetables. "Tell me about it, I didn't get time for lunch today and breakfast seems like a long time ago."

Megan tossed the poultry into the pan, grimacing at the cold slimy feel of it, and turned to wash her hands. She was just relieved to have avoided another one of the suspicious looks Jayne had been sending her way. She never could lie to her, her friend knew her far too well. She was having a difficult time keeping her mind on their conversation. All she could think about was the fact that Jack was an honest-to-goodness real-life shapeshifter. That, and the fact that he was, at this moment, hiding in Jayne's walk-in closet. She was bursting to tell her friend but she knew Jack wouldn't be happy. In fact he was not going to like it when he found out that she had already confided in Jayne.

Wouldn't like it... She shook her head ruefully. Furious is what he'd be. That was not really something she wanted to witness. Normally she was confident in her ability to handle men, but then there wasn't usually the danger of being eaten during the argument. If Jayne saw the cat she would know that it was him, at the moment she still thought he might be crazy and that was bad enough. Maybe once Jack got to know her... Well anyway, it wasn't her secret to tell and she felt guilty enough as it was. Instead she asked, "Tough day?"

"Oh, no worse than usual." Jayne added the vegetables and turned on the cooker. "What about you? You are awfully damn jumpy for a woman who spent all morning making love." She wiggled her eyebrows at Megan and turned back to the cooker.

"I still think you're nuts for wanting to spend the night on my sofa bed instead of naked with a hot guy."

Megan began setting the table, breathing in the aroma of spices and cooking stir-fry appreciatively. "It seemed like a good idea at the time." *I wonder how good Jack's hearing is…* "I needed to think and I can't seem to do that around him. It scares me how I can't seem to control myself around him." Jayne put the two plates on the table and while Megan poured two glasses of water, she thought of Jack cooped up in the cupboard. *Maybe I should take him a saucer of milk.* She chuckled and looked up to see Jayne giving her that suspicious look again. Time to change the subject. Knowing that it would be enough to start Jayne off, she said, "So, I take it you're still having trouble with your boss?"

The manager of the store where Jayne worked was a chauvinistic pig who thought he was irresistible to women everywhere. Needless to say, he and Jayne had been butting heads from the beginning. He went out of his way to make Jayne's life a misery. The conversation lasted the rest of the meal allowing Megan to relax a little.

They were cleaning up when Megan's calm was shattered by a loud thump from the direction of the spare room. Jayne's startled gaze flew towards the door before she sent a narrow-eyed look of inquiry to Megan and went to investigate. Heart in her throat, Megan followed.

Jayne headed straight for the cupboard door and quickly opened it. The breath Megan hadn't realized she was holding whooshed out when she saw Jack sitting on the floor with Jayne's spare duvet tucked under his arms. There was a sheen of sweat on his face and on the powerful shoulders that rose and fell as he visibly tried to calm his breathing. She read relief and embarrassment in his eyes.

"Hi." Jayne said brightly, "You must be Jack."

Jack looked at the two women standing in the open door as he struggled to his feet. The tall, slim redhead regarded him with curiosity and humor. She felt…familiar to him in some indefinable way. He dismissed the vague feeling. It was probably Megan's awareness he was feeling. Her green eyes drifted over his face and the breadth of his shoulders making him grateful for the duvet that he had managed to pull from the shelf earlier. "And you would be Jayne." He cleared the hoarseness from his throat. His body felt heavy and clumsy and exhaustion descended on him as he walked wearily into the center of the room. He hadn't eaten since this morning and two changes and the loss of blood were taking their toll on him.

His mate, who had been uncharacteristically silent until now, hurried into an explanation. "Jack was...that is...we..."

Jayne looked from Megan's flushed face to him with laughing eyes. "I think I can guess what you were up to." She ignored Megan's half-hearted protest. "I would be too if he were mine."

"I got soaked on the way over here and Megan offered to take care of my clothes."

Jayne gave them a reproachful look. "And you were hiding in the cupboard because...?"

"Well...after all the fuss I made this morning, I didn't want you to know I'd given in so easily to him. So I asked him to hide until I could sneak him out."

Jack wanted to shake his head at Megan's weak excuse but he couldn't think of anything better himself. He watched both disbelief then suspicion cross Jayne's pretty face. "You are my best friend, Megan, so I'll let that go—for now. You must be hungry, Jack. There is some chicken left if you like. I'll leave you two lovebirds alone. I believe I hear a book calling my name."

The door closed behind her and they stared at each other in silence for several uncomfortable seconds. Jack approached Megan warily, cupping her chin in his hand. "Thank you." She frowned hard at him, brows drawing together in puzzlement. He still couldn't believe she was standing here with him, chose to stand here with him, knowing what he was.

"Thank you for trusting me. For lying to your friend. Thank you." Leaning forward he kissed her lips, demanding nothing in return. Her eyes drifted closed as he drew back, she shivered and he felt the soft puff of breath on his lips when she sighed softly. Jack's body stirred in response. To his surprise she rose on her tiptoes and pressed her lips to his once more. The kiss was deep and hot and wet as they explored each other's mouths. Heat surrounded them and he groaned low in his throat. Megan stilled instantly and broke away. Fingers pressed to her lips she gasped for breath. "Why don't you go take a shower, Jack, and I'll wait for you in the kitchen." She whirled away from him, leaving him hard and aching for her.

Why had she stopped? He stared sightlessly at his reflection in the dark window. The annoyingly weak part of him whispered that it was because she had suddenly come to her senses and realized what she was kissing. It hadn't been fear he had read in her eyes though, it had been determination. Mystified, Jack added yet another question to the list he had to ask her later.

Never in his life had he been as off-balance and confused, he had always been confident in himself and his abilities. Hell, he had worked his way to the top of his father's company on his own merits and now ran his own multinational company. He was grateful for the way he had been raised to believe he could accomplish anything he wanted. Aside from the fact that he was from a family of shapeshifters, his childhood had been disgustingly normal, maybe too normal. His parents still lived in the same house in the suburbs that he had grown up in—far enough from the city to be peaceful while still close enough for his dad to commute daily. They had money so he had wanted for nothing but there had been no cooks, cleaners or nannies. His mom had stayed home with him and Nick until they were at school then gone to work part-time in an antique store.

Though open about their heritage and what it would ultimately mean for their sons, his parents had tried to give them as normal a childhood as possible. As a result he knew he wasn't as accepting of his heritage as he could be and now he was beginning to realize just how unprepared it had left him. He could almost hear Nick's voice saying "I told you so". Where Jack had been happy to accept what his father taught them, his brother had actively sought out other shifters to find out as much as he could. Nick would no doubt find his self-assured, focused older brother's present situation highly amusing. Wearily Jack turned from the window and went in search of the shower.

Megan paced the kitchen floor restlessly. What was it about Jack that she couldn't seem to resist? One kiss and she had practically jumped on the man. Even now she was aware of parts of her body that she wasn't normally conscious of. Her nipples were peaked under the soft fabric of her T-shirt and bra. Her clitoris pulsed with every beat of her heart. She had already washed the few dishes that she and Jayne had used and put Jack's clothes in the dryer—she was running out of distractions. Down the hall the shower started and her imagination immediately provided her with an image of Jack naked. Hot water coursing over his golden skin and down his muscular torso, following the trail of dark hair over his flat stomach to... *Aaargh! No! No! No!* With a curse she turned on her heel to resume pacing and caught sight of the kitchen waste bin. It needed to be emptied, it wasn't her favorite job but it would definitely take her mind off of Jack. What could be less sexy than emptying a bin?

Pleased with her restraint but mind nevertheless still filled with fantasies about her naked shapeshifter, she carried the bag of rubbish down through the quiet building. The back of the flats—where the dumpster for the residents rubbish sat—was usually lit by a floodlight above the back door. The door had swung shut behind her before she noticed that the light was out. The night air was cool and damp from the earlier storm, and a few gardens away she could hear a dog barking furiously.

Feeling a bit like a character in a horror movie, she stood in the patch of yellow light that shone through the window in the door and stared into the inky blackness. She knew that the dumpster was only about twenty-feet away, she could just make out the outline of it as her eyes began to adjust. The hair rose on the back of her neck, reminding her that the characters who went off into the dark alone in horrors usually got killed first. *It's a good thing this isn't a horror movie then, isn't it?* Megan thought, with uneasy amusement. She weighed the bag of rubbish in her hand, took a slow breath to calm her jittery nerves and walked quickly to the large rubbish container. In one movement she tossed the bag into the top, turned, and dashed back towards the door.

About halfway across the yard she began to feel ridiculous and forced herself to slow to a walk despite the frantic racing of her heart. She reached for the handle of the door and a callused palm suddenly closed over her mouth, hauling her against a large, hard body. Her scream of fright was muffled as he swung around so that his back was to the wall by the door and she was facing the darkness. She began to struggle, kicking at his shins with her heels and thrusting her elbows back towards his stomach, trying to break the bruising grip he had on her mouth. Something sharp pricked the skin of her throat. A knife. Her eyes widened in fear and she tried again to shout.

"Be still!" he whispered harshly, and there was a sharp sting as he pressed the blade more firmly to her neck. Breathless from her exertions, Megan froze. She thought of Jack bleeding on Jayne's floor just a few hours ago, it seemed she might be next. She fought back her rising panic locking the knees that threatened to buckle under her. *This neighborhood is really going downhill.*

The man behind her sniggered nastily in her ear, "Ah telt him it was worth watching the back door as well as the front." The stubble of his jaw prickled against her cheek and the sour stench of old sweat and tobacco clung to him. "Where is your friend? Ah could'a swore ah got him but unless you've got his body hidden in there somewhere ah must'a missed." It took several seconds for the meaning of his words to become clear to her, this was one of the men who had mugged Jack. *They know who I am and they must have been watching the flat all evening. Why?*

"Ah bet you if we just wait here for a wee while he'll be right down. Then ah can kill twa birds with wan stane." He was right. Any moment now Jack would get out of the shower, find her missing and come looking for her. At the thought of Jack being hurt again by this man, anger swept through her, clearing the fog of fear from her brain. "You are a feisty wee bitch though…maybe we could have a bit of fun. Efter ah take care of your man."

Megan began looking for ways she could stop this, or at least warn Jack. Obligingly her brain supplied the image of her letting herself go suddenly limp, breaking her captor's hold. Unfortunately the knife pressed firmly against her throat dampened her enthusiasm for that move. From the corner of her eye she saw the door open a tiny crack and she knew time had just run out.

Jack was here.

Chapter Eight

Megan tensed, waiting for the big brute to see the opening door but there was no reaction. He hadn't noticed. She knew that Jack would need some kind of diversion otherwise he would never get out unseen. Taking a breath she closed her eyes and leaned back into the unwashed stink of the man's body. The hard ridge of his erection rested just above her buttocks, and pushing back revulsion, she rubbed herself against him and moaned low in her throat.

"Aye, ah knew you'd be hot for it. Like a bit of rough, dae ye?" His whisper was warm and moist in her ear. It made her shiver in disgust. The knife slid slowly down her neck towards her breast. *Now or never. Think heavy.* Keeping her eyes shut tight she let herself drop to the concrete and rolled away on her side.

Behind her she heard a bang as the door hit the wall. Almost simultaneously there was a sickening crack and a high-pitched shriek that chilled her blood. By the time she looked back to the scene, Jack had her captor pinned against the wall by the throat and the terrified man was trying to break the chokehold with one hand. His other hand dangled limply at his side, the wrist bent at an angle that made Megan feel slightly queasy.

Even barefoot and wearing only his damp jeans, Jack broadcast danger. A low rumbling growl emanated from him and his whole body almost vibrated with anger. Although his frame was sleekly muscled, there was little evidence of the kind of strength it took to lift a man easily onto his tiptoes with one hand, or to break his wrist like a dry twig. The man in question was about the same height as Jack but heavier, with the kind of build you might see standing outside a nightclub glaring at the people queuing. His head was shaved and his flat nose had obviously been broken more than once. *Where did this guy come from, Villains 'R' Us?*

"Who sent you?" Jack snarled at him as if reading her mind, but the thug shook his head. Before she could blink, Jack held a switchblade under the man's nose, his eyes widening at the threat from his own weapon.

"Who. Sent. You?"

"Ah dinnae...know!" he gasped. "Ah didnae...see him." When he stopped, Jack merely waited, eyes narrowed, face hard and unyielding.

"It was all...din on the phone... He called and telt us where you were... Paid cash...left it in...the gents at the train station... Half now, half efter proof..."

He ground to a halt again, and this time Megan saw Jack's fingers tighten around his throat as he hissed, "Proof?"

The man's face turned an alarming shade of purple and she thought he might actually suffocate before he could answer.

"Pictures!... Of you and the bird...efter we'd...din you," he managed. Megan drew a shocked breath. Jack loosened his grip again and, encouraged, his captive continued in a rush. "We missed the first time... Telt him a hit and run wisnae a guid bet, but that's what he wanted, said it had tae look accidental. Nothing personal, pal, it wis easy money. All we had t'dae wis show up where he telt us tae."

Nothing personal... Megan shuddered as she realized that this man had nearly killed her twice now. More terrifying was the fact that someone out there still wanted her dead. She glanced at Jack. He was visibly trembling, his incandescent eyes burning holes through the man he held. The knife in his hand was now lying just under the man's chin, a drop of blood welled up where it had nicked the skin.

Jack struggled with fury unlike anything he had ever felt. He wanted to kill the spineless idiot in his grasp who had dared to threaten his mate. The man was silent but for his harsh breathing, and the scent of fear rolled off of him in waves, inflaming Jack's senses even more. He wasn't a human being anymore, he was prey. It was primitive and irrational and Jack didn't care. For endless seconds he teetered on the edge of control until he heard Megan approach him from behind.

"Jack. Let him go, he's not worth it." Her gentle voice and the scent of her calmed him. He jerked his wide-eyed captive against the wall, satisfied when his head hit it with an audible thump. "You better run far and fast 'pal' because the next time I catch up with you will be the last." He let go, and the man crumpled to the ground with a yelp before springing back up and scrambling away cradling his injured wrist.

Jack closed his eyes and simply breathed. Never had he come close to killing someone before, he was as tightly strung as a piano wire. Though he could feel the heat from Megan's body as she stood behind him, he still jerked when she laid a soothing hand on his shoulder. After finishing his shower, he had gone to the kitchen to ask her about his clothes and had seen the empty bin immediately. It hadn't taken a genius to work out what she was doing, especially when he tuned into her thoughts. Concerned for her safety, he had only paused long enough to retrieve his jeans from the dryer and pull them on before following her. He had been halfway down the stairs when she had been grabbed. Her thoughts from then on had become maddeningly disjointed but he caught enough to know that he was dealing with one of the two knife-wielding thugs who had attacked him. It had been all he could do to hold his concentration long enough to send an image to help her break the man's hold.

Reaching up, he took her hand and brought her round in front of him. He traced the outline of a small bruise forming on her cheek and had to rein in his useless anger again. Part of him wanted to be mad at her too, for coming out here at this time of night on her own, but he reminded himself that she hadn't been aware of the danger. Desire and possessiveness radiated through his veins mingling with relief and fear, and he claimed her mouth in a hungry kiss. Nibbling at her lips, demanding entry, plunging his tongue deep when she complied. The taste of her went straight to his head—both of them. When she responded by sucking gently on his tongue, he thought his hard-on would burst straight through his jeans. He wasn't sure if it was the sudden lack of blood to his brain that made him dizzy or the sheer intoxication of desire. Their mouths separated reluctantly, both stealing nips and licks until Megan took a small step back. Her pupils dilated, cheeks pink with excitement, she ran the tip of her tongue over red, swollen lips.

Jack stifled the impulse to pull her back into his arms. He had to find out who was after them and why, and he needed to keep his mate safe while he did it. With his family out of contact, there was only one other person he could think to go to for help and he lived right here in Scotland. Cameron Murray would not be happy to see him, though, and taking Megan there might be like jumping from the frying pan to the fire.

"Jack?" Megan looked at him, passion fading from her eyes, brows pulled together in concern. "Who would want to hire someone to kill us?"

Jack returned her gaze, giving a small shrug of his shoulders. He was still as clueless as she clearly was. "I don't know, but I'm going to try to find out. Right now we have to get out of here, it's not safe and if we stay any longer we might put your friend in danger, too." He expected her to argue, saw the intent in her eyes, but anxiety about her friend's safety seemed to squelch it. He took her hand and led her back inside before she could change her mind, making plans as he climbed the stairs.

"Where can we go?"

"I have a friend who lives in the north of Scotland. Cameron Murray. He has a big house with a lot of security. So even if we are followed—" *and we probably will be*, he thought, "—you'll be safe." Megan came to an abrupt stop a few stairs behind him, her grip on his hand threatening to topple him backwards. "You mean we will be safe, don't you? Because if you are thinking of dumping me in a stranger's house and going off on some macho crusade, you have another think coming."

That had actually been very close to his plans but one look at the mutinous expression on her face made him revise them. Jack swore he could feel his blood pressure rising again. If the bad guy didn't kill him, his mate surely would! Muttering under his breath, he tugged on her hand and continued on up the stairs.

* * * * *

Jack studied his mate as she slept soundly in the passenger seat of her car. She had tilted the seat back as far as it would go and was curled up on her side. The seat belt fastened around her, knees pulled up towards her chest. It had taken longer than he wanted to get started on their journey since he had to collect his things, change clothes and check out of the hotel. He'd offered to take Megan to her apartment so that she could pack a few more belongings but she'd said it wasn't necessary. Instead she'd borrowed a few things from Jayne to add to what she had already packed, insisting she could buy anything else she needed. He knew she couldn't afford it and had silently resolved to pay for anything she needed himself. It was his duty now to provide for his mate—though he didn't look forward to her reaction when he told her that.

Jayne hadn't been happy with his intention to whisk her friend away in the middle of the night with no explanation. In the end he had to tell her that someone was following him and now Megan, and that he needed to take her somewhere safe until he found out why. Jayne hadn't been entirely happy about that either but since Megan had unhesitatingly backed him up, there hadn't been much she could do about it. Before they left, though, she had gotten the last word. His lips curved as he remembered them.

"You hurt my friend, or let someone else hurt her, and I will hunt you down, cut off your balls and feed them to you."

With a quiet chuckle he turned his attention back to the dark road, checking again for headlights in the rearview mirror. The sky was still cloudy but occasionally the moon shone through the gaps and gilded hedgerows and fields of livestock with silver. They had left the busy motorway behind them long ago and joined the winding maze of dark country roads leading to Cameron's estate. There were so many twists and turns that a clever enough pursuer should be able to stay far enough back that he wouldn't be seen. He could count the number of cars they had passed in the last hour on one hand, so it should be easier now to spot anyone following them. Jack wasn't taking any chances, though.

The closer they got the more anxious he became, for himself, for Megan and for his friend. He didn't know how Cameron would react to Megan's presence. In fact, he didn't even know how welcome he would be himself — he hadn't had any personal contact with Cam for months. His friend had locked himself away in his house, rarely seeing anyone anymore. Before last August, he had at least received a phone call every few weeks. Now there wasn't even that. Jack suspected he still held himself at least partly to blame for Nick's disappearance despite Jack's efforts to convince him otherwise. Frustrated, he had asked Cameron's housekeeper to stay in touch. As long as he kept receiving those e-mails, he knew Cam was all right.

The radio played quietly in the background and the weather report distracted him momentarily. Cool night air mussed his hair as it blew in the slightly open window. It brought with it the scent of the rain promised by the bulletin and the unfamiliar smells of the countryside. He welcomed the chill since it helped keep him alert. God, he was so tired. This couldn't go on. How could he protect his mate if he spent half the time exhausted from shifting? Megan must trust him, all of her actions said that she did even though she didn't seem to believe it herself. Yet he was still reluctant to tell her about the blood exchange. Why? He looked at her sleeping form and a wave of tenderness washed over him.

I love her…and I'm afraid to lose her.

The realization stunned him. His fingers tightened on the steering wheel as he acknowledged the truth of the words. He had known it was a possibility, after all, it was one of the reasons he had searched for so long. He just hadn't expected to fall for her so soon. Megan was attractive and funny and fiercely independent. Already he could hardly picture his future without her in it. Dearbh Ceangal or not, Jack was very much afraid that when he gave her the choice she would not feel the same.

He pushed aside his concerns as the hedgerows bounding the road gave way to the edge of the thick pine forest that surrounded Murray House. The only access road was a rutted one-lane track leading through the trees. It was well concealed and he almost drove past it.

Megan woke as he hit the first pothole, she blinked gritty eyes and sat up stiffly. Her mouth felt like it was filled with cotton and she licked her dry lips and wished she'd thought to pack a drink. She glanced at Jack's profile in the dim light inside the car. He said nothing, just concentrated on navigating the narrow dusty gravel road illuminated by the headlights. Pine trees towered over them on either side and she shivered as she stared through the bushes at their base into darkness thick enough to cut. Their fresh, distinctive smell wafted in the open window mixed with the moist smell of earth. She'd always had a good imagination and thoughts of what could be lurking in there made the back of her neck prickle.

"Where are we?"

Jack flicked a glance at her before turning his attention back to the road and answering. "We're almost there, the house is about half a mile ahead."

The car bounced into another hole and she winced at the potential damage to her small vehicle. "You've been here before then?"

"A few times, but it has been a while," he said and fell silent again.

Questions clamored at her, she was desperately curious about their destination but Jack didn't seem to be in the mood to talk. They were nearly there anyway. She could be patient. There was a sound suspiciously like a snort from the other side of the car and she looked sharply at his impassive face. Jack glanced at her, his expression inquiring. "What?"

"Nothing." She shook her head and stared out into the trees, soft music from the radio filled the silence again. A short time later they rounded yet another bend in the road and stopped in front of a large set of black, spiked, iron gates. They were set into a red sandstone wall that must have been at least ten feet high. The red eye of a security camera glowed from the top of the wall on the right. Beyond the gates a long paved driveway curved away towards the dark silhouette of an enormous mansion house. Two of the windows she could see had light shining softly from them, even at this ungodly hour — one on the second floor and the other on the ground floor. Beside her Jack rolled down the window and pressed a button on the telecom that was mounted on a post beside the road. The speaker hissed as it was activated but no one spoke. The gate was already opening when Jack announced, "It's Jack, Cam."

His expression grim, he rolled up the window and drove through the gates. He didn't look happy at the prospect of seeing an old friend. In fact he seemed worried. Perhaps understandable since he hadn't phoned to tell him that they were coming, despite Megan's request. Jack seemed to think it was a better idea just to arrive. However, it was the trace of nerves she could feel from him that she found more disturbing. *What exactly were they heading for here?* After the last few days, Megan didn't think her stress levels could get any higher but they were climbing again now. Her neck and shoulders were tight with it.

The headlights showed well-trimmed grass on either side of the road stretching off into the darkness. As they rounded the driveway, the lights swept over the house and she saw it was constructed of the same stone as the outer wall. Jack eased the

Cait Miller

car to a stop at the foot of the stone steps and switched off the engine.

The atmosphere vibrated with tension as he climbed out of the cooling vehicle, and after a few seconds Megan followed. She shivered slightly both from the breeze and nerves. Jack wrapped his arm around her, enveloping her in the comforting heat and scent of his body and they climbed the stairs to the heavy wooden front door together.

To Megan's dismay, Jack simply opened it and pulled her into the house, closing it gently behind them. Before she could sputter in protest, he murmured, "Trust me." Then transferred his grip to her hand. She missed the closeness of the embrace even though the entryway was pleasantly warm. And silent. There wasn't a sound save for the ticking of the grandfather clock that stood against the wall at the bottom of the staircase on her left. If she didn't know better, she would swear the big house was empty, but someone had let them in. *Get a grip, Megan. You're behaving like the heroine of a gothic romance*, she scolded herself. Resolutely she straightened her shoulders, determined to shake off her strange mood, and took in her surroundings.

It was all very tasteful and very masculine, so far, at least. The walls and the doors, as well as the few pieces of furniture, were all wood, the shining brass wall lights made it glow with rich color. A dark red patterned carpet covered the floor, continuing on the stairs to the open landing of the first floor and out of sight. In front of them an unlit hallway led away towards the back of the house. Her curiosity made her long to explore further.

Jack's grip tightened on her hand and as she turned to look at him, movement on the landing caught her eye. A man stood there, unsmiling, both hands leaning on the wooden banister. The two men stared at each other in silence. Megan gasped in surprise.

He was a big man, tall and broad at the shoulders, his golden hair shone in the soft light that drifted up from the hall.

As if he sensed Megan's appraisal, he switched his amber gaze to her. She swallowed nervously. With that one look into his eyes, she instinctively knew this man was like Jack. With one difference. Until now she had thought Jack had an air of danger about him, but this man, this man personified danger. She could feel it radiating from him like pressure in the atmosphere. His voice, when he spoke was smooth and deep, American, flavored with a hint of Scottish. It was a beautiful voice, but his words destroyed her appreciation of it.

"What the hell is she doing here, Jack?"

Chapter Nine

Jack didn't react to the curt words. In fact he seemed to expect them. Megan on the other hand was astonished. She didn't even know this man. What could he possibly have against her? Something in her wanted to cower at the barely suppressed animosity in his tone and that only made her angry. As if sensing her reaction, Jack soothingly caressed the back of the hand he held with his thumb.

"I needed to bring her somewhere safe, Cam," he answered calmly, not taking his eyes off of his friend.

Cameron gave a harsh, humorless bark of laughter. "You know better than that, Jack."

Again the words drew no reaction from Jack other than the soothing caress on her hand that seemed to urge her silence as he continued. "Someone is trying to kill us." He relayed the close calls they had had of the past couple of days ending with the information that he had obtained from the man who had attacked her. "I need your help to find out who and why." Emotion flickered across the other man's face too quickly interpret.

"Do you want me to call the team?"

Jack paused, considering. The team was a group of shifters who helped ensure that their species remained a secret. If there was any threat to their way of life, be it from humans or other shapeshifters, they dealt with it. They wouldn't hesitate to come if Cameron called them, after all, he used to be one of them. Still was, in some ways.

"No," he answered. "Not yet, let's see if we can deal with this on our own first." Jack knew most of them, but not well enough to know if he could trust their restraint around Megan.

Cam nodded, his eyes narrowed on Megan. "Keep her away from me."

Megan stared after him, bewildered by the exchange, as he turned and walked silently back into the darkness towards the next floor. As his friend disappeared, Jack sighed deeply and his shoulders dropped with the release of tension. He lifted a hand to rub the back of his neck and turned to face her. "Stay here while I go get the bags." With a final squeeze of her hand, he left her standing in the empty hallway waiting in vain for an explanation.

She barely had time to gather her thoughts before he returned and wordlessly led the way to the first floor and into a softly lit bedroom. He dropped the bags on the floor at the foot of the oak four-poster bed and went to the window. Frustrated at his continued silence, she shut the door behind her with more force than was necessary. Not that he seemed to notice as he continued staring out at the dark night with his back to her. It was all it took for Megan to reach the end of her rope.

In the last few days she had gained a crazy American admirer with the persistence of a mosquito and been overtaken with lust for him. Nearly been run over by a car and been terrified by a wild creature in her apartment. Given first aid to a stab wound, been shown her crazy admirer and the wild cat were one and the same. Been held at knifepoint and threatened with rape. Found out someone was trying to kill her then dragged halfway across the country to the house of a man who didn't want her anywhere near him and no one was telling her why!

A hard tremor shook the length of her body heralding the emotional storm that was bearing down on her. Megan wasn't a crier. After her parents' death she had thought she had no more tears left, and she refused to do it in front of Jack. She yanked her nightshirt from her bag. Eyes burning, struggling to rein in her wayward emotions, she flung it on the foot of the bed. There was really no point in crying, after all she was here, she was alive, and so was Jack. What good would it do? With swift angry motions she stripped off her clothes and perched on the edge of the mattress in her peach satin bra and panties.

She was winning the battle when Jack left the window and knelt in front of her, his desire for her evident in his eyes and the reaction of his body. This was why she was here, this enigmatic man who had turned her world upside down and made her abandon the rules and routine she had fallen into. She wanted to berate him for it but it was becoming more than obvious that he was as lost in this situation as she was.

His expression remained somber and when he spoke his voice was tinged with regret. "I'm sorry I got you into this, Megan, but I can't be sorry that I found you."

He leaned forward, cupped her face and claimed her mouth with a tenderness that emptied all her concerns from her head. She poured all her feelings into the kiss, sucking gently on his tongue, clutching his shoulders through his dark T-shirt. Arousal rushed through her, stealing her breath and her reason, leaving her panties damp. She moaned as Jack ran callused fingers through her hair, over her shoulders and back, pausing to unhook her bra. He broke away from her lips, murmuring to her and brushing tiny soothing kisses along her jaw. With impatient hands, she pulled his T-shirt over his head leaving his dark hair tousled, and allowed him to urge her back onto the mattress behind her.

She loved the weight of him when he laid his body the length of hers, surrounding her with his musky male scent. *God he smells so good.* She ran a hand along his jaw, smiling when he rubbed against her like a cat seeking her caress, his dark stubble prickling her palm. Soundlessly he yielded to the pressure of her hand against his shoulder and rolled so that she straddled him. Through the soaked satin of her underwear, she felt the hard bulge of his erection straining against his zipper. She rocked her hips against him, tearing a harsh groan from his lips, and began to explore his broad shoulders and hair-dusted chest.

Her hands were pale against the dusky gold of his skin, and smiling, she traced her finger down from the dip at the base of his throat and along the curve of his pectorals. She raised her eyes to his face, meeting his molten silver gaze as she circled his nipples. They beaded instantly at her touch and she slid down his body and ran the tip of her tongue around each of them. Jack's mouth twitched in a half smile that promised recompense. Keeping her eyes on his face, she traced the path of dark hair down the center of his hard belly until she reached the waistband of his jeans. He sifted his fingers through her hair and she took his hands in hers and guided them to the bed.

"Let me do this, Jack, please."

"Megan, you don't have—"

She interrupted his protest. "I know, I want to. Let me taste you, Jack." A muscle twitched in the hard line of his jaw and he released his grip allowing her to unbutton his jeans. Megan watched with undisguised fascination as his erection forced the zipper the rest of the way down until his cock sprang free to bob against his abdomen. "You're beautiful, Jack." Smiling wickedly, she captured the velvety hard flesh in her hand and stroked him from crown to base slowly. Jack moaned, eyes closed, and lifted his hips into her touch. Circling the base of his shaft she leaned into him and raised her eyes to see him looking at her. Deliberately she licked her lips drawing his attention to her mouth, the expression on his face causing her nipples to tighten painfully. The muscles of her womb clenched in anticipation, releasing a trickle of moisture down the inside of her thigh.

His body trembled with restraint when she ran her lips and tongue around the blunt head of his cock, savoring the salty taste of his flesh and the smooth, hot feel of him. When she investigated the little triangle underneath, a harsh gasp escaped him, his hips thrust helplessly upwards. "Megan, please..."

Stretching her mouth wide to accommodate his girth, she took him in her mouth, taking as much of his length as she was able. Her tongue caressed the vein-ridged flesh on the underside as she withdrew, sucking gently. She repeated the motion, this time using her free hand to stroke and explore his lightly furred sack. Jack was panting now, "Harder..." His hands grasped her head and urged her on, his hips thrusting in tempo with her mouth as he reached blindly for his climax. She could taste the salty-sweet of his pre-come on her tongue, feel the throb and pulse of her own body, and moaned.

"Oh, fuck...Megan...Meg... I'm coming!" he gasped and tried to pull away. She held him firmly, swallowing his seed as it erupted from him, reveling in his harsh groan of completion.

Tenderly Megan kissed the pink scar on his side, marveling at how quickly the wound was healing. At the time she had been sure she was going to watch him bleed to death. She ignored the memories that wanted to distract her and crawled up to rest her head on his chest, listening to the thumping of his heart as it gradually slowed to its normal rhythm. Jack hooked a finger under her chin and tilting her face up to his, he kissed her. "Thank you."

Effortlessly he turned them so that they both lay on their sides, her bottom nestled against his sex. She rubbed against him feeling the coarseness of his hair against the smooth skin of her back. "Your turn," he whispered. Turning her head, she kissed him, hissing when he nipped her lip then soothed the small sting with his tongue and kissed his way along her jaw to her neck. Her head tilted instinctively to give him access while his hand roamed over her breasts pausing to torment her nipples into tingling berry-red peaks.

"Have I ever told you I love your breasts? I love the way your nipples darken and bead when you're turned on...and I love it when all that creamy white skin flushes pink with embarrassment...or arousal." Jack's soft words and the touch of his warm breath on her neck made her heart pound and shivers of awareness tingle through her body. His hand slipped lower to the notch of her thighs, petting her dark curls, sliding over the already wet entrance to her body.

Megan whimpered and rocked against his hand then cried out when his fingers circled her clitoris. "Jack!"

"You're so wet for me, baby, what is it you want? Tell me Meg." His fingers moved again, tracing gently along her labia, and her inner muscles clenched again in reaction.

"I want you inside me, Jack...please." Against her bottom she could feel his soft cock and she rocked her bottom into him.

Jack chuckled wryly, "I'm afraid he hasn't recovered quite yet, honey, but..." He eased two fingers inside her. "I'm sure we'll think of something else."

Her inner muscles clasped his fingers as he began to move them, tension already building in her body. His thumb began circling her throbbing clit, she could hear his ragged breathing next to her ear mingling with her own moans. "Come for me, Megan!" He pressed harder with his thumb and a third finger joined the other two, filling her unbearably. Her muscles tightened, tightened until she came in a rush, arching soundlessly into his fingers as pleasure stole her breath.

Little aftershocks continued to pulse through her body as Jack withdrew his hand and wrapped her in his embrace, his cock now semi-hard against her hip. They lay in silence for endless moments, each wrapped in their own thoughts. With a suddenness that startled her, he wrenched himself away, leaving her gasping for breath. Belatedly she registered the furnace-like heat of Jack's body, far overpowering the natural heat their lovemaking had generated.

He began to scratch, leaving red welts on his golden skin. His gaze seemed to turn inward as he groaned, "No. No. Not now, dammit!" Her heart lurched in her chest at the agonized expression on his face and the harshness of his exclamation. She rose to her knees, reaching for him, desperate to ease the pain somehow but he scrambled away from her. His back slammed against the solid oak headboard in his haste to escape her touch. "NO! Don't want to hurt you." His voice had already lost its humanity, the last words almost unintelligible.

The change was no easier to witness than the first time, the tears she had managed to fight back rolled unheeded down her cheeks as she perched helplessly on the edge of the bed. When it was over, he lay panting on his side, exhausted. Megan moved beside him, swiping at the useless tears, before fondling his ears and stroking his face. "Oh Jack, how do you do it? Why? Isn't there anything you can do to stop it?" He licked her fingers and heaved a huge sigh. Megan smiled sadly and shook her head at the futility of their situation. Lying down on the thick comforter beside him, she sank her fingers into the soft fur on his side and fell into an exhausted slumber.

* * * * *

The vast entryway didn't look forbidding at all, Megan decided. She paused halfway down the stairs and turned back to admire the beautiful round, stained glass window pouring color onto the landing. It featured an unfamiliar coat of arms, presumably representing the Murray family, and was a detail she had completely missed last night in the darkness. Not to mention the fact that their reluctant host had been standing in front of it and had had all her attention. She turned again to look up to the second floor where she had glimpsed an identical window and wondered what other unexpected surprises the house held.

At the foot of the stairs she caught the faint scent of coffee and followed it towards the back of the house hoping to find Jack somewhere nearby. When she woke there had been no sign of him. *If he has left me alone in this house with his bad-tempered friend, there's going to be hell to pay.*

At the end of the hallway she found a large, bright kitchen. The cabinets were a golden-hued pine, the walls tiled in white and the floor in slate. There was a glass conservatory attached to one side allowing soft gray light to fill the room and reflect off of the polished surfaces of a multitude of appliances and gizmos. The conservatory itself held a large pine table and chairs and the windows were lined with well-tended plants. Sitting there to eat would be like sitting outside, Megan thought, only without the rain and bugs.

The door was open, leading onto a patio with what looked like beds of fresh herbs. Further on a wide lawn sloped down towards a bank of pine trees and a blue-gray loch was just visible through them. This was obviously a room someone loved and was equipped to prepare for dinner parties, small or large. Somehow she could not see the man from last night on his hands and knees pruning herbs or spending hours cooking so she assumed he must have staff...somewhere. Ordinarily a room like this charmed her. *And it will,* she thought, *as soon as I get my hands on that coffee.*

The machine sat on the counter directly in front of her so she quickly helped herself to a mug from the stand beside it, filling it with the fragrant brew. As she raised the mug to her lips she felt the hairs on the back of her neck rise to attention. Turning quickly, she found herself pinned again by the golden gaze of Cameron Murray. The man was even bigger than she had thought. He towered over her from just a few feet away dressed in faded jeans and an oatmeal-colored knitted sweater. She took a quick step back and was brought up short by the kitchen counter, then immediately berated herself for letting him intimidate her. *It's a tragedy that such a babe should have such a bad attitude.* Throat suddenly dry, she croaked out a greeting, "Morning."

He continued to stare at her in silence, broad chest expanding as he inhaled deeply. A barely perceptible tremor ran through him as he exhaled. Megan watched his pupils expand and was suddenly grateful that she had showered before coming downstairs. It seemed increasingly likely that he was a shapeshifter like Jack and no doubt would have been able to smell the scent of last night's lovemaking. He lifted his hand and her muscles tensed in anticipation of his touch. He clenched his fist briefly, seeming to fight some internal battle then took the mug of coffee from her fingers instead.

"Jack is a friend so I guess I'm stuck with you for now. You can go wherever you like in the house but stay away from me and keep out of the second floor!" he commanded softly. His eyes flicked briefly towards the conservatory and he turned abruptly and stalked out of the room.

Megan watched him leave, mouth open in astonishment, barely resisting the urge to check and see if she had somehow been transported to the enchanted castle from the Beauty and the Beast fairytale. *What the hell have I gotten myself into here?*

Following the path of Cameron's gaze, she was unsurprised to find Jack watching her. What did surprise her, though, was that he was still a cat. A wave of apprehension swept through her. Megan had never seen him transformed for longer than a few hours before and although he hadn't said how long the changes lasted, something told her this was not normal. The transformation seemed to take so much energy and she recalled how tired he had looked last night. Was it possible he just didn't have enough strength to shift back again yet? Even as she completed the thought, she dismissed it. The change wasn't voluntary so how much strength he had wouldn't really matter, would it? So why was he still standing before her on four legs instead of two?

She looked into Jack's eyes and what she saw there worried her even more. *Fear.* It was gone so quickly she might have imagined it, though she knew she had not. As she watched, a shudder rippled through the sleek body and he started towards the door.

"Wait, Jack!" He turned back towards her as she approached. His body still poised for flight, even as another tremor shook him. "It's happening, isn't it? Please, don't leave. I know I can't be much help, but I want to stay with you." She placed her hand on his powerful shoulders and felt the heat that was becoming so familiar radiating through his thick fur. After a moment, he took a few steps away from her and laid down.

Again the transformation lasted only a few agonizing minutes, but to Megan it seemed like hours as she knelt on the cold tiles watching with silent empathy. When it was over, she crawled to his side. His whole body was trembling with exhaustion and his eyes were dull with the remnants of pain. He lifted one hand and cupped her face. "Just once, I would really like to wake up in a bed with you," he whispered hoarsely.

She laughed half-heartedly. "You aren't missing much. I'm really not a morning person."

Jack's hand fell back to his side and his eyes closed, a small grin tugged at one side of his mouth. "Bet I could change your mind," he mumbled. She felt color suffuse her cheeks at his words and smiled at the reaction, after the last few days she had no reason to blush. She brushed her fingers over his silky hair and listened with surprise to his deep rumbling purr. The skin under his eyes was even more bruised by fatigue and his cheekbones stood out in sharp relief. He climbed stiffly to his feet and tugged her up along with him. Everything about his appearance said all was not well in Jack's world. Though he had said that shapeshifting was normal and natural for him, Megan was becoming more certain that there was something else he had not told her.

"I'm going to take a shower." He bent and kissed her, just a soft brush of his lips. And, she silently admitted to herself as she watched him walk away, she had fallen in love with the man.

Drawn back to the garden, she poured herself another coffee and perched on the low brick wall surrounding the patio. *I still can't believe that...swine! Stole my coffee!* Megan pushed the thought away and simply enjoyed the unpolluted highland air. Though the granite wall and the stones of the patio were dry, the air smelled damp, suggesting rain wasn't far away and the cloudy, gray, late morning sky was beginning to darken with the promise of it. She marveled over the changes the last few days had wrought on her life. Jack Douglass had swept through it like a charming wrecking ball.

It was a little tough to take, and still that little voice in the back of her mind said it wasn't over yet. She had all but turned her brain inside out searching for some reason why anyone would want her dead and come up with nothing. Cameron Murray, unpleasant though he was, apparently had resources which would help them find out. As well as a safe haven for them.

It grated on her independent nature to turn the reins over to someone else but there seemed to be little else she could do at the moment but wait. Part of her hoped that Jack and his friend would quickly find out who was after them so that she could go back to her nice, normal—safe—life and pretend none of this had happened. But that would probably mean never seeing Jack again and that was unthinkable. How was it possible to come to need someone so much in such a short time?

Chapter Ten

Jack climbed out of the shower and dried himself off with brisk swipes of the towel. A quick study in the mirror told him that his knife wound was completely healed, not even leaving a scar to mark its seriousness. One of the benefits of his species. He began to dress, trying to shake off the tension that gripped him. It was obvious that Megan was beginning to realize something was wrong. Something other than being the target of a mysterious assassin, that is, he thought with dark humor. But the fear would not be brushed aside this time, there had been a point in the early hours of this morning when he had thought that it was over and he had waited too long. The cat had taken over completely. He couldn't wait any longer, he would ask her today if she would complete the bond with him, and if she chose not to...the thought shook him... Then he would leave her in Cameron's care and use whatever time he had left to find and stop whoever was after them.

The idea of leaving her with his friend wasn't one which sat easily, and he growled in instinctive protest. Cam was beginning his mating cycle and though he had no intention of taking a mate, even Cameron's formidable will would be tested. Jack trusted him to find somewhere safe for Megan before he lost control but there was little he could do about any shapeshifters who might seek her out in the future. In the end, it had been fairly easy for *him* to track her down. It might be wise to take further advantage of Cam's skills and wipe mention of her birthmark from her medical files.

The thought had barely formed when he heard the bedroom door snick shut, but it wasn't Megan's presence he felt. A cool breath of air slid through the half-open door causing the steam to swirl and eddy and bringing with it a familiar scent.

Prepared for the conflict that had been building since they had arrived, he pulled on a sweater and walked into the bedroom.

Cameron lounged against the wall, his tone and posture deceptively relaxed, but Jack had known him too long not to feel the barely restrained anger and worry.

"So, how long have we got before I have to call your parents and tell them to start building a cage?"

Jack's laugh was sharp and bitter as he turned his back and stared out of the window into the misty gray morning. Trust Cam to get straight to the point.

His silence seemed to push his friend over some invisible line and the calm façade disintegrated. "Dammit, Jack! They have already lost one son this year, they do *not* need to lose the second! What were you thinking?"

As his friend no doubt intended, mention of his missing brother provoked instant reaction. Jack rounded on his friend and growled, "Nick is *not* dead."

He drew in a calming breath, guilt, fear and anger swarmed in his veins. "It was time. They know I was looking for a mate, I couldn't put it off forever." He shot a glance at his friend who had every intention of doing that very thing. "She's the one, Cam. I felt it the minute I saw her, a Dearbh Ceangal. I know you don't believe in it but it's real."

Cam shook his head in his usual stubborn denial and began to pace out his agitation. "If you believe that, then why haven't you finished it?!"

"I will not force this on her, Cam, she has to choose." He faced the other man knowing his sharp mind would eventually reach the logical conclusion.

"How can she let you do this? She is your mate, how can she stand back and let you throw away your humanity…your life, like this!" The pacing halted abruptly. "She doesn't know, does she? Why the hell haven't you told her?!"

"I was going to tell her… No, the hell with it, that's a lie. I was just going to take her, seduce her, complete the bond then tell her what I had done to her!" Jack's voice rose to a near shout, rich with disgust at his own arrogance. He ran a hand through his dark hair and said softly, "Then I fell in love with her…and I couldn't do it. If I tell her what happens to me if she walks away, she'll stay. She's too good, Cam, too damn nice! I want her with me because she feels the same way I do. If that means I have to let her go, then so be it."

An uncomfortable silence fell around them thick with unspoken anxiety. Cameron was the first to break it. "I'm making some progress into finding out who is after you but I don't have anything concrete yet." He blew out a frustrated breath and stalked to the door, halting with his hand on the doorknob. "I don't want to lose anyone else I care about either, Jack. Tell her…or I will."

He found Megan just closing the conservatory door in the kitchen. Droplets of moisture clung to her dark hair like diamonds from the light rain that had begun to fall. His feet were silent on the tiled floor as he stalked towards her, drawn by the fierce urge to take her, possess her. Her scent filled his lungs mixed with the fresh tang of Highland air and his cock hardened painfully.

She turned towards him taking a quick startled breath. "Jack." Her hand went to her chest. "You scared the life out of me. I am definitely going to have get a bell for around your neck," she drawled, her rueful grin taking the sting out of her comment.

With effort, Jack reined in the demands of his body. This was definitely not the time. Taking her hand her led her to the table and before she could take another chair, pulled her onto his lap. Their gazes met when she felt the evidence of his desire and she grinned and rocked her hips. "Good God, woman!" he ground out, "Hold still!" Jack closed his eyes and fought to cool his unruly body. The problem would be easily solved if he moved her to the other chair but he wanted her closer than that.

"I need to talk to you," he said quietly. Absently he traced a finger over her jeans high on her thigh where he knew her birthmark lay, making her shiver. Her fingers played in the hair at the nape of his neck and he leaned into the caress and purred.

Megan laughed delightedly, "You do that a lot recently." Jack's arousal vanished as he realized the truth of her words. He hadn't even noticed he was doing it. More and more the behavior of his counterpart was seeping over outside of his shifting. It only emphasized how little time he had left to finish this, one way or the other.

"When we first met... You were right to think I had been sitting in front of that door waiting for you." She stiffened and her fingers withdrew from his hair. He mourned the loss but pressed on. "The fact that you could hear my voice in your head had nothing to do with an active imagination. I was testing you." She tried to pull away from him and he held on, looking into her angry eyes.

"Don't, Jack, I don't know how you found that out but there is no such thing as telepathy."

Yeah, right. That's what you said about shapeshifters.

Her eyes widened. Astonishment and acceptance replacing anger, she demanded, "Do that again."

You told me shapeshifters didn't exist, either.

"Oh, good grief. Can you do that to anyone?" The tinge of excitement in her voice surprised him.

"No, sometimes with close family and friends I feel their emotions. Finding someone who is...compatible with you is...difficult."

A crimson flush of embarrassment washed over her face. "I suppose you...read thoughts as well?"

"Only yours and at the moment it's like a badly tuned radio. The closer I am to the signal, the more easily I receive something." Hers were a blur as her mind worked to accept the new information but he saw the instant she put two and two together.

"Wait a minute. You said you were testing me...and what do you mean, 'at the moment'?"

Jack paused, gathering his thoughts and ignoring the nerves that tap-danced in his stomach he again caressed her jean-clad thigh. "Have you ever noticed how your birthmark resembles a cat's paw print?"

Megan's hand closed over his, ceasing the restless movement and he thought she was going to demand he answer her questions. Instead she said warily, "Yes, it does but...what does my birthmark have to do with this?"

"When my kind reach adulthood they have the ability...the need...to form a bond with a mate, a connection that joins the couple for the rest of their lives." She listened intently as he tried to explain. "So when the time comes, we begin to search for someone bearing the birthmark that tells us they can be mated. I searched for a long time for the right person, all over the world."

She frowned at him and he felt her tension rising as she made the connection. "So it's just a lucky dip? You find a girl who has this mark and that's it, she's the one?"

"Well...yes, it can be. The physical attraction between a pair is usually very strong—"

"But--"

He carried on before she could protest further. "Wait, please, I'm not finished. It can just be about sex but if you're patient, and very lucky you can have a Dearbh Ceangal. A true match in every way, heart..." He placed his hand on her chest. "...mind..." His hand moved to touch her forehead and down to tilt her face up, his lips a breath away from hers. "...and soul." He kissed her gently. "You're my Dearbh Ceangal, Megan."

When she pulled away this time he let her go. "Why me? I mean how do you *know* I'm your...Derv Ke-an-gal? I mean, I have feelings for you, Jack." She gave an uncertain smile. "Big scary ones, but we barely know each other."

Jack's heart turned over in his chest at her admission. He was becoming well acquainted with those kind of feelings himself. "The first things you already know about—the birthmark and the telepathy, those are present for any couple.

When we meet our *true* mate, it's like all the magical energy that makes us what we are becomes supercharged and reaches out for her. It's an unmistakable feeling and many of us never get to experience it."

For an eternity she stood in silence, hands fisted in her unruly curls, absorbing the implication of his words, before she faced him. "How do you do it? I mean, what exactly is involved in 'bonding'?"

She's asking questions. Asking questions is a good sign, isn't it? A tiny seed of hope took root in Jack's heart. She hadn't agreed to do it, but she wasn't running away either...yet. "The moment we touched that first time it started."

Her eyebrows rose and she dropped her hands to her sides. "I remember feeling something, like the shock you get when you take your laundry out of the drier, only stronger. When we shook hands..." She looked at him for confirmation and he nodded. "You know you freaked me out that day, Jack. I thought I was having some sort of paranoid delusions. I convinced myself it was my imagination."

"I know." He shrugged. "You are my mate, and sometimes your thoughts are loud."

Her cheeks pinked again and she scowled at him. "Little did I know, my life was about to get a lot stranger. So what else do you have to do to finish it?"

"We need to exchange a few drops of blood."

"Exchange? Exchange how, Jack? Transfusion? Slice our palms blood brothers style? Hell, the way things tend to go in our conversations, it probably involves drinking it..." Her voice trailed off and she read the truth in his face before he said a word.

"Oh, no! Yuck! Jack, that is just disgusting! Do you have any idea how many blood-borne diseases are out there? How can you do that with a stranger?"

Jack's mouth curved in a reluctant half smile, it wasn't quite the reaction of horror he had anticipated and she still hadn't refused him. "First of all, you're not a stranger. Second, I can't get those diseases and third, after the exchange, it won't matter to you, either." Her mouth dropped open and he almost laughed. This woman never reacted the way he expected. "If you bond with me, you become like me."

The amusement evaporated like water in the desert when he caught Megan's immediate and unguarded thought. *Well. Bet Jayne never thought about this when she encouraged me to believe him...* She slapped a hand reflexively over her mouth. Anger shot through him. "You told Jayne!"

Megan threw up her hands. "Well, look at it from my point of view. I thought you were a fruitcake and I had just had sex with you on my kitchen table! Women share those kinds of events. It's almost the law!" She paced away towards the windows and back again, remorse warring with indignation with every step. Jack tried to put himself in her position and though he didn't want to admit it, she had a point.

"I don't think she really believed it anyway and even if she did, she wouldn't tell anyone. You saw her library, she loves all this stuff!"

Jack began to calm down. There was nothing he could do about it now. He didn't have a clue what Megan meant by the library comment since he'd been a little busy at the time to pay much attention. Something about Jayne Davis niggled at him. He couldn't quite put his finger on what it was, but it told him he could trust her. It was time he started to trust his instincts. After all, ignoring them had gotten him nothing but trouble so far. "All right! Okay! About the bonding thing?"

Megan looked at him, her relief clear at the change of subject. Her expression became serious. "What if I don't want to be furry and telepathic?"

Despite the lighthearted phrasing, a shaft of fear thrust through as he answered. "Then you walk away and I'll never come near you again."

He held his breath, unsure of her intent as she walked back over to the chair. Hands on either side of his head, she leaned down and kissed him. Immediately her tongue demanded access and he provided it, parting his lips while she teased and explored his mouth for too short a time before straightening and stepping away from him. He ached to gather her to him but the distance of her body told him it wasn't what she wanted so he kept his hands clenched at his sides. He expected questions, protests or both but she surprised him again.

"Thank you for telling me, Jack, for giving me the choice. I'm guessing you didn't really need to. I'm asking you now to give me a little time to think about it." She left the room quickly, leaving him alone and praying like he'd never prayed before.

Megan's head was spinning by the time she reached the bedroom. *Just when I think I have things under control, Jack Douglass finds new ways to turn my life upside down!* She sat on the edge of the bed and flopped backwards staring hard at the ceiling as if she could somehow find some answers there. She thought back to her conversation with Jayne about whether or not shapeshifters could be real. *Yeesh, was that just two days ago?* Now, here she was actually considering becoming one, worse still she had not even hesitated in believing it was possible. What did that say about her sanity, she wondered vaguely. Was she becoming so open-minded her brain was in danger of falling out? She still wasn't entirely sure why she hadn't turned him down flat and ran for the hills or laughed at him. A few days ago, that was exactly what she would have done.

Speaking of open-minded… The man could read her mind! She might never have privacy ever again. How could she accept the fact that her thoughts might not be her own? She shuddered to think what Jack might have heard crossing her mind the last few days, especially concerning her lustful thoughts about him. At least now she had an explanation for the immediate attraction between them. *His Dearbh Ceangal…* It sounded as if it might be Gaelic, even mentally she struggled with the pronunciation. Was she, with her romantic streak, reading too much into those words? Definitely too many paranormal romances. How many mates could he actually have? After all he hadn't actually said anything about her being his one and only, though it was implied. Would he turn her into a cat and leave her to go find someone else with a funny birthmark?

Questions, questions...*now* she had questions! Where were all these thoughts a few minutes ago in the kitchen? Instead her mind had gone blank and all she could think of was what it would be like to spend the rest of her life with Jack. She ought to get a pen and paper and write them all down. Her fingers drummed on the soft quilt and the room suddenly felt too small. Jumping up she grabbed her jacket and raced down the stairs and outside, quietly pulling the heavy front door closed behind her.

Heedless of the light misty rain that brushed her cheeks, Megan hesitated on the wide curving driveway. She wasn't entirely sure where she wanted to go, only that she needed to get outside and away from Jack and his mysterious friend for a while. Indecision nagged at her until she remembered the loch. Sweeping her already damp hair away from her face, she made her way around the building and headed towards the screen of pine trees.

Ever since she had been a child, the castles, lochs and the pine forests that often surrounded them had fascinated her. Her mother had loved the history of the buildings and her father the natural beauty surrounding them. Though she still loved to visit the castles, it was her father's world that had captivated her. Megan still remembered most of the stories of enchanted woods and loch monsters he had charmed and, as she got older, scared her with. It was to those places she still gravitated when she felt a need to escape.

By the time she found a path, her shoes were wet through from walking on the damp grass. Second thoughts assailed her when she saw the trees were denser than they had seemed, the loch not quite as close as it had looked. Too busy thinking about Jack's revelations, she hadn't stopped to consider the wisdom of straying from the house. But, she reasoned, he wouldn't have brought her here if he didn't believe it safe. Reassured, she allowed her memories and her innate stubbornness to lure her into the shelter of the trees.

Though ferns and other greenery grew around the edges, the ground underneath was bare but for a thick, springy brown carpet of fallen needles. A heavy growth of branches above her head dimmed the daylight and gave any sounds a muffled quality. In fact the steady drip of collected rainwater from the boughs above her was all she could hear beyond the scuff of her own footsteps. Megan felt watched. It caused the hair to stand up on the back of her neck though she could see a good distance through the trees on either side. *That seems to be happening to me a lot recently.*

She steadfastly refused to recall any of the eerie stories from her father and walked quickly on towards the water. Still, her heart was pounding and she nearly leapt onto the narrow pebbly beach. She chuckled and cursed herself for being ridiculous and letting her imagination run away with her. The windows of the house were still visible through breaks in the trees and if anything, that was the most likely source for the feeling. Hands in her coat pockets she walked to the edge of the loch letting the tiny waves lap at the toes of her shoes. It was small, small enough for a decent swimmer to cross it and the dark gray-blue of its center suggested depth. She could see now that the woods circled it and stretched much further on the other side, following the incline of a large hill. No doubt they were the same trees which bordered the road they had entered Cameron Murray's property on. She wondered idly how much of this he owned.

The mist was thicker now, making it look as though the clouds were caught on the steepled tops of the pines. *I am going to be soaked.* She closed her eyes and let the breeze blow moisture against her face, thankful that it wasn't cold. Her jacket was waterproof but it was summer weight and wouldn't provide much protection. In a few months when there would be snow coating the ground and frosting the branches it would be beautiful. Maybe she and Jack could come back then. Jack. It was inevitable, she knew, that her thoughts would lead her back to him. She doubted that even this serenity could calm her thoughts under these circumstances.

He was asking her to give up part of her humanity and form a connection with him that would last a lifetime whether she spent that time with him or not. The lure of experiencing life as a cat was tempting though she wasn't sure the pain he seemed to suffer with the transformation was worth it. As to the telepathy thing. Well, there must be someway to get around it or live comfortably with it. What had his parents done all this time? *I don't care how much you love someone, you still need your privacy sometimes.* He said the ability was intermittent, but would it get stronger if she was like him? Megan suspected it might and part of her was excited about that. The bottom line was that she loved him, but just how much was she willing to risk for that love when it might not be returned?

Lost in her thoughts, she didn't hear the shifting of the stones behind her until her face was covered by damp fabric. Something wrapped around her chest pinning her arms to her sides. She drew in a breath to scream and choked on the sickly, sweet odor. Coughing, she dug her nails into a dark nylon-clad arm, trying to push the cloth from her face and kicked back with her heel. Her captor grunted when she connected with his leg but her rush of satisfaction was short-lived. The world began to spin around her, her limbs felt like lead and her vision grayed. Megan's last thought as she slid into the darkness was that it was her own damn fault.

Chapter Eleven

Conscious of time running out, the ticking of the grandfather clock in the hall mocked Jack. He stalked past it and into the sitting room and threw himself down onto the hunter green leather sofa. A couple of sheets of A4 paper on the coffee table caught his eye. There was a sticky yellow note on top with his name printed in Cam's bold handwriting. He must have left them here rather than interrupt the discussion in the kitchen. It was a printout of names, a few of which sounded familiar. He noted that a small percentage of them seemed to be related, whether they were married couples or family members. Near the bottom of the first page he came to "Nick Douglass" and his heart nearly stopped in his chest. These had to be names of missing people. The terse handwritten statement at the bottom of the following page confirmed it.

"These are names of known shapeshifters who have disappeared or been killed in accidents or under unsolved murders in the last two years."

There had to be close to sixty names on the pages. How had this gone unnoticed? Papers clutched in his fist he raced to the second floor and Cam's office where his friend sat in his accustomed place in front of his computer. "How many of these deaths can we be reasonably sure were genuine accidents?"

Cam swiveled around in his chair, turning his back on the information scrolling down the screen and folded his hands behind his head. He nodded his head towards more printouts on the desk. "I eliminated the ones I don't believe are connected to this. *That* is the twelve that are left, six couples." Jack picked up the list, scanning it while Cam talked. "All but one couple died in what looked like accidents but police were suspicious enough to keep the cases open. On the surface they are all different, the only similarity is that they all occurred in the UK. Unless you know that at least one half of the pair was a shapeshifter and the other carried the cat paw birthmark. Since they also occurred sporadically over the course of two years, no one has connected them."

He didn't question how the man had got his information. He had yet to come across anyone who had as much talent with computers as Cameron Murray, and working in the computer industry he had met his fair share. "What about the other couple?"

"Two years ago, Paul Spencer and his new bride drank champagne laced with enough sedative to drop an elephant and were shot and killed in their honeymoon suite. The couple obviously assumed the bottle was complimentary, the champagne left in the room before their arrival. No one was seen entering or leaving the suite. No one was ever arrested for the murder. Whoever killed them knew enough to use a powerful drug that was odorless and sweet enough to be disguised by the champagne. They were both shot repeatedly in the head, leaving no chance of survival. Had they been human, a single shot to the chest would have done the job if the sedative hadn't already. I think this murder started it all. Whoever killed them knew what they were. What all those couples were. That first one was personal, he just doesn't like to get his hands dirty anymore."

Jack tossed the list back onto the table. "So find out who murdered Mr. and Mrs. Spencer and we find out who is after us." He paused, his brother's name had been on that list too. "Do you think the missing people on the list could be connected?"

"I don't know, Jack, my head says no. Our species isn't always as sociable as you and I." He smiled wryly, "We do have a tendency to live in isolated areas, given our nature. We can probably also rule out a lot of these as victims of the mating cycle. Anyway, Nick and two other men are the only ones to disappear here in Britain." He shrugged and rubbed his eyes. "I just don't like loose ends."

Although Jack was aware that Cameron was still talking to him, he was no longer listening. Since she left him in the kitchen Megan had been a steady and reassuring presence in the back of his mind. Now as if someone had flipped a switch, that link had suddenly vanished. He had been aware of a powerful wash of anger and fear and now, nothing.

"Megan!" Jack raced for the door, cursing himself for not paying closer attention to her. Instead, he had given her the privacy she feared she would lose. Torn between needing and not wanting to know what her decision might be, he had worried that he would be unable to resist influencing her and deliberately distanced himself. Now terror filled him at the thought that he may have cost his mate her life.

Allowing his senses to guide him he followed her scent from their bedroom, outside and into the light misty rain that already threatened to wipe away the trail. He followed as quickly as he dared. Deep menacing growls rumbled through him by the time he reached the edge of the loch. A dull red haze of fury descended, stealing his control and bringing the beast closer. The scent in the woods had been tinged with fear but here it was stronger. Someone else had been here. There was something odd about the male's scent, though. Mingling with the odor of chloroform was something unidentifiable that made the hair on Jack's body stand on end. A hand clamped down hard on his shoulder as he turned back to the woods where the trail continued. Snarling, he faced his attacker only to find Cameron standing behind him, his face carved in grim lines.

"Jack, stop. Think." Cam's hand hovered near his arm. "He knows what you are and yet he hasn't even attempted to cover his tracks!"

Jack shook his head and forced himself to calm as his friend's words pierced the fog of murderous rage around him. It was harder than it should have been. The cat wanted to hunt and kill. It had no interest in trying to reason. Cameron was right. Megan's captor had to know Jack was capable of tracking him. So why had he not at least waded into the water? Instead his scent was blazing strongly through the trees where even the rain would take longer to wash it away.

That someone knew enough about his species to hunt mated couples and have them killed was incomprehensible to Jack. How did he find out? The implications for all shapeshifters should their existence be exposed were horrifying.

"He wants you to follow him, Jack." Cam dropped his hand to his side satisfied he had Jack's attention for now. "Otherwise he would have killed her here. He wants both of you."

Jack shifted his feet, his entire body tensed against the urge to find Megan. His sharp eyes scanned the shoreline and trees around them. "I have to go after her, Cam, he knows that. But he won't expect both of us. We have to be quick, it won't be long before I shift again and it will be out of my control."

* * * * *

Consciousness leaked back slowly. The first thing Megan became aware of was the pounding in her head. It felt like someone was ramming ice picks into her brain. Not that she'd ever actually had an ice pick rammed into her brain... She was lying on her side and her hands and feet were tightly bound. Memory flooded her and she blinked blurry eyes until her surroundings came into focus. Careful to move as little as possible, she let her gaze roam around her. It looked like an abandoned house. She faced an open door leading into another dim room and the floor beneath her was wood covered by a thin layer of dirt. Piles of leaves had gathered in the corners.

A spider scurried across the floor in front of her and she tried not to think about her unbound hair and what might crawl into it. Wallpaper was peeling from the walls in damp strips and the one window she could see was cracked and dirty. The battery-operated lantern on the floor next to a rolled-up sleeping bag and a backpack near the fireplace told her she was not alone. Nausea rose, thick and oily in her stomach and she fought it back. Was her kidnapper the person who had tried to kill them?

She suspected she was about to find out as footsteps echoed through the doorway.

When he entered the room, Megan realized he had made no effort to conceal his appearance and he wasn't what she expected. Medium height and rail-thin, he looked around sixty years old with short steel-gray hair surrounding a bald patch on the crown of his head. He was dressed in new-looking jeans and boots and a black nylon windbreaker, and looked like he could be someone's grandfather. Until she saw his eyes. A dark muddy brown, they were filled with such malice she instinctively shrank back against the concrete behind her.

"Ah, I see you are awake." His voice was frighteningly calm and there was something familiar about the cadence of his voice. "I am sure we won't be here long, your mate will be here soon." He took a gun from his pocket and sat it on the floor by the lantern. He was right, Jack would come after her and he would be walking straight into a trap. "Who are you?" she demanded, struggling up into a sitting position against the wall. "Tell me what you want with us!"

He didn't react to her questions, just continued talking in that soft tone. "Such a shame really, you were very young. A pretty young girl just like..." He paused and looked away, taking a seat on the top of his sleeping bag. "Well, they usually are, that's why I have to stop it." He fixed his eerie eyes on her again, peering at her with unnerving intensity before quickly shifting his gaze to a point just above her head.

"How much of your humanity is left, I wonder? He hasn't finished with you yet or you would not have succumbed so quickly to the chloroform." Suddenly Megan realized why his tone was so odd. He was talking to her like she was an animal! Somehow he knew about Jack. "Let me go!" She struggled against her restraints twisting her wrists and pulling against the coarse rope until her flesh burned but there was no give. All the while the old man continued murmuring at her. Infuriated, she shouted, "I'm not an animal, God dammit! Let me go!"

He was on his feet in an instant, towering over her. His face scarlet, eyes bulging from their sockets, he drew back a hand and hit her, knocking her to the floor. Spittle flew from his lips and his eyes glowing with madness, he roared, "Do *not* take the Lord's name in vain! You are an *abomination*! Not fit to speak His name to me!"

He began to pace agitatedly. "I will succeed, Lord. You showed my path when the Demon took my daughter. I will see the souls these creatures pollute freed."

Megan struggled upright once more and watched, terrified. Tears streamed unchecked from her eyes and her face throbbed where the blow had landed and a trickle of blood ran from the corner of her mouth. "Bastard!" she spat at him.

He crouched next to the rucksack and extracted a capped syringe from a zipped pocket before walking purposefully back towards her. "He will be here soon, the trail was clear enough for him to follow. It's time." His calm was restored as if the outburst had never occurred. "I see now that once again He wishes His act of mercy to be carried out by my own hand." He smiled gently. "I'm going to send you home. The good Lord will cleanse your soul."

He's going to kill me.

Adrenaline flooded her system and her brain screamed at her. *Escape!* She started to shuffle away from him and he grabbed her with the same wiry strength he had subdued her with before. Megan screamed and cursed him with the fury of someone who *was* possessed. Avoiding her bound feet when she tried to kick at him, he rolled her onto her stomach and held her with his knee. The fight drained out of her when she felt the sharp sting of the needle as it pierced the flesh of her upper arm. Panting, she lay face down on the dirty floor, her arm stinging. His weight lifted from her and he hauled her roughly back to sit against the wall. She glared at him through the tangled, dirty strands of her hair. Her body ached with a new collection of bruises and her throat was raw but she didn't feel anything else. Yet. "What did you do to me?" she hissed.

He too was breathing hard when he sat back down. He ignored the question, picking up the gun instead and fixing his attention on the door. It didn't really matter. From his ranting she thought that whatever it was, he probably meant it to kill her. *I'm going to die.* Her thoughts went to Jack, and letting her head fall forward she closed her eyes and concentrated. He had said that picking up her thoughts was like listening to a badly tuned radio. With that in mind, she focused her thoughts and made sure her signal was as clear as possible. *Trap. Gun. Trap. Gun. Trap. Gun…* Over and over she repeated the words in her mind in the hopes that Jack would pick up one or both and be warned.

Jack studied the derelict cottage through a screen of ferns and brambles. What had once been a cleared garden was now being gradually reclaimed by the woodland and Jack was confident that he couldn't be seen crouched in the tree line. He and Cameron had delayed long enough to collect waterproof jackets and a small safety rucksack Cam kept packed for when he hiked. It contained a first aid kit, torch, matches and a few other bits and pieces that came in handy in emergencies. The comforting weight of the handgun under his jacket was something else he had his friend to thank for. Jack had been grateful, but unsurprised when Cam had appeared carrying it and a hunting rifle for himself.

They had easily tracked Megan and her kidnapper around the loch and up the hill to the house, leaving no doubt in either of their minds that it was deliberate. As they had approached she had nearly knocked him on his ass with a forceful mental warning. It had still taken his friend's cool head to convince him not to charge ahead and into the house when they had gotten close enough. The relief of feeling her alive was shadowed by the knowledge that she was terrified and hurting. He swore to himself it wouldn't be for much longer.

Since only one of the rooms had four walls and a roof, they had decided this was the most likely place for him to be holding her. Cam was maneuvering into a spot where he could see into the room with the riflescope. Jack gave him a few minutes head start and drew his gun before approaching the building, staying clear of the cracked window.

The disturbing scent of the kidnapper was strong here and beneath it he felt Megan's fear and a trace of her blood. Sweat broke out on his brow as he fought for control and looked into the room. She was leaning against the wall, knees drawn up and shoulders hunched as though trying to make as small a target as possible. As if she sensed his regard, her head lifted and she looked at him with frightened blue eyes. Tears had made tracks through the dirt on her bruised face and dried blood marked the corner of her mouth. Jack's hold on the cat slipped and he growled deep in his throat. Megan glanced to the other side of the room and back to him in a clear signal, confirming what his nose had already told him. He stepped across the threshold and looked into the eyes of a madman.

This, Jack realized, was what tainted the old man's scent and caused such a primal reaction in him. Megan was silent, her mind filled now with a jumble of images, her concentration broken. Reluctantly he closed her out and focused his attention on the man before him. The kidnapper stood easily showing none of the weaknesses his appearance suggested. His voice and face were emotionless when he spoke, "Drop the weapon."

Jack eyed the gun pointed at him and did as he was told, sliding his own weapon across the floor towards the door. He didn't need it, anyway. Moving slowly, he approached the fireplace, drawing attention away from his mate and snarled, "Why are you doing this?"

The blank expression cleared from the man's face and was replaced by determination. The gun twitched in his hand and he moved away from the wall in order to keep Jack in his sights. "The Lord has charged me with delivering you back to hell. I will not fail Him."

The light of true belief glinted in his eyes and even though he knew it would be pointless, Jack retorted, "We are not demons! What about the girl? She isn't one of us. Why are you punishing an innocent?"

"Your victims' souls must be freed from eternal damnation. They shall not suffer!" His voice dropped to a whisper. "I make sure they don't suffer. She didn't suffer."

Jack inched further around, slowly herding him into the center of the room "Who didn't suffer?" He watched the old man warily as he began reciting "The Lord's Prayer", his voice rising with every repetition. Drowning out anything Jack might say, his finger tightening on the trigger of the gun. A trickle of sweat ran down Jack's spine and he prepared himself to take action.

From the corner of his eye, he saw Megan gather herself and knew she intended to pounce as soon as the kidnapper was in range. *Stay down. Don't move.* He heard her tiny gasp at the strength of his order but she didn't move. Instead she stated in a precise voice, "Your daughter was an innocent, too. When you killed her, you marked your own soul for damnation!"

"*Lead us not into temptation!*" The old man's face flushed and body trembling with rage, he took a step backwards and arced the gun around to aim at her.

"*...Deliver us from evil!*"

The words echoed off the bare rafters of the room, Jack saw the intention to fire flash across his face and leapt towards Megan.

"*Move!*"

His fingers grasped the front of her jacket and his knees connected hard with the floor. The blast of a gunshot filled the room and there was silence.

Jack raised himself up off of Megan's trembling body and onto his elbows. She glanced to the side at the still form of her kidnapper and her blue eyes met his.

"Amen," she whispered in a shaking voice.

Jack sat up, pulling her with him and freed her from her bindings with a small pocketknife. He hissed at the damage done to her wrists, bringing them to his lips and gently kissing the raw flesh. He brushed the tangled hair from her face and devoured her lips hungrily, relief rushing through him. Footsteps pounded and they broke apart when Cameron rushed through the door. Jack smiled, rising to his feet, and grasped his friend's arm. "What took you so long?!"

Cam grimaced and shook his head, "You did. It was your job to get him in range of the window. I was getting worried for a while there." Jack picked up the sleeping bag from the floor and unwrapped it, laying it over the body. Megan hadn't seemed too worried about it yet, but once the shock had worn off it might be a different story. As if in confirmation, she said in a small voice, "Uh, guys? I don't feel so good."

Chapter Twelve

Jack looked at her. She was sitting against the wall, her eyes were closed and face chalk white. "We had to kill him, Megan. The man was beyond reason, there was no way he was letting us out of here alive. I've covered him up, you can open your eyes."

Her words were slurred. "You…you don't understand. He g-gave me something." Her eyes opened slowly and she scanned the floor, nodding at an empty syringe.

Jack knelt at her side, engulfing her in his embrace, adrenaline flooding his system. "Did he say what it was, baby?" She slumped against him and he tilted her pale face to his, alarmed by the sheen of sweat on her face and the dilation of her pupils.

She shook her head and pushed herself upright, scrubbing a hand over her face, "I'm so tired."

"Do *not* go to sleep yet, Meg. You hear me?" Jack glanced up as his friend let loose a string of curses.

The contents of the old man's bag were scattered on the floor and Cam held a glass vial in his hand with powder residue on the bottom. "It's a veterinary tranquilizer, Jack, the same one used to drug Paul Spencer and his wife two years ago. There is enough concentrated in this vial to kill a normal human." He threw the container against the wall, shattering it. "So unless you change her, he's killed you both anyway."

Jack jerked back as if his friend's words had physically hit him. He gathered his mate up in his arms and carried her out into the night air. The wooden porch was still quite sheltered and he sat with his back to the wall and held her on his lap. Cameron could still hear him out here, after all, his ears were every bit as sensitive as Jack's, but Jack knew he would do his best not to eavesdrop. At least they would have the illusion of privacy. Their time had been cut brutally short and he knew he would have to take the decision from her hands after all.

Megan struggled to throw off the insidious weariness that seeped through her body. She really was going to die. Adrenaline flooded through her system helping to stem the tide, she was not giving up without a fight. "What was he talking about, Jack?"

He looked at her, silver eyes filled with resignation and regret. "I can save your life, Megan, if we complete the blood exchange and I make you one of us."

He closed his eyes, pressed his forehead against her, and said fiercely, "I wanted to give you a choice, Meg, but I can't let you die."

Joy sparked within her and she lifted a leaden hand to cup his face. "I have chosen. I made my decision by the loch before I was kidnapped." He opened his eyes and lifted his head and a wary hope crept into his eyes.

"It's true. If you had been listening like you said you could, you would already know." She smiled lopsidedly at him and said, "Do it, Jack."

His pupils flared, eyes heating at her words and leaned forward and kissed her, the heated strokes of his tongue causing her sluggish heart rate to pick up. It amazed her that this man could turn her on so much with a simple kiss. She could feel him shaking as he drew back from her slightly, proving that she wasn't the only one affected. He fished in the pocket of his jacket and withdrew the little knife, quickly piercing the tip of her index finger. She hissed at the sharp pain and then moaned as Jack sucked her finger into the warmth of his mouth, caressing the small wound with his tongue.

"My turn." Megan took the knife from him, fumbling slightly. Unsure whether she was breathless as a result of what he was doing to her, or because her body was struggling against the tranquilizer. She repeated his actions, surprised that the taste of his blood in her mouth didn't disgust her as she thought it would. Instead she reveled in the intimacy of the act, knowing that it would bind her to Jack in ways she had never imagined.

The bleeding stopped quickly and with a final swipe of her tongue, she released him and lay back in his embrace, soothed by the thump of his heart beneath her ear. She was exhausted, frighteningly so, and this time she knew her shallow breaths had nothing to do with arousal. "Jack? What happens now?"

He tightened his embrace and she felt him lift his shoulders. "Nothing. We wait, I suppose."

Megan considered the times she had seen Jack transform and tried to brace herself for the pain that was sure to rack her own body. With weakness already spreading through her, she wasn't sure how she would cope with it. Pins and needles tingled in her hands and feet and she shifted, trying to ease them, and unzipped her jacket to let the breeze cool her heated flesh.

Instead of easing, the tingling spread, up her limbs and through her body until even her scalp prickled. Megan realized abruptly that the transformation had started. Behind her, Jack gave a startled oath and the hand that had been behind her back appeared in front of her. Her mouth went dry as she saw that he too was beginning to change.

He lifted her from his knee. "Take your clothes off." She gaped at him and he began to strip her briskly. "If you don't get out of them now, they'll be ruined." Heat and strength radiated through her and the tingling sensation multiplied as she obeyed him and knelt on the rough wood planks. It didn't hurt. A fact Jack seemed to realize at the same moment she did. He lifted his startled gaze to her face. "There's no pain…" His voice was deep and rough in his throat. Feeling strangely lightheaded, she looked at her hands and saw that they had almost completely changed. Panic whispered through her so she closed her eyes and let her body take over.

Sounds suddenly assaulted her from every direction. Birds, rain, the wind shushing through the trees, Cameron moving around inside the cottage. She smelled the damp wood beneath her feet, the damp earth and grass and the tang of pine. A multitude of other scents and sounds surrounded her that she couldn't yet identify. Fascinated, she opened her eyes. Jack sat in front of her, five or six inches taller than her even in his feline form. In fact it startled her how much bigger everything seemed.

Megan looked down at herself and saw that like Jack she had midnight black fur and a sleek, muscular body. Though hers was more compact than his powerful build. She stood on wobbly legs and heard Jack's deep chuckle in her mind. *Are you all right?* She glared at him and bared her teeth giving an experimental growl and he laughed at her again. Wondering if the telepathy now went both ways, she threw a few curses his way. *Is that any way to speak to your mate, Megan?* Happiness radiated from him as he licked her muzzle and rubbed his cheek against hers.

A new smell reached her and she turned towards the scuff of booted feet. Cameron stood in the doorway and for a fleeting moment she thought she saw jealousy in his eyes. There and gone so quickly it was impossible to be sure. His grudging smile transformed his broodingly handsome face into a male model perfection that was wasted on someone who shut himself away. "Congratulations, Jack. Why don't you two head back to the house? I'll clean up here and bring your clothes." He seemed to sense Jack's reluctance and continued. "Go on, unless you'd like to eat the evidence?" Jack growled and Megan felt her ears flatten and her hair bristle at the idea. He laughed and walked back inside. "Didn't think so."

Megan turned and jumped off of the porch, landing lightly on her paws. A small animal scurried away through the undergrowth and she had the powerful urge to chase. Just to see if she could catch it, definitely not eat the poor little thing she assured herself. She turned back to the porch and saw her mate still staring after his friend. *Jack.* He turned and looked at her.

Come show me the woods.

He leapt down beside her. *Is that anything like come show me your etchings?*

Megan swiped a paw at him and bounded into the trees. *Maybe later.*

* * * * *

Megan wiped the steam from the bathroom mirror and examined the face reflected there. She didn't look any different. There was no bruise on her cheek, no swelling and her wrists were no longer marked by her struggles with her bindings. Apart from the dirt she had just scrubbed off in the shower, there was nothing to suggest the ordeal her body had just been through. Only the warm glow of Jack's presence in her mind suggested her life had been changed forever. The mind-link had surprised her, rather than feeling threatened by it, she found it comforting. At the moment she only heard things that her mate directed at her but she knew in time she would be able to sense his emotions and pick up his surface thoughts. Jack, on the other hand, was more adept but she had quickly found that by imagining a door between his mind and hers she could shut him out.

So this was it, the mystery had been solved, the bad guy was defeated and the hero and heroine had gone off into the sunset together.

Happy Ever After.

Except she knew her mate was still hiding things from her. Some of his behavior in the last few days just didn't add up.

Four feet, she had discovered, were definitely faster than two and it had not taken them long to reach Murray House. She would happily have spent a little longer in the woods…there were quite a few things she'd like to try in her new form. Megan flashed a grin at her reflection. Who'da thunk it? Jack, however, seemed to be in a hurry to get back.

When she had first asked him about shifting, he had told her he couldn't control it. Imagine her surprise when, upon reaching the wide lawn of the house, Jack had stepped back from her and after a few moments of concentration…shifted. Not that this was a bad thing. She was happy to know she might not change at random, as he had led her to believe. It just added one more thing to the list of secrets. Following his urging she too had reluctantly changed back. For the first time in her life, she had felt like a giant, clumsy and awkward, but after a few moments the feeling had faded.

Her mate had been jubilant, laughing loudly and throwing his arms around her. Caught up in his enthusiasm she had hugged him back and allowed him to carry her upstairs to their room. His hands had trailed all over her naked body, allegedly looking for injuries, but the heat in his eyes told a different story. They had both been aroused by the time they got there but instead of making love to her, he had placed her on the bed, kissed her gently and asked her to meet him downstairs. Then he had left her there. Aroused, frustrated and suspicious. Oh yes, he was definitely hiding something.

She dressed quickly in a clingy scoop-necked cotton top and an ankle-length skirt, not bothering with underwear since she had no intention of being dressed for long. She paused for a moment in front of the mirrored closet door and unbuttoned the row of buttons on the front of her skirt to just above her knee. Satisfied, she gave her reflection a nod. *Take that Jack Douglass*…and went in search of her mate.

Cameron threw his jacket over the back of an armchair and walked wearily to the cut crystal decanter on the side table. Jack watched as his friend poured a healthy shot of brandy and tossed it back with a grimace. The smell of pine and smoke overlaid the slight taint of less pleasant odors hinting at the lengths he had gone to for him. "Thank you."

Cam filled his glass again and faced him, expression serious. "I would have done worse." His gaze turned inward and Jack felt his sorrow. "I have done worse." He took another sip of his drink. "I found his identification and a few other personal papers in his bag…" His voice trailed off and both of them looked up as the door opened and Megan walked in.

His Dearbh Ceangal.

At first glance her white top and sky blue skirt looked modest enough but as she approached him he saw the way the top clung to her. Her bra-less state was obvious as her breasts swayed with her movements and her peaked nipples were outlined against the soft fabric.

No panties either… her voice whispered into his mind.

Jack's mouth went dry and every bit of blood drained out of his head and into his cock. She sat beside him on the leather sofa and crossed her legs, her bare foot grazed his calf and the long skirt parted to pool around her thighs. With a monumental effort, he dragged his eyes back to her face. Her cheeks were pink as she turned to his friend, ignoring him, and asked, "You were saying, Cameron?"

Jack didn't need to be able to read minds to see the desire in the other man's amber eyes as he stared at Megan with open admiration. A low growl escaped him and Cam glanced at him with amusement and cleared his throat. "His name was James York, he was a vet. Ann Spencer was his daughter." Megan looked at him questioningly and he relayed to her what he'd found out about the murders.

"We may never know how he found out what Paul Spencer was, but what worries me more is that he found out about others. He knew a lot about us, Jack. He had notes about the mating cycle. It's going to take some time but I'm going to try to find out where he got his information."

Megan's eyes narrowed dangerously and she looked at Jack and then back at his friend. "Mating cycle?"

With a less than sympathetic look on his face, Cam swallowed the rest of his brandy. "Don't look at me, I told him to tell you." He headed for the door, grabbing his jacket on the way. "Play nice, you two."

Jack barely heard his friend leave the room. He was too busy watching his very determined looking mate as she sat beside him, one eyebrow raised in silent scrutiny. "Meg, it was for your own good…" Her brows drew into a scowl. *Okay, not a good start.* "I told you most of this. I just left out a few details."

She continued to stare at him, this time a sheen of tears in her eyes. Jack developed sudden empathy with the men he had previously mocked for giving in to the power of their wives' silence. A little desperately, he filled in the facts he had neglected to tell her about how the mating cycle began and how it would have eventually ended if she had turned him away. By the time he had finished, she stood with her back to him, she had shut him out of her thoughts and he was beginning to get a little worried. "I'm sorry I had to deceive you, Megan, but if I had to do it over I would do the same thing. I knew you wouldn't hesitate to bond with me if you knew what would happen. You are my Dearbh Ceangal, I love you… I couldn't accept less from you."

She turned back to him and his heart melted when he saw that the anger he expected was absent from her expression. Lord help him, this woman never reacted the way he expected. Life with Megan was going to be interesting. He started to go to her but she motioned him to stay where he was and knelt between his spread legs. Tears trickled down her cheeks as she said softly, "I love you, Jack." Her pale skin was blotchy and her nose red but Jack swore he had never seen a more beautiful face in all his thirty-two years. He wiped the moisture from her face with the pads of his fingers and leaned forward to kiss her. Megan, his mate, his heart, his life.

She returned his passion. Humming in renewed pleasure, her fingers grasped the edge of his sweater and pulled it over his head. She brushed her fingers lightly through the hair on his chest and down to unfasten his jeans. He lifted his hips so that she could pull them down. Groaning when she let his erection glide against her cheek.

She stood, and lifted her long skirt higher to slowly unbutton it and he caught glimpses of the neatly trimmed hair between her legs. He slid forward as she reached the final few fastenings and stilled her hands with his own. "Let me."

She nodded and while he undid the last to let her skirt pool around her ankles, she took off her top. Her firm breasts bounced slightly as she shook her unruly curls from her face. Jack sucked in a breath and just stared at her for a moment. "You're so beautiful. I love to look at you." He gripped her hips and pulled her closer rubbing his face against her soft abdomen and her hands went to his head holding him closer. He savored the smell of her arousal and blew gently on the curls concealing her mound.

She shivered against him, fingers tightening briefly in his hair. "I want you, Jack. I want your hard cock so deep inside me I don't know where I end and you begin." With gentle pressure, she urged him backward onto the couch so she could straddle him.

The supple leather of the couch was still warm from his body and Jack sat back into it without protest. Megan followed him and they shared another kiss, this one hungrier than the last, a melding of lips and tongues. She grasped his shaft with one hand and guided him into her body. Jack gasped, hips surging forward at the first touch of her moist heat until he was seated fully within her and they both cried out at the completeness of the union.

He waited, trembling, his forehead resting on hers, for her to adjust to him. She arched her back so that her breasts thrust forward and he laved and sucked her nipples until she whimpered and began to move. She took her time, rising up on her knees as far as she could without freeing him from the tight clasp of her body and sinking slowly back down. Her inner muscles tightened around his cock, increasing the pressure until she nearly finished him off. In desperation he gripped her hips and increased the pace, tilting her so that he stroked against that hidden spot deep inside her.

"Yes, God Jack! Again."

He felt his balls draw tight against his body in impending release and with one hand he reached between them and thumbed her clit. She cried out and her muscles clamped down hard on his cock, taking him over with her.

* * * * *

Jack woke in the early hours of the morning, his skin flushed and body hard with the desire that pulsed through him. Megan was sprawled over him, her head resting under his chin, a lock of curly hair tickling his nose. They had been too busy last night to shut the curtains and he could see the clear, star-filled sky outside had lightened to a dusky blue as the sun began to rise. He thought fleetingly about closing them but a vision of Megan's creamy skin bathed in the golden morning light flashed across his brain and he reconsidered. Megan stirred and her hand caressed his chest in lazy circles.

Jack began to purr and he felt her smile against him. Resigned to the fact that the annoying habit was here to stay, he ignored it. It made her happy. For the first time in a long while he felt as if his body was his own again and if he had developed a few new habits to go with it then that was fine. The feeling he had when he had discovered that he was able to shift back from his feline shape was indescribable. Instead of draining him, the transformation had energized him. His father had been right when he had said things would change when he and the cat merged. He thought about Megan's playful teasing in the woods as they had both made their way back to Murray house. His dad had been right about a lot of things, he decided.

Images from the dream flitted through his mind and he realized not all of them were his ideas. "Jack?" her voice was thick with sleep. "Is there something else you might have forgotten to tell me?" His hand drifted down her hip as he considered his reply and he smiled. "Well...there's this thing about our dreams coming true..."

Epilogue

Jayne Davis marched into her flat and slammed the door behind her. What a lousy damn day! She'd had another row with her boss after the little swine had come up behind her and brushed his sweaty little hand over her backside while she bent over to stock shelves. She'd restrained herself from hitting him, barely. She had, however, pushed him backward into some boxes. He had threatened to fire her, she had threatened to sue him for sexual harassment.

Stalemate.

He knew she needed the job and people who sued their bosses for sexual harassment wouldn't find another one very easily. All the same he didn't really want to risk forcing her hand. A good thing too because she'd definitely do it.

At the end of her shift, she had headed out into the wet windy day and her umbrella had blown inside out before she got to the end of the street. Valiantly she'd pulled her coat around herself and continued on anyway. Then she had an argument with an obnoxious and unhelpful store clerk who was reluctant to wrap the two boxes of books she had bought in plastic to keep them dry. That one too, was a draw. The clerk had grudgingly handed over the wrap and she had done it herself. A good thing, too, because when she stepped onto the pavement outside, a bus had driven through a puddle in the gutter and soaked her from head to foot. Even her shoes squidged.

Brushing her wet hair back from her face, she shrugged off her coat and set her packages down on the phone table. The answering machine light was blinking and she crossed her fingers and pressed the button, hoping that it would be Megan.

She had worried about her friend since she left with the very mysterious and sexy Mr. Douglass.

"Jayne, it's me. I'm calling to let you know it's over and I'm safe." Jayne gave a small sigh of relief. "You would not believe what's happened to me since we left! But first, congratulate me, babe, I'm getting married!" Jayne paused the tape and absorbed the impact of her friend's words. Megan was the only person Jayne had been close to since her family died. The idea that she was going to have to share her with someone else was bittersweet. "Jack wants me to meet his family, we fly out tomorrow. I'll see you soon, oh, and Jayne? Believe in the magic."

The End

About the author:

Cait Miller lives on the West Coast of Scotland in the same small town where she was born. She shares her home with a large collection of dragons and a miniature Yorkshire Terrier who has convinced the postman she's a Rottweiler. Cait dreams one day of living in a castle filled with history...or at least a house with a library.

Books and writing have played a huge part in Cait's life since she was very young. Encouraged by a mother with similar interests and one of the world's greatest English teachers, she began writing her own stories. Unfortunately she inherited a practical side to her nature from her grannie—who once told her at a party, in front of her teenage friends, to cross her legs not her fingers.

Cait went on to become one of the first people in her family to graduate from University where she trained for a medical profession. Writing became something she did for her own pleasure, never dreaming it could be anything else. Then, one day, she showed one of those stories to a group of online friends who taught her to Believe In The Magic...

If you are ever looking for Cait you only have to find the nearest quiet corner and she'll be there, book or pen in hand, wrapped up in another world.

Cait welcomes mail from readers. You can write to her c/o Ellora's Cave Publishing at 1337 Commerce Drive, #13, Stow, Ohio 44224.

Why an electronic book?

We live in the Information Age—an exciting time in the history of human civilization in which technology rules supreme and continues to progress in leaps and bounds every minute of every hour of every day. For a multitude of reasons, more and more avid literary fans are opting to purchase e-books instead of paperbacks. The question to those not yet initiated to the world of electronic reading is simply: *why?*

1. *Price*. An electronic title at Ellora's Cave Publishing runs anywhere from 40-75% less than the cover price of the <u>exact same title</u> in paperback format. Why? Cold mathematics. It is less expensive to publish an e-book than it is to publish a paperback, so the savings are passed along to the consumer.

2. *Space*. Running out of room to house your paperback books? That is one worry you will never have with electronic novels. For a low one-time cost, you can purchase a handheld computer designed specifically for e-reading purposes. Many e-readers are larger than the average handheld, giving you plenty of screen room. Better yet, hundreds of titles can be stored within your new library—a single microchip. (Please note that Ellora's Cave does not endorse any specific brands. You can check our website at www.ellorascave.com for customer recommendations we make available to new consumers.)

3. *Mobility.* Because your new library now consists of only a microchip, your entire cache of books can be taken with you wherever you go.

4. *Personal preferences are accounted for.* Are the words you are currently reading too small? Too large? Too…**ANNOYING**? Paperback books cannot be modified according to personal preferences, but e-books can.

5. *Innovation.* The way you read a book is not the only advancement the Information Age has gifted the literary community with. There is also the factor of what you can read. Ellora's Cave Publishing will be introducing a new line of interactive titles that are available in e-book format only.

6. *Instant gratification.* Is it the middle of the night and all the bookstores are closed? Are you tired of waiting days—sometimes weeks—for online and offline bookstores to ship the novels you bought? Ellora's Cave Publishing sells instantaneous downloads 24 hours a day, 7 days a week, 365 days a year. Our e-book delivery system is 100% automated, meaning your order is filled as soon as you pay for it.

Those are a few of the top reasons why electronic novels are displacing paperbacks for many an avid reader. As always, Ellora's Cave Publishing welcomes your questions and comments. We invite you to email us at service@ellorascave.com or write to us directly at: 1337 Commerce Drive, Suite 13, Stow OH 44224.

Discover for yourself why readers can't get enough of the multiple award-winning publisher Ellora's Cave. Whether you prefer e-books or paperbacks, be sure to visit EC on the web at www.ellorascave.com for an erotic reading experience that will leave you breathless.

Printed in the United States
40063LVS00002B/1-3

9 781419 951428